MW00577628

MISTER TIMELESS BLYTH

A Biographical Novel

Alan Spence

TUTTLE Publishing

Tokyo | Rutland, Vermont | Singapore

"Books to Span the East and West"

Tuttle Publishing was founded in 1832 in the small New England town of Rutland, Vermont [USA]. Our core values remain as strong today as they were then—to publish best-in-class books which bring people together one page at a time. In 1948, we established a publishing outpost in Japan—and Tuttle is now a leader in publishing English-language books about the arts, languages and cultures of Asia. The world has become a much smaller place today and Asia's economic and cultural influence has grown. Yet the need for meaningful dialogue and information about this diverse region has never been greater. Over the past seven decades, Tuttle has published thousands of books on subjects ranging from martial arts and paper crafts to language learning and literature—and our talented authors, illustrators, designers and photographers have won many prestigious awards. We welcome you to explore the wealth of information available on Asia at **www.tuttlepublishing.com**.

Published by Tuttle Publishing, an imprint of Periplus Editions (HK) Ltd.

www.tuttlepublishing.com

Copyright © 2023 by Alan Spence

Library of Congress publication data is in progress.

ISBN: 978-0-8048-5635-5
ISBN: 978-4-8053-1757-0 (for sale in Japan)

26 25 24 23
10 9 8 7 6 5 4 3 2 1   2211CM
Printed in China

Distributed by
North America, Latin America & Europe
Tuttle Publishing
364 Innovation Drive
North Clarendon, VT 05759-9436 U.S.A.
Tel: (802) 773-8930; Fax: (802) 773-6993
info@tuttlepublishing.com
www.tuttlepublishing.com

Japan
Tuttle Publishing
Yaekari Building 3rd Floor
5-4-12 Osaki Shinagawa-ku
Tokyo 141 0032
Tel: (81) 3 5437-0171 Fax: (81) 3 5437-0755
sales@tuttle.co.jp
www.tuttle.co.jp

Asia Pacific
Berkeley Books Pte. Ltd.
3 Kallang Sector
#04-01, Singapore 349278
Tel: (65) 6741-2178; Fax: (65) 6741-2179
inquiries@periplus.com.sg
www.tuttlepublishing.com

CONTENTS

To
DAISUKE MATSUNAGA
with gratitude

senryu —   (p 363-306)

Lee   p 82-84, 92-93
              379

1

TIMELESS

Blyth.

The Japanese pronounced it Buraisu.

Buraisu-san.

Suzuki-sensei had sent me a letter, the name spelled out on the envelope in his elegant, vigorous calligraphy, at once delicate and bold, unmistakeable.

This, Suzuki explained, had three meanings.

First, a simple rendition of my name in Chinese characters. Bu-Rai-Su.

Second, it meant Not-Come-Person. In other words, You have not come to see me in a long time.

Third, it could mean You are not-coming, not-going, not-born, not-dying. You are Mister Timeless Blyth.

How I signed myself thereafter.

Mister. Timeless. Blyth.

RH Blyth.

Reginald Horace.

This particular incarnation of my timeless self took birth on December 3rd 1898. *Fin de siecle.* I was a child of the Nineteenth century, though only just – born in a modest house in Leytonstone, South East London. 93 Trumpington Road, to be exact – a splendidly *English*-sounding street name, I always thought, comically pompous and overblown. Trumpet. Trumpery. Trumpington.

Trumpington Road. East Eleven.

Equally English were those names with which I was christened. Reginald Horace. Reginald Horace Blyth of Trumpington Road. The house overlooked two cemeteries, one Christian, one Jewish. That might account for the strong sense of mortality I possessed – though I was never a morbid child – and the sense too that religion was not something absolute: it came in many forms. (For a time my father, God bless him, took us to the mission hall of a rather fundamentalist sect, where he sometimes read the lesson or led a hymn. *Give me oil in my lamp…*) There was a certain melancholy beauty in walking through those graveyards. Whatever the trappings, it ended here. Dust to dust. I read the inscriptions on tombstones, each one a *memento mori*, carved in stone.

> *Thou painted piece of living clay,*
> *Man, be not proud of thy short stay.*

The sense of transience was never far away. Time's winged chariot hurrying near.

There's something I've observed that always unsettles me. On the title page of a book, in the small print under the publishing details, it gives the author's name and dates. Wordsworth, William (1770-1850). Arnold, Matthew (1822-1888). So there it would be: Blyth, Reginald Horace (1898-) The name, the date of birth, the blank space waiting to be filled in. The brackets closed.

I may not know the date, but I know where I will be buried. I can visit my own grave. (The last time I did so was on a fine spring morning, earlier this year, the cherry blossoms already in bloom). I chose the site myself, bought and paid for it years ago. I will rest alongside Suzuki-sensei who has also reserved a place. It is in the graveyard at Tokeiji temple near Kamakura, and Suzuki's wife is already buried nearby. I hope I am not tempting the fates, the furies, the angry gods, by saying I hope I have just a little more time before my passing.

I cycle to Tokeiji from Kita-Kamakura, alongside the railway track, and leave my bicycle at the gate. The climb to my grave is long and steep, an arduous ascent with steps to the highest level of the cemetery. Recently I've found myself having to stop halfway to draw breath and gather my strength.

Another neighbour in my long rest will be the philosopher Tetsuzo Tanikawa, who has also booked his little plot of land. He was born before me, and, like me, he is still on earth.

Tanikawa, Tetsuzo (1895-).

He is a good man, and will be amiable company. His date of departure too will be carved in stone, as mine will be soon enough. Soon enough.

The haiku poets all wrote a *jisei*, a death verse. In fact I have often thought that every good haiku, every true poem, is a kind of death verse.

I have already written mine, or one that will suffice.

It begins,

> *We that change,*
> *Hate change.*

It ends:

> *Ashes,*
> *Darkness,*
> *Dust.*

But on re-reading, perhaps it is rather self-consciously portentous with its dying fall. (Its dying fall!) I may substitute an unattributed haiku which was recently drawn to my attention. I like the fact that it is anonymous. It was written in Japanese, and I have made my own translation.

> *Sazanka ni kokoro nokoshite tabidachinu*

> > *I leave my heart*
> > *to the sasanqua flower*
> > *on the day of this journey*

Sasanqua flower. Tokeiji temple. It is all a far cry from Leytonstone

My father worked as a clerk for the Great Eastern Railways, and that gave me access to the station platform – after school and on Saturday afternoons – where I supplemented the family income by selling bars of chocolate to passengers. I was a strong boy – stocky and robust, not easily knocked off my stride. The speed and resilience I'd developed on the running track and the rugby field stood me in good stead as I ran and jinked along the platform. An artful dodger. The best time was rush hour when the platform was crammed, chocabloc. (Chocabloc for chocolate blocks!) I'd be blocked and buffeted as I shouldered my way along, touting my wares, shouting out the prices in best barrow-boy style.

Get yer chocolate bars here, only tuppence the quarter-pound!

The trains ran to and from Liverpool Street, or in the other direction, Southend-on-Sea. (Southend with its sandy beach and mile-long pier – we'd go there on a rare outing, on some long summer Sunday – God, so long ago now – with free tickets my father had acquired).

I'd be braced and ready as a train pulled in, engulfed in its own smoke and steam, wheels grinding and screeching to a halt, sparks and cinders thrown into the air. The doors would be flung open and, it seemed, hundreds of men would disembark or push their way on. And yes, the passengers were almost all men, on their way to work, or on their way back, and all, as I remember it, in workday suits and coats, and wearing hats – tweed caps, bowlers, even top hats for those that travelled first class.

I'd push through the crowds, keeping my balance. I'd be cursed and sometimes shoved by some irate commuter, anxious not to miss his train. But somehow enough of these men would stop and buy, and we kept the enterprise going, even though it can't have made much money.

I suppose my father bought the chocolate from a wholesaler, perhaps somebody he knew. It was always the same two varieties in simple chunky bars – Dairy Milk and Bourneville, the one pale and creamy, the other deep and dark. I ate both, equally greedily, but I knew which I preferred – the dark one, bittersweet, in its red wrapper.

My mother said I ate all the profits, and it was true I scoffed the odd
bar to keep me going. My father would say, He's a growing boy, and
she'd say that was true, especially around the waist. But the love of
chocolate never left me.

On one of my first visits to the Imperial Palace in Tokyo, Her Maj-
esty Empress Kojun sought to put me at my ease by commenting
on my girth. Mister Buraisu, she said, smiling. You are very fat.

Nonplussed, I nevertheless gathered myself and replied that it must
be because of my vegetarian diet. Even elephants, I said, which eat
nothing but leaves, grow to an enormous size. The Empress, who
had been described to me as somewhat reserved, laughed and re-
peated my remark to one of her attendants.

An elephant! she said, delighted.

Thereafter the Empress greeted me with friendliness and a kind of
wry amusement.

An English elephant in a tweed suit.

Some rogue incarnation of Ganesha, perhaps, the Hindu god of
wisdom, with his pot belly and his elephant head.

That cartoon character in the little French books my daughters read.
Histoire de Babar. I read it aloud to them and translated as I went.

My daughters, Nana and Harumi.

How did it all come to pass? How did I come to end my days here
in Japan? How did I get from Trumpington Road to the Imperial
Palace? Why did Bodhidharma come from the West?

Suzuki-sensei would have some profound non-answer.

Why did Buraisu-san come from the West?

Suzuki-sensei taught me not to teach. He taught me everything I
don't know.

I began making these notes at my home in Oiso before the illness took hold, before I was brought to hospital. I wrote in my bright study, overlooking the garden, surrounded by my books and papers – a lifetime's accumulation, my own library and archive. I sifted through old notebooks and diaries, letters, newspaper cuttings. The dross and residue of a life, of this life.

My home in Oiso. There is an outhouse I built myself, round a living tree that grows up through the roof, its branches reaching towards the sky.

There are days when I fear I may never see the house again, that this is the end.

I am writing this introduction, as I have written the rest of these pages, on sheets of old lined paper, foolscap size. The pages are yellow, like the paper I used for the drafts of the Emperor's speech in 1945. Ningen Sengen. Declaration of Humanity.

Novel on Yellow Paper. That was by the English poet Stevie Smith. I picked up an old paperback copy, years ago. The things that lie buried in the memory, only to float to the surface, unbidden. Smith wrote that remarkable poem 'Not Waving but Drowning.'

I remember, word-for-word, the very beginning of her novel. *I should like then to say: Goodbye to all my friends, my beautiful and lovely friends. And for why? Read on, Reader, read on and work it out for yourself.*

Indeed. This is my Goodbye.

Read on.

I have always written, though not about myself. Why would I do that? A shilling life would give you all the facts, if such a thing existed. But it does not, and if it did, of what interest would it be? What purpose could it possibly serve? So why, now, these scribbled notes, on yellow paper?

Why this, why that? Why anything?

Let me put it simply. In my life I have followed what felt like an inner destiny. This predisposed me to pass through a number of phases which were not, however, mutually exclusive. In coming to an understanding (or un-understanding) of these phases, I have written extensively and continuously.

In my time, I have been prolific. The list of my books is long and I believe, in their way, they have been influential, though my critics have accused me of being a mere anthologist, lacking proper scholarship and academic discipline. To which I might reply that they misunderstand my intention, and leave it at that. (I have also been called problematic and terminally eccentric. I would accept either description as a compliment!)

When I'm too tired to read or write, I can sometimes listen to the radio. The nurses are kind and help me tune it to different stations. Most of the broadcasts that come through are Japanese, and I just let it wash over me. But sometimes there's an American Forces network, or the BBC World Service, and increasingly there are reports from across the South China Sea in Vietnam.

There had been an incident in the Gulf of Tonkin where an American destroyer came under attack. As a result, a US resolution was passed paving the way for the deployment of ground forces, a strategic bombing campaign, the declared intention being to contain the spread of communism. It's hard to make sense of it, if any sense can be made. But whatever the rhetoric, it is about ideology and power, the control of resources.

It's Korea all over again and may be even bloodier. I remember the boy Lee and what became of him, and I find I have tears in my eyes.

There are students and Buddhist monks protesting in the streets. The newspapers carried that photograph of the monk who sat down calmly in the centre of Saigon, and had petrol poured over him. Then deliberately, with absolute focus, he struck a spark from a cigarette lighter and was engulfed in flames.

Some film crew managed to record it and it was broadcast on television news, again and again. The monk seated in meditation as the fire consumed him.

His name was Thich Quang Durc. He was protesting against the treatment of Buddhists in the South. He chanted *Nam Mo A Di Da Phat*, the Vietnamese form of *Namu Amida Butsu*. Homage to Amitabha Buddha.

He was the same age as me, going on sixty-six. Close to the allotted span. Three score and ten. When a younger monk offered to take his place, he pulled rank. It was a matter of seniority. The right to self-immolation was his and his alone. He stepped from the back of a saloon car which had brought him to the place. A hundred other monks formed a circle around him, praying and chanting as he set himself alight.

His body swayed and wavered in the flames. It blackened as he burned, and gave off a thick oily smoke.

Namu Amida Butsu.

I bow to the Buddha of the Pure Land.

The Buddha's Fire Sermon.

All is burning. And what is the all that is burning?
All forms are burning.
Burning with what?
Burning with birth, ageing and death.

The whine and crackle of static on the airwaves, the old radio struggling to maintain a steady signal. Then suddenly there's a clear passage of my beloved Bach. It sounds like the Goldberg Variations, the version by Glenn Gould. I have the recording – the one where Gould can be heard singing along, to the outrage of most purists. I find it glorious and anarchic and utterly human. It makes me smile.

In spite of it all, in the face of it all, there is this. *This* is still possible.

But don't you know there's a war on?
Sadly, there always is.

All was far from quiet on the Western Front. The Great War, the War-to-end-all-wars, was running its bloody course – carnage and mass slaughter on an unprecedented scale. Between Verdun and the Somme there were a million dead. Blown to bits or drowned in mud or poisoned with chlorine gas.

Your Country Needs You.

They needed replacements, more cannon fodder, more young men for butcher meat. I wanted no part in it. I would categorically refuse to go.

There was a long table by the far wall, beneath a framed photograph of His Majesty the King. Behind the table sat four men. They ignored me as I came into the room, continued their muttered conversation. Facing the table, in the middle of the floor, was a single straightbacked hard wooden chair. I stood behind it, waited. Eventually one of the four, the oldest – stiff wing-collar, *pince-nez* pinching his nose, thin hair brilliantined to his scalp – looked up and glared at me.

Name?

Blyth, I said. Reginald Horace.

He looked down at a sheet of paper in front of him, ran his finger down a list of names, stopped.

Address?

93 Trumpington Road.

Date of birth?

December 3rd, 1898.

Which makes you, by my reckoning, eighteen years and two days old.

Yes sir.

You are therefore, under the terms of the Military Service Act, liable for conscription into His Majesty's Service.

Yes sir. Indeed.

Indeed, he repeated.

I closed my eyes, took in a long, deep breath, continued.

However...

Yes?

Time passed, then I came out with it, blurted it all-in-a-rush.

I wish to be excused from active military service.

I became intensely aware of the heavy ticking of an old clock on the wall, sombre in its mahogany case.

On what grounds?

I cleared my throat, articulated my words carefully.

I have a conscientious objection to the war.

Again he glared.

You have no medical condition that would render you unfit to serve? No sir.

He banged the table, startled the others, made me jump.

Damn it man! What is wrong with you?

Bloody coward, said one of the others. Damned disgrace.

He was redfaced, neck bulging over his collar. A caricature, a Colonel Blimp. I expected him to hand me a white feather, a denunciation. Instead he hissed out *Spineless!*

As if in response, I drew myself up, stood to attention.

Sit! said the first man, nodding towards the chair, and I did.

Before I could settle, he said, Are you a religious man, Mr Blyth?

I...

Speak up, man! said redface.

Perhaps not in the accepted sense of the term, sir.

God give me strength!

I am sure he will, sir, if you pray to him wholeheartedly.

If you are being insolent, the man said, you will be held in contempt.

That was not my intention, I said. Sir.

Well answer the question! Yes or No?

It comes back to me now, down almost fifty years, this exchange, this interview, this interrogation, inquisition, clear in my memory, word perfect as a scene in a play.

Are you a religious man, Mr Blyth, Yes or No?

It was like the old lawyer's question – Have you stopped beating your wife yet? Answer yes or no. Whatever way you answered was wrong. A hiding to nothing.

It was what I would now call a *koan*. Does a dog have the Buddha-nature? Yes or No.

I am not a church-goer, I said. But I believe there is much truth in the scriptures.

Much truth? said the first man.

The teachings of Christ are exemplary, I said. Blessed are the peacemakers.

And you regard yourself as a peacemaker.

I'm a pacifist, sir. I had hoped I was making that clear.

What do you actually do to further peace? Or is your attitude the only peaceful thing about you?

I speak out, sir. Like this.

Are you some kind of revolutionary? A Bolshevik?

No sir.

What books do you read?

Apart from the New Testament! said redface.

I read widely, I said.

What books in particular?

At the moment I am especially fond of Dickens.

What else?

Wordsworth, Stevenson, Marcus Aurelius, Blake, Matthew Arnold, George Bernard Shaw...

Are you trying to impress us with your erudition?

Emerson, Thoreau, Milton, Keats...

I'm surprised you have time for anything else.

George Herbert, Henry Vaughan, John Clare...

Enough! said redface.

And all this...*reading*... said the chairman, pronouncing the word with something akin to distaste... has led you to the noble conclusion that it is wrong to defend your country against a savage and brutal enemy?

I don't believe mass bloodshed is the answer.

The other two men, both thin-faced and nondescript, had not yet spoken, but they suddenly joined in, a double-act, battering me with their rapid-fire questions.

Are you afraid of having to fight? Is that it?

What would you do if you yourself were attacked?

What would you do if your mother and father were attacked?

If you had children, who would defend them?

Would you rather be defeated than use force?

I don't know, I said. I truly do not know. These are difficult questions for anyone to answer.

So what gives you the certainty that your thinking and your feelings are right?

Are you a sheep, Mr Blyth? Or do you see yourself as a lion, or a lone wolf?

Sorry?

Do you see yourself as a follower, or a leader, or a solitary?

All of those, I said. None of them.

Are you prevaricating, Mr Blyth? Are you being wilfully obstructive?

They say that of all the senses, smell is the most evocative in terms of bringing back a memory, conjuring up a remembered scene – the particular moment, vivid and distinct. How it was. So now, some five decades on, it's the scent of the room I recall – the fustiness of the old worn carpet, furniture polish from the heavy oak table, metallic tang of *Brasso* from the fittings, and overlaying it all, the cloying musk of stale tobacco. Any of these can pitch me back to that dreary committee room in Leytonstone on a cold December afternoon. They reawaken a sense of bleakness, and apprehension, and fear.

There was a brief silence. The older man, the chairman of this *ad hoc* tribunal, looked down at the piece of paper in front of him, unscrewed the cap of his fountain pen and scribbled something at the foot of the page. Then he fixed me with his gaze, unmistakably hostile.

Mr Blyth, he said. Are you prepared to go to prison for your beliefs?

The smell of the room. The hard wooden chair. The cold.
Yes, I said. I am fully prepared.

Shades of the prison-house begin to close.
Wormwood Scrubs. The Scrubs. I always heard it like that, in a
broad Cockney accent. Dahn the Scrubs.
That wonderful old character actor from British comedies in the
black-and-white Fifties, Ealing comedies. I watched them in a film
club in Shinjuku, a smoky dive that didn't even aspire to being a flea-
pit. I watched and I laughed and was overwhelmed by a ludicrous
nostalgia for something I'd never known.
What was the actor's name? A boxer's pug-face, battered and re-
silient.
Arthur Mullard. That was it! Arthur Mullard! A name and a char-
acter worthy of Dickens at his best. An Alfred Jingle, perhaps. Or
a Bill Sikes.
Dahn the Scrubs.
Jack Dawkins, the Artful. Chameleon poet shocking the virtuous
philosophers. Sent down by the magistrates and railing at them.
*You'll pay for this my fine fellers. I wouldn't be you for something! Here,
carry me off to prison! Take me away!*
Never was a character so full of life. So full of Zen.

There's the word again, rearing its head. What is this thing called
Zen?

I had said I was fully prepared. But how could I have been prepared?

A stinking, straw-filled mattress, no more than two inches thick,
stretched over bare boards and covered by a coarse blanket. A
wooden stool. No table but a built-in shelf. A hole in the door with
a shutter that slid open at floor level so the food could be passed
through, though calling it food would be an exaggeration. Rations
were meagre enough anyway. (*Don't you know there's a war on?*) The
best on offer would be a bowl of indeterminate murky sludge that
purported to be stew. But for vegetarians like me, it was even worse.

Breakfast was a thin porridge, no more than a gruel, like diluted wallpaper paste, doused with sour milk. Lunch was a bowl of tepid scummy soup. Dinner would be a few potatoes in a watery gravy (a watery grave!) and a hunk of stale bread scraped with a thin smear of rancid margarine.

Glorious food.

Oliver.

Back to Dickens again – I keep circling round him.

The last was a S, Swubble I named him. This was a T, Twist I named HIM.

Mister Bumble the Beadle.

So the food in the Scrubs was grim, no other word for it. I make light of it, but people sickened, some died. I was robust and I made the best of it, I survived. It was possible by working overtime to earn extra rations – a mug of cocoa, another chunk of hard bread to dunk in it.

I have always prided myself (and pride is the very least of my besetting sins) on the clarity of my memory. If I read a passage that interested or affected me, it would stay, lodged or filed away until I called it to mind, or it came to me unbidden for who-knows-what reason.

They call it photographic memory, but that is not quite accurate, suggests only the visual. This faculty is also auditory, olfactory. It can be triggered by a scent. The smell of that fusty committee room that came back to me just then. Or a taste. Dark chocolate. I'm like Monsieur Proust with his famous *madeleine* – one taste and he was transported to his childhood, dipping sweet cake in a cup of tisane.

Dunk.

A good word.

Spongecake in tea. Stale bread in cocoa.

Some things I remember in the depths of my being, in my very cells. I reinhabit a place, a time. I am there.

In my cells.

The Scrubs.

There was a garrulous Scotsman in the cell next to mine. The first
night he shouted out a joke.
Did ye hear about the lonely prisoner?
He was in his cell!
It worked in his Glasgow accent. In his sel'. In his self.
It took me a moment or two to get it, but when I did, I laughed.
He spoke to me the next day as we queued to slop out our own waste
down the communal sewer. The stink was overpowering.
Pish and shite, he said, emptying his chamber pot. That's what they
feed us. Slop in, slop out. You'll also find it's the two languages most
folk speak in here. If they're not talking pish they're talking shite.
I made some kind of noncommittal grunt.
But you, my friend, he said, strike me as an intelligent man.
Thank you, I said, not knowing how else to respond.
Robertson's the name, he said. Davie Robertson.
Blyth, I said. Reginald.
He laughed.
Quite a moniker! I'll call you Reg, then.
He held out right hand, the empty chamber pot in his left. He saw
me glance at it and hesitate, and again he laughed, wiped the free
hand on his overalls, held it out again. We're all in it, he said, and
I shook his hand, the grip firm.
Reg.
Davie.
All in it.
Right in it!

Picking oakum was as wretched and tedious a job as it sounded. For
me It harked back again to Oliver Twist – the boys in the workhouse
were set the selfsame task, and told it was serving their country.
This was a B, Blyth I named HIM.
The oakum was a tarry fibre used in shipbuilding for caulking tim-
bers, wadding the deck planks.
We sat on hard benches at long wooden tables and worked for hours

unravelling old tarred ropes and cordage, painstakingly unpicking and taking them apart, separating out the fibre that could be used.

Robertson took me to task for it, said I was assisting the war effort. He was an absolutist and refused to do any work that supported the war machine, directly or indirectly.

I had never encountered such intensity of purpose, and I admired him for it.

It was an imperialist war, he said. The ruling classes made the war, but the workers had to fight it. I would fight for a cause I believed in, he said. But not this. Not this.

As well as picking oakum, we made mailbags, stitched the rough canvas with thick twine using sailmakers' needles that were often blunt. There were no thimbles or hand-guards and our fingers first blistered then calloused as they hardened to the work. Sometimes after a long shift my hands would clench, go into spasm as if arthritic. All for an extra hunk of bread, a mug of cocoa.

Dunk.

Glorious food.

Robertson and I were joined by another outcast, another Objector, by the name of Archie Bishop. Perhaps surprisingly, he was a butcher by trade and had even worked in a slaughterhouse. One of the guards berated him.

Wouldn't have thought you'd be squeamish, mate. I thought spilling blood would come natural.

That's it exactly, said Bishop. I've killed pigs, and I know how that feels, and I'm damned if I'm going to kill men.

The three of us were utterly different in character, but we bonded together in a kind of solidarity. The conshies.

Three became four with a new arrival, even younger than me (by a matter of weeks).

We were pointed out to him, and he came and sat at our table. Introductions were made, each to each. His name was Paul Dickson.

All right young fella, said Robertson, tell us your story.

I was called up on my eighteenth birthday, said the boy. The very day. And I said I had a conscientious objection to the war.

As we all do, said Robertson. As any sane person would.

So the chairman says, how old are you Mister Dickson? I says, Eighteen sir. Then you are clearly not old enough to have a conscience, he says. Dismissed.

That's a bloody disgrace, said Robertson. An outrage. Did you protest?

I got as far as But... said the boy, and they said I would be held in contempt. I opened my mouth again and they had me taken out and brought here.

Bastards, said Robertson.

Robertson liked to tease me about being vegetarian. He could understand it as a philosophical position, and even as a a political statement.

Your man Shaw, he said, puts the case very well. Animals are his friends, and he's not in the habit of killing and eating his friends.

That's certainly memorable, I said, if a little sentimental.

Hark at you! said Robertson. So what's your argument?

I believe he said he chose not to make a graveyard of his body for the rotting corpses of dead animals.

Very persuasive!

He also said – and here I tried to intone the words in an Irish accent – A mind of the calibre of mine cannot derive its nourishment from cows.

Robertson laughed. He's not one for hiding his light, is he?

He spoke out against the War, I said, and has been much criticised for it.

He said one side was as bad as the other, and he wasn't far wrong.

So you agree with him about that but not about vegetarianism?

Ach, said Robertson. It's all well and good in theory. But in practice, I don't see how it could be made to work.

It would take time, I said. Like most good things. Like the universe itself.

He laughed. I may not agree with you on this, but I like your style!
And Mr Shaw's?
And Mr Shaw's.

Next day at the mid-day mealtime in the canteen, I had brought a
little note. I had copied it, from memory, on a scrap of paper I'd
salvaged from a bin, written with a blunt stub of pencil I'd picked
up in the prison library.
It's Mr Shaw at his most persuasive, I said, and I read.
*We cut the throat of a calf and hang it up by the heels to bleed to death so
that our veal cutlet may be white; we nail geese to a board and cram them
with food because we like the taste of liver disease; we tear birds to pieces
to decorate women's hats; we mutilate domestic animals for no reason at
all except to follow an instinctively cruel fashion; and we connive at the
most abominable tortures in the hope of discovering some magical cure
for our own diseases.*
You trying to put me off my food? said Robertson. Then he laughed
and shovelled another spoonful into his mouth, from his bowl of
'stew' he admitted was mostly gravy and gristle.
Mind you, he said, It wouldn't take much!
Robertson had a way with words, and he wrote a limerick for me.

> *There was a young fellow named Reg*
> *Who was frequently heard to allege:*
> *'Eating meat is a crime*
> *Without reason or rhyme*
> *And that's why I eat nothing but veg.'*

He wrote about the others too, Archie Bishop and Paul Dickson.

> *A butcher named Bishop, one night*
> *Replied when they asked him to fight,*
> *'I've killed pigs, it's no joke*
> *And I won't kill a bloke.*
> *I'm sorry, it just isn't right.'*

Couldn't find a rhyme for Archie! said Bishop. But he laughed, delighted with it. And young Dickson was just as pleased with his verse.

> *There was a young conshie named Paul*
> *Who refused to answer the call*
> *To take up arms,*
> *Not a fly would he harm.*
> *That heroic young conshie named Paul.*

That one word *heroic* made him stand tall, and from then on I saw him walk with more of a swagger.

One night I lay awake on my palette, or rather half-awake, in that zone between waking and sleep – unable to drift off, unwilling to get up. I listened to the noises around me – the clang of an iron door far off, the footsteps of a guard on the metal walkway, now and then a shout, another prisoner perhaps, calling out in troubled sleep, or emerging from a nightmare.

Then cutting through it I heard a single voice raised in song.

> *I didn't raise my boy to be a soldier,*
> *I brought him up to be my pride and joy.*
> *Who dares to place a musket on his shoulder,*
> *To shoot some other mother's darling boy?*

I recognised the voice then as Robertson's, with its unmistakeable Glasgow gutturals. Then another voice joined in, Bishop by the sound of it.

> *Let nations arbitrate their future troubles,*
> *It's time to lay the sword and gun away.*

A third voice came in then, a younger voice that must be Dickson.

> *There'd be no war today,*
> *If mothers all would say,*

And although I was tired, my throat dry, my voice rough, I added my tuppenceworth.

I didn't raise my boy to be a soldier.

There was a racket as some of the other prisoners shouted us down, called us conshie bastards and bolshie scum, and one said, so help him, he'd swing for us. Then the guards came round and banged on the cell doors to shut us up.

Perhaps Dickson was feeling particularly heroic, buoyed up by the singing, full of bravado. But he kept singing after the rest of us had stopped and one of the guards yelled at him he'd get what for in the morning.

We had all been given the regulation prison haircut, shorn close at the back and sides, up almost to the crown, leaving a little clump on top that we'd try to flatten with water. Young Dickson always seemed to have a wiry tuft that stuck up and refused to lie flat, and it made him look like a scruffy schoolboy, or a character from a cartoon, and somehow peculiarly vulnerable.

That tuft of hair.

The day after we'd been bawling out those songs, I was queuing in the canteen for my bowl of watery slop, my hunk of stale bread, when I saw him up ahead of me, that tuft of hair unmistakable. Then there was a sudden commotion, a clatter as a tray crashed to the ground, and immediately two of the guards appeared and, incredibly, dragged young Dickson away.

I heard about it later from Robertson. One of the other prisoners, a brute by the name of Hoskins, had taken the boy to task about the singing

He's the youngest of us, said Robertson, and the smallest, and the weakest. And they call *us* cowards!

I never saw Paul Dickson after that fracas in the canteen. We heard he was in solitary, then that he had been released.

He must have friends in high places, said Bishop.

Just the opposite, said Robertson. He's done his three month minimum. Good conduct, apart from that wee rammy. They say they're letting him go.

But...?

Once he's outside, they'll say he should be with his regiment, the one he'd been assigned to. If he won't go...and he won't...he'll be rearrested as a deserter. Then he'll be court-marshalled and he'll end up back in here, starting the whole thing all over again.

But why would they do that? Bishop was genuinely perplexed.

Because they can, boy. Because they can.

God damn the warmongers, I said, so puffed up, so full of themselves. If only we could laugh them to scorn, laugh them down into hell.

If only, said Robertson. If only.

Through all the time I was in the Scrubs, Pa seldom came to visit. He found it too unsettling but said he was praying for me. Ma came when she could, though she couldn't always manage the visiting hours.

But even in the midst of darkness there is light. There was Dora, my dear cousin.

Dora.

Her face appears before me, just as she was, her dark hair centre-parted, her bright eyes that looked into my soul, intense but divinely playful. I once told her she reminded me of Dorothy Wordsworth and she laughed and said she took that as a great compliment, for she could see I was halfway in love with the poet.

And the other half? I asked.

Well then, sir, she said, I shall appropriate that for myself, and she laughed again, linked her arm in mine, quoted Dorothy.

I would not circumscribe your love:
It may soar with the Eagle and brood with the dove...

Dora came to visit me every week I was in prison. I felt sorry that she had to see me in such a place, but I was grateful for her presence, her grace. My friends saw her in the visiting area and Robertson declared she was a right wee smasher. Bishop winked and young Dickson looked away, flustered. And she smiled at them all, light in the darkness.

Woman much missed, how you call to me, call to me...

Dora.

So much unspoken.

There was a passage in Wilde's *De Profundis* which I had copied out on another salvaged scrap of paper with another blunt stub of pencil.

One of the many lessons that one learns in prison is, that things are what they are, and will be what they will be.

What would be, would be.

Time passed, as time does, and my years at the Scrubs came to an end, as did the war-to-end-all-wars. (Did we ever think that was true?) I had done time, served time, marked time, wasted time. Time had hung heavy, it had rarely flown.

I had written poems, of a sort, since my boyhood. Now I submitted two or three to the *London Mercury*, more in hope than expectation. To my astonishment, two of my verses were published.

I still have a copy of the magazine, which also contains an early poem by one William Butler Yeats.

O body swayed to music, O brightening glance,
How can we know the dancer from the dance?

Alongside was my own poem, *Mortality*, the one I just thought I might use as my *jisei*, my death verse. (Or then again, I may not).

We that change,
Hate change.
And we that pass
Love what abides.
Summer and winter,

Day and night.
All times and seasons,
Winds and waves,
Vex our spirits
With an image
Of its waning,
And bequeath
In dying beauty,
Ashes,
Darkness,
Dust.

I managed to secure a teaching post at my old school, Cleveland Road, through the good offices of my teacher there, Mr Watson. He was himself a pacifist, a Quaker, and far from being hostile towards me, as so many were, he held me in high regard for what he saw as my principled stand.

It took courage, he said, of a different order from facing bayonets and mustard gas, but courage nonetheless, and great resolve.

But there were those who disagreed, for whom Conshie was still a dirty word, like Commie, or Coward, hawked out like a cough, a curse, and often enough they'd add yet another word beginning with C. It still took me by surprise. I'd go into the little corner shop at the end of our street, aware that the jangling of the bell above the door had interrupted a conversation, and fully expecting it to continue. But the talk would stop. Abrupt. A tense awkward silence would fill the cramped space, the air thick with the fug of cheap cigarettes, Woodbine, acrid. I would pay for my newspaper, or a bar of chocolate, with not one word spoken, and I would hear the talk starting up again as the door closed behind me.

Then there were the girls.

It was unexpected and it caught me off guard, on the blind side. I had gone out in the evening to take the air, clear my head after a day's teaching at the school. It was a Friday night, and on my way home I stopped off at The Bell, an old pub on the High Street, where I made the most of a half pint of cider, all I could afford on my meagre wage. In truth it was the only thing I felt like drinking. I didn't much care for the taste of beer-in-itself, be it mild or bitter. And as for spirits, they were firewater and rotgut, held absolutely no appeal. For all Pa's born-again fundamentalism, his temperance and sobriety, he would on rare occasions fall off the wagon, come rolling home *fou and unco happy* – tipsy, half seas over. The effect was always to render him maudlin, sentimental. He would sing, not hymns but music-hall songs, not *Bringing in the Sheaves*, but *She's Only a Bird in a Gilded Cage*. A beautiful sight to see? It was not.

The next morning he'd be hungover and penitent, signing the pledge. And Ma never once upbraided or nagged him, except by an over-loud clattering of pots and pans in the kitchen, a harangue more powerful for being unvoiced.

But there I was, nursing my half-pint. The place was busy and I was content to lose myself in the warmth, the anonymity. At the far end of the bar an old fellow led a raucous singalong.

Come, come, come and make eyes at me…

I lingered over my half-pint, stepped out with some reluctance into the night.

The walk back led past a stretch of parkland called The Flats, dark and unlit. I heard footsteps behind me, two women by the sound of it, the unmistakeable clack of heels on the pavement. There was giggling, then a sweet voice calling out my name.

Reggie! Reggie Blyth!

I turned and saw them, arm-in-arm. It took me a moment to recognise them as girls who had been in my class at school, Molly and Beth, one dark one fair. Molly was the dark one and I remembered her well. She had sat two rows in front of me in class and I had often been distracted by the turn of her head, the way she would coil a strand of that dark hair round her finger as she gazed up at the teacher, occasionally darting a glance at me over her shoulder then looking away again with a faint half-smile.

Now here she was, a young woman, calling my name, a siren-cry. I was all awkwardness and tense excitement as I nodded to them, ran a hand through my hair. They stopped and whispered to each other, laughed again, surprised me by hurrying across the road, light

on their feet, and disappearing into the park. I was confused. Did
they expect me to follow? Then fair-haired Beth was crossing the
road again, coming towards me.
She handed me an envelope and flashed me a look I couldn't read.
Amusement, perhaps, but tinged with malice? She ran back to join
her friend.
She was the go-between, delivering the *billet-doux*.
The envelope was scented, faintly floral. Violet.
I tore it open, and inside was a single white feather.
I heard the girls laughing together, a shriek, as they ran off and left
me there, burning.
Expense of spirit in a waste of shame.
What shocked me most was the thought that they must have
planned it. Did they carry the white feather with them on the off
chance they would encounter a known Conshie? Or had they seen
me go into the pub, hurried home to pick up the feather, then waited
for me in the street outside?
Once as a young boy, before my pacifist principles had taken root,
I fell into an argument with another boy who challenged me to
step outside for a fight. He said he would sort it by knocking my
block off. Full of bravado I agreed and followed him. I had barely
raised my fists when he hit me with one hard sickening punch to
the solar plexus, drove the breath right out of me so I gasped for air
and doubled over and that was an end of it. The boy laughed and
turned away.
And that was how this felt now, the shock of it, the sudden punch
to the gut, the not-being-able-to-breathe.
Scent of violet. A single white feather falling to the ground. The
taste of cider sour in my mouth.
I never mentioned any of this to my parents or to Mr Watson or
anyone else at the school. I told some of it, in edited form, to dear
Dora as we strolled of an evening in the park. She intuited that I
was a little morose, which was not generally in my nature. I told her
what had happened, trying to make light of it, playing up my own
sense of foolishness.
She stopped and took my hands, looked into my eyes.

You are strong, she said simply, and this will pass. Then she linked her arm in mine and we walked on across the park.

Dora.

If we had not been cousins, tied by bonds of consanguinity.

If.

I have written somewhere that I came to Zen through disappointment in love.

It would have been a marriage of true minds (and bodies) to which I would not have admitted impediment. But she, for all her liberal ideas, was troubled at what might be the outcome, especially if we were to have children.

If.

I knew I would move on. There was a wide world out there and I sensed it was my destiny to travel through it (and to travel *hopefully*). I was grateful to Mr Watson for the teaching job at the school, but the thought of working there all my days, growing old and chalky-white, filled me with a kind of melancholy dread. I could feel it physically, in the pit of my stomach.

Encouraged once more by Mr Watson – he gave me a reference that was almost excessively positive – I applied to study English Literature at University College. My application was successful. I was awarded a scholarship. I had taken the first step.

University would bring changes I could never have foreseen, open up possibilities I couldn't even imagine, and it was where I met Annie.

Annie.

I see her face, suddenly, intensely *there*.

Initially (*initially!*) we were a happy alphabetical accident – Berkovitch A and Blyth RH, assigned to the same tutorial group, seated together.

Blyth and Berkovitch. Berkovitch and Blyth. I said later it sounded like a two-piece comedy act, she said more likely a dodgy firm of East-end solicitors.

She arrived late for the first seminar – a flurry of agitation, a rush of air as she pushed open the door, let it crash behind her. It was a cold October afternoon, grey and dank, and she brought the outside in with her.

She was small, wore a big old heavy overcoat, buttoned up, and a long scarf wound round her neck and over her head. She took off the coat and unwrapped the scarf, shook out a dark tangle of curls.

Sorry, she said, to the lecturer, to the room in general.

I moved along the bench to make room for her, and she flashed that smile at me, bright-eyed.

Thank you, she said, something *mitteleuoropaisch* in the accent.

Don't mention it.

I just did, she said.

She settled, took out some papers from a canvas shopping bag.

To continue... said the lecturer.

I could feel the warmth emanating from her, smell her perfume, something light and fresh overlaying her own smell, unique and particular, musky.

To continue...

When the session was over, she held out her hand. Annie, she said, Annie Berkovitch.

Reg, I said, Reg Blyth.

We shook hands with what felt like an excessive formality and she laughed. Reg, she said. Good.

Her hand was small in mine, but the grip firm, warm.

Good.

We began by meeting in the student canteen, comparing notes over bitter coffee or stewed tea from an urn that was constantly topped up – one tin mug could endlessly be refilled at no extra charge. (Perhaps that was what began to put me off tea and coffee). Or we'd swipe extra slices of bread and margarine from the stack beside the soup pot. Miraculously, Annie was vegetarian, like me, and she too had been against the war. She found me funny, I found her enchanting, and fascinating, and exotic.

It's good we met, she said.

Yes, I said.

It must be meant, she said. Fated.

Perhaps.

Whatever the underlying cosmology, I found that my happiness was more and more predicated on seeing her. I felt a lightness in my being when she appeared at classes. We looked out for each other, sat together at lectures or for those long coffee breaks. We talked, and laughed, sometimes just sat silent, drinking each other in. She was like nobody I had ever known, not even Dora.

We shared a love of Bach. We talked about books we had read – I introduced her to the peculiarly English wisdom of Matthew Arnold, she offered me the dark mysticism of Meister Eckhart.

Gott ist namenlos, she said, and I asked her to say it again, not because I didn't understand, but for the sound of the words, her mouth shaping them.

We spent more time together, went to free concerts, recitals, glad in each other's company. The attraction grew into intimacy, the *frisson* was undeniable, her hand on my arm as she spoke, bright-eyed, about something, about *anything*, animated and passionate, holding my gaze. Our knees would touch as we sat talking, talking, or side-by-side at a seminar. Our bodies would be thrown together as we travelled to the city by bus whenever it lurched round a corner. We grew close.

I was inexperienced and felt clumsy the first time, in her rented room, on a Sunday morning when her landlady was out at church. The room was shabby, smelled damp. The wallpaper was yellowed, the floral pattern faded except for a rectangle where a picture had once hung. Beside it, above the bed, was a little framed painting, a Russian ikon depicting the Virgin Mary, adding to the sense of the sacrilegious. (Her own background was Jewish, but there was something in this image of the Madonna she found comforting).The house backed onto a railway line, the main route into King's Cross, and the trains juddered past with grinding regularity.

It was less than idyllic. In truth, the act itself felt slightly ludicrous, verging on the absurd. But we were swept along by it, the sheer urgency, and in the moment heedless of consequences. We gave no thought for the morrow. The fear came later, an anxious wait till the all clear.

After that first time I took what were known as *precautions*, purchased prophylactics from the barber's shop. *Will that be all, sir? Something for the weekend, sir?*

And if things had been otherwise, if Annie had become pregnant, what then? How would that responsibility have changed our lives, the road, or roads, we would travel? We would certainly have married, we were agreed on that, and having agreed on it we went ahead anyway, were married within the year.

We loved each other, that was clear. There was no need for any great romantic declaration. I don't even think I formally proposed. Annie was nothing if not pragmatic. We weighed it up, pro and con.

We could do a lot worse, she said, and I laughed. Yes, indeed we could.

The ceremony was a simple one, not to say perfunctory, at the local registry office.

When I try to recall the day, the memories are like snapshots in black and white, the ones I used to keep in a big old photo album, held in place with little paper mounts at each corner, dates and captions handwritten underneath. That album travelled with me to Japan, must have been destroyed with much else in the Summer of '44, but I can still bring the images to mind.

Myself in a three-piece tweed suit, a dark tie, my thick hair slicked down with water but springing back, unruly as ever. I stood, upright and serious, the pose formal, fixing my gaze on the camera with focussed intensity, unwavering, unsmiling, but perhaps with a glint in the eyes. A confident uncertainty. My parents must have paid the photographer whose sole admonition to us was to freeze and not to move. So we froze and did not move.

Annie beside me, half a head shorter, leaning into me, her arm linked in mine, her head to one side. She wore a high-buttoned coat, a soft bonnet with a cloth flower on the brim, a little posy of real flowers in her free hand. She too maintained a seriousness, but there was something in the set of the mouth, the bright eyes, suggesting a barely restrained mirth.

There were photos of both of us individually, separate. There was a group shot, set up and posed as if in a studio. My parents standing to attention, my grandmother between them. On the other side a wistfully smiling Dora next to Annie's mother who looked small and lost in an old too-heavy overcoat. Slightly behind, standing back, self-deprecating as ever, Mr Watson peering through his glasses, for all the world like a character from Dickens, hands clutching his lapels.

That time. That place. These people.

How it was, how we were. So very long ago.

We moved into a rented ground floor two-room coldwater flat, the privy outside the back door in a tiny scrap of garden where nothing much grew. The back room was the kitchen with an old table and a couple of wooden chairs. Propped on its end in the corner was a big tin bath we dragged out every Friday night to the middle of the floor where we filled it with pans of water boiled on the gas stove. We prided ourselves on that luxury, a bath once a week, *whether-we-needed-it-or-not!*

Like Annie's previous accommodation, the flat was close to the railway line, and in some strange way I found I liked the noise of the trains, took a kind of comfort in it. I realise now I found it almost mantric, the regularity and repetition of it, the clatter and grumble, percussive.

In the front room was a heavy-framed bed with noisy springs. Along one wall I built a bookcase to hold all the books we already owned and the many more I was sure we would acquire.

The kitchen table was where we would work of an evening, spreading out our books and papers, sometimes looking up at each other, grinning at the ridiculous miracle of our being there. It was good, and we were content.

The way time and chance conspire to change our lives. A visitor

from Japan was to address graduating students about the possibility
of teaching English out East, not in Japan itself but in Korea. A
Bach cello recital scheduled for that evening had been cancelled,
so we went instead to the talk, Annie complaining that she had no
interest whatsoever in going to Korea.

We had discussed going abroad – we were young, and England
could feel cramped and stifling. That sense of constraint had come
upon me again, a dread at the thought of being limited, trapped.
The scholarly life held an appeal, but the academic world seemed
sterile. Nor could I imagine settling for a dull suburban existence,
never travelling beyond these shores.

There was something else too, a sense that we were both, in certain
circles, regarded as outsiders, beyond the pale, Annie for her Jew-
ishness, I for my adherence to pacifism – the white feather factor.
Often it didn't amount to much, a look, a dismissive smirk, a turning
away so we felt cold-shouldered. But the idea of moving on and out,
getting away from an England still riven by divisions of hierarchy
and class, had been in our minds.

Annie's preference was for America. She liked the idea of the life
we could make there, freedom and open spaces, a sense of endless
possibility. I had always been drawn to the East, by temperament
and inclination. India was an option, but I wanted no part of the Raj
and all its works, the brutality and arrogance of Empire. So I was
intrigued by the subject of this talk, the promise it offered.

If, if, if, if, if, if…
If that concert hadn't been cancelled, if we hadn't gone to the talk.
That singular occasion, and all that followed from it.

The speaker, Akio Fujii, was a young man of about my own age.
(I later discovered we were indeed born in the same year). I was
immediately taken with his manner, his bearing. He sat, straight-
backed but relaxed, not rigid. He was handsome and dapper, elegant
in a dark suit and tie. His English was accented, but confident,
measured, and I could understand every word without difficulty.
He spoke of Korea, its beauty, something of its history. But when

he spoke of his homeland, something else entered into the telling. There was an intensity, a quiet pride. He mentioned Shinto, the national religion, its essential animism, a kind of democracy of all things, which he said was not at all in conflict with Buddhism. He used the word Zen, and I heard it spoken for the first time. *Zen*. It was a small stone dropped in a still pool, its ripples spreading out.

We spoke to him after his presentation, were charmed by his attentiveness, his quiet grace.

So, he said at last. Would you be interested in going to Korea to teach?

I looked at Annie. She smiled, gave a little shrug.

Yes, I said. Yes.

While I was still in London, still teaching, I had another of those chance encounters that occur from time to time which seem somehow fated, like scenes from a carefully-plotted novel. My bicycle had a flat tyre so I hadn't ridden it to work. I was delayed leaving the school and missed the bus I would have caught. I decided to walk the two miles home. Halfway there I heard a voice behind me, a Glasgow voice I recognised.

Reg? Reggie Blyth!

I turned and it was Davie Robertson, my fellow conshie from the Scrubs. Older, harder, more gaunt, more embattled.

As I live and breathe! I said.

There was a young fellow named Reg...

Who was frequently heard to allege...

Still philosophising? he asked.

Afraid so, I said. Still agitating?

Always have, always will.

We were passing a pub and he suggested stopping for a pint. I said I would settle for a ginger beer. Since the white feather incident, I had lost my taste for cider, forsworn even this slight indulgence. I told Robertson I was teetotal (a wonderful word) and he shook his head, said, Ach Reg!

We talked for a bit, he swigging his pint, I sipping my fiery but innocuous brew, and he asked if I'd ever had news of the others in our little group.

Not a word, I said.

I met Archie Bishop, he said. By chance. Like us meeting today. He's back at his old job, wielding a meat cleaver.

Needs must, I said.

He told me something really…distressing, said Robertson. About what happened to young Dickson.

Paul.

I don't know, maybe Bishop met somebody in the boy's family. Anyway he heard the story and he says it's the God's honest.

He took a swig from his pint. You'll remember they let the boy out after he'd served his first three months? Well that wasn't the end of it. They said now he was out, he'd have to join his regiment, the one they'd assigned him to. He refused and was re-arrested as a deserter. You thought that might happen.

Aye. Only this time they didn't bring him back to the Scrubs. They actually took him to France with the regiment. He wouldn't fight – he couldn't fight. Suffered what they call shellshock. They court-martialled him for disobeying a military order, and they shot him.

Dear God, I said.

Not much in evidence, said Robertson. No sign of a dear God in any of this.

No, I told him, I had to agree.

As flies to wanton boys are we to the gods. They kill us for their sport.

That other young man, decades later, to all intents and purposes my own son.

Lee.

If only, if only.

I never ran into Robertson again after that chance meeting. The fates did not conspire. The moving finger wrote, moved on. But once, again by chance, by the unlikeliest of coincidences, I was rummaging one rainy afternoon in a secondhand bookshop in Shinjuku. Tucked away in a corner was an old wooden crate stuffed with books in English, mostly tattered and musty, the pages curled with damp. There was little of interest – religious tracts, pre-war travel guides, a bundle of bus timetables from the Midlands. But in amongst them was a little book of verse, written by one David Robertson and published by a workers' press in Glasgow. The title was *Prison Poems*, the title printed in red against a black-and-white drawing of a brick wall with a high, barred window.

Did ye hear about the lonely prisoner? He was in his cell!

The poems were doggerel, setting new words, anti-war propaganda, to popular songs and verses. But as I read I could hear Davie's voice belting them out, and I found myself unexpectedly moved.

I showed the book to the shopkeeper, pointing at the cover, laughing as I tried to explain the author was a friend of mine. Perhaps he wanted to humour this crazy gaijin jabbering at him, or thought I had written the book myself and was what the Americans call a jailbird. Or, more likely, as a simple gesture of kindness he insisted I take the book and refused to accept payment.

That book must have been destroyed in '45, along with so much else.

But once again I get ahead of myself in the telling.

I have been writing this after the fashion of some of the modern novelists, in the first person, meandering here and there as the fancy takes me, as memory dictates. And if I cannot remember exactly, I shall make it up to the nearest approximation.

Was it like that?

Yes, it was exactly like that. More or less.

2

LAND OF MORNING CALM

I cannot recall in exact detail our preparations for the move to Korea. Annie had been swayed by my enthusiasm, decided to give it a go. What did we have to lose? We waited till after we had graduated, then made our plans, booked our passage, packed our worldly goods – a box of books, a few clothes – to be shipped on ahead. What life awaited us we had no idea.

To be young!

I thought we were to travel by train, get to Moscow then on across Asia by the Trans-Siberian Railway. With all the enthusiasm of that small boy whose father had worked for the Great Eastern, I threw myself into planning the journey, imagining it. I traced the route on a map, spread out on the kitchen table. I pored over timetables. Moscow to Kurgan, Omsk, Irkutsk, Lake Baikal, Manchuria and on to Vladivostok. The very names were thrilling and I intoned them in a gravelly voice in my best Russian accent, arms folded like a Cossack dancer, all for Annie's sake, to make her laugh.

Idiot! she said, in her own best Russian accent. Ee-dyot!

To make her laugh. There were times when I thought that was my main goal in life.

But the journey for her was no joke. For various complicated reasons I could never quite fathom, the long haul was not overland but by boat. Annie was a creature of fire, not water, and she did not travel well. (Nor did she travel hopefully, but rather in desperation to arrive). By the time we made landfall in India, docking at Bombay, she was wretched and close to despair. The seasickness had left her washed-out and weak, unable to keep down food which in any case was unpalatable. My iron constitution enabled me to survive more or less unscathed. My years in the Scrubs had taught me to survive on next to nothing, and on the voyage I supplemented the miserable fare on offer with a supply of chocolate I had stashed away in my suitcase. Annie found even that hard to stomach, the smell of it too sickly-sweet. She subsisted on black tea without milk or sugar, charred slices of dry toast. For my part I was helpless to ease her suffering (apart from fetching the tea and toast from the galley). I quite literally soothed-her-fevered-brow, cooling her forehead with a damp cloth.

At Bombay, we disembarked and had a few days to rest and recover before the next stage of the journey. Annie felt a little better for being on dry land, but was still not strong enough to go outside and walk around. So I headed out alone, followed my nose and my instincts. The place was quite simply overwhelming, a cacophony of noise, kaleidoscope of colour, an olfactory assault, rancid and stagnant, intoxicating and fragrant. I had never known anything like it, was completely unprepared.

It was only a few short years since the Amritsar massacre, Jallian-wala Bagh – hundreds of unarmed demonstrators, among them women and children, herded into a walled garden from which there was no escape and gunned down by British troops. Reading the accounts of it had made me feel physically sick. Man's inhumanity. I had always been uncomfortable with the whole idea of colonial-ism, nations subjugated, plundered for their resources in the name of democracy, or civilisation, or God help us, Christianity. It was an abomination, especially when imposed by brute force on a culture as ancient, as sophisticated, as India.

I had with me a little pocket edition of the *Bhagavad Gita*, the Song of the Lord, published in the series *Wisdom of the East*. (I have it still, its cover faded, pages yellowed and dog-eared). I had read it on the voyage and could quote passages by heart.

It slays not, nor is it slain. It is born not, nor does it die.
Weapons cannot cleave it, fire cannot burn it, water cannot drench it,
wind cannot dry it.
For him that is born, death is certain, and certain is birth for him that is
dead. Therefore when a thing is unavoidable, grieve not.
Grieve not.
I wondered how many of those slaughtered at Amritsar had faced
death sustained by that teaching.
Thinking of me when he goes forth leaving the body, he attains the highest
way.
How many had invoked the Lord as they ran in panic and the En-
glish bullets tore their flesh?
Even by me they are already slain.
And these words were spoken by Krishna to Arjuna on the battle-
field at Kurukshetra.
I happened on a little statue of Krishna at a wayside shrine and I
stopped in front of it. The figure was graceful, depicted the god with
his flute raised to his lips.
Unheard melodies.
Someone had garlanded the statue with a string of yellow flowers,
placed a few more blossoms at his feet. Unbidden, I folded my
hands and bowed.
Namaste.
As I turned away I saw a portly Englishman, a caricature in khaki
shorts, glaring across at me with a look of utter disdain as if he had
just detected a particularly fetid smell right under his nose. I couldn't
help myself. I folded my hands again and bowed to him, just as I
had bowed to Krishna.
He took a step forward and for a moment I thought he might ac-
tually strike me. Instead he spat out, Damn fool! and strode off in
high dudgeon.
He was the epitome of a certain kind of pigheaded John Bull Eng-
lishness, imbued with an innate and unfounded certainty of its own
superiority. God was in his heaven and all was right with the Empire
on which the sun never set. I imagined there were many of his type
in India. He also reminded me forcibly and uncomfortably of the

members of the panel who had interviewed me, long ago and in another world, that cold committee room in Leytonstone, before I was consigned to Wormwood Scrubs.

Are you a religious man, Mr Blyth, Yes or No?

I continued, away from the main roads, down side streets and narrow lanes, past hawkers and street vendors, beggars in rags, some crippled or maimed, and worst of all children, scrawny and malnourished, hands held out, eyes beseeching.

I was not prepared, had no money to speak of. Hands tugged at my sleeve, and I felt if I stopped I would be swamped. And which one to choose, to bless with my feeble largesse, my few miserable pennies? I bowed to them all, said Sorry, kept my head down and pushed on, took refuge in a small temple, stepped into its coolness and found myself in front of a statue of Ganesh, the elephant-headed Remover of Obstacles, and once again I bowed.

Namaste.

Of all the Hindu gods, pot-bellied Ganesh was the most benign, the most warmly human. There was strength here, that elephant strength, solid, indomitable. But there was kindliness and compassion, a twinkle in the eyes. I looked at him long, smiled back at him, filled with an immense and unexpected sense of wellbeing. There was a rich fragrance of incense in the air, heady and sweet, perhaps sandalwood. A sadhu in yellow robes appeared beside me, folded his hands and began to chant in what I took to be Sanskrit, a rapid singsong incantation, a mantra that sounded like *Aum Ganeshaya Nama*. I began to feel lightheaded, whether from the journey or the heat, the sheer exhaustion of it all, but behind that was a wonderment at the sheer otherness of everything. It was utterly dreamlike yet utterly real, and here I was, Reg Blyth, in the midst of it, walking through it. I entered another temple, passed through a courtyard and up a flight of worn stone steps, stopped in front of a statue I recognised as Shiva in the form of Nataraj, Lord of the Dance. The incense here was deeper and darker, musky, the smoke thick. This was the god of destruction, of transformation, *that moves and moves not*, dancing in a circle of flame, dancing through aeons, dancing whole worlds, the universe itself, out of existence before the cycle began again, death and rebirth, endlessly. The face of the god was impassive, looking out, looking on.

This was openness to all of it, to everything and nothing, the void in the full and the full in the void.

I had read of a mantra adopted by a particular school of Vedanta philosophers, who embraced an extreme form of *Advaita* or non-dualism. They would repeat *Neti, Neti...* meaning *Not this, Not this...*

It was not nihilism, but transcendence, a constant going beyond.

Not this.

Not this. Not this, but more, always more.

Beyond. Beyond the beyond...

For a moment I felt I was losing my bearings. I didn't recognise myself, didn't know who I was. And that was the truth of it, the heart of the matter. I didn't know who I was. But I had been given a glimpse into something vast, something timeless.

Back out in the street I looked about me at the teeming flow. *So many, so many...* Drops in the ocean.

India itself was a reality. Not this. Not the multitudes. Not the swaggering arrogance of the Raj and all its works. Not the politics of the place, not the history. It was behind and above and beyond all these, a great being, a living consciousness.

I made my way back to the docks, to our lodgings, to Annie, to our life.

Given the importance Japan was to assume later in my life, the intensity of what I would experience there, it is strange to think back to our arrival in Kobe. Of course we were still very much in transit, en route to Seoul, and perhaps the long voyage had finally taken its toll on me as well as Annie. Nothing felt quite real.

I do remember Akio being at the dock to meet us when we arrived. He was not an effusive man but his joy at seeing us was evident. He seemed unsure whether to bow or shake hands, so he did both at once, laughing.

Welcome to Japan!

In retrospect the words resonate – Japan my home now these many long years, and soon to be my final resting place.

Welcome.

Akio took charge, quietly, efficiently, dealt with our luggage, our passports and paperwork, all the formalities that had to be negotiated. He had a cab waiting and sped us to a pleasant hotel.

If we thought we would have time to rest and recuperate after the journey, Akio had other ideas.

You have to see a little of Japan Proper, he said, before you travel on. We can make quick tour. You say whistle-stop?

Indeed we do.

He took us first to Kyoto, just an hour and half by train, and we found ourselves standing on the verandah of the great temple Kiyomizu-dera, jutting out from a hillside, built on huge wooden pillars. We looked out, awed, at the view across the city as Akio explained that the present building – a mere 400 years old – had been constructed without the use of a single nail, on the instruction of the Tokugawa Shogun Iemitsu.

Akio said there was an expression, Jumping off Kiyomizu Stage. It means what you call Taking the Plunge.

Like what we're doing, I said.

Yes!

Kiyomizu, he said, means clear water, and he showed us where we could drink from a waterfall that flowed down from the hill. He said drinking it would bring long life and good luck. There were wooden ladles and I took one and leaned out, laughing as I soaked my sleeves but gathered enough to share with Annie.

The water was clear and cold.

Kiyomizu.

Another day we travelled further, took the train in the opposite direction, to Hiroshima.

It is impossible to say the word now, or write it, without conjuring the image of the cataclysm, devastation. *Now I am become death…* But back then it was just another port city with a rather beautiful name that sounded to my ears like waves on a shore.

We went there en route to another famous beauty spot which Akio insisted we see, the island temple of Miyajima. From Hiroshima there was a short ferry crossing and there it stood, apparently floating on the water, a huge red torii gate.

It's an image much used, perhaps overused, to conjure an aspect of Japan for the tourist. But seeing it there, rising above the incoming tide, it was a thing of immense beauty, a portal to some other realm. Beyond the gate, in the temple grounds, a few little deer grazed, delicate and graceful, utterly enchanting.

Akio would have loved to show us more of his country – but for now it was just a staging post, a stop on the way to Korea.

Some day we come back together, he said. Spend more time.

I would like that, I said.

Some day.

If merely breathing the air of India and Japan had opened my eyes (all three of them!) then being in Korea – living there – was to enter fully into another world, another reality altogether, and from the outset I found that *otherness* intoxicating. I was in a waking dream, though at times I felt as if my life in England had been the dream and I had awakened to this.

I was happiest just walking the streets, taking in the sights and sounds and smells. The men here and there dressed in long white robes gathered at the waist, wearing high-crowned broad-brimmed hats. They all seemed to walk with a kind of swagger, meeting my gaze with a look of amusement, secure here in their own place, their own land, where I was the interloper, the alien, the stranger. Little children in bright tunics, carrying smaller children on their backs. All unashamedly curious. Clearly the foreigner, particularly the round-eye westerner, was still an unusual sight. I did my best not to terrify them (but did not always succeed, and often sent them scurrying).

I found the markets a particular delight, the tradesmen and pedlars and food stalls, merchants selling everything-under-the-sun. In one stretch there was a scribe writing letters for the illiterate, a barber offering close shaves with an open razor, an old wizened medicine man dispensing potions and elixirs. There was even a dentist plying his trade (plier-ing his trade!) right there on the dusty pavement. (No anaesthetic, just a stoic acceptance of necessity, a grim trust in the man's efficiency and skill, making it quick). I caught the scent of clove oil, perhaps all they had by way of antiseptic and painkiller, and I felt my own teeth clench.

There were stalls selling food and drink, noodle bars and tea shacks, the smells hanging pungent in the air, fried fish and seared meat and all manner of spices. Outside one place the carcass of what I took to be a pig was roasting on a spit over an open fire. Annie covered her nose and mouth, turned away.

I thought it was a dog, she said.

It was not a good sign.

Initially we stayed in staff accommodation at the University, a little self-contained apartment, clean and compact. Akio apologised for the lack of space, the smallness of the rooms, but it was larger than anywhere we had lived in London, and we set about making it comfortable. Once a week Akio invited us to his own home where his charming wife Motoko prepared vegetarian food for us, introduced us to Japanese cuisine. She had a brightness about her, a kind of quiet poise. If all Japanese women were like this, I thought, I was in danger of being severely smitten.

The University was called Keijo, the Japanese name for Seoul.

Why not Seoul? I asked him.

He said Keijo was Japanese for Capital City – in Korean that was Gyeongseong. Before the arrival of the Japanese, it had been called Hanseong, Chinese City, and Hanyang, Chinese Light.

Most Korean people, he said, are happy not to call it by those names.

Most? I said.

I suppose, he said, there is small minority who look to China. And some old people still say Hanseong. Or Hanyang.

I rather like the sound of those, I said. Especially Hanseong. It sounds more musical. More true.

Perhaps, he said. But now it is Keijo.

Or Gyeongsong.

Not so much used, he said. Keijo is best.

Not Seoul?

Not Seoul.

The city was surrounded by mountains, a protective presence. It did the heart good to see them there, timeless. It was thrilling to look up, past buildings, see distant vistas opening out, hills beyond hills receding, and every day different, depending on the time, the light, the weather. It was always changing, always the same.

The old hymn came back to me. *I to the hills will lift mine eyes.* I had sung that in London as a boy, never having seen an actual hill, only flat never-ending cityscape all around.

This was something else entirely and I found it invigorating.

On my first day teaching, Akio introduced me to the class of boys, all in uniform, tunics buttoned up to the neck, Japanese-style. They were uncertain, curious, respectful, polite.

They stood to attention, chorused, *Good morning Mister Buraisu,* bowed in unison. No doubt they were weighing me up, this alien dropped into their midst from another world.

Akio had said they most certainly would not know what to make of me. My appearance, he said, stocky build, large head, had something of the Slav about it, and they might think I was Russian. He said Russians often appeared in the city, the military in uniform, businessmen in their dark suits. He said perhaps to the boys I might appear similarly imposing.

Very well then, I said. I must try not to impose.

I did not mean...

Stocky? I said. Big-headed? Slavic?

He looked concerned, then realised I was teasing him.

Still.

By comparison with his own slight build I was indeed on the solid side.

Like an elephant. Like Ganesha the Remover of Obstacles. Head like a battering ram.

So.

My lessons, and much of my conversation, would naturally be in English. But out of necessity, or at least simple courtesy, I felt I should acquire a smattering both of Korean and Japanese.

Annie mimicked the sounds she could hear, nasal and clanging, singsong. She said (reluctantly I thought) she would try to master the basics, enough to get by in the marketplace.

I noticed from the outset that the two languages were similar, at least in syntax, so learning them in parallel was made that little bit easier. The sentence structure, for example, the word order, was the same. Subject, object, verb.

Focusing straight away on what for me would be the essentials, I learned to say in Japanese, *Watashi-wa niku o tabemasu.* And in Korean, *Na nun kogi run moguo.*

I eat meat.

And even more important, *Watashi wa niku o tabemasen,* and *Na nun kogi run anmoguo.*

I do not eat meat.

To most of my colleagues this would better be rendered in English as, I am decidedly odd, probably untrustworthy.

With the boys, it was important that I conduct the lessons in English, and I tried from the start to instill a love of the language, its musicality and its rhythms. (Sense, I thought, would follow). There was no better way of doing this than introducing them to poetry, poetry and more poetry.

I would often stride to the front of the room, motion them to sit down (for they would be standing as I entered). I would scribble the title of the poem on the blackboard, perhaps the name of the poet (even if that was the ever-prolific *Anon*). Then I would simply declaim.

Who killed Cock Robin?
I, said the Sparrow,
With my bow and arrow.
I killed Cock Robin.

Who saw him die?
I, said the Magpie,
With my little eye.
I saw him die.

And so on.

From day one I made a point of identifying the boys individually, learning their names. This, I believed, was a pleasant surprise to them. My predecessor, an American missionary by the name of Kerr, had made no such effort. Akio also told me Mr Kerr had been difficult for the boys to understand, with his American accent and his tight-lipped delivery. By contrast, said Akio, they found my voice musical and easier to follow.

I had no sooner congratulated myself on my success, when an incident took the wind out of my sails. I was in full flow, delivering a lesson (I use the term loosely) when I noticed a change in the atmosphere, a kind of tension.

Is something wrong? I asked.

Nobody spoke.

One boy cleared his throat, another meticulously straightened the sheets of paper on his desk, a third arranged his pens in a row. Nobody met my eye, until the first boy caught my gaze and looked quickly away.

I addressed him directly.

Well?

He seemed to hesitate a moment, gathering himself. He took a quick sharp intake of breath and stood up abruptly, his chair scraping behind him. He bowed.

I nodded. *Hai.*

Sumimasen

What was it I could read in his face? Anger? Apprehension? Fear? Exasperation?

He composed himself, made his face a mask.

What is it? I asked.

He began by speaking in Japanese, then, remembering the rule of the class, he tried to express himself in English.

We don't understand, he said. Talk fast. Too many things.

It had taken a great deal of courage. The nail that stands up gets hammered down.

I felt great respect for the boy, even though his words stung me.

What about the rest of you? I asked. Do you feel the same?

Again there was that moment of hesitation. The boy looked round, and all the others stood up as one, bowed in unison.

A year or two ago, in that little cinema in Shinjuku, I saw the Hollywood film Spartacus, a splendid story of the Slaves' Revolt in ancient Rome, starring the redoubtable Kirk Douglas (of the craggy jaw and cleft chin). At one point in the action, after the revolt has been crushed, the Roman general in charge asks the defeated slaves which of them is Spartacus. The intention is to make an example of him by crucifying him at the roadside. The real Spartacus (played by Douglas) gets to his feet and says *I am Spartacus*. But immediately another slave stands up and says the same. *I am Spartacus*. Then they all stand up, one by one, the old and the young, and each one calls out *I am Spartacus*.

This is what comes to mind now as I remember that day in the classroom at Keijo.

The boys stood there in silent challenge. The Students' Revolt. I was taken aback, but at some level I was impressed that they had the gumption to stand up and make a protest. Then I noticed something even more extraordinary, even more impressive. In the far corner of the room, in the very back row, was one boy who had not stood up. He had resolutely stayed in his seat, not joining in. He sat in defiance of his peers, eyes fixed ahead.

The others had clearly agreed their strategy in advance. They would show solidarity, they would stand together. For this one boy to resist was an act of real courage and defiance.

I remembered myself, not much older than these boys, standing in that dingy committee room in Leytonstone, stating my conscientious objection to the Great War.

Bloody coward. Damned disgrace.

I motioned to the rest of the class to sit down.

The boy who had not stood up – his name was Kasai – was one of the brightest in the class, one of the most imaginative. At some

level he understood what I was trying to do in the lessons. He got
to his feet.

Like the other boy he spoke first in Japanese, *sotto voce*, his words
in a rush, with much bowing to his classmates. Then, remembering
the protocol we had established, he spoke in English, softly at first,
his voice a little shaky, but gaining in confidence as he continued.

Buraisu-sensei is not always easy to understand. But maybe that
is our fault. And even small part of what he says is more better...

...is better, I corrected.

...is better, he said, than other teachers. He make us laugh, he make
us think.

For a moment I simply did not know what to say. The young man's
stumbling eloquence had touched me deeply. I bowed, felt real hu-
mility in the face of it.

Thank you, I said. I shall try to be more aware.

I clapped my hands together, said, Well then! Shall we continue?

Most of the boys looked round, at each other, at the boy in the
corner, at the one who had led the protest. They looked at me.
Tentatively they nodded.

So desu, I said. Let us continue. And I promise I shall take account
of what has been said. Now, where were we?

When I told Akio what had happened he laughed and said the boys
showed spirit.

I resolved, as far as I was able, to rein myself in, curb my tendency
to orate and declaim when I was teaching the boys.

Those boys. I see their faces before me. Young Mr Kasai, who had
spoken out in my defence, was serious and quiet, did not look in
good health. I saw him in the street one day, not long after the in-
cident, and I bowed and thanked him sincerely for his courage in
speaking out.

I will not forget you, I said, and he was genuinely flummoxed that I
should speak to him in this way, not as a superior, but simply, man
to man.

This was the reaction when I met any of the boys outside the class-
room. The Korean boys especially seemed taken aback. One young
fellow – his name was Kim – bumped into me in the department

store at the end of the day. I asked if he was shopping and he said, Yes. I said, Me too. I told him I was looking for chocolate and socks, and both were absolutely essential.

Even the boy who had led the little rebellion, Isshiki, spoke to me one day in the street. He had seen me waiting at the tram terminal and tentatively, mustering his courage, he approached and said, Hello Mister Buraisu.

Hello Mister Isshiki, I said, and gave a little bow.

He indicated an unlit cigarette held awkwardly between his fingers. Can you please lend me fire? he asked, pronouncing his words carefully.

No, I said, I'm sorry.

He looked disappointed, then I continued.

But I can give you a light.

I didn't smoke, but as it happened, I had a box of matches in my pocket – we needed them at home for lighting the stove.

His eyes brightened as I lit his cigarette and he inhaled, laughed, coughed.

In time the boys grew more relaxed with me and I less rigorous with them.

At the beginning of each class, I took a roll-call. I read out the names, alphabetically, and each boy would call out a smart Yes! when his name was called.

From time to time, especially on a Friday afternoon, there would be more responses than there were boys in the room, and I quickly re- alised a few of them were playing truant and had asked a classmate to call out on their behalf. They even took the trouble to disguise their voices.

I knew what was going on, and they knew I knew. But I let it pass. I understood the absentees had gone to a matinee at the cinema, and part of me thought they had made a good choice.

Looking back now, I realise some of those boys would be sent to the Pacific War, and some of them would never return, and I am glad I let things be, allowed them their few hours of freedom, their Friday afternoons.

The boys of summer.

Given my objections to British colonial rule in India, it was ironic that I could live happily in Korea, effectively annexed and colonised since the Meiji era by Imperial Japan. Of course it was described as a protectorate rather than a colony, a fine distinction no doubt lost on native Koreans who saw their own culture subsumed if not suppressed.

When I brought up the subject with Akio he was reluctant to discuss it. For all his openness, his experience of the wider world, he still held to the view that Japanese culture was innately superior in its essence, its refinement, its aesthetic sensibility, its pragmatism, all of it and more, embodied in Zen. So of course, he said, it was natural for Japan to extend its influence for the good, bring civilisation to its neighbours.

Whether they want it or not, I said.

We had been sipping Japanese green tea, *bancha*, with a wonderful smoky flavour, from exquisite glazed bowls, each one unique in its colouring, its texture, the feel of it cupped in the hand, just so. Even I, who was not in the habit of drinking tea, found it pleasant.

Akio set his bowl down, looked at me as if struggling to understand. And why would they not want it? he said. Japan really does give protection, from Russia, from China. These are very powerful, very dangerous neighbours.

And in return? I asked.

Again he gave me that look.

Japanese firms build their factories here, I said. Labour is cheap. They make huge profits.

And make jobs for here, he said. Is good for the economy.

And Japanese farmers, buying up the land?

Again, he said, it's good. Good relationship. You say symbiotic?

Perhaps, I said.

There was a little silence between us.

Motoko had been sitting quietly, not joining in. Now she leaned forward and picked up the teapot, swirled the leaves, smiled.

More tea?

I suppose right from the beginning I took to the place more readily than Annie.

We walked one day out of town, along the banks of the Han River and looking upstream I was elated by the vista, the landscape, the distant hills, the river itself with its traffic of little boats. I said it was timeless and looked for all the world like an old Chinese painting.

Yes, she said, It's beautiful in its way. Then she pointed downriver towards the city, the port with its shipyards, its plumes of dark smoke rising from factories.

Yes, I said. This too.

I resolved to make sense of the country and its culture through its stories, which I did my best to translate. There was one about the end of the world.

Some time in the future the last day will come. A large red sun will rise, and heaven and earth will join together in the form of a millstone, turning round and round. Every human being on earth will die, and new creatures will be born.

I read it to Annie and she shuddered.

Wonderful, she said. Just what I need to cheer me up.

She said she felt it in her stomach, visceral, and I did too – the elemental power of the image, the physicality.

The large red sun, the grindstone obliterating everything.

It's suffocating, she said.

I thought I might lighten the mood by reading some humorous stories.

There's a formula to them, I said. They end in, *As you well know...* A nudge and a wink to the reader.

All living creatures came from water, I read. Even human beings come from water. As you well know. Heaven moves, the earth does not. In the case of human beings man, in the upper place moves, but woman, in the lower place, does not. As you well know.

That's it? she said. That's the story?

This is the story of the Three Foolish Brides, I said, hurrying on.

Three brides who had been divorced from their respective husbands met together, and the first one asked the second, Why were you divorced?

It was nothing at all, came the reply. One night my mother-in-law told me to throw away the pipe ashes, so I took the pipe into the garden and knocked out the ashes on a round stone. Unfortunately the round stone was the bald head of my father-in-law, and I was divorced.

The first woman said, In my case too it was a mere nothing. My mother-in-law told me to bring in some live charcoal for smoking, so I carried it in a sieve, and I was divorced.

The third woman said, Mine was less than nothing. I couldn't get rid of the fleas in my petticoat so I steamed them in the rice-saucepan. They said I shouldn't have done that...

And I was divorced... said Annie.

Perhaps they lose something in translation, I said.

Not at all, she said. They're like your music hall routines.

I say, I say, I say...

Yes.

Take my wife...please.

I look back now at those early years in Korea, and more than any other time they have a dreamlike quality, a sense of unreality. I had taken this huge step out of my old world and everything I knew. I made a new life, or it was made for me. I was well paid and greatly valued. My salary was far in excess of what I could have earned at home, enough to buy a house and almost half an acre of land.

It was a little way out from the town centre, towards the Han River. But it was close enough to the University. I would buy a bike and could cycle to work and back.

When we first saw the site, on a low rise overlooking a field, the house was just being built and that meant we had a say in the lay-out. I even helped with the work, cutting and fitting wooden beams, laying down floorboards to be covered with tatami mats, installing sliding shoji screens. In essence it was a traditional Japanese house, which appealed to me greatly in its simplicity, its sense of proportion and space. But, partly for my own sake and partly out of deference to Annie's taste, we allowed for a living room and a study that were more western in style, rugs on the polished wood floors, a couple of armchairs, four smaller kitchen chairs and a dining table. On the wall she hung the little Russian icon she had brought with her from London.

I built in bookcases from solid pine, sturdy, ready to take my expanding collection of books. I made a workshop behind the house kitted it out with an old bench and an assortment of tools I had picked up in the market. Next to that I put up a garden shed.

From where to where? I said, when we moved in. We called to each other, from room to room, amazed.

It's hard to believe it's ours, said Annie.

But it was. Our home. Entirely our own.

We began by growing our own vegetables and they thrived in the warm, humid climate, the rich soil. We bought a dog, and I suggested to Annie, half in jest, that we could keep some hens and geese for their eggs, a goat for its milk. She laughed, said Why not? So we went ahead.

Akio was also amused. He said I was becoming a gentleman farmer, an English country gent. It was the perfect counterpoint to my teaching work, the life of the mind. The simplicity of it, the sheer physicality, was exhilarating and deeply satisfying. We bought another dog, a second goat, and finally, a horse – an old good-natured grey mare. Annie was resistant at first, thought a horse was taking things too far. But I brought her to where the beast was stabled, let Annie see her great sad knowing eyes, and clinched it by saying we would be saving her from the knacker's yard. We called her Martha and the back garden became her paddock where she could graze and move around.

On occasion I would saddle her up but lightly, without a bridle and bit. She was happy enough to carry me round the field where she might even break into a gentle trot. Riding my trusty steed, my ancient nag, I fancied myself some latter-day Don Quixote de La Mancha, a true man of zen (or Man of Zen) if ever there was one. *Doubtless you look on me as a madman, a crazy fellow, and my conduct*

*would testify to that. But let me tell you, I am not so crazy or half-witted
as you would suppose.*
This madman surrenders himself to the flow of life, that is, to the
Will of God.
He rode on his way, going where it pleased his horse to carry him.

Akio had a great enthusiasm for Zen, a deep knowledge of the phi-
losophy, which stimulated my own interest. But I have to say it was
Motoko who fired my passion for the culture and inspired me to
learn Japanese. She also kindled my lifelong love affair with haiku.
I had been blessed with an innate aptitude for languages. I had
picked up enough Korean to get by. I was even compiling a basic
Korean grammar for English speakers, thinking it might be useful.
I had also kept up my reading in Spanish, German, Italian, tackling
Cervantes, Eckhart, Dante. I had no sense that there was anything in
Japanese literature to compare with these, and I thought, foolishly,
that it was simply not worth the effort. (The arrogance of it!) To be
fair to myself, I had been subjected to the likes of Lafcadio Hearn
and his humourless romancifying of Japanese sentimentalism.
It was on another evening at the home of Akio and Motoko – Annie
and I had joined them for dinner – and the talk turned, as it often
did, to poetry. Motoko asked, all innocence, who was my favourite
haiku poet and I had to admit, feigning shame and making her
laugh, that I wasn't really familiar with the form or with any of the
poets who practised it. I think I had read one or two insipid transla-
tions, found them thin and wishy-washy, lacking in substance. With
great charm and persistence, Motoko introduced me to the haiku of
Basho and it was my moment of conversion, my road to Damascus.
She began by unrolling a paper scroll on which a single poem had
been written, the exquisite lettering trailing languidly down the
page. I asked if the calligraphy was her own and she gave a little
bow, said it was. I complimented her, said she had already made the
poem beautiful and she gave a delighted laugh, bowed again. Then
she read the words out loud, chanting them, her voice sweet and
musical. She chanted the poem again, tracing the flow of the lines

with her slender hand, finger pointing. I was captivated.

Furuike ya kawazu tobikomu mizu no oto

Had I just heard her chanting, her delivery, I might have assumed the poem spoke of things poetic, the full moon perhaps, the wind in the pines. But when she translated it I was stunned.

Old pond, she said. And frog jump in. Water make a sound.

A line of Herbert came to me. *Something understood.* And that was it, something was understood, I knew not how. Basho's frog in the poem leapt into the pond in my head, in my heart, in my consciousness, made a tiny frog-shaped *splash* that resonated, sent ripples out and out.

Yes, I said. Yes!

With Motoko's help, line by line, I made my own translation – the first of many.

The old pond:
A frog jumps in –
The sound of water

as av or p302

I knew it wasn't perfect but it was something, it was a beginning. I was as pleased with it as if the poem were my own. I bowed to Motoko. Akio clapped his hands. Annie looked uncomfortable. But a door had opened. I would learn Japanese and I would learn haiku, and Motoko – with Akio's approval – would teach me both.

Even now, after decades of immersing myself in the subject, I am amazed how often I am asked the same question. Do you think foreigners can ever understand haiku? And even after publishing volumes of my own haiku translations I am still asked, Do you think haiku can ever be translated into English? I have always found both questions infuriating, but my answers, respectively, would be, No they can't, and Yes they can. At first I would give both answers through gritted teeth, but in time I could give them quite calmly and with an unaffected smile. So perhaps in this at least I have made some progress.

The more Motoko taught me about the subtleties of the language and the intricacies of the form, the more enamoured I became, paradoxically, with the utter simplicity and, at the same time, the universality of haiku. *Multum in parvo.* Infinite riches in a little room.

No frog jumps into the same pond twice.

In the middle of the forest, if a frog jumps into an old pond, and if nobody is there to hear it, does it make a sound?

Mizu no oto.

I was in the school staff room one rainy afternoon, preparing to teach a class, when Akio came in carrying a book which he placed on the table in front of me.

This is it, he said. This is the one.

His eyes were bright with kind of suppressed excitement and he couldn't keep from grinning.

The book was in English, published in London. The title was *Essays in Zen Buddhism* and it was written by a Japanese scholar, DT Suzuki.

It is for you, said Akio. A gift. Please, keep it. Read it. It will change everything.

He was right.

I took the book home and read it straight through, staying up all night, by the light of my desk-lamp. (Annie took herself off to bed and left me to it – she had long since given up trying to understand my whims and foibles, my sudden incomprehensible enthusiasms). I didn't know anything of Suzuki or his work, but it was intriguing that it had been published at all (at a time when very little writing on Zen was available). It was edited by one Christmas Humphreys (a splendid name, I thought!), President of the Buddhist Society in London, and it pleased me to think of this physical object, this book I held in my hands, being produced in my home town and by chance – by chance! – finding its way to me here, halfway round the world. From the opening pages the book gripped me. There was clearly a

formidable intellect at work, but there was no attempt at obfusca-
tion, intellection for its own sake, thinking-too-precisely-upon the
event. The language was clear and direct, the style engaging.

It is the object of Zen, he wrote in the preface, *to save us from going
crazy or being crippled.*

I was, as they say, hooked.

Dr Suzuki was not averse to subjecting Zen to the light of the an-
alytical mind, to scrutiny and philosophical argument. But he was
adamant, it seemed to me, that this could only go so far

*Appeal to the intellect is real and living as long as it issues directly from
life. Otherwise no amount of literary accomplishment or intellectual
analysis avails...*

What came across more than anything was his sense of Zen as a
kind of enlightened common sense, albeit interwoven with all man-
ner of affirmations that seemed relevant, inappropriate, irrational
and downright nonsensical. And yet, this was the whole point (and
the paradox) – to drive the intellect beyond itself.

A monk asked Joshu, *When the body dies and returns to dust, one thing
eternally abides. Where is this one thing?*

Joshu answered, *It is windy again this morning.*

As it happened, (How I have grown to love those three words!) the
wind was shaking the trees outside the house. I looked up from my
reading and laughed, and must actually have shouted *Yes!* out loud,
for I heard Annie stirring in the next door room.

Yes, I said, this time in silence. *This*, I said. *Here*, I said. *Now.*

There was so much in the book that chimed with my own way of
thinking, my own way of seeing. The very act of reading was a kind
of awakening. Behind the words there was the sense of a great con-
sciousness expressing itself, an openness, an inclusiveness.

I was delighted too to find that the good Doctor made reference to
western poets and thinkers, in fact to some of those I held closest to
my heart. The book might have been written for me and me alone.
There was Blake, of course. *To see a world in a grain of sand.*

There were passages from Eckhart – I would tell Annie in the morn-
ing. *The eye with which I see God is the eye with which God sees me.*

He linked that to Plotinus – *That which mind, when it turns back, thinks before it thinks itself.*

Then it was back to Eckhart again. *What a man takes in by contemplation he must pour out in love.* Then Suzuki's own comment that in Zen he must pour it out in work. Mysticism had to be grounded, down-to-earth. Then the most thrilling leap of all, for me, back to Herbert.

Who sweeps a room as to thy laws makes that and the action fine.

I could have wept from sheer gratitude, an overwhelming sense of recognition.

By first light I had read the book from start to finish and was ready to begin again.

Breakfast? said Annie, standing in the doorway, rubbing her eyes.

Yes, I said, seeing her there. Yes, I said. Thank you, I said. That would be wonderful.

Yes.

It was not just that Suzuki's book had awakened something in me, deepened my understanding (or non-comprehension) of Zen. More than that, it filled me with a sense of possibility. It shone a light, showed me the kind of book (or books!) I could write myself. I was overwhelmed with gratitude and told Akio as much when I saw him the next day.

I thought so, he said, and added that he had once heard Suzuki lecture, in Tokyo, said he was wise and kind, a true Zen man.

Perhaps someday if we go to Japan you can meet him.

I bowed, said I could think of nothing that would give me greater joy.

Nothing.

Alongside haiku, the zen writings I loved best were the koans, those unanswerable questions, madly illogical, designed to push the rational mind beyond breaking point, beyond limitation into something expansive and inclusive, an awakening to the here and now. One commentator described them as *catechistic paradox*, which made me smile.

I asked Akio about the origin of the word. What did koan mean?

He said it was from the Chinese, and literally meant public record or public document. He supposed that meant it was something official and binding, not to be challenged.

Kind of like a legal case, with the master as judge?

Perhaps.

Joshu was asked, *Does a dog have the Buddha nature?* For various reasons, to answer Yes was wrong, and to answer No was just as wrong. It was like the old lawyer's question, *Have you stopped beating your wife yet?* Answer Yes or No and it's a hiding to nothing.

Joshu's answer was the single syllable *Mu*, meaning nothing. Nothing. The nothing that opens up when you realise the impossibility of answering Yes or No. Neither and both.

Cutting off the Cheshire Cat's head. The executioner's argument was, that you couldn't cut off a head unless there was a body to cut it off from.

When you've understood this scripture, said the Cheshire Cat, throw it away. If you can't understand this scripture, throw it away. I insist on your freedom.

Does a cat have the Buddha nature?

Mu.

Music. *Mu*-sic. *Mu (Sic).*

I have always been grateful for the gift of music. We had an old upright piano at home (more or less in tune) and I had been given lessons at school where there was also an assortment of recorders, violins, a cello, even a trombone. I seemed able to get a tune out of whatever one I picked up. I recognised in myself an admirable combination of aptitude and enthusiasm (allied to dogged determination). I wanted more than anything to have instruments of my own.

Every Good Boy Deserves Favour.

I have a letter Ma sent to me years ago.

I so wanted to give you music, and buy you musical instruments, and we managed it somehow out of the housekeeping and your pocket money. Your dad was never mean, not really, but very careful, and rightly so.

She added, *There is much of Pa in you.*

I found that very affecting, and still do.

I so wanted to give you music...

Was it a memory of all that which motivated me in those early heady days in Korea? That love of music, and of musical instruments, was innate, or at least had been with me from my youngest days. But there was also my father's practicality, even his frugality, the ability to make do and mend. So now that I could afford to buy instruments without having to penny-pinch as my mother had done, I found I preferred to buy instruments that were old and in need of repair.

I had another excuse to buy them. Akio had told me he wanted the pupils at the school to have music lessons with the intention of forming an orchestra. Resources were limited and there were no funds for such luxuries. That was all the incentive I needed. I told him music, like poetry, was not a luxury but an absolute necessity. The markets were a great joy to me. I picked up old books and pottery and knick-knacks – a carved wooden Buddha, a little brass figure of Ganesh, translations of Confucius and Lao-Tsu, a hanging scroll inscribed with calligraphy which someone translated for me as *Form is Emptiness*. But I felt perhaps the greatest excitement when I found a musical instrument I could patch up and restore. The first one I bought was my precious silver flute, still in its hard black case lined with red velvet. The label read *Boosey and Hawkes, London*, which gave me a momentary sense of nostalgia. (It quickly passed). The head was intact, the mouthpiece undamaged, and I could blow a single note on it, pure and clear. (One note of Zen!) I laughed and the shopkeeper laughed too, quoted me a price. I showed him how much work it would take to make it functional. He shrugged his shoulders, noncommittal but willing. I haggled him down and we shook hands on it, laughed again. Over a few days, somehow I found the materials I would need and I set to work. I replaced missing screws, some of them irritatingly finicky. I made new finger pads, gluing them into place. I oiled the joints and the little hinges. Finally I rubbed the whole thing with silver polish, the tang of it like Brasso from my childhood, and I buffed it with a soft cloth till it shone. I pieced it together and once again played one single note, purer and clearer than before. Then I played from memory a passage from *Syrinx* by Debussy, not perfectly, but Annie applauded, delighted.

After that the shopkeeper, Mr Gan, would beckon me in every time I was passing. He knew the kind of thing I was looking for and the kind of price I was willing to pay. I bought a cello and a clarinet, a second – wooden – flute and three recorders, a snare drum and two violins (one without strings – a zen fiddle!) I bought a mandolin and a balalaika, a little xylophone on a wooden base.

Mr Gan found me amusing, thought at first I was some kind of madman, perhaps in a way that must be peculiarly western. He asked me – genuinely curious – if I had many friends who were musicians and if I was making an orchestra. I told him that might well be the end result, but initially I was buying them for boys at the school who couldn't afford to buy instruments for themselves.

After that he was even more helpful, kept a look-out, offered more and more instruments at knock-down prices. I bought a viola and a third violin, a trumpet and a piccolo, two more recorders, a guitar, an accordion and a trombone. I drew the line at a great beefy tuba missing its valves, in fact I thought perhaps I had bought enough (and Annie was inclined to agree). But one day Mr Gan said he had something special to show me. He indicated I should follow him through to his storeroom at the back where something sat in the middle of the floor, covered with a tattered sheet of cloth. He raised a finger in anticipation, his eyes twinkling, and with a certain amount of ceremony, a flourish worthy of a stage magician, he whipped off the cloth to reveal an old battered harmonium in a carved box-frame. I laughed out loud at the sight of it, the incongruity. How in God's name it had ended up here was beyond me. A relic, perhaps, from some Christian enclave, a little mission-hall? I pulled up a low chair and sat in front of the keyboard. There were stops, ivory-handled, to change the tuning. The air through its reeds was driven by bellows, operated by foot pedals. I pressed down on them, tried playing a note or two and it wheezed and groaned into life, making me laugh again. It would take a great deal of work but

I was sure I could make it sing.

Mr Gan had it loaded onto a cart and delivered to my home, placed in the middle of the workshop. I saw him looking round at all the other instruments he had sold me, in various states of repair, dismantled and reassembled, and for a moment I saw it through his eyes, as if the harmonium might be the centrepiece in some infernal Heath-Robinson contraption, not a one man band but a one man orchestra.

He looked beyond the room, out through the window to the little field at the back of the house, took in the menagerie out there, the dogs and geese, the goats, the horse, all happily co-existing. He looked back at me, perhaps returning to his earlier opinion that I was quite, quite mad (and in that he was not far wrong).

Annie looked in on me later that afternoon, found me cross-legged on the floor, in the midst of the harmonium in pieces around me, and I thought she might well be in agreement with Mr Gan about my state of mind. She closed the door and left me to it.

I realise I was often at my happiest absorbed in some piece of work like that, hand and eye coordinated, mind focused, myself at rest. There was something too in the physical posture – a kind of cellular memory. I felt like some sadhu in meditation telling his beads, or an old Jewish tailor seated in his workshop, engaged in a different kind of meditation, a meditation-in-action.

Happy is the man who has found his work.

Watching my father at his workbench in the shed, behind the house in Leytonstone, sawing, drilling, turning something on a lathe. He was never happier, making and repairing, salvaging and rebuilding, and nor was I, learning from him, being his apprentice. Make do and mend. An entire philosophy in itself.

He always wore tweeds, as I have done all my adult life – sturdy and practical, rough to the touch but comfortable, and, or so I tell myself, timelessly stylish.

There is much of Pa in you.

The smells were a joy, cut wood and sawdust, turpentine and linseed oil, intoxicating as any incense, smells you feel in your teeth, that make you want to bite. I feel it now, and with it another sensation, another smell like burning, I remember it, the friction-burn of the wood in the lathe.

All forms are burning.

The telegram from Ma arrived unexpectedly, as telegrams always do.
PA DIED PEACEFULLY IN SLEEP LAST NIGHT STOP FU- NERAL NEXT FRIDAY STOP NOT POSSIBLE FOR YOU GET BACK BUT THAT'S ALL RIGHT STOP YOUR LOVING MA STOP END.
The pared-down message, printed out on a slip of paper, was stark, unembellished apart from those two words, PEACEFULLY and LOVING. And I heard Ma's voice in the THAT'S ALL RIGHT, reassurance and absolution.

Pa holding my hand on the station platform at Leytonstone, waiting for the train to Southend. Pa working in his shed, at his lathe. The smell of him, tweed and tobacco and carbolic soap. Pa standing at the pulpit in the little church mission hall we attended, leading a hymn, reciting scripture. *I am the resurrection and the life*. Pa the quietly evangelical fundamentalist, born again, but never fanatical. Pa, who should not perish, but have everlasting life.
Pa. Gone.
I showed Annie the telegram and she held me, ruffled my hair. She had hardly known Pa but she said she thought he was a good man. All he needed by way of epitaph.

It took time, perhaps weeks, but I fixed the harmonium, rendered it good as new (or rather better, as I was sure it had improved with age and with my loving ministration). I brought Annie into the workshop, sat her down on a kitchen chair, dusted off specially, and I gave a little recital for her and her alone, ran through a rep- ertoire of old hymn tunes – *Bread of Heaven, Bringing in the sheaves, Give me oil in my lamp keep me burning* (in honour of Pa, perhaps).

The noise rose and swelled and outside the dogs began to bark and howl, joining in or trying to drown me out, and Annie clapped and clapped, laughing till the tears ran down her cheeks.

Annie, Annie, Annie.
How young we were. How little we knew.

I was happy to provide the musical instruments for the school. I had the joy of finding them in the first place (the joy known to all collectors, the hunt, the quest, the search for lost treasures). Then there was the added joy of repairing the instruments, restoring them to full functionality. (And the work itself, the labour of love, was restorative in terms of my own wellbeing). Finally there was the joy of seeing the boys being given the instruments for the first time, tentatively trying them out, delighted at plucking a string, blowing into a mouthpiece. In the beginning was the sound.
In the teaching I had found my work. The Buddhists spoke of *right livelihood*, the Hindus of *Karma Yoga*, selfless action.

I began giving lessons to a few of the boys, basic instruction how to play their instruments, the violin and viola, tenor and descant recorders. We would meet after school in one of the empty class-rooms and practise for an hour. For the first few weeks I insisted they play nothing but scales and arpeggios. Over and over again, concentrating on technique and tone, again, the same runs, again, till it was second nature. Again.
Sometimes one or other of the boys couldn't stay behind, so I arranged for them to come to the house in the evening or at the weekend.
Mr Gan had found me an old upright piano which I managed to tune and it sat, imposing, against the wall of our back room. I put the boys through their paces, the scales and arpeggios. Again.
I would know the hour was over when I'd hear Annie, irritable, banging and clattering in the kitchen, letting me know she'd had enough of the screeching and scratching of strings, the morose wailing of recorders.
In the name of God, she said one night. Can't you at least give them

a tune to play?

The boys themselves asked the selfsame question (albeit without the tetchiness). They were irked by the tediousness of the repetition.

When can we play tune?

When you are ready, I said. But eventually I relented, gave them *Three Blind Mice*, and *Twinkle Twinkle Little Star*, and they went to it with a will.

I have never been good at time. I have never been good *with* time (as I have never been good with numbers). I have no mind (no-mind!) for dates, no clear memory of when this or that happened. In fact I have always been slipshod and lackadaisical about such things.

Some time ago (some time ago!) I read Mr Beckett's *En attendant Godot* and found this:

One day we were born, one day we shall die, the same day, the same second, is that not enough for you?

My answer would be Yes, it is more than enough, thank you very much.

Time passed, inevitably, inexorably.

Motoko had a child, a lovely daughter they named Katsura.

By this time it might have been expected that Annie too might have become pregnant. We had long since stopped taking precautions, deciding what would be would be, and nature would take its course. But time continued to pass and she was not, as they say, with child. If this was our lot, to be childless, then so be it. I felt no desperate need to propagate my species, my race, my particular bloodline. The planet was over-populous as it was.

But Annie, dear Annie, took it hard. She had always thought, always imagined, always assumed she would be a mother.

We walked on a grey afternoon in the grounds of Myoshin-ji temple, wandered through the graveyard, stopped before row on row of small stone statues depicting the Bodhisattva Jizo in his guise as protector of children – the miscarried, the stillborn, the aborted, the ones who simply died young.

And the unborn? said Annie. The never-were? The never-to-be? What of them?

In amongst the statues, placed in front of them, were offerings from grieving mothers, heartbreaking in their ordinariness, their banality – a doll, a toy animal, a paper parasol, a wrapped bean-cake, a small bottle of some dark fruity drink. Some of the statues had even been given little knitted baby-hats, touching and ludicrous and sad. I don't know, I said, taking her small cold hand in mine. I truly do not know.

There's nothing brings home the passage of time quite so forcefully as seeing a child change and grow. So quick. So quick. We watched little Katsura blossom into herself, now a baby, now a toddler, now an infant bright and alert and wanting it all. The Fujii's home was walking distance from where we lived, and they would often bring her round, at weekends, or in the evening after school. She would eat berries from our garden, or chestnuts we roasted – oh, the smell! – and she liked nothing better than playing with the animals. She'd feed the hens, chase the dogs, sit in front of me astride Martha our old grey mare and we'd trot round the field, content and at ease.

I am quite sure Annie was as fond of Katsura as I was. But I noticed when the child was with us, after a while there would be a change in Annie's mood. She was still all kindness, all smiles as she chatted to the girl, made her welcome. But her eyes clouded, her attention turned inward, and I knew with certainty that she still ached and yearned for a child of her own (a child of *our* own).

Akio had told me they were appointing a new member of staff and I would like him very much. Akio brought the new man to meet me in the staff room on the morning of his arrival and his eagerness was almost overwhelming.

Shinki Masanosuke, he said, bowing, grinning. He was short, compact, wore a neat grey suit.

Shinki-san, I said, returning his bow. I am very happy to meet you.

And I you, Buraisu-sensei.

He made a very good attempt at pronouncing the *th* in my name.

Fujii-sensei has told me so much about you, he said, and he shook my hand. I am dying to work with you.

I hope it doesn't come to that, I said.

He looked momentarily puzzled, then realised. Ah! You are making a joke, yes? This is pun!

He laughed, nodded vigorously, clearly delighted. By Japanese standards he was effusive in the extreme, and without further prompting he launched into his life story, telling it all-in-a-rush.

He was born in Nagasaki in 1904. (Six years my junior, then, which would have been impossible for me to guess). The family had moved to Manchuria when he was three years old, then to Seoul when he was eleven. From high school he had gone to university and studied English literature. He had taught briefly in Kyushu then applied for the post at Keijo. And here he was, back in Seoul, and most glad he would be working with me. He thought we had much in common, many things to share. English literature was the love-of-his-life. Perhaps you and I, he said, shall be like Wordsworth and Coleridge. Perhaps, I said, a little taken aback. But his enthusiasm was utterly engaging.

I think it is fate I come here, he said. Fate we meet. Fujii-sensei has told me you have a great interest in Zen.

Indeed I do.

I began Zen practice at age of seventeen, he said. Right here in Keijo, at Myoshin-ji temple. Now I am back I will resume sitting. Very happy if you join me.

I would like that very much indeed, I said. Thank you.

Good, said Akio, his eyes twinkling. Good!

It emerged that Shinki's practice as a young man had consisted of nothing too rigorous. He had not advanced as far as koan study, but had sat in meditation once a week and listened to the master's dharma talks. He had also done what he called practical zen – the physical work of cleaning and sweeping, weeding the garden. Down-to-earth, he said.

Grounded, I said.

So.

The abbot's name was Hanayama Roshi. I suppose I had expected someone older, gaunt and gnarled like a winter tree. But the Roshi, I thought, was not much older than me. He was a formidable presence, gave the impression of contained strength. The first time I attended a lecture at the temple, I could follow almost nothing of his discourse. My Japanese was still rudimentary, conversational, and the abbot's language was sometimes arcane. From time to time Shinki would whisper something in my ear if it seemed a particularly important point was being made. Then at the end of his talk, the Abbot grew very serious, his voice admonitory and harsh. Shinki sat to attention, and I felt this was it, some profound spiritual truth was being uttered, an essential teaching passed on.

Shinki explained to me that the admonition was in two parts, both equally important.

The first was that we must never, and he emphasised it, *never*, smoke a cigarette while passing water.

I must have looked confused, Shinki shrugged.

OK. And the second thing?

When the Abbot or any of the monks call out to you, *Oi!* you must reply immediately, with no hesitation, *Hai!*

And that's it?

That's it.

Oi! and *Hai!*

Yes.

When the session was over, the Abbot got to his feet and we all stood and bowed. As he was leaving he paused in the doorway, turned and looked directly at me.

Oi! he said, his voice gruff and challenging.

Shinki nudged me and, somewhat self-consciously, I blurted out *Hai!* But I had been too slow, the Abbot had gone, out through the door.

Never mind, said Shinki. Next time!

When I was a boy, like all other English boys I read Robinson Crusoe. But I think I read it more often, more earnestly than most. What really appealed to me was the idea of living alone, like a Wordsworth or a John Clare, or even better like an old Chinese or Japanese hermit poet, a Han Shan or Chomei. It was a desire for nature and poetry and loneliness, a desire for solitude.

There is a charm in solitude that cheers...

In that spirit, I would sometimes steal away from Annie and the house and the whole cacophonous menagerie I had gathered. On a Saturday or Sunday when I was not teaching, I might escape, leave Annie with the place to herself (albeit with said cacophonous menagerie). I had acquired a little flat-bottomed skiff and patched it up, rendered it shipshape and watertight. I would take with me a bento box packed with rice and vegetables, a flask of miso soup and a bar of chocolate. And more important even than the food, I would take a few books – Thoreau perhaps, Stevenson, Matthew Arnold – and my old silver flute with a few pages of sheet music, and I would launch my little boat on the Han River. I would stay close to shore, paddle upstream a way, then drift with the current, read poems aloud and play the flute for nobody, feeling for all the world like an old Chinese hermit-poet in a watercolour painting by T'ang Yin, or Ch'iu Ying.

The philosopher-poet with his flute on the Han River.

OR

At his ease on the river with music and verse.

OR

The fat Englishman enjoys his self-indulgent delusion.

Whatever the reality, I returned home towards evening refreshed, restored to myself.

3

BUT A DREAM

The winters could be a struggle. The temperature fell well below freezing. Two feet of snow. Icicles on the roof-tiles. Well water frozen solid. But I resolved to go again with Shinki to sit in zazen at Myoshinji temple. On the way in at the gate, we had to pass by, or even step over, the beggars, homeless, huddled there for shelter, a place to sleep.

My neighbour, how does he live?

The meditation hall was heated by a single brazier at one end, and we were issued with thin threadbare blankets to wrap round our shoulders. But the cold cut to the bone as we sat numbed, trying to go beyond it, our breath clouding as we chanted sutras.

I told myself I should be able to use energy from my meditation, keep myself warm. And at some point I succeeded in focusing all my attention on the navel chakra, generating a little heat and feeling inordinately pleased with myself.

After the session I stepped out, back aching, legs stiff. Again we had to pass the sleeping beggars and we realised that one of them was *really* asleep, frozen to death. There was no mistaking it, the angle of the limbs, the gaunt features locked in a final grimace, a grim rictus. I was shocked at the fact of it, the finality, the body just lying there in the cold. One of the other beggars had already appropriated the dead man's flimsy cover, a piece of old sacking, left him exposed and vulnerable, unutterably sad.

I stopped Shinki who was about to walk on.

There's nothing to be done, he said. It happens all the time. Some of the younger monks will be dispatched to take the body to the cremation ground for disposal.

Lug the guts into the neighbour room, I said.

There's nothing to be done, he said again.

And yet.

It was the manner of it, the lack of care, of simple humanity. The coldness.

Inasmuch as you have done this to the least of these my brethren, you have done it unto me...

Nothing to be done.

Coldness and cold.

When I returned home I didn't immediately tell Annie what had happened. She was struggling with just being there and hadn't warmed to the place or our life in it. I had no wish to fuel that particular fire. We ate a simple supper of rice and vegetables, seated at our low *kotatsu* table, our legs tucked under its quilt to keep warm. The words I use in writing this. She hadn't warmed to the place. To fuel the fire. We ate, keeping warm.

The deepest level of Dante's Hell is not fire, but ice, intense cold.

We ate, and made small talk, but she knew me well enough to tell I was at odds with myself. So I told her the story, described the old man, dead outside the temple gate.

She sat a long while in silence then let out a sigh that was almost a sob.

So sad, she said. So very, very sad.

The foxes have holes. The birds of the air have nests. Only the son of man has no place to lay his head.

The first of the Buddha's Four Noble Truths: Existence is suffering.

The manner of the old man's death, the sheer misery, the unremitting poverty. To be born for this.

That night the dead man haunted my dreaming. Now he was my father. Then somehow he was myself, and although I was looking at him, and knew it was a dream, at the same time it was real, and his face was my own, looking back at me, grimacing.

I woke in a panic, with no idea where I was, only aware of the cold and dark surrounding me. Then there was Annie beside me, human warmth, holding me, calming me, bringing me back to this life we were living.

The experience at the temple had shaken me. But I recalled the parable of the young Prince Siddhartha, who would become the Buddha, going out from his palace with Channa his charioteer. He is full of the joy of being alive, on a beautiful day. But one after the other, Siddhartha encounters an old man, a sick man and a dead man. He comes to realise absolutely that humanity's lot is to age and sicken and die. *Existence is suffering.* He vows to go beyond, to conquer death.

If Zen could be said to be *about* anything, it was about that, a going beyond suffering and death, but a return to this, the reality of suffering and death. It was a coming to terms with that reality.

This and that. And the next thing.

When I next went to the temple, Shinki was reluctant to speak about the dead man, but I brought it up, told him I had been deeply affected by it.

It is not just something that happens here, he said. I am sure you would see the same thing outside the great cathedrals of northern Europe.

I said that was true, but it didn't make it palatable, or right.

No, he said. It is neither. So we work to make ourselves better human beings. And we do that here.

He bowed and we entered the temple, bowing also to the other figures still huddled by the gate.

All through the meditation I had the passage from Lear going through my head.

> *Poor naked wretches, whereso'er you are,*
> *That bide the pelting of this pitiless storm,*
> *How shall your houseless heads and unfed sides,*

Your loop'd and window'd raggedness, defend you
From seasons such as these? O, I have ta'en
Too little care of this!

It was my mantra, my sutra. It drove out everything else.

From time to time, at the end of the working week, I would go out
to eat with Akio and Shinki and a few other colleagues. On special
occasions – a birthday, the end of term – we would go to the Chosun
or the Keijo Hotel, in the Japanese enclave downtown. These were
often unsatisfactory for me as a vegetarian. While my companions
gorged on sukiyaki and thick steaks, my choice was limited to vari-
ations of vegetables and rice, perhaps enlivened by some marinated
beancurd. They found it hard to understand that I didn't even eat
fish (for fish too were living creatures, sentient beings). This made
it doubly difficult for me as even the simplest of dishes – a bowl
of noodles for instance – was almost certainly cooked in a broth
seasoned with little *bonito* fish-flakes.
Occasionally (only occasionally I hope!) this made me a little tetchy
and I would launch into a tirade against everything that irritated
me about the Japanese, especially their headlong rush to embrace
Western manners and customs. I remember once delivering a rant
about forms of greeting, praising the inherent politeness and deco-
rum of bowing. What was the norm in the West? I asked. Shaking
hands or kissing, both practices filthy and animalistic, unhygienic
and downright barbaric.
Akio led the laughter at my expense, led the others in a toast to me,
raising a glass of sake.
Kanpai!
I raised my own glass of clear water.
Cheers.
The company, of course, was male. No women were invited.
Akio said perhaps I did protest too much.
Perhaps he was right. I have been accused of prudishness in my
time, and there may after all be some truth in it, at least as far as

my public pronouncements went, my writings, my pontifications.
I can see myself, a little pompous, faintly ridiculous, declaiming,
holding forth. Protesting too much.

Kanpai!

My own favourite eating place, the *Sushi Hisa*, was not for away in
busy Honmachi Street. It was a haven, and the chef, Momota-san,
was a master. In fact I addressed him as such, called him *Sensei*.
He returned the compliment, knowing I was a teacher.

Momota-sensei.

Buraisu-sensei.

Oi!

Hai!

He was a true man of zen (if not Zen), the embodiment of zen-in-
action. (And what other kind of zen is worth its salt, its *gomasio*?)
He did everything with gusto – that's the word – with life-more-
abundant.

It was not simply that he offered me more than the usual fare, it
was the consciousness he brought to making and serving the food.
My favourite dishes were *norimaki,* tight little rolls of rice wrapped
in thin sheets of toasted seaweed, pickled ginger at the centre, and
inari-zushi – dried beancurd compressed and somehow puffed up
into little rectangular pockets when they were fried. These too were
stuffed with rice and served with pickled ginger, a sprinkle of sesame
seeds, and they were served with that flair, that dash of panache that
marked him out as a master.

There were no tables around the place – the customers sat on stools
at a counter like a bar-top encircling the central space where Momo-
ta-Sensei worked and moved and had his being. This was his temple
but also his stage, and he owned it utterly.

I never tired of watching him at work, totally absorbed in it, fo-
cussed and at ease. He would cut and dice vegetables with swift
efficiency, fan rice with a bamboo paddle to cool it. His knife was a
precision instrument, steel blade fine and honed as a samurai sword
as he sliced raw fish into the thinnest of slivers for sushi.

In retrospect I wonder about the time and energy expended on
splitting the atom and I think perhaps the same result could have

been achieved by giving the job to Momota-san. One stroke of his redoubtable blade might have done the trick, cleaved the particle in two, sundered worlds. But then Momota-san himself would have been whisked off with his trusty knife to some research station in Omsk or Arizona, making his atomic sushi.

Instead he moved with ease and grace in the cramped space of his kitchen (where he most definitely *could* take the heat), the air thick with the scents of hot sesame oil and dark soya sauce, the fresh tang of ginger. He was the Bodhisattva Manjushri, wielding the sword of discrimination. He was master Hakuin dicing his demons and pounding them into miso to make soup. But at the same time, *at the same time*, he was the chef Momota, grounded, light on his feet in the here and now.

There was always something bubbling and boiling, something deep-frying in blackened iron pans – agedashi tofu in batter, gyoza dumplings, crisp-coated tempura fritters.

Momota-sensei the lord of his domain, calling out to me across the counter.

Oi!

Hai!

For all his eagerness and enthusiasm, Shinki-san could also behave with a kind of formality, a certain reserve. He never called me anything but Blyth-san and I, likewise, called him Shinki-san.

He spoke to me one day in the staffroom, asked, tentatively, if it might be appropriate for him to give me a gift.

I said that would be most kind, and I would be honoured, and I asked him what the gift might be.

It is nothing special, he said. You will see.

Next day he brought it, a flat package, maybe three feet square, carefully wrapped.

I knew he had studied brushwork and calligraphy as part of his Zen practice, and his gift was a painting he had made, a watercolour landscape in the Chinese style, a river in the foreground, a suggestion of trees, distant mountains through mist.

He said, It is called Autumn on the Han River.

Yes, I said. You have caught it just so.

I noticed he had not signed the painting, not even stamped it with a seal. I mentioned this and he was suddenly awkward.

My teacher said is not good to sign. Means you think it is finished, is perfect. Too much ego!

Perhaps just a little ego is necessary I said.

I took the painting home and hung it on the wall of my study. Annie glanced at it, said the brushstrokes could have been more vigorous but it was not bad, it was something, better than nothing, better than a blank wall.

I invited Shinki to eat with us at home and he was delighted, brought a little box of exquisite mochi sweets, made with red bean paste. Annie accepted them with genuine good grace, said they were her favourite. But after we had eaten she excused herself and said she would leave us to it, our discussion of poetry and zen, the poetry *of* zen, the zen of poetry.

By the time I went to bed, after Shinki had gone, Annie was already asleep, or that was the impression she wanted to create as she lay almost too still, turned away, her back to me.

I don't know when it began. Perhaps it had been happening all along and I had simply ignored it. But Annie grew more and more listless, irritated, out of sorts. I finally brought it up, asked her what was the matter.

It's everything, she said. It's us. It's this place.

But we've made a life here.

You have, she said. Not me. I might as well be in purdah.

We have friends.

They are your friends, not mine. This is your world, not mine. It has never been mine, not any of it, not ever.

Akio and Motoko invited me to the Sushi Hisa for the birthday of little Katsura. Annie was also invited but felt a little squeamish, said she wouldn't come. I offered to stay home with her but she shooed me out, said, Go! Go! So I went.

Katsura was happy to see me, her Oji-san. I gave her as her birthday gift a copy of *Alice's Adventures in Wonderland and Through the Looking Glass*, in one volume, with the wonderful illustrations by Tenniel. She turned the pages, eyes wide with delight.

Read to me please, she said, holding out the book to me.

It will be an honour, I said, and I cleared my throat and read (or rather, recited, for I knew the words by heart).

> *'Twas brillig, and the slithy toves*
> *Did gyre and gimble in the wabe:*
> *All mimsy were the borogoves,*
> *And the mome raths outgrabe.*

Katsura laughed and clapped her hands.

What does it mean?

I have no idea, I said. But it sounds wonderful.

She looked puzzled and intrigued, as if trying to solve a riddle.

You won't be able to read it all just yet. But stay with it. The more you read it the more it will grow.

How big? she said, spreading her arms. This big?

Bigger, I said. As big as you. It will grow *with* you.

Her parents had ordered tuna sushi for the three of them, my favourite inari zushi for me. When we'd eaten we took our leave of Momota-san and moved on to a nearby sweetshop, Meiji-Seika, for dessert. Katsura said she wished she could do this every week.

Then it wouldn't be special, said Motoko. It's not your birthday every week.

Ah! I said. But it is your *un*birthday.

What's that?

It's right here, I said, taking the book from her and turning the pages. You see?

I pointed as if at some irrefutable proof. It says we only have one birthday a year. That means we have... (I made a show of counting on my fingers)...three hundred and sixty-four unbirthdays.

And they are special days?

Katsura! said Motoko, seeing where this was going and trying to rein her in.

Indeed they are, I said. And obviously it couldn't be *every* day, but I see no reason why we can't have sushi and sweets from time to time, to celebrate.

Well... said Akio.

How about a month from now?

He nodded to Motoko, said All right, it's a date.

Katsura clapped her hands again, and I raised my glass of water by way of a toast.

Unbirthdays!

From then on, whenever Katsura came to the house to hear stories or learn songs or practise the recorder or play with the animals, she would say, So, today is my unbirthday.

I would check the calendar and say, Yes, you're right, and we'd head for Sushi Hisa and Meiji-seika.

One week she looked thoughtful, working something out.

Oji-san, she asked me. When is *your* birthday?

December, I said. Juuni-gatsu.

Her eyes widened.

So today is *your* unbirthday too!

You're right, I said. That's wonderful!

And it was.

Was it around that time that I met Professor Yoshishike Abe? It must have been. He was Head of the Law Faculty at the University so there was no reason for our paths to cross. But Akio told me Professor Abe was responsible for negotiating the rates of pay for teaching staff. So it was due to his efforts that I was being paid what was effectively a professorial salary.

You are an asset, said Akio. They know this.

At a reception following a graduation ceremony, Akio took the opportunity to introduce me to the Professor, and I took the opportunity to thank him.

He was clear-eyed, gave the impression of resolute strength. He dismissed my thanks, businesslike, said I was doing a good job. And that was that.

Akio came to me one day and told me there was a plan to provide scholarships for boys who showed promise but whose parents were too poor for them to continue at the school. He asked if I would contribute to the fund, effectively sponsor a student or two, and I said yes without hesitation. (It occurred to me I should have asked Annie first, but fortunately she was in agreement, adding only that she hoped in time there would be a girls' school offering the same kind of support). By our own standards we were well off and it was good to be in a position to help. My monthly salary was 400 Yen (at the time a princely sum). The cost of one scholarship was 20 Yen a month, so without hardship we could fund four or five. .

The first time I met young Lee Insou was when he was brought to the classroom by Akio. He was one of the handful of boys who had been given scholarships, and I was assigned to be his mentor, in part because I was effectively funding his education but also because he was something of a prodigy. Akio had told me the boy was an orphan from the poorest background, but had already showed himself to be something special – bright and gifted, eager to learn.

I took to him right away, and he to me (after perhaps an initial wariness at this looming tweed-suited foreigner benignly concerned about his welfare).

Not long after his arrival, I told Annie I wanted her to meet him. He came to our home for an evening meal and everything just fell into place.

Annie was clearly taken with the boy, as he was with her. Suddenly she was more fully alive, more fully herself, the Annie I had first known. It was she who made the suggestion. We had plenty of space, a spare room. Why should the boy languish in a dormitory at the school when he could move in here?

She took it on, with a will. She enlisted Akio and Motoko to help with the formalities, the paperwork, the bureaucracy – the tedious detail that was anathema to me. In a matter of months it was done. Lee Insou was a member of the Blyth family, our adopted son.

I fitted out a little back room for him on the ground floor, gave it a lick of white paint, put up some shelves and a low table we'd found at the market, a futon and quilt he could roll up and store in the corner during the day. It was both touching and humbling to see him in the space, looking around him, not quite believing it was his own. His belongings were meagre – his school uniform and other basic clothes, a handful of books, some in Korean, some in Japanese. To those I added a few in English, *Alice in Wonderland* (another copy!), Stevenson's *Child's Garden*, Blake's *Songs of Innocence*. He took them as if they were sacred texts (which, of course, they were), touched each book to his forehead before placing them beside the others on his shelf. We left him to settle, to make himself at home, and the next morning Annie took him to the department store, bought him shoes and a sweater, a warm winter coat. He took them with the same acceptance and wide-eyed gratitude, still perhaps not quite believing how his life had changed.

He clearly loved being with us, being in his new home, being with the animals in our little menagerie. His life had been unsettled, full of contradictions, and I felt the animals helped him stay grounded, connected to something essential. He helped us feed the geese and hens, walk the dogs, milk the goats. And most of all he enjoyed grooming Martha, brushing her tangled coat. He found it deeply calming, as did I.

Lee had an aptitude for music. He picked up the violin and managed to make sounds that were not excruciating. This was a rare gift and it argued an innate ability, a musical ear. Not surprisingly then, he was equally fond of poetry and loved nothing more than hearing me recite to the class.

I had compiled a little folio of simple poems that were catchy and easy on the ear and yet had a resonance and a depth that would repay many readings – poems for life. I plundered Wordsworth and Clare, Blake and Christina Rossetti. Lee loved them all, but his favourite was Stevenson.

Of speckled eggs the birdie sings
And nests among the trees:
The sailor sings of ropes and things
In ships upon the seas.

The children sing in far Japan,
The children sing in Spain;
The organ with the organ man
Is singing in the rain.

I wrote the words on the blackboard for the class to follow as I read aloud. Then I read again and had them join in, reading as best they could. Lee could still recite the poem from memory years later, delighting in it.

One day in class I decided to teach the boys *Row, row, row your boat*. The melody was straightforward and enough of them could hold the tune, so they sang along with gusto, belting it out.

Row, row, row your boat,
Gently down the stream.
Merrily, merrily, merrily, merrily,
Life is but a dream.

I was even inspired to teach them to sing it as a round, a canon in two parts. This was something new to them, so at first it was more difficult. Then they got the hang of it, the stronger voices leading, and before long, with me beating time, they were giving it their all, utterly joyful, enjoying the shimmer and resonance of the simple harmonies. *Merrily, merrily…*
The afternoon sun poured into the dusty classroom.
Again! they shouted when the song came to an end. Again!
Life is but a dream.
Myself in a boat on the Han River with my poetry and my flute, utterly content.
A dream.

For a time, then, all was well, or so it seemed. God was in his heaven, all was right.

How long did it last? We had two good years of it, no more than that. Then it all began to unravel once again. I became ever more immersed in the teaching, in trying to write my book, in grappling with the maddening illogicalities of Zen. Annie had found some solace, some fulfilment, in looking after Lee. She had picked up a little more Japanese, more Korean, so it would be easier to talk to him. But beyond that, she was even more cut off, more isolated than ever. She began to take issue with things I said. One time she objected when I called her feisty, objected even more when I said it was meant as a compliment. I added that the way she objected was feisty in the extreme.

Feisty, she said. Feisty! I speak my mind and you call it feisty. Have you any idea how condescending that is?

I said I had thought I was being simply affectionate, she dismissed it as patronising.

It was difficult.

It came to a head when I came home one day from teaching at the school. She was sullen, had a look in her eye I had come to recognise. I could feel it, the anger held in check.

I hate this place, she said. This place, these people, all of it.

I agree the people have their flaws, I said, grandly. I find them a mixture of placidity and vehemence...

She had been stirring a pot of vegetable stew and she'd turned, clutching a ladle in her hand, brandishing it at me.

They're brutal and cruel, to the point of sadism.

Again I agree, I said, they have that propensity. But there's kindness too, and there's something to be said for their... *earthiness*.

Their grossness is unbearable, she said, her voice rising, and she threw down the ladle, set it clattering on the draining board.

Has something happened? I asked.

She gathered herself

I was at the market, she said, buying the vegetables for this – she indicated the stew simmering, innocent.

I heard a commotion, she said. Shouting and a pitiful wailing and whining. Right there in the market square, in full view, a squat little brute of a man had hung up his dog by the nose. He had hung it up on a hook, and he was slowly, methodically, beating it to death with a stick.

I'm sorry you had to see such a thing, I said.

And the worst part, she said, the worst part of the whole business, was that a crowd had gathered round to watch. It was a sport, a public entertainment. There were children, looking on and laughing.

She was crying now, and I took a step awkwardly towards her, reaching out. But she pushed past me and hurried out of the room. I picked up the ladle and carried on stirring the stew so it wouldn't stick to the pan.

At the dinner table later I told her a story about Stevenson. One day he had seen a man in the street, beating his dog with a stick. Stevenson had intervened, and told the man, It's not your dog, it's God's dog, and I am here to protect it.

Isn't that a thrilling story? I said.

Quite, quite thrilling, she said, her eyes sad, her voice dead. With you there's *always* a story, or a poem, or a piece of scripture. But wasn't that God's dog in the market today? And who was there to protect it?

I had no answer.

Does a dog have the Buddha nature?

Are not two sparrows sold for a farthing? And one of them shall not fall on the ground without your Father.

I can't do this any more, she said at last. I can't stay here.

This is painful to remember, even after all these years. I was committed to teaching till the end of the year. Annie wasn't. I wanted to see out the time, she didn't. She wanted out, if possible on the next boat. I couldn't leave, was unwilling. Fine, she said. You stay, I go. There was a finality in it. She was resolute, determined, her face set, her mind made up.

What about the boy? I said. I can't possibly look after him on my own. I have my work...

Of course, she said. You *can't possibly*... You have your *work!*

I heard the sarcasm in her mimicry, all the more cutting for the truth in it.

The boy, I said again. We're responsible for him. We can't *unadopt* him.

No, she said, quietly. We can't.

We sat in silence, separate. It was a koan, insoluble.

Eventually she broke it. He can come with me, she said.

I was flummoxed.

We want him to learn English and get an education, she said. Where better? And it would take him away from here, from this Godforsaken place.

I looked and Lee was standing in the doorway, his head to one side, listening, uncertain.

What do you think, Lee? she said. Would you like to go to England?

If it was a koan, was it Nansen and the cat? Two monks were arguing over the ownership of a kitten, and they came to Nansen to solve the dispute. He took the cat in one hand, a sword in the other, said if either of them could say one word of Zen he would spare the cat. They choked, unable to speak, and he cut the cat in half.

Poor poor Lee. Did we cleave him in two?

One word of Zen.

Would you like to go to England?
He nodded his head, said Yes.

There are times in our lives we find hard to recall, perhaps because we have no wish to recall them. To think of them is too painful and leaves us empty and bereft. Now when I try to remember that year, the year Annie left, it has the quality of an unsettling dream, or a black-and-white film in which I played myself – or a version of myself – as the weeks and months passed by, fading into one another and leading nowhere.

I suppose I had not quite believed Annie would go. But she was determined. One day she was there, one day she was gone. (*Is that not enough?*)

I was alone in what had been our house, our home, now suddenly too large, all life and meaning drained out of it. My teaching work-load was as heavy as ever and I couldn't manage that and at the same time maintain the house, look after the animals. So Akio and Motoko helped me sell the beasts to a farmer with a smallholding outside town. They even arranged for them to be taken away while I was at work so I didn't have to see them go. They did this out of deference to my state of mind, a fragility born of tender-heartedness but verging on sentimentality and tinged with self-pity. I was feeling sorry for myself.

I once wrote that being sentimental means having more concern for things than God does. So, Guilty as charged, Your Honour. I couldn't bear the thought of the animals being butchered, of our old nag Martha ending up in the knacker's yard. Akio assured me that would not happen, I had his word, and I chose to believe him. He told me he and Motoko were concerned about me. They said I was not myself.

So whose self was I?

My face in the mirror was gaunt, haggard, the eyes desolate.

Who is it that can tell me who I am?

I had little appetite, found it hard to sleep. Akio took to bringing me a little bento box Motoko had made up for me, packed with my favourite sushi and pickles. The kindness of it almost undid me and I ate the food gratefully.

Shinki was also anxious on my behalf. He even summoned the courage to knock on my door one evening, uninvited, bearing a basket of fruit – apples, persimmon, pears – for which, again, I was inordinately grateful.

I missed my lunches and dinners at *Sushi Hisa,* my unbirthday celebrations with little Katsura, but I couldn't face either, thought I would not be the best company.

Akio made some enquiries on my behalf, found an older Korean woman, Mrs Gyeong, who would come and clean my house once a week, make simple vegetable soups and stews that would last a few days.

The first evening she placed a steaming bowl of food before me on the scrubbed table, said simply, *Meokda*.

Eat.

Something in her manner – gruff and direct, no-nonsense, innately good-natured – broke through the carapace I had constructed. The thud of the bowl as she set it down on the table was a jolt. It shook something loose, like a blow to the head in an old zen story.

Meokda.

I laughed and did as I was told.

I do not know what I had expected, what I had hoped – that Annie would have a change of heart and come back to me? I only knew that I did not want to leave things as they were, unresolved. Communicating by letter was slow. Telephoning was impossible. So I decided, nothing else for it, I would go to London. I made arrangements with Akio to take indefinite leave, on the understanding I might yet return to Seoul. Akio was sad but sympathetic. He said he would keep my post open for me, rent out the house during my absence. He drove me with my luggage to the docks where we'd first arrived in Korea, and Shinki came too, to say goodbye, to help with my bags. Akio had brought me a bento box from Motoko. Shinki – bless him – had brought chocolate. Both men gave me books to read on the journey, Shinki a copy of Hermann Hesse's *Siddhartha* in the original German, Akio an English version of the Heart Sutra.

Form is Emptiness.

They both wished me a safe journey and a speedy return.

After the crossing to Vladivostok, I travelled by train, making, in reverse, the journey I had imagined all those years ago when we first left London, taking the Trans-Siberian Express through Manchuria, to Lake Baikal, Irkutsk, Omsk, Kurgan and on to Moscow.

I had the books my friends had given me and I also had Suzuki's book of essays (now well-thumbed and annotated) and a copy of

Anna Karenina that had been Annie's. She had left it behind and – who knows why? – I had picked it up and brought it with me. Perhaps I thought its heightened mood of desolation, its high tragedy, appropriate for the long train-ride across Russia.

By way of total contrast I brought *Alice in Wonderland* and Stevenson's *Fables*.

The train rattled and clattered for days across bleak featureless terrain, snow-covered fields. I slept, woke, slept again. At the different stations armed guards came aboard and checked everyone's documentation, their manner gruff, suspicious. One or two of them peered at my passport, had a look at my books. (Tolstoy seemed to meet with their approval). Then, no doubt deciding I was a harmless academic, they let me be and moved on. But I found the experience unsettling.

There is a passage I remember reading, though I am never certain if it was written by Churchill or Orwell. But it argues that we in so-called civilised societies sleep easy in our beds at night because some thug with a gun patrols a distant border to keep us safe.

The image, like the argument, is a powerful one, and thinking back on those guards I feel the strength of it, the challenge.

My abiding memory of that journey, however, is of reading *Anna Karenina*, in particular a chapter where Anna is travelling by train and reading an English novel! I huddled, cold, in my heavy overcoat, hunched over the book, and read the extraordinary description of Anna's experience as she tries to enter into the life of the book she is reading.

I thought of Tolstoy himself dying after a long train journey in winter at the age of 82. He quarrelled with his wife one last time and simply walked out into the night, ill clad in the freezing cold. He boarded the train with little thought for his destination, travelled for more than 24 hours growing ever weaker. Bronchitis developed into pneumonia and finally he collapsed, was taken from the train and died at a remote station after uttering a few final words of wisdom. I read on, losing myself in the book as Anna had tried to do in hers. At first she is distracted by the conversations around her, the other passengers, the noise of the train. Then she tries to engage with the book and is overwhelmed by the urge to identify with the characters, to live what they live. She asks herself, *What am I? Myself or someone else?* Then with a sudden realisation she awakens to the very life she is living. At a station she steps down onto the platform, exhilarated by the cold air and everything she sees.

With pleasure she drew in deep breaths of the snowy, frosty air and, standing by the carriage, looked around the platform and the lit-up station...

As I write this account on my lined yellow pages, I allow myself to imagine it being published, years into the future when I am long gone. I further imagine a reader carrying the book on a train journey, reading these pages about me on a train reading about Anna Karenina, on a train reading an English novel....

Matryoshka. Russian dolls.

As we pulled out of a station, I wiped a clear patch on the steamed-up window, saw myself reflected in the glass, the bright-lit carriage as if projected out there, and I leaned closer, looked further out, beyond the brightness to the snowy landscape, the dark night.

Ma, dear Ma, was overwhelmed when I arrived, almost couldn't speak for joy. She welcomed me like, well, like a long-lost son. She fed me (a lentil pie with bubble-and-squeak!) She ran a bath for me, then let me rest in my old bed, in my old room redolent of fustiness and damp, which I yet found a comfort. I slept deep and woke in the middle of the night, disoriented, thinking I was in Korea (dis-oriented!) but unable to understand why my room there had been superimposed on this one from another life. Or had there been some slippage in time? Had I been propelled back to this, awakening from a dream? I sat up, set my feet down on the cold linoleum, took my bearings. I switched on the bedside lamp, saw in its tired light the room bare and clear, the very objects resting in their own dream, there, things-in-themselves. The candlewick bedspread. The faded floral wallpaper. There.

In the corner was the desk where I had worked as a boy, and above it a bookshelf stacked with a few books I had left behind. *Meditations* by Marcus Aurelius. *Pickwick Papers*. If I returned to Korea I should take them with me. (*If* I returned).

I picked down *Robinson Crusoe*, opened it at random.

How strange a Chequer Work of Providence is the Life of Man! and by what secret differing Springs are the Affections hurry'd about as differing Circumstances present!

I got back under the covers and read till I fell back into sleep.

At first Annie had moved in with her mother, just for the first few weeks till she found accommodation for herself and Lee. We had made arrangements – a bank account in her name – so she could get by. She had her degree and would be able to teach. In the meantime she had taken a job as a secretary in an insurance office, and Lee was attending school.

Visiting them in their rented rooms, in Camden, was dispiriting. Annie was civil to me, we made small talk, but there was nothing between us, an emptiness. She had already moved on, consigned me to the past. Any hopes I might have held of reconciliation were dissipated. There was no possibility of her returning to me or to the life we had tried to make.

The furniture was old and heavy, the curtains drab. But on a sideboard wee a few cut flowers in a glass vase, and on the wall I recognised the Russian ikon from the first rooms we had shared, so long ago. She had kept it all this time, carried it to Korea and back, still turned to it for protection and grace.

I told her I had been reading her copy of Anna Karenina, said I would return it.

Keep it, she said. It's a wonderful book but I don't think I'll be reading it again. Karenina is a strong woman, so of course that means she is punished. She is not allowed a fulfilling life of her own. So…. She gave a little dismissive wave of the hand, a gesture I knew so well.

Lee came home from school, looked surprised to see me. He was the same bright, earnest young fellow. But he too had grown distant, looked on me as a stranger, someone he had once known. I asked about his school and he said it was fine, he liked it well enough.

Do they teach you poetry? I asked.

Some, he said. A little.

Not Stevenson I suppose? Of speckled eggs the birdie sings.

No, he said, uncomfortable, looking at me again across a great distance. He had put away childish things.

Wordsworth?

Westminster Bridge, he said. And the one about the daffodils.

Well, I said. That's something.

Yes.

Better than nothing.

Actually, said Annie, Lee has homework to do.

The boy looked grateful, relieved, as he picked up his schoolbag, went through to the other room.

I think he's going to be a scientist, said Annie, or an engineer.

Where did I go wrong? I said.

For a moment there was a flicker, almost a smile. I used to make her laugh.

Annie.

The moment passed and was gone. She closed herself to me once more. said we should discuss what she called our *situation*, come to an agreement about the best way to proceed.

The whole business was unbearably sad.

Earth hath not anything to show more fair? London felt grey and drab, unfamiliar. It was more than just my own sense of distance, alienation. There was something in the atmosphere, oppressive as the dank pall that seemed to hang in the air. The country had emerged from the Great War into years of depression, poverty, unemployment, presided over by a national government. Now, incredibly, there was the threat of another Great War with Germany, as if mankind had learned nothing and was hellbent on its own destruction.

Dora laughed when she opened her door to me.

Well, Reggie boy, she said. Here we are.

She took my face in her hands, kissed me full on the lips.

Everything else fell away.

I would not circumscribe your love.

Here we are.

We fell into it naturally, took to walking out together, arm in arm.
She worked in a bank but finished in the late afternoon, had week-
ends off. We strolled in the park I had known as a boy, The Flats, or
we took the tube into town and walked by the Serpentine in Hyde
Park, took tea in a Lyons Corner House.

We went to the cinema – the pictures – usually a matinee at the Ri-
alto in the High Street. (Many a time and oft in the Rialto!) We saw
Robert Donat in the Thirty-Nine Steps, Ronald Colman in a Tale
of Two Cities. We watched Richard Hannay escape from the train
on the Forth Bridge, Sydney Carton climb the steps to the guillotine.
A far far better thing. Dora cried and we held hands in the dark,
came out blinking into unexpected daylight, the late afternoon sun.

There was another call I had to make, to pay my respects. Mr Wat-
son had retired from teaching, but he lived in the same house, in
Ilford, close to the school.

He answered my knock at the door, squinted at me, unsure.

Yes?

Reg, I said. Reg Blyth.

He brought me into focus, subtracted the intervening years.

My God, he said. Reg! Dear boy! Come in, come in!

In his front room he cleared a space for me on an old sofa, shifted
a pile of newspapers and magazines.

Sit, he said, bustling. Please sit. I'll put on the kettle.

He made a pot of tea, then another. I sipped a cup out of politeness.
We talked the afternoon away.

Shoes and ships and sealing wax, he said.

Cabbages and kings.

He asked if I was home for good.

Or ill, I said.

I told him the whole story – or my side of it – of Annie and the boy, our life in Korea and how it had come to this.

Loggerheads, I said. Stalemate.

The eternal note of sadness, he said.

I still read Arnold, I said, recognising the quote.

I'm glad, he said. He is somewhat out of fashion these days.

I laughed. I remember an exam question from my student days. *Dover Beach is a plangent threnody. Discuss.*

And did you?

At great length!

Now, he said, speaking of books that are very much *in* fashion, have you seen these? This is the latest publishing venture from Penguin. Novels and other works in soft covers, and selling for sixpence each. Can you imagine? A tanner a book! I bought all ten for five bob.

He passed the pile of books to me and I leafed through them.

Agatha Christie, I said. I didn't know you read crime fiction.

Guilty as charged, he said. It's a pleasant diversion, and somehow comforting.

The mystery is solved, I said. All's right with the world.

Exactly. Now this is something else entirely.

He picked out one of the other books, handed it to me. Ernest Hemingway. *A Farewell to Arms.*

A story of love and war, he said. A tragedy.

How could it be otherwise? I said. Love and war.

It's well written, he said. The prose is lean and spare.

He insisted I keep the book as a gift.

Are you sure?

No expense spared, he said. A whole tanner!

I shall read it, I said, and let you know what I think.

Sadly, he said, a farewell to arms was unlikely in these times. Pacifism was in danger of becoming a dirty word once again. He said for a time after the War there had been signs of hope. Swords into ploughshares. Now? Germany had withdrawn from the League of Nations and was once more embracing militarism. Britain was ready to commit, albeit reluctantly, to re-arming on a grand scale. So soon.

War and the pity of war.

Collective madness.

All we can do is hold to the light, dear boy. Hold to the light.

I told him of my interest in Zen, that it was not something exotic, or esoteric.

How can I put it? I said.

It feels very like the thing, he said.

Exactly!

So you'll go back there, he said, out East?

I think so.

I think so too, he said. It's where your work is.

His simple words had a curious effect on me. I felt a kind of awakening, or recognition, a kindling of that sense of destiny I have mentioned before in these pages.

I found myself one day in Great Russell Street, beside the British Museum. I popped into Collet's Chinese Bookshop and was delighted to find a recently-published volume by Arthur Waley, his translation of the *Tao Te Ching* which he called *The Way and its Power*.

I picked it up and turned the pages.

The Way that can be told is not the Unvarying Way;

The names that can be named are not unvarying names.

It was from the Nameless that Heaven and Earth sprang...

I bought the book, lost myself in it on the train, rattling out to Leytonstone on the Central Line.

Only he that rids himself forever of desire can see the Secret Essences.

He that has never rid himself of desire can see only the Outcomes....

I knew I would have to go back to Korea, at least in the short term, to deal with what I had left behind – my commitment to Akio and to teaching, the house in Seoul and everything in it, years of accumulated books and papers, my writings. My work.

But in behind that, beyond it, was a sense of something more, something deeper I had to pursue, my own Journey to the East

And yet there was the problem of this life here in London. Annie and Lee, Dora and Ma. So much unresolved.

For Annie there was no going back, not in any sense, not to Korea, not to me.

Spring had given way to summer, muggy and enervating, the heat unforgiving. Annie wanted clarity, finality. She asked if we could meet one more time to discuss what we should do. She suggested meeting in Hyde Park so we could walk as we talked, and I agreed. I saw her as I approached and at first had the strange sensation of not recognising her. She wore a summer dress and a light jacket, her hair loose about her shoulders. A stranger. Then a familiar movement, a turn of the head, brought her into focus, and I saw her, Annie, my wife. I waved and saw her look up and recognise me in the same way, and she caught my eye and waved back, and for a moment I was quite undone. But it passed, a faint glimmer then gone. We walked round the Serpentine. (I didn't mention that I had recently walked there with Dora, but I myself was conscious of how different that had felt). We walked, past children feeding the ducks, past two girls on horseback, past a young man sculling across the water, everyone absorbed in their own dream.

Annie said Lee was fine. She asked after my mother, and I said she was in good health. We stopped by the statue of Peter Pan and she said she had spoken to a lawyer.

She had told him we were separated, and living in different countries. He had asked if there was any possibility of reconciliation now that I was here. She'd said, No, absolutely not. It was over. She wanted an ending, a divorce.

Although we were undeniably estranged, the word still stung. It cut, abrupt – cold legalese.

Divorce.

I found myself, ludicrously, inappropriately, recalling the ancient jokes I had read to her in Korea, the old folk tales.

As you well know…

Unthinking, I asked if she remembered them too, and she did.

How could I forget? she said. The three foolish brides, each one more stupid than the one before.

And I was divorced.

There are cultures still, I said, where it's just a matter of saying three times, I divorce thee…

If you're a man, she said. And even here it's more difficult for a woman. The lawyer talked about suing, and going to court. He talked about burden of proof. He talked about getting a decree *nisi* and then a decree absolute.

Again it was the coldness of the language, the harsh abstraction. It drained all colour from the day.

She was looking across at some children playing around the statue, one small boy, intrepid, climbing up on the base.

But the lawyer did say there was hope, she continued. He said the law is to be changed, this year, maybe next. The new law will say desertion for more than two years is good cause. Sufficient grounds. So…

So if you do go back to Korea, and stay there, and don't contest it, that should be enough.

Simple as that.

Again there was that sense of destiny, necessity. I had to go to Korea. That much was certain (as much as anything was). But for how long? Ma was here, and though she was still robust, that could change. If she grew frail as she aged, would I have to come back to look after her? Then there was Dora.

It's a koan, I said.

Annie rounded on me, her voice no longer matter-of-fact but hard, angry.

A koan? she said. One of your stupid zen riddles? Next you'll be telling me there's a story or a parable. Well there isn't. This is the story. This. Us.

The children's voices carried, clear. Another young man rowed past, his boat cleaving the water, trailing light, bright droplets dripping from the oars.

This. Us.

I'm sorry, Annie, I said.

That doesn't help, she said.

Years later – decades – I found myself in that film club in the little flea-pit cinema in Shinjuku, watching Brief Encounter. And for all its sentimentality, the cut glass accents, the overblown Rachmaninoff soundtrack, I found myself moved by it. The scenes where the couple go to the cinema, walk in a London park, took me back to that year. Between the Wars. Annie and I irrevocably estranged. Dora and I, briefly, happy in each other.

I asked Dora if she would consider coming back with me to Korea. She thought long and hard, said No, Reg, I can't. You know I can't. Why not?
So many reasons. I have my job.
In the bank. How exciting!
She tensed and I changed tack, hammed it up like Ronald Colman, Robert Donat.
Come away with me!
She managed a smile but shook her head.
No.

We are who we are. We live as we live. We do what we do.

That smile, rueful. The shake of that lovely head.

No.

4

LIGHT OF
THE FIREFLIES

I arrived back in Korea a year after I had left, almost to the day. Once
again I travelled on the Trans-Siberian Express, from Moscow on
to Kurgan, Omsk, Irkutsk, Lake Baikal, Manchuria, Vladivostok.
Instead of Tolstoy I read the book I had bought in London, Waley's
translation of the Tao Te Ching. It made me resolve to learn Chinese.

I couldn't face going back to live in our old home, *sans* Annie, *sans*
the animals. Akio helped me sell the house and the land to the
young family who had been renting it. I found another house I could
rent for myself, closer to the University – a compact Japanese-style
two-storey building that opened out on a little garden. Akio and
Shinki helped me move my belongings, my worldly goods. Mrs
Gyeong resumed cooking and cleaning for me.
Meokda.
I settled back into routine, picked up, as far as possible, where I
had left off.
A fresh start, said Shinki.
Indeed.

Akio invited me to his home again where Motoko was quietly de-
lighted to see me. I asked if we might continue our haiku lessons
and she said that would make her very happy, but who would be
the teacher and who would be the pupil?
Little Katsura had grown in the time I was away. At first she was
almost shy of me, then I said we had missed many unbirthdays and

would have to make up for lost time, and she laughed and clapped her hands.

At school I felt strangely detached to be back, standing in front of a class of boys. Everything as it was, nothing as it was.

One young fellow named Jo made a point of waiting for me after class. Tentatively, a little self-conscious, he bowed to me, said he was very happy to see me.

Thank you Jo-san, I said.

We thought you will not come back.

Would not, I corrected. Or *might* not.

Would not, he said. Might not.

But here I am.

Yes, he said. And is good.

Jo was Korean, came from a poor family and was very bright. Like Lee. But as a young boy he had been sent to train as a monk. It was one way for a family to manage – the boy would have food and lodging at the temple and be given basic education. In Jo's case he was later awarded one of the scholarships to the school. (Again, like Lee). But his early Zen training, I thought, showed in his bearing, a certain lightness.

I asked Shinki about sessions at Myoshin-ji, and although he had not been attending regularly himself, he was keen for me to resume my practice and he copied out for me, in his immaculate script, a full schedule of dates and times.

Every Sunday, *zazen*, sitting meditation at 5 a.m.

Every month, on 3rd, 13th, 23rd and on 8th, 18th, 28th, evening *zazen* (after dinner) followed by a talk given by Hanayama Roshi

I asked Shinki if there was some esoteric significance to the dates, all ending in 3 or 8. He said No, it was simply a way of dividing the month so there was a gap of five days between sessions. I told him I trusted his arithmetic.

I read it all through, said Yes, count me in.

For which sessions?

All of them.

The early morning air was cold when I set out in the pre-dawn dark, wrapped in my heavy overcoat against the chill. I walked once more through the temple gate, stepped up onto the verandah, remembered vividly the man who had lain there, frozen to death.

Too little care....

Perhaps the problem had been addressed or was simply less severe than in winter. Whatever the truth of it, there were only two figures stretched out on the verandah, against the wall, each huddled under a thin blanket, head pillowed on rolled-up sacking. I checked, made sure both men were breathing, wished them the protection of the compassionate Buddha. I slid open the door and stepped inside.

In a way I could not quite understand, I was overwhelmed with a sense of familiarity. The dark wood of the pillars and beams, the polished floor, were all imbued with the ancient scent of pine incense, ingrained down the centuries. To breathe it in was itself an act of meditation. I took off my shoes, put on a pair of wooden geta, the sandals the monks wore. I stood in line to receive my breakfast, a bowl of watery porridge. I remembered my time in the Scrubs. The lonely prisoner. Here it would be the lonely monk. In his cell.

The old monk who ladled out the gruel recognised me from my previous visits, acknowledged the fact with a nod. I smiled. He looked stern, said *zazen* would begin at 5 o'clock.

There was that story of a monk coming to Joshu for teaching.

Have you eaten? said Joshu.

Yes, said the monk.

Then wash your bowl, said Joshu.

And that was it, that was the teaching.

The monk became enlightened.

I ate my gruel, washed my bowl and dried it, placed it upside down on a shelf beside the sink.

I made my way into the meditation hall, found a spot and sat on an old black *zafu* cushion, crossed my legs as best I could, knees creaking. I straightened my back, breathed in, breathed out.

A bell rang.

To begin again.

The first time I attended an evening session, I found myself queuing up beforehand for another meagre repast, dished out by the same stern-faced monk. This time it was a handful of rice and a few boiled vegetables topped with three slices of what I recognised as *takuan*, pickled *daikon* radish. Whatever the reason – the colour (bright yellow), the texture (overly crunchy) or the taste (bittersweet), I found this particular pickle unpalatable and would always, if I could, leave it at the side of my plate. On this occasion, however, that reaction would be unpardonable and rejecting the food freely offered would cause offence. I bowed to the monk, braced myself for the ordeal. Then I heard a quiet voice behind me.

Buraisu-sensei.

I turned and saw young Jo, the boy who had spoken to me at school. He had been brought up at the temple, had lodged here, and he still liked to join in the sessions.

Jo-san.

We sat together at the long low table, offered silent unironic gratitude for the food. I glanced at Jo's bowl and saw in a moment he had been sent, he was my saviour, my salvation. He was a growing boy for whom the portion of food was minuscule. I would perform an utterly selfless act of kindness by giving him my allocated three slices of the offending *takuan*.

I was just about to effect the transfer when Jo bowed, said *Dozo...* Please...

And deftly with his chopsticks he picked up the pickle from *his* bowl, transferred it to mine.

There was nothing I could do but thank him and set to, grudgingly crunching the pickle, a double portion.

Arigato gozaimasu.

I told Jo later that I didn't in fact like the pickle and had been on the point of offering him mine when he pre-empted my move. His eyes widened and he told me he too hated the *takuan* and had been grateful to get rid of it. I mimicked our polite exchange.

Dozo.

Arigato gozaimasu.

We laughed, bowed, laughed again.

Over the weeks and months that followed, I looked forward to the sessions more and more. It was hard work, no arguing with that, body aching, mind ready to scream at the endless intrusions, distractions. But I was determined to see it through.

My Japanese was adequate for most purposes, but when it came to Hanayama Roshi's talks there were still times when I struggled to understand (though perhaps that struggle was the whole point and having another obstacle to overcome was a positive advantage). I followed what I could, carried along by the almost incantatory power of the Roshi's delivery, a kind of measured rhythmic monotone. At times I let it wash over me, then the words would come into focus, ring clear and true.

Awaken the mind without fixing it anywhere.

My first great breakthrough (or so I thought it at the time) came at the end of a morning session. We chanted, as we usually did, the sutra to the Bodhisattva Kannon, said to bring consolation in times of adversity.

Enmei Jikku Kannon Gyo....

I joined in, added my tuneless *basso profundo* to the collective sound. The chant came to an end, a bell was struck, and I experienced it, my moment of awakening. I was quite simply aware of myself sitting there, nothing more (but also nothing less). It was extraordinary and at the same time nothing special. I just sat there as if I just sat there.

One of the younger monks caught my eye as we left the zendo. Perhaps he saw something in my demeanour, sensed a change.

Oi! he said.

Quicker than thought, I responded. *Hai!*

In time I heard that *Oi! – Hai!* so many times I began to wait for it. It became a kind of joke, and as soon as I saw it that way, it was like seeing the light, like *getting warm* in some remembered childhood game. It was like launching a ship down a slipway. Release the blocks and the ship moves.

I have a piece of calligraphy by Suzuki, lines from *As you like it*, laid out like a tanka poem in the master's brisk script, bold and cursive, black ink on handmade paper.

> *O wonderful.*
> *wonderful,*
> *and most wonderful wonderful!*
> *and yet again wonderful…*

That was the way of it. Wonderful.
I was seriously considering becoming a monk.

If I had gone straight home from school that day instead of taking a detour. If I hadn't stopped at the department store, parked my bicycle and gone inside. I wasn't even looking for anything-in-particular. (And isn't that the way, that we find what we're looking for when we're not looking?) I was simply killing time – an odd expression but an apt one. Whatever the non-reason, I was not in any hurry to go home.
I passed through the drapery department – it smelled of camphor from clothing and bales of cloth, a faint mustiness, a hint of incense. Beyond that was kitchenware, bamboo ladles and graters, bowls and chopsticks, sharp-bladed knives in little wooden sheaths. Then there it was, the goal of my non-search – the stationery section. I looked longingly at brushes and ink-stones and handmade paper. I imagined myself composing haiku and illustrating them, working on my calligraphy and brushwork. Then I thought of my previous cack-handed ham-fisted efforts, blotched and botched. Perhaps not! Instead I bought a few functional lined notepads, a set of pencils and one indulgence, a little hard-covered notebook made from rough-textured paper which opened out like a concertina. I opened and closed it, opened it, closed it. The young woman behind the counter had been looking on, politely amused, watching me make my mind up. Now she bowed and smiled, began wrapping my purchases in soft tissue paper. Then I remembered there was something else I had wanted to buy, but I had forgotten the name of it. A kind of wrapping cloth that folded to make a bag. My students would

use it to carry their books or bento boxes.

I tried miming, laying out the invisible cloth, gathering the ends and folding them. She laughed, covering her mouth with her hand.

Hai! she said. *Furoshiki desu.*

Yes, that was it. *Furoshiki!* I said, with huge satisfaction.

She ducked down behind the counter, reappeared with the cloth in her hand – simple linen, a subtle deep green. She folded it and was about to wrap that too in paper. I managed to indicate she should instead use the cloth to wrap my other purchases. Again she had to stifle her amusement, but she did as I asked, and I looked on, captivated, as she wrapped what I had bought, placed it on the counter like an offering.

I paid and she gave me my change, a few coins, and as she did so she cupped her hand, small and soft and warm, beneath my own hand as she put the coins in my open palm.

It was a gesture of indescribable delicacy and refinement, the slightest touch, and it sent an electrical charge right through me. I was stunned, smitten. I even felt myself blush, flustered. I bumbled out some stumbling banality about the weather and the season, translating badly from English instead of thinking in Japanese. I was tongue-tied, quite undone.

I managed to ask her name.

Kijima Tomiko.

Kijima-san.

Tomiko.

The shapes her mouth made, forming the words.

I told her I was *Buraisu-san*, (pointing to myself) and English, *Igirisujin.*

Buraisu-san, she said, and my name had never sounded so beautiful.

I went back a few days later to buy another notebook I didn't need. This time I was more composed and managed to hold a polite conversation. I told her I was a teacher at Keijo University. (She had guessed as much). She had been born in Japan, in Hagi, Yamaguchi, but the family had moved to Korea when she was 10, because of her father's business. I assumed he allowed her to work at the store to add to the family income, but also perhaps to get-her-out-of-the house, give opportunities for her to socialise. And however unlikely it might have seemed, here she was, meeting a potential suitor, this divorced *gaijin,* besotted-at-first-sight.

I looked up the meaning of her name. It was in two parts – *Tomi* meaning wealth, blessings, good fortune, and *Ko* meaning child. Blessed child, then. Child of Good Fortune.

Tomiko.

Tomiko.

How many notebooks did I buy? They probably had to re-stock from their suppliers, wondering at the sudden increase in turnover. In my rather old-fashioned, gentlemanly fashion, I was courting her. I liked the word. It had echoes of courtesy, and courtliness. Courting.

I had no idea as to the protocol, the formalities. I simply asked her one day (as she wrapped yet another notebook for me to place in the *furoshiki* cloth) if she would like to accompany me to a concert at the school, a performance of Bach by some of the young students I had been teaching.

For the first time I saw her look uncertain, and I wondered if I had made some social gaffe. Then I realised she was just making sure she had not misunderstood and that I was indeed asking her out.

In London, in another life, Annie and I had intended to go to a Bach concert that was cancelled, and we'd gone instead to hear Akio speak about teaching opportunities in the East. Another life and half a world away. Now Annie was back there, and I was here with Tomiko, at a concert of Bach. As I listened to the students, haltingly, imperfectly playing the music, I had an overwhelming sense of the randomness of things sometimes resolving itself into a kind of coherence, a pattern endlessly repeated but with infinite variations. A fugue. Yes it was like this, we were infinite, as the music was, and we experienced it here in this drab school hall, in this our only life, in the best of all possible worlds.

I had no idea if Tomiko would appreciate the music. She sat next to me in a wine-coloured kimono, her sheen of black hair caught up and gathered, held in place with a red lacquered clasp. Our arms were touching. I could feel her warmth, smell her perfume, sweetness of jasmine. When the music ended we joined in the applause. I turned to her and saw her eyes were shining.

Tomiko's father, Kijima-san, was a successful businessman, managed a construction company. He was among those Japanese bringing *progress* to Korea, dragging it into the modern world, *developing* its resources, industrialising on a grand scale. He had doubtless, as they say, made a killing. I recalled my conversations with Akio about the nature of this progress and exactly who stood to benefit most from the development. I resolved not to pursue the matter with Kijima-san.

He was in many ways my polar opposite – stolid, materialistic, grounded in that world of work, mechanistic, governed by profit and loss, getting and spending. His wife looked like an older version of Tomiko, in fact not so much older, with that ageless quality I saw in so many Japanese women. But her eyes were tired and she was self-effacing almost to the point of negation, deferentially bowing when she entered or left the room.

I had been invited to the family home so that I could be vetted and assessed, weighed up. The evening was awkward. There was little to talk about. The latest building materials? The knocking down of the old city walls to allow extended urbanisation? Could I counter with the metaphysical poets? My love of Bach? The importance of koan practice in Rinzai Zen?

Then there was my refusal to drink alcohol or eat fish. Kijima-san and his wife seemed genuinely bemused by this tweed-suited gaijin in their midst, confirming their worst fears.

On the other hand, as a Professor at Keijo I was clearly a fellow of some standing and something of a catch for their daughter.

At one point I caught Tomiko's eye and she flashed the quickest sweetest smile, amused and complicit.

The wedding was a very Japanese affair, conducted at a Shinto shrine. We were a small group – a dozen or so – and we entered in procession through a red torii gate, led by a priest in his white ceremonial robes. He clapped his hands and chanted, invoking the *kami*, the benevolent deities, particularly the gods of marriage, Izanagi and Izanami, themselves a married couple. All this Tomiko had explained to me in advance. She wore a red kimono and a white silk headdress, equivalent of the bridal veil. I wore a formal suit instead of my usual tweeds, a wing-collared shirt and black bow tie. We exchanged rings and bowed. The priest placed a branch of *sakaki*, Japanese evergreen with its bright yellow flowers, on a little altar in front of the shrine, and chanted a verse invoking long life and fertility. Tomiko's parents looked on, reconciled to the match, smiling their approval.

Akio was here in the role of Best Man, *nakodo*, literally a matchmaker. I had told him that as he was responsible for bringing me here in the first place, that was entirely appropriate. Motoko and Katsura looked on and Shinki beamed at everyone, delighted and benign.

In deference to my status as gaijin (whether that was something to be admired or pitied!) I was allowed to choose a reading, which Akio did his best to translate.

I read from Paul's Epistle to the Corinthians.

Love suffereth long, and is kind; love envieth not; love vaunteth not itself, is not puffed up, doth not behave itself unseemly….beareth all things, believeth all things, hopeth all things, endureth all things.

The wedding guests stood listening, attentive and polite. They suffered long and were kind. I caught Tomiko's eye and she smiled at me, the white veil framing her face.

My love is like a red red rose. An extravagant statement if ever there was one, and yet…

The priest was chanting again, intoning a sutra, a final blessing in the name of Izanagi and Izanami. We drank sake (it could not be avoided) and exchanged cups. The priest clapped his hands three more times, and it was done. We were married. Mr and Mrs (Timeless) Blyth.

Tomiko loved the house, the simple Japanese style of it with wooden walls and sliding shoji screens, tatami mats on the floors, a low ko-

tatsu heated table where we would dine. But her father had bought
us, probably through the store where she worked, a western-style
writing desk and chair, as well as two upholstered armchairs and
a standard lamp. In the market I had found two tall bookcases.
Already they were half filled and more boxes sat waiting to be
unpacked.

I sat in one of the armchairs, slapped the arms, laughed.

Your father begins to know me a little, I said. For although I loved
the *Japaneseness* of the house and its artefacts, the wonderful ele-
gance and spareness of it all, the old armchair was damned com-
fortable!

Outside was the little square of garden, ready to be tended. We
stood there a moment, enjoying the evening air after the heat of the
day. We came back inside.

The bedroom too was Japanese, the low futon with its mattress, its
quilt patterned with stylised cranes.

I felt the moment called for a haiku, something sensual but subtle.
But what came to mind, unbidden, was a crude senryu, shouldering
its way into my awareness.

> *The long summer night,*
> *We'll tumble together*
> *In sheer delight.*

My version of it came out rhymed, like some old East End pub song.
Come, come, come and make eyes at me... Perhaps the sake from the
ceremony had gone to my head.

The occasion deserved better. There was a poem written by Hakuin
as a young man.

> *Miss Fuji –*
> *Cast aside your hazy robe*
> *and show me your snowy skin.*

I had not yet seen Fuji (in the flesh, as it were!) but I imagined that
response, that mix of tenderness and awe was just right. It felt just

right for this too.

This.

I spoke the words now to Tomiko, in English, then more haltingly in Japanese.

She laughed, and she came to me, and oh, the sweetness, the sweetness.

By some miracle we had found each other. The age difference between us was not so great as to be grotesque – I was 38, she was 22 – and all would be well and all would be well. I was sure of it. All manner of things would be well. My friends – Akio and Motoko, Shinki – took to her, found her charming, engaging, down-to-earth. They were happy for me.

We settled to a routine. I had my work, she had hers. I read and wrote and taught. She seemed more than happy to clean and cook. She didn't mind making vegetarian dishes for me but had no intention of becoming vegetarian herself. She was too fond of fish and could not imagine giving it up. I said she should try, and she screwed up her face, laughed and said, *Doshite?*

Why?

In the face of her laughter I had no answer.

I don't think Tomiko ever fully understood my interest in Zen. (For that matter, did I ever fully understand my interest in Zen?) If anything she found it amusing (and I suppose that in its way showed a true zen spirit).

I told her I was planning to return to the temple, resume my practice.

Doshite?

Why indeed?

How to explain my experience of koan practice? How to put into words what cannot be put into words?

In any case, it is understood that such practice is secret and sacrosanct, so to describe it to others would be a breaking of trust.

(I *could* tell you, but then I would have to kill you!)

So don't expect me to go divulging inner meanings and esoteric truths. No spilling of beans, no sir, not here.

Shinki told me with genuine horror that there existed a book-of-answers to the best-known koans.

What was that description I had read? *Catechistic paradox.* That was one way of putting it.

On the other hand.

Does a dog have the Buddha-nature?

Joshu's answer was *Mu*. Nothing.

Meditate on this. *Become* this nothing.

Mu.

I was nothing but gratitude to Hanayama Roshi who tolerated my bull-in-a-china-shop blundering into the practice. (Ten bulls in ten china shops?) He challenged my un-understanding, prodded and probed my presumptions. He responded to my efforts, sometimes with encouragement, more often in silence with a kind of controlled exasperation, an exaggerated sigh. There were moments when I thought I had broken through, only for the Roshi to disabuse me with a grimace, an admonitory glare.

Not this. Not this.

Mu.

The sessions of zazen, paradoxically (!) became easier. Perhaps my muscles and joints, my sinews, were growing stronger, getting used to just sitting. (And yes, that experience was again vouchsafed, the sense of simply being there and nowhere else).

Nowhere? Now-here.

But the hours of sitting could also leave me struggling, at a loss. More than once I left a session close to tears.

I thought of asking the Roshi about this but it was not appropriate. He was the one asking the questions. I looked at the *unsui*, the trainee monks, saw no light in their faces, only anger and meanness held in check.

But the young monk who had noticed me before, and had done the

Oi! / Hai! routine, spoke to me after a morning session. He said his name was Gibun. Bun-san.

Buraisu-san, I said.

Yes.

The way is long, he said. It may take a lifetime. Or more. You should not be discouraged.

I was deeply moved by his kindness, saw in his face none of that tension I saw in the other monks. He offered to sit with me and said if I had questions to ask he would do his best to answer them.

Does a dog have the Buddha-nature? I asked.

Perhaps not that!

But he said I could ask anything arising from our practice or the teachings.

We sat facing each other, formal. I bowed and asked, Bun-san, do you cry?

The question, I could see, was unexpected, caught him by surprise. What do you mean by this? he asked.

I cry often, I said. I cried yesterday when the light of the setting sun shone on our verandah. The bamboo poles turned red in the evening light. I saw this, and I thought of my mother, and I cried.

Ah, he said. If that is what you mean by crying, then I also cry. Everybody cries.

No, I said. Those who really cry are few.

Is that so?

And those who do not cry are no good. They cannot be trusted.

Perhaps, he said, you should not be so quick to judge!

Perhaps, I said. Then I framed another question.

I watch the trainee monks, I said, the *unsui*. And this means cloud – water.

Yes, he said. From a Chinese poem. To drift like clouds and flow like water.

Very good, I said. A very pure and noble aim. But what I want to ask is, Why do they have such angry faces?

I think this is only how you see them, based on your own ideas.

No, I said. They glare at everyone. Their faces are mean.

He smiled, said, You should try to see them with nothing-in-mind.

It was a little moment of reluctant insight, a thorn being removed.
Yes. I myself could be cantankerous and curmudgeonly.
He who treads the path in earnest sees not the faults of others. But from
morning to night I saw nothing else!
I threw back my head and laughed.

We spoke often after that, and our exchanges filled me with a kind
of exhilaration. I realised that all my life I had sought a friend like
this, a David to my Jonathan, a Goldmund to my Narziss, a Han-
shan to my Shih-te. (A Laurel to my Hardy!) I thought in Bun-san I
had found such a friend and one morning I hurried to the temple, a
lightness in my heart, eager to resume our conversation. But on this
occasion he treated me with coldness, responding to my greetings
by giving a curt nod then ignoring me, turning away to busy himself
with other things.
I went home feeling quite wretched. My expectation had been fool-
ish, and I resolved – the sourest of sour grapes – that I did not need
a friend at all and was perfectly fine without one.
That evening I ate little – I did not have much of an appetite – and I
sat in my study, trying and failing to read a page of the Mumonkan.
I heard a knock at the door – we were not expecting visitors – and
Tomiko answered then called up to me that my monk-friend had
come to visit.
I went downstairs and there was Bun-san, bowing and smiling with
what I could only describe as a malicious twinkle in his eyes.
I told him how I felt and how his behaviour had affected me.
He smiled again, said, That's because you wanted something from
me!
Then he told me of a poem by Hakurakuten.

> As I wandered round the lake and gazed at the fishes gliding to and fro,
> I came across some boys fishing in a boat.
> Both they and I loved the fish, but our state of mind was different:
> I had come to feed the fish, they to catch them.

Here ended Bun-san's lesson on attachment.

The way was long. A lifetime or more. I should not be discouraged.

The idea of a book had been growing in me. Suzuki's writings had impressed me greatly, in fact they had inspired me, not to do what he had done – which in any case would have been impossible – but to follow what I can only call an inner voice. He had opened doors for me through which I might walk into limitless possibility, finding my own way, my own necessity.

I wanted, if not to justify the ways of God to men, then to illuminate the ways of Zen to a wider readership in the West. Nor would it be merely for scholars and academics – it was far too important for that.

I had already written the first words of what would be my preface. *Zen is the most precious possession of Asia.*

There! I had thrown down the gauntlet (to myself as much as to any other reader). I continued.

It is the strongest power in the world. It is a world power, for in so far as men live at all, they live by Zen. Wherever there is a poetical action, a religious aspiration, a heroic thought, a union of the nature within a man and the Nature without, there is Zen.

I had nailed my colours to the mast, set sail for open seas, let the currents carry me where they must. I would show that what I called the spirit of Zen was something universal, something which infused all great literature, and I would draw on the works in which I had immersed myself. I would quote freely from Dante, Eckhart, Cervantes, but my main emphasis was the literature of the English language and its relation to the cultures of India, China and Japan. The title was fixed, all high seriousness: *Zen in English Literature and Oriental Classics.* Shakespeare, Dickens, Wordsworth and Stevenson were my guiding lights. But I would lead my readers through the looking glass with Alice, into the dock with the Artful Dodger, into heaven and hell with Blake, and always, always, let paradox be my watchword.

I took delight in chapter headings that would challenge and intrigue: *What is Zen? Directness is All. The Unregarded River of Our Life.* And further in, *Words, Words, Words. The Pale Cast of Thought.*

In my university days, back in England, in another life, I had realised that the world of scholarship and research was not for me. I lacked the inclination for nit-picking specialisation and – dare I say it (of course I do!) – the requisite dullness. I had also been granted a kind of revelation, an insight you might say, and it was this: Whatever connections a researcher might endeavour to make in pursuit of a thesis, he would eventually discover there was no end to it. One thing led to another, and another, and on ad infinitum, everything connected to everything else. (And that way madness lies!)

It was like Indra's Net as described in the Vedas – the entire universe a net strung with jewels, linked together, reflecting off each other endlessly, a web of interconnection and interdependence – the universal in the particular, the world-in-the-grain-of-sand.

This revelation (let the word pass) opened up the way for me, showed me I had the capacity to make the *necessary* connections for my aim and purpose. It gave me the confidence to proceed.

The other day I came across a little notebook from those days. It was the size of a pocket diary, the kind of thing I used to carry around with me for scribbling down random thoughts, ideas, observations. This one had a brown cover on which was embossed a stylised lotus. God knows where I had picked it up, but inside, over the first few pages I had written a little note, an injunction to myself.

When you write a book, don't worry about whether it will ever be published or whether anyone will ever read it. All that is God's worry. Let God worry about it.

After that, something had been scored out, then the thought continued.

When you work just work. Don't worry about whether others are working or not, or whether the temple will burn down next week or not. Just work, that's all.

Act, but surrender the fruits of your actions. Just work. That's all. With no thought for the morrow.

And I did. I threw myself into it, *con gusto*. I wrote in the early mornings, in my lunch breaks at school, at the kitchen table in the evenings after dinner, and when I wasn't writing I was thinking about it, giving it shape (or finding the shape it wanted to take). I had never felt so engaged, so happy. Once again I had found my work, which was also play. (And as Herbert wrote, *By mere playing we go to Heaven*).

The book had a life of its own. It grew, chapter by chapter, into its own form. I looked on my work and saw that it was good.

For a time my schedule was such that I had no classes on a Friday afternoon. By happy coincidence (or perhaps through clever manoeuvering) Akio was in the same situation, and so too was Shinki. We would often spend the time together, eat lunch – our favourite haunt was the *Sushi Kyu* – and we might even take in an art exhibition or watch a film.

One Friday Shinki said he wanted to take us to a gallery-museum set up in an old palace building in the centre of town. He said it specialised in what he called *Mingei*, roughly translated as popular craft. So, he said, it's the Korean Folk Art museum. It had been established by an eminent Japanese art collector, Soetsu Yanagi, with the aim of preserving and displaying indigenous arts and crafts. It is about the beauty of *zakki*, said Shinki. Ordinary, miscellaneous objects. Everyday things.

Shinki was in his element, expounding on the anonymity of the creator (a subject close to his heart). He spoke of the similarities and differences between Zen and Pure Land Buddhism, said *Mingei* drew on both.

Pure Land is for everyone, he said. Not just for few.

Akio picked up a little tea-bowl, said he liked the feel of it in his hand.

Shinki said Yes, it was for use.

Akio passed the bowl to me and I felt the weight of it, satisfying, the roughness of the glaze, the not quite regular shape.

Pleasing, I said.

Because it is natural, said Shinki. And making it was also natural, unselfconscious. No ego.

Everyday mind, I said. Nothing special.

Yes!

Next time I was in the market I noticed a stall selling local pottery, among it a box of tea-bowls not unlike the ones I had seen at Mingeikan. I started looking through them, examining them, weighing each one in my hand.

The stallholder, an old Korean woman, watched me, eyes crinkled, lips turned up in a faint smile. I shrugged, indicated I did not know what to choose.

She said they were all good. Every one was the best.

I laughed, chose two at random. She wrapped them carefully and I carried them home.

The Zen master Bankei recounted how one day he was walking through the marketplace near his temple and he overheard a dialogue between a butcher and his customer.

The customer asked which cut of meat was the best. The butcher said, All of them. They are all the best.

On hearing this, Bankei became enlightened.

Remembering the story, I laughed again.

In our kitchen Tomiko unwrapped the bowls, looked slightly bemused. I explained they were like ones I had seen in the museum.

So, she said, noncommittal.

She washed the bowls and dried them, put them on the table, used them at dinner for our miso soup.

So.

I came into the staffroom one day and saw Shinki sitting with a journal open in his lap. I said Hello and he glanced up, distracted, a look in his eyes I had not seen before and which I could only describe as desolation.

I asked if something was wrong, and he brought me into focus, said simply, This world.

He had been reading an article about the Great Kanto Earthquake.

A terrible thing, I said. And not so long ago.

The earthquake had happened just a year before I arrived in Korea. It had hit Tokyo and Yokohama, left more than 100,000 dead. I had read about it, seen images of the devastation, the reconstruction that followed.

Earthquake was bad, said Shinki, But this was worse.

He passed me the article, a sombre account of the aftermath, a state-orchestrated massacre of Koreans living in Japan on the pretext they were exploiting the earthquake, looting and pillaging, committing acts of sabotage and terrorism, poisoning water supplies, all with the aim of undermining the state. Thousands of Koreans were murdered, executed, lynched, in what was effectively a pogrom.

I knew about the earthquake, I said. But not this. Not this.

I spoke of it later to Akio and he nodded, said quietly, Yes, it was a very dark story. He said there were Korean students at the school whose families had escaped here from Yokohama.

It has made these last years even more difficult, he said. Much hostile feeling against the Japanese

Understandably, I said.

He sat silent, serious, then spoke again.

It was partly why I was willing to come here and teach, he said. Give something to Korea, teach these young boys our culture is good.

A noble aim, I said.

Yes, he said, nodding. Noble.

Things were changing. Akio looked deeply troubled as he spoke of a rising tide of militarism in the homeland. In recent years Japan had annexed Manchuria in the name of economic necessity. Now there was war with China, brutal victories hailed as glorious triumph. He said some of our own boys would be enlisted and sent to fight. (Already they had been ordered to use the Japanese forms of their names to facilitate their conscription to the army).

The thought made me sick to my stomach.

From time to time Ma would send me an English newspaper, usually the Times, and the news from Europe was equally dispiriting. It reinforced everything Mr Watson had told me in London, the rise of Nazi Germany, the seemingly inexorable move towards yet another war, the same dark forces at work – greed, rapaciousness, the plundering of resources.

Was this, then, what the Hindus called the *Kali Yuga*, the epoch of darkness and destruction, annihilation?

It escalated quickly, Czechoslovakia, then Poland. Mr Chamberlain's *Peace in our time* proved not so much a mantra as a vain and desperate hope, now replaced by the grim banality of the announcement. *This country is at war with Germany.*

No *Cry Havoc.* No *Let slip the dogs.* No rhetoric or oratory, just the statement, dull and factual but cataclysmic in its impact.

This country is at war.

In Korea too, our lives were suddenly less comfortable, more unsettled, the whole situation more volatile. Anti-Japanese sentiment was on the rise. The writing was, quite literally, on the wall – slogans daubed on government buildings, factories, the railway station. *Free Korea. Japanese overlords out now.* There were acts of sabotage, an assassination attempt on a Japanese general.

The numbers 3-1 appeared everywhere. In Korean that was *Sami-Il.* Akio explained it was a date, March 1st, the date of a historic uprising against Japanese rule, back in 1919. Akio was concerned, for himself and his family, but also, genuinely, for Tomiko and me. He warned me there was a danger my contract might not be renewed. He himself was planning to return to Japan and he suggested I might want to follow him. With his contacts he was sure he would be able to help me find work.

It was another koan, trying to decide what was for the best. Stay in Korea? Move to Japan? Go back to England? Then something happened that cut through everything, everything, everything. Akio had a heart attack and died. That was it, the stark fact of it. Akio died, aged 42. *Angina pectoris.*

Akio died.

I wept and Tomiko could not console me.

Why should a dog a horse a rat have life and thou no breath at all?

Mu.

This little life of ours. What to do with it? What to do next?

Tomiko's father, mindful of his business interests, had already moved back to the family home in Yamaguchi. Motoko and little Katsura had also gone, home to Kyoto. Everything, it seemed, was telling us to go.

Tomiko agreed.

That early poem of mine began, *We that change, hate change.* But Dickinson wrote, *In insecurity to lie is joy's insuring quality.*

We made our preparations to sell up and move out, move on. We would take our chances in Japan.

I made a final visit to Myoshin-ji, paid my respects to the Abbot, said goodbye to Bun-san.

It was time.

We would travel by train to the port of Pusan and from there by boat to Kobe. So many years since my arrival with Annie, Akio welcoming us. So many years. Our lives passing.

Shinki said he would be at the railway station to say goodbye and so too did Kasai, that young boy who had spoken up for me when his classmates rebelled. Now he was a grown man, teaching at the school. Time and change.

Tomiko and I stepped from a taxi cab in front of the station. I looked round expecting to see Shinki and Kasai, perhaps a few of their students come to see me off. Instead I saw, assembled in the square, ranks of boys in their uniforms, lined up as if in military formation. Shinki and Kasai approached, bowed.

They are from whole school, said Shinki.

To say goodbye, said Kasai.

They turned and Kasai shouted out a command. The boys stood to attention and began to sing.

I knew the melody, the tune of *Auld Lang Syne* that had stirred me as a boy.

In Japan it was also a song of parting, sung at every graduation ceremony, *Hotaru no Hikari*. Light of the Fireflies. It told of poor students studying by the light of fireflies, the moonlight reflected on snow. Now they were graduating and moving on.

Light of the fireflies, moonlight on snow…
Many suns and moons spent reading.
Before we know it, years have passed.
Now resolutely we open the doors and depart.

The whole thing was unremittingly sentimental but I was completely undone by it, overwhelmed by the surge of emotion in my chest. Beside me Tomiko was sobbing and I knew if I looked at her I would be helpless.

It was the sheer unexpectedness of it, the innocent intensity of the boys, the swell of the young voices raised as one, and beyond that the simple humanity of it all, ritualised, formalised, timeless but of the moment, *this* moment.

This.

I looked out across the square, to the hills beyond the city, for all the world like a stage set, a painted backdrop, and I knew in my bones I would never return, would not see this place again. This part of my life was over.

The song came to an end and the boys bowed. Shinki and Kasai turned to me, expecting me to make some kind of farewell speech. But I could not. All I could do was bow and say, Thank you, my voice breaking.

Thank you.

I had nothing more to say. No more words.

5

PERSONS IN A BELLIGERENT NATION

Novelists know this. There are times when the passage of years can be rendered in a paragraph, while a single moment may require pages.

So those first few weeks in Japan are a blur, so quickly did they pass. I suppose they were a time of transition. (Though what time is not?) We stayed with Tomiko's family in her hometown of Hagi in Yamaguchi prefecture. The town itself was beautiful, overlooking the Sea of Japan. Tomiko's parents were overjoyed to see her, and they were hospitable and welcoming. Right from my arrival in Japan I once more had that sense of familiarity – it felt like coming home. But I was also driven by a restlessness, a need to move on.

I had worked like a fiend on my book. The manuscript was almost complete. I was inexorably drawn to Tokyo where I thought it would be easier to find work and perhaps also interest a publisher. I made the decision. Three months after arriving in Japan we found a small house to rent in Ueno.

The very name thrilled me. I had translated Basho's famous haiku.

A cloud of cherry blossoms.
The temple bell –
Is it Ueno? Asakusa?

And on the way to Tokyo by train, I had looked up, seen through the window a great mountain flash past. Moved to tears by this glimpse, I bowed to great Fuji-san, grateful to have seen it at last. Then a few moments later the *real* Fuji-san came into view, unmistakeable, vast. My sense of foolishness was immediately subsumed in a moment of initiation, the mountain suddenly there, overwhelming, this huge, otherworldly presence, in this world and yet somehow beyond it, archetypal, sublime. This time I was overcome with emotion and again I bowed, this time in deep obeisance. One or two Japanese passengers had not been looking up, not paying attention to this great being in their midst, taking it for granted. They noticed me, this foolish tearful gaijin, and they smiled, took a sudden pride, and they too bowed, remembering.

In Ueno I felt instantly at ease. Our house was near the railway station – again I heard that clatter and rumble of trains I had always loved, a comfort to me, a mantra. And around the station was the sprawling market in the narrow lanes and alleys, the arches under bridges, all random and ramshackle, every inch of it crammed to bursting, teeming with raucous life. To walk through it all was to step into a woodblock print, a Hokusai or a Hiroshige, the riot of colour and noise, the floating world.

In Ueno Park was the Zoo. I could hear the animals, the trumpeting and roar of them carried on the wind, but I could not bear to go in. I agreed with Blake: *A robin redbreast in a cage / Puts all heaven in a rage...*

At the edge of the Park I looked up at the looming bronze statue of legendary samurai Saigō Takamori. It was all solid strength, enduring, but what appealed to me was the figure of his dog, given its due, its rightful place beside him on the pedestal.

Did this dog have the Buddha-nature? Without a doubt.

Another reason for moving to Tokyo was to be closer to Suzuki-sensei. His home, I discovered, was in Kamakura, a short train ride away, beyond Yokohama. I wrote to him care of Engakuji temple where I understood he lived. He replied, *mirabile dictu*, on a handwritten postcard, said he was just about to travel to his hometown of Kanazawa where he had agreed to do some teaching. He would be delighted to meet me on his return to Kamakura, or earlier if the opportunity arose for me to come to Kanazawa.

I replied that I would be in Kanazawa the following week (I made sure of it!) and we arranged to meet at the inn where he was lodging.

I arrived in Kanazawa, excited, beside myself, as they say. (And which self would present itself to this esteemed teacher?)

I imagined Suzuki might be fierce, a ferocious Zen patriarch, a Hakuin, a Bodhidharma. a hard taskmaster like Daito Kokushi, who would – physically and not just figuratively – rap his students on the knuckles if they gave an unsatisfactory answer to the question, *What is Zen?* And for Daito Kokushi, any answer at all was unsatisfactory. (As, for that matter, was no answer).

What is Zen?
The cherry tree in the yard.
Rap!

What is Zen?
Who wants to know?
Rap!

Feeling anticipation and trepidation in equal measure (a fluttering, like electricity, in the heart, a dull churning in the gut) I walked the half mile or so from the little ryokan near the station where I had booked in on my arrival.

I felt overdressed in my tweed suit, my collar-and-tie, but the occasion was formal and I was aware how ludicrous I would look in Japanese clothes. I was still sometimes the subject of a certain curiosity, the portly round-eye, the *gaijin* in their midst, and I had no wish for that to turn to mockery or animosity.

I found the address and stood on the threshold, uncertain whether to open the door and announce my arrival. Suddenly the shoji-screen panel slid open and a small middle-aged Japanese woman was bowing and smiling at me, bowing and smiling, and she indicated I should take off my shoes and step inside.

She led me to an inner room where Suzuki-sensei himself was waiting, and he stood to greet me, bowing with a little half-smile. I turned to thank the woman but she had already gone, closing the shoji behind her with a quiet *swish*.

I was here, alone with the master, and he nodded to me to sit facing him on a small *zafu* cushion like the one he himself was using.

So, he said. Buraisu-san. Welcome.

How to find the words – the right words – to describe him?

He was small and extraordinarily thin with prominent cheekbones and unruly eyebrows. Far from being ferocious, his manner was gentle, sympathetic, kindly. He asked after my health, and the journey to Kanazawa, and my lodgings, and I began to feel he was more interested in me and my everyday life than in philosophising.

He reminded me of a character from fiction, Mr Heyhoe, the minister in a story by TF Powys, who never spoke to anyone for the purpose of teaching them (for God had his own time for that!) Rather he was always ready to speak of the most trifling matters, for who could tell in what little way the joy of religion might enter the soul.

The joy of religion.

The shoji swished open again and the woman came in carrying a tray with a teapot and two cups, a little plate of mochi sweets. Again she bowed and smiled, bowed and smiled, as she poured the tea, placed everything just so, her movements deft, efficient, unhurried. He introduced her as his landlady, Mrs Yazaki, and he praised her kindness as she quietly took her leave.

We sipped the bitter green tea. (On such occasions I felt it would be impolite not to). We ate the sweet, soft mochi. I felt content, at peace.

He noticed me looking at a framed photograph of a very striking Western woman, older but with a directness and strength in her gaze, self-contained, smiling for the camera. He told me it was his wife Beatrice, an American, and that it was only a year since she had died.

I said I was sorry and he said that was not necessary. Their time together had been long and happy.

A blessing, I said.

May I ask you, he said after a silence, how you came to be interested in Zen?

I replied with a certain eagerness (which might have seemed gauche had it not been so heartfelt) that it was through reading his *Essays on Zen Buddhism.* I said the book had changed my life and I was hugely indebted to him.

I have never forgotten his response. He bowed his head, and I cannot say how much that simple action impressed me. It was not modesty, not even gratitude. There was humility in it, but more than anything it was an expression of the inevitable, an acceptance that might be summed up, *Is that so?*

I was deeply moved, but composed myself and said the book had led me on to further study.

As you know, I said, I have just come from Korea, where I studied under Hanayama Roshi at Myoshinji Betsuin.

As I spoke the words I heard them as faintly ridiculous, as if I were puffed up and full of myself, announcing my credentials.

So, he said simply. Can you tell me what is Zen?

I believe I have already mentioned this exchange in these pages. But it seems to me important, and worth revisiting. What is Zen?

As I understand it, I said, there is no such thing.

Ah, he said. I can see you know something of Zen.

Thank you, I said, and could think of nothing else to say.

No such thing as Zen, he said. Now, have more tea, another mochi.

It is hard to believe that first meeting with Suzuki was almost a quarter of a century ago (although there are times when I feel I have always known him).

Suzuki who taught me all I don't know.

Suzuki who can read what I can't write.

Suzuki most definitely put in a good word for me at his old school. I also had exemplary references from Keijo. So as if by magic (things unfolding as they must) I was employed as an English teacher at the Fourth Kanazawa High School. Once again we were on the move. We settled in accommodation provided by the school, as Annie and I had done in Keijo all those years ago. My salary was fixed at the same amount I had been paid before. Once again I felt somehow protected, almost as if by some higher force, shaping my destiny, guiding me towards I knew not what.

There was something about Kanazawa I liked, something in the air, a certain mildness. The weather was often misty and perhaps that as much as anything else reminded me of London (unlikely though that may sound). The boys I taught also had a mildness and a kind of earnest straightforwardness. When I told them their city reminded me of London they didn't understand. London was a metropolis, and their image of it, if they had one, would be of Buckingham Palace and Tower Bridge, Horseguards on parade, red double-decker buses, bowler-hatted city gents. Kanazawa, they said, was like Kyoto but smaller – *Sho Kyoto*, Little Kyoto, with its temples and gardens, its maze of narrow lanes beside the city walls. I understand, I said. But still, there is something....
Hai, they said, humouring me. *So desu*.

Just as I had done in Korea, I bought an old bicycle and fixed it up, made it roadworthy. I rode it to work and at weekends went further, exploring the city. One afternoon I emerged, leisurely pedalling my bike, into the square beside the railway station. There was some kind of gathering opposite the main gate, a speech being made through a loudspeaker. It brought to mind my departure from Seoul, those boys singing their song of farewell, *Hotaru no Hikari*.
I dismounted and crossed the square, pushing my bike. It was difficult to make out what was being said, the sound crackling, the words broken up by the wind which was also tugging at two banners, raised at the front of the crowd. I stopped, caught my breath as the flags unfurled, a Rising Sun and a Nazi Swastika.
I turned away, unsettled, and cycled home.
Didn't I know there was a war on?
There was a newspaper article the following day. What I had seen was not some military rally, a show of force. Rather it was a welcoming party for six young visitors from Germany, members of the *Hitler Jugend*, visiting Japan to learn something of its culture. From Kanazawa they would be taken to the great monastery of Eiheiji to experience firsthand the way of life there, the rigorous discipline of the monks. The abbot said he hoped the boys would take away

something of the spirit of the place, an understanding of Zen.

The hope, I thought, was optimistic. But what did I know?

The monastery had been established by Dogen, the revered founder of Soto Zen.

Like all great teachers Dogen was a poet. I would use one of his verses on the first page of my book.

> *The water bird*
> *Wanders here and there.*
> *She leaves no trace*
> *But never forgets*
> *Her path.*

I had been working steadily on the book. Now I resolved to throw myself into it even more.

Suzuki-sensei had returned to his home in Kamakura and I sent him the first few chapters. He kindly invited me to visit him there whenever it might be convenient. As soon as I could, I made the journey by train, once again bowing to great Fuji-san (the real one!) on the way. As instructed, I alighted from the train at the little station of Kita Kamakura and walked the short distance towards Engakuji temple, breathing the clear air, uplifted by birdsong.

The path to Suzuki's place led through an avenue of tall trees – magnificent cryptomeria, Japanese cedar known as *sugi* – up a flight of worn stone steps, past wild magnolia, azalea and camellia to his retreat, a three room house looking out across the tree tops, beyond Engakuji to the sea. It was like entering another world.

Suzuki welcomed me, bade me sit facing him on a thick zafu cushion at a low table. So, he said. Here we are!

And there we were indeed.

There were bookshelves filled to overflowing, stacks of books on the tatami-covered floor. A single scroll hung in a tokonoma alcove, and on a shelf was the same photograph of his wife Beatrice I had seen in his lodgings in Kanazawa.

I asked if he was well, and he said Yes, he was very well. He had been to the dentist that morning. And he had pain in his eye. And he had taken a dose of worm powder. And it had been necessary to call in a carpenter to repair some rat-holes in the ceiling. But apart from all that, yes, he was well!

His expression was at once stern and benign, the corners of his mouth turned down, the eyes beneath those bushy eyebrows twinkling.

And you, he asked, how are you?

I too am well, I said. All things considered.

Good, he said. It is good to consider all things!

It was remarkable to see, this austerity tempered by humour.

Now, he said, shall we eat?

The kitchen at the temple had delivered two bento boxes, one vegetarian for me, the other for him with a serving of raw sliced fish.

He bowed. *Itadakimasu.* I humbly receive this. All that was needed by way of grace.

Bon appétit.

I feasted on rice balls with umeboshi plum, tofu pockets, cold noodles in a sesame dressing, a little sliced omelette. On the side there were pieces of pickled ginger but not, mercifully, my unfavourite *takuan.*

Oishii, I said. Delicious.

When we had eaten, I was anxious to hear what Suzuki thought of the chapters I had sent him, my work-in-progress, but I was reluctant to ask. As if reading my mind, he smiled, gave what felt like a benediction.

I think your book is excellent.

I said it owed a very great deal to his own work.

Thank you, he said. That may be so. But you have made something entirely your own.

I was humbled by the generosity, the kindness of his comments.

I think, he said, we are doing the same work, opening doors.

Or *shoji* screens!

Perhaps it is important we bring Zen to the world.

He indicated a pile of manuscripts on his desk.

My own books have been translated. They are published in England,

America and Germany.

At a time like this, I said, that is something wonderful

Yes, he said, that is the word. Wonderful!

I am sure they bring light into the darkness.

Let us hope, he said.

I told him about the gathering I had seen at Kanazawa station, the delegation, the flags.

He looked concerned, his forehead furrowed.

And you say these young Germans went to Eiheiji?

Yes.

He was silent for a moment.

I wonder what Dogen would make of that?

Heartened by Suzuki's response, I worked even harder on my book, in the early mornings before Tomiko woke up, in the evenings when I came home from school, at odd moments in the staffroom between classes. In a matter of months I had completed a draft. I had it typed and mimeographed, ready to go. I took a copy to Suzuki, carried it up that long flight of steps to his home at Engakuji, a gift delivered with gratitude.

Over the next few visits I made, he gave me the wisdom of his response, sharing his insight, his erudition but also his humour. Occasionally he would correct a mistranslation, a misinterpretation. But more often than not he simply encouraged, with a word, a silent nod. When we got to the end of the book he let out a great sigh of satisfaction.

So, he said. This is your Sacred Treasure. This is why Buraisu-san came from the West!

In these darkest of times I was pursuing the light. Word had filtered through about the blitz on British cities, particularly London. I woke often in the night, worried for Ma and everyone else back home. But Ma's letters reassured me. She was fine and in good spirits. These were indeed dark days and poor old London was taking a battering. She supposed she shouldn't say it, but she didn't think Leytonstone was much of a strategic target. Elsewhere the damage was terrible, but she felt in her bones all would be well, in time, in time. She said she was actually glad I was not at home. She ended, Send your prayers for us all. And I did, at Engakuji I prayed for all sentient beings, but especially for Ma and Dora, for Annie and for Lee. Let them all be safe from harm.

Suzuki had said more than once I must meet his friend Yamanashi-san, as in *Admiral* Yamanashi, late of the Imperial Japanese Navy.

At first I was reluctant, uncertain. What would a lifelong pacifist have to say to a military commander? Nation shall not lift up sword against nation, neither shall they learn war any more?

But Suzuki was adamant and could be most persuasive. He said in his own way the Admiral was a man of peace. He had consistently opposed Japan's naval programme, the increasing of its capacity, its preparation for war, which he said would be suicide. He had argued in favour of a treaty with the Western powers. There had been a high-powered meeting in London where he had put his case. But he had been overruled, a voice crying in the wilderness. He had been forced to resign, replaced by what Suzuki called fire-breathing nationalists.

And now?

Most interesting, said Suzuki. He was appointed President of Gakushuin, the Peers School. This has close connection with the Imperial household. So he most certainly has the approval of the Emperor himself.

Suzuki could see I was intrigued, not least by his own insistence.

He is a very cultured man, he said. I think you will like him!

I have often thought back to that meeting, at Suzuki's home, and in retrospect I see how pivotal it was, how monumental its importance (at least in terms of my own little life!)

I had made a few visits to the house since that first time, and though he always put me at my ease, I still treated him with great deference, saw each visit as a kind of pilgrimage, to sit at the feet of the master. Now there was to be this added dimension, the presence of

Yamanashi, a man who had been in a position of great influence and power and who still moved at the highest levels of a rigidly hierarchical Japanese society.

I was not sure what to expect, but my trust in Suzuki was absolute, and if he had chosen to introduce me to the Admiral, he must have his own very good reasons (or un-reasons).

I arrived at the exact time we had arranged, going so far as to be there a few minutes early and check my watch, counting down to the second before sliding open the door and calling out my greeting. *Gomen kudasai.*

Suzuki himself called back, Buraisu-san, welcome! Come in, come in!

I should not have been surprised that Yamanashi-san was already there, but it was gratifying to see that he too treated Suzuki with great respect. He stood and greeted me, gave a slight bow, spoke to me in English.

Mister Blyth, he said. I am very happy to meet you.

And I you, I said, responding with a deep bow. *Yoroshiku onegaishimasu.*

So, said Suzuki. Here we are!

Yes, said Yamanashi, smiling. Here we are.

He was quite unlike anyone I had ever met, had a poise about him, an air of contained strength. He looked younger than his sixty years, his hair just beginning to turn grey at the temples, a neatly trimmed moustache still dark. The face was lean, almost gaunt, skin taut over high cheekbones. But what struck me most about his appearance were the eyes. I could imagine him scanning horizons, looking out across immeasurable distances. Then when he focussed on me with that same intensity, the gaze was piercing. I fancied he was looking into my soul, assessing me in an instant. It should have been unsettling, but the judgement was kindly, almost amused.

Please, said Suzuki, indicating we should sit. A teapot sat on the table with three blue-glazed bowls, each one different. He poured, and we drank, and we talked the afternoon away.

Yamanashi's English was fluent. He spoke with great fondness of the time he had spent in England as a young man, studying in

London.

Earth hath not anything to show more fair, he said.

He mentioned he had returned to London just a few years ago but had not had time to enjoy the city for its own sake, being constrained by duty.

I recalled what Suzuki had told me, of the Admiral being in London, his attempts to negotiate a treaty, his resignation.

No doubt you would have found the place much changed, I said.

No doubt, he said.

Nevertheless, he wondered what could have made me want to leave London and come to Japan.

Fate? I said. Destiny? Karma? Or perhaps sheer chance!

Perhaps, he said, then left a little silence before continuing.

Suzuki-sensei has told me about your book on Zen in English Literature. It sounds fascinating.

A small contribution, I said, to understanding across cultures. Or to creating further *mis*understanding!

I should very much like to read it, he said.

I would be honoured, I said. I shall make sure you receive a copy.

Throughout the afternoon we spoke and relaxed into each other's company. We discovered much common ground. I sensed a keen and incisive mind, a generous spirit of inquiry. To my delight he also showed a great love of English poetry, particularly Shakespeare and Wordsworth, but also Blake and my beloved Matthew Arnold. I felt that, like Suzuki, he would be an insightful reader of my book, and I, in turn would have much to learn from him.

Towards the end of the afternoon, when there was a natural pause in the talk, the three of us sat in a kind of companionable silence. It was then that I felt something quite extraordinary take place. It is difficult to put into words – like any profound, or profoundly simple experience.

I can only say it felt like a deepening, a recognition, a familiarity. We were in the moment, and yet we were somehow beyond time. It was as if we knew each other and had sat like this before.

Two Chinamen, behind them a third...carved in Lapis Lazuli.

In the timelessness there was a stillness, a fulness-in-emptiness.

We sat, as if in zazen. We just sat there as if we just sat there. That was all. Eternity in love with the productions of time.

So, said Suzuki, breaking it, and clapping his hands. When shall we three meet again?

Later Suzuki told me I had made a good impression on the Admiral, adding, And he is not a man who is easily impressed.

I was equally taken with him, I said.

I thought of telling Suzuki about my little moment of awakening, or satori, or delusion, call it what you will, but I decided against it for the moment.

Suzuki's eyes glinted with a kind of amusement, a look I had come to recognise.

I was glad you introduced yourself, he said, with *Yoroshiku one-gaishimasu.*

Yes, I said, a little hesitant, aware of that twinkle in the eye.

It was most appropriate, he said.

It means, I am happy to meet you, does it not?

Indeed, said Suzuki. But words can mean much more than they say. As a poet, you know that! So this simple expression can also mean, You are my superior and it is a great honour to meet you.

I see. So far, so respectful.

It can also mean, Please help me. Be kind to me.

Really?

Or, taking it further, it can mean, I am in your debt and look forward to working with you.

I had no idea.

Finally, it can mean, Thank you in advance for all the help you are going to give me.

Good God, I said. All of that in two little words?

You are discovering just how subtle Japanese can be.

And maddeningly allusive and complex.

I hope the Admiral did not think I was bing pushy or obsequious.

Not at all. They were the right words to use.

The best words in the best order.

Exactly so.

I had no idea at the time just how prescient Suzuki's words would prove to be. I would indeed be endlessly indebted to the Admiral for all his help. Yamanashi, I discovered, was in contact, not just with the Imperial household, but with some of the most powerful and influential men in the country. He moved comfortably among them, and was part of their world. And yet he took to this unqualified *gaijin*, this barbarian. He gave me his hand. He reached down and helped me up. He opened doors. Without him I would not have survived.

He read the completed manuscript of my book (passed on to him by Suzuki) and he declared himself Most Impressed. The book, he said, was important, especially at this time. He introduced me to an editor at Hokuseido publishing house in Tokyo and recommended the book to him. In time, and largely, I suspect, as a result of the Admiral's influence, the book was accepted for publication. Who would read it? I had no idea. But that was not my concern. It would be out there in the world and for that alone I was simply grateful, felt blessed.

And as if that were not enough, Tomiko told me one evening, quietly and without fuss, that she had been to see the doctor and he had confirmed what she had already known (and I had hoped), that she was expecting our first child.

I held her and she wept for joy.

My cup runneth over, I said.

She didn't understand and I didn't think I could explain. But she could see I shared her gladness.

I tried to mime the fulness in my heart, cupping my hands. Then a little gospel song came back to me, from my early childhood when Ma and Pa would take me to church.

I sang it as best I could.

> *Running over, running over,*
> *My cup's full and running over.*

Tomiko laughed, delighted, clapped her hands.

> *Since the Lord saved me*
> *I'm as happy as can be.*
> *My cup's full and running over.*

Happy as can be.
Pass the tambourine!

I was much distracted by the imminent arrival of our child. Tomiko was almost at full term and the baby was due any time. So when the postman brought a small rectangular package along with the usual mail, I did not at first give it my full attention as Tomiko set it down on the kitchen table. Then I noticed the package was from Hoku-seido Press and I picked it up with some excitement. I felt it in my gut, a stirring, a quickening, and part of me, quite detached, looked on with some amusement as my hands actually shook, fumbling to tear the thing open without doing damage to the contents. I peeled away the paper wrapping, the stiff protective card, and there it was, an advance copy of my book.

I have heard other writers say that moment is always a kind of disappointment to them. They have worked long and hard at the book, put their very souls into it, now time has passed and here it is, somehow reduced, laid out between boards, the life gone out of it. I can only say I have never experienced this with any of my own books, and least of all with this, the first.

I held it in my hands, felt the weight of it, the solidity. It was here. It existed. It was real. It had actually come to pass. A cream-coloured dust jacket with my name and the title in blue lettering across the top. *Zen in English Literature and Oriental Classics. RH Blyth.* The same underneath in elegant Japanese characters.

I took off the dust jacket, admired the rich blue cover, the title printed in a panel on the spine. I replaced the cover, opened the book at the frontispiece, a monochrome watercolour painting by Thomas Girtin, titled *Fields in Flood*. It looked for all the world like a Japanese brush drawing, and underneath was a haiku by Onitsura.

I know well
  That the June rains
    Just fall.

It was exquisite, the juxtaposition just perfect.
I flicked through the pages, smelled the paper. I laughed.
I could eat it! I shouted.
Tomiko didn't quite understand but I mimed taking a bite out of the book, rubbed my stomach. Then she laughed too, at her husband the crazy *gaijin*, and she patted her own stomach.
A good time for us, she said.
Yes, I said. Yes!

When Tomiko's contractions began I was useless – headless chicken, dog chasing its own tail – all the cartoon cliches of bumbling male ineptitude. What price my years of Zen practice? But I ran next door and summoned our neighbour Mrs Tanaka who had three children of her own. She immediately took charge, brisk and efficient, dispatched me to the public telephone across the road to call the hospital. We had decided in advance Tomiko would go there and she had already packed a bag with a few things she might need. The ambulance arrived and I watched, in a daze, as she was helped into the back and the doors were closed. I silently chanted the Nembutsu as the vehicle eased off down the street. Mrs Tanaka made me tea, told me Tomiko was strong and everything would be fine.
Not worry, she said, in English.
I sat up half the night, tried to read, to pray, to meditate, to not-worry.
At first light I got on my bike and went to the hospital. Tomiko had just given birth to a baby girl. There was no way on earth that I, a mere man, could begin to understand what she had gone through. The doctors said everything had been straightforward, insofar as such a thing is possible.
Later they allowed me to visit the ward. I could see Tomiko was exhausted, but her eyes shone. I stood at the end of the bed and she held up the baby for me to see. I went closer and she let me hold the little bundle. I looked in awe at the lovely puckered face, the tiny, perfect hands.
Our daughter.
I was overwhelmed, felt a joy I had never known.

We called her Harumi, the two kanji meaning Spring and Beauty. Harumi, our little Spring Beauty. Or, even more poetically, they might mean Spring Sea, as in the name of a piece of music by Michio Miyagi – *Haru No Umi*. Then there was a haiku by Buson, one of my favourites. *Haruno umi Hinemosu Notari Notarikana*. I had made my own translation.

> *The sea of spring*
> *Rising and falling*
> *All the day long.*

Harumi. Harumi.

Suzuki-sensei and Yamanashi-san both suggested I apply for Japanese citizenship. They would give their backing, and they thought Harumi's birth and the publication of my book would both weigh heavily in my favour.

The war in Europe was running its bloody course and I entertained no more thought of returning home to England. My responsibility, my duty, was here in Japan, with Tomiko and now Harumi. The fear was that the collective madness of nations, this insatiable bloodlust held in check these twenty years, would spread, a conflagration, over the whole world. I knew Japan had its own dream of a pan-Asian empire and was in conflict with the US and the UK (itself no stranger to colonising the continent).

I renewed my application for citizenship, citing my new circumstances. I cycled to work every day, continued to teach the children in my charge. I wrote. I prayed. I meditated. I was at peace. I lived in hope.

However much we had anticipated the escalation, it was the suddenness of it that was such a shock.

The newspaper report, under the headline VICTORY, stated that Japan's Imperial Forces had made one splendid strike after another in historic surprise attacks on Pearl Harbour, where the bravado of the US Asia fleet met with sudden defeat, and off the Malaya Coast,

where the main forces of the British Asia fleet were utterly annihi-
lated. In a third strike, Hong Kong Island, England's strategic base
for its 100-year exploitation of East Asia, fell in a matter of days.

Suzuki told me when Yamanashi heard the news, he wept.

Japan was now officially at war with the US and the UK.

Three days later I was arrested. Two policemen came to the house
and I was taken to Naka police station.

The chief officer spoke English.

You will be taken to Kobe, he said, and institutionalised as persons
in a belligerent nation.

Oh well, I said. If you put it like that.

Tomiko had left Harumi with our neighbour and followed me to the
station. She was distraught but composed herself, tried to explain. I
was a respected teacher and author, I had important friends, I would
soon be a Japanese citizen, we had a young child. But the man was
unmoved. The regulation was clear. There was nothing to be done.

Don't worry, I said to Tomiko, with an assurance I didn't feel. It
will be all right.

Yea though I walk in the valley of the shadow.

They led me to a cell.

Persons in a belligerent nation.

Among my papers I have an old typed copy of the letter Churchill
sent to the Japanese Ambassador in London, confirming the dec-
laration of war.

Sir,

*On the evening of December 7th His Majesty's Government in the United
Kingdom learned that Japanese forces without previous warning either in
the form of a declaration of war or of an ultimatum with a conditional
declaration of war had attempted a landing on the coast of Malaya and
bombed Singapore and Hong Kong.*

*In view of these wanton acts of unprovoked aggression committed in
flagrant violation of International Law and particularly of Article I
of the Third Hague Convention relative to the opening of hostilities, to
which both Japan and the United Kingdom are parties, His Majesty's*

Ambassador at Tokyo has been instructed to inform the Imperial Japanese
Government in the name of His Majesty's Government in the United
Kingdom that a state of war exists between our two countries.
I have the honour to be, with high consideration,
Sir,
Your obedient servant,
Winston S. Churchill

Churchill later wrote that some people did not like the ceremonial
style of the letter. But after all, he said, when you have to kill a man
it costs nothing to be polite.
I once told Yamanashi there was much Zen in that statement.
Samurai spirit, he said.
Yes, I said, but with a kind of droll bleakness, a sense of irony and
paradox. Like something by Stevenson. Churchill holding his lit
cigar to the fuse of a loaded cannon.
Perhaps, he said.
Now it brings to mind the passage from the Gita where Krishna
tells Arjuna to fight and slay his enemies who are also his kinsfolk.
Krishna tells him to have no fear because they are already dead.
Krishna, as Time and Death, has already destroyed them.
Time and Death. Time and Death.
Thou shalt not kill. Or if thou must, then thou shouldst be polite
about it.

They kept me at the police station for two days. Tomiko came to
visit. She was tearful but resolute, determined. She had not given up
hope that it was all a mistake and I would be released. But if I was
indeed to be sent to Kobe for the duration, for God-knows-how-
long, she would get her father's help. She would move to Kobe, find
somewhere that she and Harumi could live, near where I was to be
interned.
Poor Tomiko. What she went through for my sake.
She brought me a change of clothes, a heavy coat against the coming
cold. (If it came to it, the coat could serve as a blanket). She also
brought a case containing some of my books and papers, the ones I

had told her were most important (and including a copy of my *Zen in English Literature*).

The chief officer looked through the contents, checking the papers, picking up individual books, putting them back with a noncommittal grunt. I half expected he might refuse to let me take the books. But perhaps he was indeed swayed by my status as respected-man-with-important-friends. Perhaps he was impressed at seeing my own book, and by the fact that some of the volumes – the *Manyoshu*, the *Mumonkan* – were in Japanese. For whatever reason, he grunted again, closed the lid of the case, said OK, you take.

Tomiko cried, with relief I guessed, and maybe a glimmer of reassurance. We embraced and I was led away, carrying the case and my bag of clothes, back to my cell.

Next morning I was taken in the back of a van, to Kobe where I had first made landfall in Japan, so many years ago, in another life.

The Daruma doll was brightly coloured, a child's toy I had bought in the market in Kanazawa, the robes rendered in deep red, the features crudely drawn like a caricature, a cartoon version of the fierce Zen patriarch Daruma, Bodhidharma.

The eyes were staring, lidless, for according to legend, Bodhidharma had cut off his own eyelids so he wouldn't fall asleep in meditation. Where he threw them a tea-plant grew up, so the monks could drink tea to keep awake. A less drastic solution, and a good story.

Another legend was that he sat so long in zazen that his legs atrophied and fell off, hence this depiction as a doll rounded at the bottom. If you knock it over it rolls back up.

Get knocked down, bounce back up.

Before I was taken away I had showed it to Harumi. Down...up. There was a little chant that went with it.

Nana korobi ya oki... Seven times down, eight times up.

I sang it to her, made her laugh. She knocked the doll over, watched it bounce back, clapped her hands.

The clothes and blankets Tomiko had packed for me were in an old kit bag – Pack up your troubles! (*What's the use of worrying? It never was worthwhile...*) At the bottom of the bag, wrapped in a towel, she

had placed the Daruma doll. To remind me.
Nana korobi ya oki...

6

EIGHT TIMES UP

The authorities had taken over a ramshackle old mansion known locally as Mark's House after its original owner, an American businessman who had gone back home when he saw the way the wind was blowing. The house was set back from the road with a courtyard and high surrounding walls. There I was to be interned along with other persons in belligerent nations, mostly Americans

Shades of the prison house. Again.

The camp commander, Mister Higasa, seemed like a decent man, serious and conscientious, making the best of a difficult job. He assembled us one morning in the courtyard in front of the house.

It was the kind of scene that would later be replayed in numberless British or American war films. But here there was no brutality, no overt threat. Higasa did not rant or try to intimidate us. He explained that our situation was unfortunate and that he hoped our internment would not last long. He also said we would be treated well and that our co-operation was essential. Restrictions on our freedom were regrettable but necessary and if we accepted this there would be no problems. He then bowed to the rising sun flag above the building, and we were dismissed.

His office was on the ground floor, next to the main entrance. He must have had a gramophone in there and from time to time, when the window was left open, we could hear his music blaring out. Most of it was martial – patriotic marching songs, with now and again some popular piece of sentimental trash. Occasionally he would play something western, a sombre passage from Beethoven, or a march by Sousa. But one recording he played every day was an unsettling piece called *Roei no Uta*, the Bivouac Song.

It was a paean to glorious death, bloody sacrifice on the battlefield, and I grew to loathe every note of it, its tinny jingoism jangling my nerves.

It began, *Katte kuru zo to isamachiku*... To prevail with utmost courage.

Then came *Asita no inochi o dare ka shiru*... Who knows what tomorrow shall bring?

Next was something about being soaked in blood, saluting the rising sun. And finally the triumphant *Tennoheika banzai to!* Long live His Majesty the Emperor!

Ten thousand years. The rising sun flag. *Banzai!*

I was allocated a corner of what had been an office. In an alcove there was room for a simple wooden palette bed, covered with a thin mattress and an old quilt. I could draw a curtain across the space to close it off, transform it into a monk's cell.

Did ye hear about the lonely prisoner?

Next to the bed was a makeshift desk knocked together from two old packing cases. It was definitely more comfortable than my cell in the Scrubs. I would make the best of it.

We arranged for Tomiko to move to Kobe for the duration. We could afford to rent a small house not far from where I was imprisoned and where she and Harumi could be comfortable enough. With the help of her father and some of my colleagues from Kanazawa, we even managed to transport my entire library, packed in crates and loaded into a borrowed truck. Tomiko was allowed to visit me one day a week (sometimes with little Harumi in a harness on her back). Every time she would bring a few books, my papers and notes, pens and a stack of lined notebooks for writing.

Translations of haiku in English had begun to appear – Asataro Miyamori's *Anthology of Haiku, Ancient and Modern* and a little volume by HG Henderson, *The Bamboo Broom*. I found much to admire in both books. I could even (almost) forgive Henderson his talk of 'Basho's eternal concentration on the beauties of the Absolute.'

(I had no idea how much Henderson would come to figure in my

life, or the nature of the task we would undertake together. That
would be years ahead, in a yet uncertain future).

I resolved to keep working on my own translations and commen-
taries, towards another book. By effort of will, or by simple accep-
tance, letting go of expectation, I would lose myself in writing or in
the focus of zazen. War was raging over half the world and I was
locked away here, not free, but otherwise unharmed. And in that
very constraint, the limitation placed on my outer life, my *inner* life
came powerfully to the fore. I recalled Suzuki's quote from Eckhart
– *What a man takes in by contemplation he must pour out in love* – and
Suzuki's gloss, that in Zen he must pour it out in work.

Well then, this was my work, and I would go to it with love.

I settled to a routine, *zazen* every morning, early before anyone else
was awake, a little exercise walking round the yard, some physical
work sweeping and cleaning the floors. I washed dishes, I even took
my turn scrubbing the latrines, holding my breath against the stink.
(In fact I rather took a pride in that as a kind of monastic duty!) But
for hours every day I had time to read and to write. This would be
my life, my discipline, as long as the war might last.

Two years passed.

I endured.

I was seated one day, cross-legged on my bed, absorbed in my work.
As I recall, I was translating a passage on *senryu,* and a particular
poem had made me laugh.

When the Buddha was born,
the first thing he did
was blow his own trumpet.

I looked up and saw a young man who had just come into the room.
He was clearly American, a new arrival.
He looked at once eager and apprehensive.
Mr Blyth? he asked.

The very same.

My God!

I sincerely hope not, I said, otherwise you're in trouble!

I looked at him more closely, saw he was frail and thin. His breathing was wheezy and laboured, asthmatic.

He said his name was Robert Aitken and he'd just been transferred from another holding centre.

I said I hoped he had not been too harshly treated.

No, he said. Not at all. Apart from the loss of my liberty. And the inadequate rations. My health has suffered somewhat.

I nodded in sympathy, cleared a space beside me on the bed and motioned him to sit down.

Thank you, he said, and he caught his breath before continuing. But I know we've been lucky, and things could have been much worse. Indeed.

In fact, he said, one of my guards showed me a great kindness, and that's why I was hoping to find you.

I'm intrigued.

This particular guard was a young man who actually spoke some English. One evening he came into my room, quite drunk, waving a book in the air. *This book!* he shouted. *My English teacher...*

As he spoke, Mr Aitken opened a little canvas bag he was carrying, and brought out a book to show me – a battered and much-read copy of my *Zen in English Literature*.

My book! I said. How extraordinary!

It was! You'd taught this young fellow in Kanazawa, and he actually loaned me the book. I think he wanted corroboration that his English teacher was in fact a man of some importance.

Hardly.

You sell yourself short, said Aitken, his eyes shining with what I feared might be the zeal of the acolyte. I must have read the book straight through ten or eleven times, he said. I memorised my favourite passages and could turn right to them. The guard gave up on even trying to get it back from me, and bought himself another copy.

Aitken flicked through the book again, laughed, amazed at his luck in finding me. He had heard a rumour I was here but he didn't dare believe it.

Every time I finished reading the book, he said, I just started again at the beginning. I suppose it was my First Book, if you know what I mean. The way *Walden* was for some of my friends.

You put me in exalted company, I said.

Would you have had a First Book? he asked.

I've never thought about it, I said. But perhaps Arnold. I read him when I was still at school. *Dover Beach. Culture and Anarchy.* I still find myself revisiting him from time to time. *Life is not a having and a getting, but a being and a becoming.*

Yes! said Aitken, clenching his fist in a little gesture of affirmation. I think there's a great deal of Zen in that.

And even more in this. *We are here on earth to do good to others. What the others are here for, I do not know.*

For a dreadful moment I thought he was about to start taking notes, but he just laughed again, shook his head, still coming to terms with the fact that we were actually sitting here talking.

Zen is the most precious possession of Asia... he said, returning us to *my* book, and quoting its opening sentence. *It is the strongest power in the world.*

I hope you're not planning to sit there and recite the whole damn thing to me, I said. All four hundred pages.

He laughed again, coughed, recovered himself.

Maybe not, he said. But I do love that opening paragraph.

It is a world power, for in so far as men live at all, he continued, *they live by Zen. Wherever there is a poetical action, a religious aspiration, a heroic thought, a union of the nature within a man and the Nature without, there is Zen.*

Bravo! I said. I do rather like to get up on my soapbox, don't I? Or climb into the pulpit for a bit of a rant!

That's what I love about it, he said. It's wonderful!

Nevertheless, I said, noting again that slightly fevered glint in his eye, I hope you will take this too with more than a pinch of salt. Or would do if such a thing were available in these straitened times.

He licked his top lip, tasting the salt of his sweat. He glanced down at the book I had put down, the papers I had pushed aside.

You were chuckling when I came in, he said. Can I ask what was making you laugh?

Ah! I said. *Senryu!*

As a form? Or one particular poem.

Both, I said, and I read him the poem in question.

When the Buddha was born,
the first thing he did
was blow his own trumpet.

He nodded, smiled. That's good, he said. I like it.

I once thought, I said, and rightly enough, that poetry was the most important thing in the world.

I picked up the book of *senryu*, still bent back, open at the page.

Now I think, also rightly, that humour is the main thing. The real thing.

The thing itself, he said.

Exactly.

I'm not so familiar with *senryu*, he said. I haven't come across many in translation.

I laughed, said I thought the most popular would find it hard to get past the British or American censors.

And why is that?

The best…and worst…of them are decidedly…earthy.

He shook his head.

There's so much I don't know, he said, so earnestly I laughed again.

That's a good place to begin, I said.

So, he said. Can you teach me?

I gave it a moment's thought, said, Perhaps we can unlearn together.

I mentioned to Bob, half reluctantly, that I did my best to sit every day in zazen, at least for half an hour in the early morning, before the place came to life. He asked if he might join me from time to time, and if I might teach him. Perhaps even more reluctantly, I agreed, with the proviso that I was no kind of teacher.

That couldn't be better, he said. No-kind-of-teacher is exactly what

I need!

I tended to meditate sitting up on my bed, my rough curtain drawn, but for Bob to join me there would have caused consternation among my neighbours, and would also have been rather difficult to explain. Bob's accommodation was even more cramped. As a late arrival he had been allocated a corner in a larger room, sharing with six other internees. We agreed I would stick to my routine, do my own meditation every morning first thing. We would try to find a space, a niche, a little corner when we might be able to sit together, perhaps of an evening after the sparse evening meal. If we found such a place, I said, I would endeavour to un-teach him the little I didn't know.

That would be just dandy, he said.

I should have known he would find something – he was keen to learn (or unlearn), with all that aforementioned zeal. He felt somehow it was fated that we should meet, that it was beyond co-incidence, not chance but sheer grace. For my part I had no reason to disabuse him of the notion. For all I knew, it might well be true. He took to exploring the building so far as he was able. Some areas, housing the commandant and the guards, were off limits, out of bounds. The rest was made up of the dormitories, the kitchen and bathrooms, the communal area and canteen. All this I had told him, but he was determined to look for himself.

And one afternoon fate and grace conspired together once more and he found himself part of group commandeered to carry some crates and boxes down to the basement. I had been assigned similar duties myself on occasion, knew the basement was dank and inhos-pitable, a few small rooms off a dimly lit corridor. The rooms were used only for storage, all of them, as far as I knew, packed floor to ceiling, cluttered with things they couldn't use but didn't want to get rid of – sticks of furniture, old bedding, bits of broken machinery that would never be repaired.

While he was down there, Bob had wandered along the corridor, trying the different doors. Right at the far end he had found a tiny room, not much bigger than a cupboard with nothing much stored there – a couple of palettes, a rolled up futon, damp and stained. The room was dusty and cobwebbed, smelled stale and mildewed. But in Bob's imagination it was the perfect haven, a meditation-space, a monk's cell.

The guard called him to get back to the group immediately and he did, bowing and apologising, hurried back upstairs. When he found me he was still smeared with dust from the basement, but grinning, excited to tell me what he had found.

I said it sounded like a good idea but we should tread carefully, ask the commandant most humbly for his permission. Bob bowed to my wisdom (in fact, looking back that was something he always did, rightly or wrongly) and said he was happy to be guided by what I thought best.

Deep breath.

I waited till Mr Higasa was making a routine inspection. I stood before him and bowed deeply, addressing him in the most formal language I knew, indicating I was showing him the utmost respect. He nodded for me to speak, and I explained that Mr Aitken and I were studying the precepts of Zen and endeavouring to put them into practice in our daily lives. I said this involved studying the sacred texts – here I showed him my much-read copy of the *Mumonkan* – but it also involved sitting in zazen, silent meditation, at least once a day. Bob stood behind me, gangling and inoffensive, following my lead in giving a deep respectful bow.

Mister Aitken, I said, had noticed in passing the tiny unused basement room, and we wondered if the honourable Higasa-san might do us the utmost kindness of allowing us to clean it out and use it on occasion for our practice.

He was silent then gave a little noncommittal grunt. He didn't seem to engage but I thought there was a faint flicker of amusement in his eyes.

The room really is small, I said. Maybe two-tatami size. I mimed small with my hands. *Ni-jo.*

At this he threw back his head, let out a sudden, unexpected laugh. He copied my mime, indicating how tiny the room must be.

Ni-jo! He laughed again. *Zen Gaijin!* The he spoke in English.

You get all gaijin here do zazen. Then camp become zendo. You sensei. Be very good. No need for guard!

I bowed even more deeply than I had before and Bob did the same. Then I offered the most humble thanks I knew – respect, gratitude and obeisance gathered into one word.

Osoreirimasu,

Higasa-san acknowledged it with the slightest nod.

The next morning Bob turned up as I sat cross-legged on my bed reading Suzuki's book of essays. He was accompanied by one of the youngest guards who was doing his best to sustain a peremptory gruffness of demeanour, ordering Bob, quite unnecessarily, to move quickly.

Hayaku! Hayaku!

The boy – for he was little more than that – explained to me that we should go with him to the basement, as ordered by Higasa-san. Perhaps because I was a little older, or because he had heard Higasa-san speak of me with a modicum of respect, he was slightly less aggressive, less brusque in his manner, trying instead to maintain a kind of impassivity. The effort, conversely, made it clear just how young he was. I realised, with a pang, he was not much older than Lee, and I bowed to him and thanked him, let him usher us out of the room, along the corridor and downstairs to the basement.

I had only glanced at the room before – a casual saunter downstairs, a quick look behind the door. Now it looked even smaller. There were no windows at this level, but the room had a working lightbulb, albeit weak, that gave off a dim glow. It was enough, and Bob's enthusiasm was undiminished. We set to, dragging out the contents, lugging the junk along the corridor to a bigger room while the young guard stood and watched, overseeing our efforts, maintaining his detachment. When we had cleared everything out, shifted it along, he looked at the newly empty space, then showed us to a broom cupboard with an old sink in it, ragged mops and bamboo brooms and scrubbing brushes, scraps of torn-up cloth. He mimed that we should get a move on, clean out the room for our use, then with a little snort of disdain he took himself off, back upstairs, and left us to it.

We wiped down the walls, got rid of cobwebs, spread water on the floor to damp down the dust, then swept and mopped as best we could. When we were done, we left it to dry out, came back next afternoon and sat down rather self-consciously on the hard stone floor. I led Bob in chanting, as I had learned to do, invoking the blessings of the Bodhisattva Kannon.

Enmei Jikku Kannon Gyo....

In our cell, our cave, our retreat, in the faint glimmer of our single bare bulb, we folded our hands in *gassho*, bowed, took refuge.

I was touched that Bob had a set of sandalwood japa beads he had picked up in Guam – a rosary for counting repetitions when he chanted a mantra or prayer. Somewhere he managed to find a couple of old worn tatami mats, threadbare but serviceable, which we laid out on the floor.

I was wrong about the size of the room, I said. It must be four tatami!

We each brought a blanket, rough, regulation issue. But folded and re-folded, each one made a cushion, not quite padded *zafu*, but they did the job.

We're in business, said Bob.

I told him the first thing I had learned in the earliest days of my practice at Myoshinji – that rule about always responding when the master called out *Oi!* Immediately, without hesitation the student must call back *Hai!*

That's it? he said.

That's it, I said. *Oi!* and *Hai!*

For the moment, and after all, everything was just for the moment, I would assume the role of the master, and Bob would continue to play the part of the student.

I couldn't imagine it any other way, he said. You do know a thing or two.

And much good it's done me, I said, Oh, there was one other thing the Abbot told us at the very beginning, a really important rule.

I'm listening, he said.

You must never, *never*, smoke a cigarette while pissing.
He looked thoughtful.
And I guess, he said, we should never piss while smoking a cigarette.
I think that goes without saying.
I think I've got it, he said.
Good, I said. Oh, Bob?
Yes?
Oi!
He laughed.
Hai!

Now, after all this time, our roles are reversed. He is the teacher, I
the (lapsed) student. As if to confirm it, he recently sent me a one-
word telegram. *Oi!*
I replied. *Hai!*

We began by sharing books. I loaned him Suzuki's *Essays in Zen
Buddhism*, English translations of The Sutra of Wei-lang, and the
Blue Cliff Record. In return he loaned me a selection of Dogen's
writings and introduced me to the poetry of Wallace Stevens.
He had the idea that Stevens had been considerably influenced by
Zen thought without engaging with it in terms of study or practice.
Nevertheless, he said, it seems to me there are moments of real
insight, the poetry of emptiness.
Or the emptiness of poetry, I said.
Perhaps, he said. Certainly there can be a cold analytical quality to
it. But he catches the other kind of coldness, the reality of winter,
and how we perceive it.
He recited.

One must have a mind of winter
To regard the frost and the boughs
Of the pine-trees crusted with snow.

A mind of winter, I said. That is very good indeed.
And the last verse, he said, is even better.

For the listener, who listens in the snow,
and, nothing himself, beholds
Nothing that is not there and the nothing that is.

Nothing himself, I said. The nothing. *Mu,*
Form is emptiness.
Bob was particularly taken with what he called the near-haiku se-
quence, *Thirteen Ways of Looking at a Blackbird.*
Again he recited, the first poem.

Among twenty snowy mountains,
The only moving thing
Was the eye of the blackbird.

The poem was a little door, he said, opening a way into vastness.
It's like a landscape painting, I said, maybe something by Sesshu.
Moving not moving.
I told him that particular poem, the first in the sequence, was closest
to Zen spirit. That and the last one.

It was evening all afternoon.
It was snowing
And it was going to snow.
The blackbird sat
In the cedar-limbs.

It, said Bob. The nothing that is.
I said, Emperor Wu asked Bodhidharma, What is the first principle
of the holy scripture?
Bodhidharma replied, Vast emptiness, nothing holy.
Nothing, said Bob.
Listen to us! I said, and we laughed, sitting there on our folded-up
blankets, on the worn tatami, on the hard stone floor, in our little
zendo, our bare basement room.
Nothing holy.

I continued with my early morning meditation, seated on my palette, my curtain drawn. Bob did the same, made the best of his small corner by rising early before his neighbours were awake. But twice a week, every Wednesday morning and Sunday evening, we sat together in our two-tatami room.

Throughout the week we met every day, talked endlessly, set the world to rights. But in those short sessions (short *sesshins*) we were generally silent, allowing the meditation to happen. It just felt like the right thing to do, recalling my meditations at Myoshin-ji, or sitting with Suzuki at Tokei-ji. When sitting, we just sat, and we seemed to draw strength from each other's silence, a shared consciousness, a sustaining power, for which I felt immense gratitude. Deep bows.

If my life in those years was circumscribed, if I suffered the constraints and deprivation of internment, Tomiko's life was equally difficult, moving to a strange city, bringing up a young child, seeing me once a week, struggling just to get by, to make ends meet. She could see I was not thriving on the food rations at the camp, and she would bring me extra supplies every week, some tofu and fresh vegetables, rice balls wrapped with seaweed, a jar of pickles, soba noodles. She even managed to bring me a little bottle of vitamin pills – *wakamoto*. She said they were good for digestion and would give me strength. I found myself growing tearful at the kindness, the trouble she took in the face of everything.

I introduced her to Bob, not long after his arrival, and she was shocked at how thin and gaunt he looked. She began bringing a little extra food, and more *wakamoto* so I could share with him.

He was deeply moved, told me I was lucky to have married such a good woman.

I told him she, in turn, thought he was a good man, very gentle and kind. She said he was not very American.

He laughed, said he would take that as a compliment.

Usually Tomiko left Harumi in the care of a neighbour, Mrs Taneda – Yuko – a young mother with a baby of her own. I understood it was difficult enough for Tomiko to come to the camp, carrying

the food for me, and the books I had asked her to bring. She would
also be concerned that Harumi might be upset and confused, not
quite understand what was going on. But from time to time she
was able to bring the little one, and for that I was hugely grateful. It
brought it home to me what I was missing, the day-to-day contact,
simply being there, being a father. But that made the visits all the
more precious, as I watched with amazement, week by week, month
by month, my daughter, this unique and particular being, growing
into herself.

The child's laugh –
 Her little hands
Grasping at everything

My relationship with Mr Higasa and the other guards was formal
and civilised. But when Tomiko came to visit, especially if she
brought Harumi, something else entered in, a kind of empathy, a
shared humanity. I was still this *gaijin*, this alien, but I had a Jap-
anese wife and a Japanese child. I had chosen to make Japan my
home, to embrace the life here, and for that I sensed in their attitude
a greater respect.
As for Bob, if he was happy to meet Tomiko, then seeing Harumi
filled him with delight. At the same time, he could see the separation
was hard for me to take.
But you know, he said, what you have is a hell of a lot. I mean....
I know, I said. I know.

Because we had no teacher, no designated path, Bob and I were
free to pick and choose, take inspiration where we found it. My
own book was a rich source of inspiration, not from my words,
but from the myriad quotes I had plundered from here, there and
everywhere, from every religious tradition, and none. We would
take a haiku as a starting point – perhaps something by Basho – or
a line from Shakespeare, or Herbert. A stone dropped in a pool. (A
frog jumping into an old pond!) We would let the words carry us
beyond the words, into silence.

Initially Bob was most inspired by the Soto Zen of Dogen with its simple but powerful quietude.

If you cannot find the truth right where you are, where else do you expect to find it?

We sat in our little basement room.

If you want to see things just as they are, then you yourself must practice just as you are.

Breathe in. This moment. Breathe out.

But Bob was also drawn to Rinzai Zen, the Zen of Hakuin, with its study of koan, those maddeningly unanswerable questions, existential riddles that had to be answered with the whole being.

What is the sound of one hand?

Does a dog have the Buddha nature?

Why did Bodhidharma come from the West?

Bob, engagingly, described them as the folk tales of Zen, and while I would not have described them in that way, the idea was a good one, made a certain kind of sense (or non-sense!) Each koan had a narrative to it, a surprise ending (a punchline!)

I thought of those old Korean tales with which I had tortured Annie (felt a pang at that).

All living beings come from water, as you well know....

But no, the koan were not stories in that sense, not parables but problems to be solved. And reading the 'answers' given by the great masters and handed down from generation to generation was no help at all.

What is the sound of one hand?

Hear the soundless sound, the sound-beyond-all sound.

Does a dog have the Buddha nature? (The answer is not Yes and it is not No).

Mu. Nothing. No-thing.

Why did Bodhidharma come from the West?

The old oak tree in the yard.

I told Bob about another response, given by the monk Hsiang-lin. A student asked him, Why did Bodhidharma come from the West? He answered, My old legs are stiff from sitting so long.

Bob laughed out loud at that. He said his own spindly shanks were one long ache when he sat in meditation, an ache that drove out all thought.

Which may be the pointless point, I said.

But Hsiang-lin's answer seemed to open a little door for Bob, let in a chink of light.

It's the humanity of it, he said, the grouchy grumbling physicality. We sit. We ache. We sit some more. It's about keeping our butts on that cushion....

That folded-up blanket....

We keep sitting. We persist.

He began writing little verses, based on Chinese *gatha*, to keep him focussed.

I sit in the meditation room,
And vow with all sentient beings
To acknowledge that this is the sacred,
This breath, this body, this bottom.

That one made me laugh.

Straight from the heart, I said.

Sometimes in the canteen, after eating our rice and vegetables (and trying to think of it as monks' rations) we batted our koans back and forth, made up our own answers. One day we continued it out in the yard, walking round and round.

What is the sound of one hand?

What's that? Speak up. I can't hear

Why did Bodhidharma come from the West?

Why did you?

Spin around till you're dizzy. Where is East? Where is West?

Does a dog have the Buddha nature?

Do you? Do I?

Seriously, does a dog have the Buddha nature?

Hear him bark!

Does he? Yes or no?

Woof!

I said I was afraid a certain lack of profundity might have entered

into the proceedings.
We need a real master to set us straight.
A real master might cuff us about the ear.
Knock us into the middle of next week!
Now that would be something!
Transcending time and space.
The middle of next week!
Thwack!
 Kwatz!
After that we returned to the work, interrogating silence.

Time continued to pass, now quickly, now slowly, but it passed. The seasons turned, months became years. Basho wrote that the days and months were travellers on eternity's road, and travellers too were the passing years, they hurried past like windblown clouds. The actual passage of time was marked for me, made vividly clear, by Tomiko's visits and the changes in little Harumi. Unable to see her day by day, and sometimes not even week by week, I would be astonished at what would appear to be a sudden transformation. It was like a speeded-up film, watching her grow and become.
Now she's swaddled in a blanket, wee face puckered. Now she's teething, biting on a rubber ring and anything else she can grab, wailing at the injustice of it all. Now her baby hair has gone and she's once again a miniature baldpate Bodhisattva, a budding Kannon, Kwan-yin.
Now the hair has grown in again, thick and dark. Now the sounds she gurgles have evolved into one clear word, delighting Tomiko. *Mama*, says the baby, a universal utterance. *Mama*. Weeks pass and eventually she says *Papa*, and I'm idiotically happy.

One day I brought the little Daruma doll, set it on the table.
Remember this?
I tipped it over and let it rock back up. Harumi did the same, laughed and clapped her hands.
I chanted. *Nana korobi ya oki...*
Seven times down, eight times up.

She knocked it over again, again.

I chanted. She laughed.

Nana korabi...

Life could be as good, as simple as this.

The number of my haiku translations had grown and would now make a substantial collection. I saw that this would indeed be my next great work (listen to me – my Great Work!) There would be four volumes, arranged by season and embellished (or diminished) by my commentary and exegesis and general meandering. I knew there was a danger, of over-elaborating, of mistaking the explanation for the poetry, the pointing finger for the moon. The aim of the explanation, the pointing finger, is to make itself unnecessary. Get rid of the extraneous so the truth can be seen.

But I felt the same excitement I'd felt when embarking on my *Zen in English Literature*, and once again there was the same commitment to the work itself, for its own sake, irrespective of what would become of it.

Don't worry about whether the temple will burn down next week...

Just the work.

Bob was almost as excited as I was, eager to have more books to inspire him.

What you're doing is important, he said.

Perhaps, I said. Perhaps not.

Not all of the American internees appreciated me or my work. Some of them regarded me as a collaborator, a turncoat, a traitor. I heard one muttered suggestion that I face a firing squad after the war.

They think you've gone native, said Bob.

In my old tweed suit?

They see you doing zazen, he said.

In my old tweed suit!

They hear you speaking Japanese to the guards.

It's useful.

They think you're some kind of apologist.

For the culture, I said. Not for this travesty of a philosophy, this wilful misinterpretation, this warmongering and brutality. If the Japanese had not abandoned their true heritage, if they spent more time composing haiku and senryu, this stupid war would never have happened.

That simple? said Bob, and even he, I could see, was taken aback by what he saw as my naiveté.

That simple, I said.

With Bob I often found myself making pronouncements, speaking in aphorisms.

The way to stop war is to show how ridiculous it is.

Yes... he said, and I saw him scribble my words down in a little notebook.

War is caused by a deficiency of food or its unequal distribution, or differences of religion, of world view – the idea of what makes life worth living at all.

Yes...

These causes are not so different, not entirely separate. Equality of distribution is itself a religious idea. Peace demands that all shall have work and all shall eat.

You're sounding like a communist!

Inasmuch as ye do this to the least of these my brethren, ye do it unto me. Zen tells us I am you and you are I. So when your stomach is empty, mine is empty too. We have to know this in the gut and not in the head. Then all our troubles – social and political, national and international, are at an end, for my troubles are yours, and yours are mine.

We realise our essential oneness, said Bob.

Exactly so. But then again, the troubles do not end there. This oneness has to extend to all sentient beings.

So, we have our work cut out!

Every time Bob came to sit with me, he would have another comment about my *Zen in English Literature*, another query, something else to discuss. His own copy of the book was falling apart

How is it possible, he said, that this could be published? A book written in wartime, by an enemy national, in the enemy's language, a language which is prohibited in Japan.

The contract was made before the war, I said. And the publisher simply kept his promise.

And thank God for that.

I am rather proud of the book, I said. All that's wrong with it is that it's too good, too rich, like a Christmas pudding or a trifle.

A very English description, he said.

There are no easy or flat bits, I said. It's all purple patches!

He fell silent for a moment, then said, I don't think I shall ever tire of reading it.

In spite of myself I was moved, and for once I had no words.

More than once Bob Aitken came to my defence if discussions grew too heated. Most of the American internees regarded me with a kind of bemused tolerance. They took to calling me Mr. B, which I thought combined formality with a kind of gruff respect that was not unfriendly. But tensions persisted. Those who saw me as a traitor would occasionally spit venom at me. One man in particular, a trader by the name of Olsen, from Pittsburgh, was particularly hostile. One evening he just came up to me in the canteen and confronted me directly, asked how I could possibly defend the Japanese.

What I defend, I said, is the real *un*military power of Japan, the *poetical* power and glory. Amen.

That made him even angrier. Now you're blaspheming, he said. Taking the Lord's Prayer in vain!

I have great respect for the Lord's Prayer, I said. I regard it as one of the greatest mantras ever written. I folded my hands and raised my eyes.

    Thy Will be done…

He thought I was mocking him, threatened to knock my goddam Limey teeth down my goddam Limey throat.

Who's blaspheming now? I said, and he stood and moved towards me, fists clenched. He came so close I could smell the stink of his sweat, the rankness of his breath. I braced myself, but Aitken and one of the other Americans intervened, led the man away.

Bob asked me later how far I would have taken my nonviolent response if the man had actually tried to hit me.

Let's hope it doesn't come to that, I said.

But if it did?

There's a story, I said...

There always is!

This one concerns a snake who terrorises the small village where he lives. The villagers live in fear of being bitten. The one day a master passes through the village and gives a talk. The snake listens and is deeply moved. He resolves to mend his ways and asks the master how he should live his life.

A talking snake? said Bob. So this is a fable?

Perhaps a parable.

In any case, the master can speak fluent snake.

Clearly. And he tells the snake he really must stop biting people.

A good beginning.

The master goes on his way, but he l passes through the village again some time later. The first thing he does is look for the snake, to see if he has made any progress. He searches everywhere, and eventually he finds the snake lying by the roadside, very much the worse for wear, badly battered and beaten.

The Master asks him, What happened?

It's your fault, says the snake. Once the villagers realised I wasn't going to bite them, they set about me with sticks and left me here for dead.

The master shakes his head and sighs. I told you not to bite, he says. I didn't tell you not to *hiss.*

Bob laughed. It's a good story. So you'll hiss at Mr Olsen if he tries to hit you.

Let's say I'll try to dissuade him.

And if that doesn't work, what then? Turn the other cheek?

The problem with that, I said, is that it would do him no favours. It would simply lead him deeper into ignorance.

It's a koan, said Bob.

Perhaps.

So what would you do?

I have no idea. But I wouldn't rule out a straight left to the jaw.

You're priceless! said Bob.

Mister Priceless Blyth.

Always a story.

I remembered Annie saying that to me, when our marriage was falling apart. There's always a story. She'd spat it out like an accusation. There was another one I told Bob, one I might have tried on our friend from Pittsburgh.

It concerns the monk Gasan, I said.

He listened, attentive.

A group of soldiers from the Japanese army were on the march, preparing for battle. Some of the officers commandeered Gasan's temple and set up their headquarters. Gasan said they were welcome and instructed the cook to make them the same simple food as he made for the monks, and to dish out the same meagre rations. The commanding officer was outraged at this lack of deference.

Have you no respect? he asked. Who do you think we are? We are soldiers sacrificing out lives for our country.

Gasan replied, Have *you* no respect? Who do you think *we* are? We are soldiers of humanity, fighting to save all sentient beings.

Bob laughed. I don't think our bull-headed friend would have been too impressed!

I can see him so clearly, Bob Aitken, earnest, sitting at my feet, or at least on the floor at the end of my palette, plying me with questions, eager to learn.

He went home after the war but continued his intense study of Zen. He went the whole hog, was ordained as a Zen priest, relocated from California to Hawaii, became Aitken Roshi. Great Dragon of the Clear Pool.

Bob.

Bob told me once that he was deeply touched by something in *Zen in English Literature* which was almost unspoken, a little aside. It was just this, that in the closing lines of my preface, I thanked my typist, Mrs. Saeko Kobayashi of Tokyo. (I recall the acknowledgement – I pointed out that she displayed more Zen in her typing of the manuscript than I did in the writing of it!) Just below that, I ended with the simple words, *Kanazawa, May 1941.* This was what Bob found so evocative and affected him so deeply.

It's a stark, matter-of-fact statement, he said, that the book was written in exile, in a place and time that could not have been less conducive to the work, at a time when Japan itself has turned its back on the precepts of Zen. Nor would the intended readership, in Britain and America, be particularly receptive.

In spite of the commendation on the book jacket, I said.

The author shows a penetrating insight and a keen judgement in the treatment of his subject...

You couldn't have put it better yourself! he said.

Indeed. (Of course I had, in fact, written it myself).

What was that *senryu*, he asked, about the Buddha blowing his own trumpet?

So I'm in good company, I said.

But seriously, said Bob. I'm just grateful you stuck to your task in a world tearing itself apart. You kept the faith.

Yes.

7

DESTROYER OF
WORLDS

Bob and I were out in the yard with a few other detainees. The guards had gone inside, left us unsupervised to take exercise. Suddenly Bob stopped, looked up and waved. There was a house next door, on the other side of the high wall, and there at the upstairs window were two young boys, looking out. I waved too and the boys, tentatively at first, then more vigorously, waved back.

The next day at the same time, we were once more walking round the yard. I glanced up at the window again and was surprised to see a flurry of movement above the wall. Two little dark heads seemed to bob up then disappear. Then one figure clambered up, followed by the other, and they straddled the wall, looking down at us. It was the two boys we'd seen at the window, and to my surprise they were not Japanese, their hair dark but curly, their eyes round. They were European, perhaps Jewish, something in them that reminded me, with a little pang, of Annie.

Bob called out, affable. Hi guys!

The boys were obviously brothers, maybe 12 and 10 years old. The older one responded, said Hi!

How'd you get up there? said Bob. The wall's high.

There's a shed on the other side, said the boy. We climbed up.

That's great, said Bob. But be careful.

Sure, said the boy. Right.

I'm Bob, this is Reg.

Alex, said the boy.

George, said his brother.

Great, said Bob. Where you from?

Here, said Alex. Born in Kobe.

How come? I mean, you don't *look* Japanese.

And you speak English, I said. And your names...

Dad's from Russia. Mom's from Lithuania.

Wow! said Bob. That's amazing.

Both the boys looked pleased, momentarily basking in the glow of being special.

You American? said Alex.

I am, said Bob. He's British.

Why are you locked up?

Because I'm American and he's British! Wrong place, wrong time. Or maybe right place, wrong time, I added. We're designated enemy aliens.

The younger boy, George, looked very serious. He asked, Are the Japs going to kill you?

Jeez! said Bob. I sure hope not!

I think it's unlikely, I said, though the thought had troubled me from time to time, in the wee small hours.

They treat us pretty well, said Bob, except for not enough food.

The high shrill note of a whistle pierced the air, and one of the guards was rounding us up to go back inside. Quick as blinking, the boys had disappeared, slid down off the wall, back on their own side, like two seals slipping off a rock into the sea.

After that the boys were there often, not every day, but two or three times a week. Some of the other prisoners spoke to them, but we had made first contact and they looked out for us. They were happy to tell us the story of their family. Their father had been in the Russian army, and after the revolution he had escaped to Shanghai. There he had met and married their mother, set himself up as a trader, eventually moving here to Kobe and opening a general store.

Sounds like quite a guy, said Bob.

Again the boys looked pleased, proud of their old man.

Bob and I spoke about it later, agreed that the father must indeed be quite a character. A Russian Jew, ex army officer, a trader moving easily from China to Japan.

Soldier of fortune, I said.

A bit of a swashbuckler, said Bob. Mind you....

What?

I suppose anyone reading about *our* lives might find them kind of exotic, don't you think?

I never swashed a buckle in my life, I said. Or buckled a swash for that matter.

Still.

One evening, when we'd been let out for a breath of air, the boys appeared, peering over the wall, and there between them was their father. He gave us a wave.

They call me Sid, he said. It's a kind of nickname and it's easy to say. So you're Bob and you're Reg?

Right.

The boys told me about you. Said you were all right.

Glad to hear it, said Bob. We like them too.

They did tell me you don't get enough food. I mean, who does these days? But looking at you, I see what they mean. You look like shit.

Gee, thanks, said Bob.

But we looked at each other and saw that he was right. While we kept to each other's company we could ignore the weight loss, the clothes hanging looser with every week that passed, the sagging flesh, the general air of exhaustion. But the gaze of this emissary from the outside world cast a harsh light on us, stripped us bare.

No more than this? We owed the worm no silk, the beast no hide, the sheep no wool, the cat no perfume. The thing itself, unaccommodated man. A poor bare, forked animal.

Here, said Sid, and he threw a small package to land at our feet. He was keeping a look out, making sure there were no guards in sight, and he signalled us to pick it up.

Bob tore off the paper, found two sandwiches filled with a kind of fish paste, two rice balls and a sweet beancake. We stuffed the food in our pockets and Bob threw the paper back over the wall.

Be careful, said Sid. I deliver little packages for the officers and the guards, you know, cigarettes, canned food. So they pretty well turn a blind eye. But like I say, watch out.

Before we could thank him he had slipped off the wall, the way his boys always did, and he was gone, and the whistle was calling us back inside.

We shared the spoils, Bob apologising because he knew I couldn't eat the fish. He ate one of the sandwiches, gave the other to a prisoner who had been poorly. I gave the same man one of the rice balls and ate the other myself, following it with the beancake. It was an unexpected feast, and I offered a prayer of gratitude to Hotei the god of good fortune.

I was sitting on my palette bed, reading a book of Suzuki's essays when I heard a commotion outside in the yard – voices raised, shouting and laughing. Bob stuck his head round the door, a huge grin on his face.

You have to come NOW!

I laid down the book and followed him outside where it seemed every single prisoner had gathered, watched by the guards who had taken up position along the wall, standing to attention, their rifles shouldered. A truck had backed in at the main gate and the more able-bodied internees were unloading its cargo of boxes.

Red Cross! said Bob, as the men ripped open the boxes to reveal their treasures – items of clothing, canned foods, dried fruit, books and magazines, cigarettes…. There was one large box marked Hershey which was packed with chocolate bars. The young man opening it started laughing, beyond himself with disbelief and delight.

Unbelievable, said Bob. It's like Christmas, Thanksgiving and everybody's birthday rolled into one!

One of the Americans, an older man by the name of McNulty, took charge and organised the distribution. In spite of the excitement and high spirits (or perhaps because of them) everyone was very well behaved as they queued for their allotted share. As far as possible we all received the same, and it would be up to us to barter and trade. So I wasn't bothered at being handed packs of cigarettes and cans of beef. I knew I could readily exchange them later for the dried fruit, powdered soup and those precious Hershey bars.

When the clothing was handed out – trousers, sweaters, workshirts – a few of the men started trying them on. Because everyone had lost so much weight, most of the garments were too big. Two of the younger men started clowning around in them, then they both squeezed into one outsized shirt and marched up and down, making everybody laugh – even the guards till their commander called them to order. The two young men were assigned to clear away the empty boxes and the rest of us were dispersed, back to our quarters, hoarding our booty. As I turned away with my own stash, I looked up over the high wall to the house next door where the two boys, Alex and George, were looking out of their upstairs window, no doubt hugely entertained by the whole business. I waved and caught their eye, held up one of the chocolate bars and pointed to it, and at them, and I mimed throwing it to them.

In the evening Bob and I did our circuit of the yard, and sure enough the boys were there on the wall, looking out for us.

We had each brought one of our bars, large, foil-wrapped. With unbelievable largesse, we threw the bars to the boys who caught them and disappeared.

Greater love hath no man, I said.

On occasion I have told the story of those days of internment and met with varying degrees of incredulity. Our guards were not kind, but I can honestly say that they were not cruel. At worst they were indifferent, but I certainly never witnessed any brutality.

We had told those young boys, Alex and George, with an air of confidence and certainty, that the Japanese were not going to kill us. Apart from anything else, if that was their intention, they would surely have disposed of us before now instead of going to all the trouble of keeping us alive.

Nevertheless, one night there was real fear as we were all woken from uneasy sleep by the guards ordering us to gather our belongings and get out into the yard. There was no explanation, other than that we were being moved. It was chaotic, prisoners stumbling around half asleep, pulling on clothes, throwing their few meagre possessions into kit bags. My services as translator were suddenly much needed as I relayed the instructions over the cacophony of voices raised in curses, deprecations, complaints. Once more the older man, McNulty, took charge of the Americans, managed to organise them to get outside and line up in ranks. I stuffed my books and papers into my old battered suitcase, packed in with the few serviceable garments I owned, my scroll reading *Form is Emptiness*, my little Daruma doll, for luck. *Nana korobi ya oki...* Seven times down, eight times up.

Outside there was confusion, and apprehension. I found Bob and lined up beside him.

What's happening?

The guards just say we're being moved, to Futatabi.

And where the hell is that?

Who knows? I think the name translates as Second time...

As in, *Here we go again*?

Outside the gates a convoy of trucks had pulled up and sat with their engines running. The guards, their rifles once more at the ready, marched us out and we were loaded onto the trucks. The scene was curiously dreamlike, the flicker of the streetlights, the too-bright headlamps, the low growl of the engines, and above it, monotonous, the cry of cicadas. Looking back, I saw the boys, Alex and George, looking out from behind their upstairs window, waving goodbye.

Camp Futatabi was on a hill at the edge of the city. Our new home was an old factory building converted into dormitories. It emerged that more prisoners were due to arrive, from Guam and elsewhere, necessitating the move from Mark's House.

I no longer had my own space – no little alcove where I could shutter myself away. I was in a long low-ceilinged room with thirty other men, the beds lined up in rows.

Hear about the lonely prisoner? Chance would be a fine thing.

The walls were high, but there was no barbed wire, no broken glass, no searchlights or electrified fences. From time to time the guards patrolled the perimeter, but most of the time they stayed in their quarters, indoors. In the beginning some of the younger prisoners would take advantage, grab an opportunity to scramble over the wall, but invariably they would come back after an hour or two of walking the streets.

I asked McNulty one day if any of them had ever tried to go further, to get away.

I think the first few guys thought about it, he said. You know, prisoner's duty to try and escape and all that jazz. But think about it. It happened in Germany – I read about it. Guys would bust out, take the chance of being caught and killed. But that was it, there *was* a chance. Brits, Americans, Aussies…with a change of clothes they could blend in, keep their heads down, maybe just manage it. Here, they kinda stand out.

Just a little, I said.

Tall Caucasian guys, skin and bone, dressed in ragged clothes.

And not speaking the language.

Exactly. Plus we're on an island. How they gonna get off it with nobody to help?

No underground, no secret network, no partisans.

Right. So what they gonna do? I guess the Japs just turned a blind eye and most of the guys got bored with the whole thing.

Here for the duration, I said, and I realised I had no idea how long that might be.

Tomiko was not in the habit of reading, beyond the pages of illustrated magazines. (She said I read more than enough for both of us!) But I asked if she might find out if there was a story behind the name Futatabi. She went to the local library, asked the librarian who found the answer.

Behind our camp was a mountain and the monk Kukai had gone there to pray at a shrine before undertaking a journey to China to study the Buddha's teaching. On his return he went again to the mountain to offer thanks. The mountain was then named Futa-tabi – Second time.

I told Bob and he laughed.

So it's all about gratitude.

Yes.
Deep bow.

Through autumn the weather had been mild, a beautiful season, right into November. I'd been told it would be colder through the winter, though not unbearable. But in January the temperatures dropped. The dormitories were freezing and it was a struggle to keep warm. I wore everything I owned, in layers – shirt and jacket, over-coat and a woolly hat Tomiko had brought me, pulled down over my ears. The constant diet of rice gruel had taken its toll, reduced our natural insulation against the cold. There was a pervading air of misery among the men. More prisoners sickened, a few died.

I woke one morning sensing something strange in the light, a brightness that cast a faint yellow glow in the room. I sat up and realised it was snowing, and had been all through the night. In spite of everything I felt a lifting of my spirits, and I sensed it in the other prisoners, as they went to the windows to look out. Even the guards looked more relaxed, chatting to each other, laughing.

I understood snow of this magnitude was a rare event and had brought the city to a standstill. It fell all morning, big flakes falling silently, snow falling and lying, snow on snow, falling endlessly into itself. There was no traffic. Nothing could come or go. We were isolated.

After what passed for lunch – rice in a watery broth – they let us out as usual to exercise, let the cold air fill our lungs. The snow covered everything, lay two feet deep, and it made a silence over all the world, made all things new. Every sound – someone shouting, the bark of a dog – carried sharp and clear.

The guards pointed to the main gate which they had opened, and they instructed us to go outside into the street.

At first there was confusion. Were they about to move us again? Were we to be taken out and left somewhere to freeze?

The guards looked amused, just kept directing us towards the gate. McNulty asked me to find out what was happening. I questioned the guards, addressing them with respect and deference in my most formal Japanese, and when I was certain of what they were telling me, I reported back to McNulty that we were being allowed out to enjoy the snow.

They were letting us out to play!

There's a haiku by Basho.

> *Come on!*
> *Let's go snow-viewing*
> *Till we tumble down!*

And that was the mood. The men became like children, or perhaps adolescents, yelling and laughing, completely caught up in the exhilaration of it all as they gathered up cold fistfuls, lobbed snow-balls at each other. Then very quickly, as if by some innate sense of organisation, they formed themselves into two groups, two warring factions. Each group built a wall of snow, three feet high, across the width of the road. Behind these ramparts they piled up an arsenal of snowballs and at a given signal they let battle commence, pelting each other across the few yards of no man's land. (Snowman's land?) The barrage was thick and fast, but one side was stronger – Mister Blockhead Olsen among them – and eventually they went over the top and charged the enemy position, kicked down their opponents' wall and won the day.

McNulty and I had stood back with a few of the other slightly older men and some who were younger but not strong enough to take part, all of us, nevertheless, taking vicarious delight in the whole thing, the sudden unexpected freedom.

Mister B, said McNulty, for a pacifist you sure enjoyed watching the battle.

Much as I enjoyed rugby as a boy, I said. Channelled aggression. Letting off steam. No harm in it at all. And look at the men, look at their faces.

And it was true. By the time the guards called us back inside the compound, the whole mood in the place had lightened. I made a point of bowing to the guards, and McNulty did the same.

When the first air raids came, I heard the planes drone overhead, the distant thump and blast as the bombs dropped. Bob said it would be a terrible irony to be blown to bits by the Americans. But I felt real fear, raw and gut-churning, for Tomiko and baby Harumi.

I sat on my bed and chanted the *Nembutsu*, invoking the protection of the compassionate Buddha.

I had translated another haiku by Basho.

How admirable
He who thinks not life is fleeting
When he sees the lightning.

How much more so when he hears the bombers.

Namu Amida Butsu.

Through the night I found it hard to sleep and when I did, fitfully, I dreamed. Tomiko was walking towards me out of a conflagration, buildings burning behind her. She carried Harumi who clung to her, crying. Tomiko was holding out to me a scroll, unfurled. I could see the lettering, the calligraphy, written in fire, but I couldn't read it, I couldn't understand. I woke afraid.

The next day I was anxious and fretful, then one of the guards brought me a letter from Tomiko. It was not one of the days when visiting was allowed, so she had handed in the letter at the gate.

The rented house had been damaged by a bomb-blast. By a miracle, Tomiko and Harumi were safe, unharmed. I thanked God, and the compassionate Buddha, who were one and the same. But the room housing my library, all my books, had been completely destroyed.

That would be a waste, I thought, my work not yet done. But in the scheme of things – or the tale told by an idiot (you pays your money and you take your choice) – it was a small matter and of no great import. I sat on my bed, read and re-read the letter in Tomiko's delicate script, a little flower-garden. I stared till it lost all literal meaning and the marks became images only, stylised representations of a tree, a house, the sun.

All forms are burning.

The images blurred and there were tears in my eyes. I stood up and composed myself and stepped outside into the yard. A single cherry tree had shed its blossoms on the ground. Of course it would be a cherry tree, with its myriad associations, its unmistakable resonance. *Sakura.* But this one was simply, resolutely itself, its bark and branches scraggy and dishevelled.

I walked round and round the small space, stunned, numbed.

I thought about my books and what they had meant to me. The crates I had shipped from London when Annie and I were hopeful and young. The volumes I had picked up in the market stalls in Korea, in the secondhand bookstores in Tokyo and Yokohama.

Shakespeare and Wordsworth and Stevenson. Confucius and Dante, Arnold and Shaw, Thoreau and Burns. Emerson and Keats. Basho and Issa and Buson and Shiki. Eckhart and Blake. Spinoza. The Manyoshu. The Bhagavad Gita. The Bible. The Dhammapada. Milton and Lewis Carroll. Herbert and Vaughan. The Blue Cliff Record. All of Dickens. All gone.

My papers and notebooks. My musical scores. Bach and Mozart, Haydn, Corelli. The recordings shattered, cracked, melted. Nothing left.

I walked, round and round. And what came to mind was a haiku written by Ryokan after a burglar had broken into his shabby hut and stolen the few meagre possessions he had.

> *The thief*
> *left it behind –*
> *the moon in the window.*

Such grateful acceptance.

> *The wind*
> *brings fallen leaves enough*
> *to make a fire.*

I stopped and breathed deep. The wind picked up, a sudden gust. It caught and swirled the white flowers all around me, an uplift, a dance, a momentary exhilaration.

There was a Japanese word for this flurry of blossoms. *Hanafubuki.* It was *all* a dance, everything in motion. All I had to do was let go, begin again, over and over, now and now and now.

Let go.

Tomiko and Harumi were safe. Nothing else mattered. Nothing. Nothing, nothing, nothing.

Back at my desk I laid out the handful of books I had with me, with their scuffed covers, their dog-eared pages. They were suddenly, immeasurably precious.

My few other possessions included the little Daruma doll that had made Harumi laugh.

I tipped it over and it rolled back up.

Eight times up…

Why did Bodhidharma come from the West?

The answer given to this by Joshu – *The oak tree in the yard*.

Why did Bodhidharma come from the West?
Why did I?

> *Fallen blossoms,*
> *caught up by the wind,*
> *dancing.*

It had been a miracle that Tomiko and Harumi had been at the house of a neighbour, Kaneko, when the bomb fell. Almost as great a miracle – at least stretching the bounds of coincidence – was the fact that Kaneko was the wife of an English naval officer, Lewis Bush, who was interned in Kowloon, and was, as it happened, a friend of my mentor Dr Suzuki.

I wanted Tomiko to take Harumi and go back to the family home in Hagi. They would be safer there. Her father could make the arrangements. But she said travel was impossible, they would have to wait. Kaneko helped her find a small rented apartment, closer to

Futatabi. I returned to praying and meditating. There was nothing else I could do.

Whenever the bombs fell Tomiko sent a message, those few kanji spelling out the same simple message. They were safe. They had not been harmed.

Namu Amida Butsu

The later raids were an all out bombardment aimed at the total destruction of the city. The area around the docks was obliterated – the most densely populated neighbourhood where workers and their families were concentrated. Word came through that central Tokyo had also been firebombed in the same way but on a much larger scale. I read about it after the war, in a US report declaring the operation a complete success. I still have the piece of paper where I scribbled down the details.

More than 300 bombers dropped almost 2000 tons of bombs, mostly 500 pound cluster bombs, each of which released smaller napalm-carrying incendiary bombs. These punched through thin roofing material or landed on the ground. In either case they ignited 5 seconds later, throwing out a jet of flaming napalm globs. Other incendiaries were also dropped, each one a 100-pound jellied-gasoline and white phosphorus bomb which ignited on impact.

Again the attack centred on the city's working class district near the docks. The first wave dropped their bombs in a large X pattern. X marks the spot. Later aircraft simply aimed near this flaming X. The old wooden buildings flared like kindling. 16 square miles of the city were destroyed and at least 100,000 people died.

A complete success.

Why did I write this down, copy out the bare facts? As if it could be grasped. As if it could be understood.

At least 100,000. Incinerated.

I read and I wept.

That humanity should have come to this. Brutality and destruction followed by reprisal, a cycle of escalation that would never end until we wiped out our species entirely.

The mood among the Americans in the detention centre was one of jubilation. They were certain the war was coming to an end and victory would be theirs. They gathered in the canteen and sang their songs – *The Yanks are coming... O say can you see... The bombs bursting in air* – till the guards broke it up and ordered them back to their dormitories, locking them in for the night.

I hoped it was true that the war would soon be over. But I feared that the Japanese would never surrender. Surrender was not in their nature. Surrender was cowardly and dishonourable. Surrender was less-than-human.

At the height of the bombing there was a thundering roar overhead, the sound of ack-ack and a huge explosion so loud we thought the camp had been hit. I stumbled outside with most of the other inmates, saw flames and smoke rising from the edge of town just a few blocks away. The guards on duty shouted at us to get back inside. They yelled and threatened us, bayonets fixed. It was the first time I had seen them so angry and afraid, and I suddenly saw how young they were.

Next morning we heard the full story. A bomber had been shot down, crashlanded in open ground just north of Futatabi. The pilot had baled out and been brought here to the camp, under guard.

Now we watched as he was led out, limping and clearly injured, blood on his face, on his shirt. Again the guards lined up, facing us, bayonets at the ready. Like them, the pilot was young, so young. He was bundled into the back of a van and driven out through the gates. The commandant, Mr Higasa, turned away, grim-faced, growled out an order to the guards who once more demanded, with menaces, that we go back inside the building.

This was the reality, this, right here on our doorstep. For us the living had been, comparatively, easy. We were non-combatants, enemy aliens, our freedom taken away. But this young man, wounded and bloodied, had been captured, was a prisoner-of-war. As they led him away, I felt a twist of fear as to what would become of him.

Didn't I know there was a war on?

I have read the stories, the accounts of life in Japanese prison camps, in Java and Malaya, in Singapore, on the Burma Road. As recently as last year, Laurens Van der Post published his novel, The *Seed and the Sower*, based on his own wartime experience. The stories are horrific, recounting acts of brutality, cruelty and torture – prisoners used for bayonet practice, beheaded for not showing sufficient respect to their officers and guards, for not bowing deeply enough to *Kyokujitsu-ki*, the Rising Sun flag. I have also read that Korean guards were, if such a thing is possible, worse than the Japanese themselves.

It is sickening. Man's inhumanity writ large. But it was very far from my own experience of internment. We were in Japan itself and not in some far-flung outpost, and we were non-combatants. In addition Higasa-san, our camp commandant. was a decent man. We experienced none of the barbarism meted out to others. In fact I would go so far as to say my treatment in Kobe was less harsh than what I had experienced as a boy in Wormwood Scrubs. Bolshie bastards and commie scum.

> *Let nations arbitrate their future troubles,*
> *It's time to lay the sword and gun away.*

I heard much later that the young American pilot, with another surviving crew member, was taken by the Kempeitai, the Japanese Gestapo. Both men were tried for the deliberate fire-bombing of civilian targets. There was no defence. They were taken blindfold from the courtroom to a lonely spot on a hillside not far from our camp at Futatabi. There they were shot by firing squad next to graves already dug for them. The bodies were covered over, the graves left unmarked.

At first it was only rumour. The Americans had developed a weapon of unimaginable power. A single bomb had completely destroyed

Hiroshima. Another had done the same to Nagasaki. Unless Japan surrendered immediately and unconditionally, Tokyo would be obliterated. The whole of Japan would be laid waste.

Newsreel film of Robert Oppenheimer, gaunt and skeletal, staring at the camera, looking out narrow-eyed from a deep dark place, quoting from the Bhagavad Gita – Krishna on the battlefield at Kurukshetra, showing Arjuna his universal form, terrifying and all-consuming. *Now I am become Death, the destroyer of worlds.*

Beyond all imagining.

The Potsdam Declaration laid down terms for Japanese Surrender as agreed by the USA, the UK and China. It was signed by Truman, Churchill and Chiang Kai Shek. Their ultimatum stated that if Japan did not surrender it would face prompt and utter destruction.

Prompt and utter destruction.

The sheer scale of it, the enormity. The blast ripping apart the very fabric of reality, tearing it asunder. Intolerable brightness that would sear they eye, then darkness blotting out the sun.
Death the destroyer of worlds.

Again there were rumours, and counter-rumours.
The Emperor has been arrested and charged with war crimes.
The Emperor has been executed.
The Emperor has been imprisoned and the military are refusing to surrender.
The Emperor has recorded a message to the Japanese people, to be broadcast on radio forthwith.
This last rumour proved to be true.
Many in the Japanese army were opposed to the war being ended in this way. It would be cowardly and dishonourable. When word spread that the Emperor's message would be broadcast, as many as a thousand officers and soldiers raided the Imperial palace to

destroy the recording. They were unable to find it, hidden in a pile of documents. It was smuggled out of the palace, rather ignominiously in a laundry basket of women's underwear, and taken to the radio station.

Even then, I heard later, a diehard group of fanatics managed to get into the building in a final kamikaze attempt to stop the transmission. They were gunned down and the broadcast went ahead, from a locked studio, with armed guards at the door.

In Kobe our years of internment ended abruptly. Higasa-san summoned us all to the courtyard one last time, the guards standing rigidly to attention. His voice quavering, he announced what had happened. Arrangements would be made, but essentially we were free to go. He bowed and turned on his heel, strode back into his office.

The doors to the camp were unlocked, the gates left open.

At first some of the Americans thought it might be a trap and we would be shot for trying to escape.

I looked across and saw Tomiko outside the main gate, hesitating then walking towards me.

I went to her, uncertain, and she stopped in front of me. She was in tears, covered her face with her hands. She bowed, then straightened up again, shaking her head, laugh-crying.

Is finished, she said, her voice choked. War is over.

It was a time of chaos and uncertainty. Nobody knew what would happen next, what kind of rule the Americans would impose. Tomiko was glad the war was over, happy I was home in our temporary rented apartment, our little family once more complete. But she was not at peace. She laughed again, cried again, seemed at times to retreat inside herself, numbed and frozen. She looked out at me from far away, not seeing or not understanding.

I knew in part what she had been through, the upheaval she had endured. But I sensed that this, now, was something more. I asked and she tried to explain. She had been in turmoil since the Emperor's broadcast.

She spoke, haltingly, of something I translated as The honourable death of the hundred million. It was an old song, she said, sung by the military.

One hundred million souls for the Emperor.

It spoke of the entire nation sacrificing itself, and as I understood it, the song had become a rallying cry, a call to mass suicide as a matter of honour if the Emperor should demand it in his speech.

But surely, I said, that could not happen. It was not possible.

Then I remembered the atmosphere in town, a heaviness in the air that was more than the intense heat, the oppressive mugginess. Tomiko had taken me by the arm and hurried me home. One old man had sat, stern-faced and rigid, outside his boarded-up shopfront, a sword on a low table in front of him. He had unsheathed it, looked long and hard at the blade, as if gauging its sharpness.

Yes, said Tomiko. Is possible.

She looked desolate, hid her face in her hands and cried, and I held her, tried to comfort her.

I heard the recorded message later when it was broadcast again. We tuned in and listened on an old radio receiver, a length of bent wire for an aerial which I moved this way and that, trying to get a better signal.

The transmission was named *Gyokuon-hōsō*. Jewel Voice Broadcast. A formal declaration. The Imperial Rescript on the Termination of the Greater East Asia War.

Tomiko sat with me, straightbacked on the tatami mat, rigid and attentive, in silent awe that once again she was actually hearing the Emperor's voice, a voice that was unreal, other-worldly, with a high singsong tonality. She bowed her head almost to the floor when the speech began.

The recording was poor, the words constantly lost in crackle and whine. And even when it could be clearly heard, it was difficult to follow the formal courtly ceremonial language. Tomiko's brow furrowed and she gave a little shake of the head as she tried to concentrate, make sense of it.

There seemed to be a heightening of intensity, a conclusion, some-
thing about the progress of the world. Then the voice cut, an abrupt
end. The national anthem was played, slow and sonorous.

Tomiko kneeled, her head bent. Once again she held her face in her
hands and sobbed, her thin shoulders shaking. Again I held her, said
everything would be all right. Harumi carried on playing with the
little Daruma doll, knocking it over, watching it rock back.

Nana korobi ya oki... Seven times down. Eight times up.

It was later still that I was vouchsafed a translation into English. I
have it here beside me as I write, the words typed and carbon-cop-
ied onto thin wartime paper. Between paragraphs are my notes /
comments, scribbled down in red pen as I read the transcript for
the first time.

*After pondering deeply the general trends of the world and the actual
conditions obtaining in our empire today, we have decided to effect a set-
tlement of the present situation by resorting to an extraordinary measure.
We have ordered our government to communicate to the governments of
the United States, Great Britain, China and the Soviet Union that our
empire accepts the provisions of their joint declaration.*

No direct statement, then, that Japan was formally surrendering.
Extraordinary measure. Accepting the provisions. The thing half-
said.

*To strive for the common prosperity and happiness of all nations as well as
the security and well-being of our subjects is the solemn obligation which
has been handed down by our imperial ancestors and which lies close to our
heart. Indeed, we declared war on America and Britain out of our sincere
desire to ensure Japan's self-preservation and the stabilization of East Asia,
it being far from our thought either to infringe upon the sovereignty of other
nations or to embark upon territorial aggrandisement.*

That was certainly one way of putting it.

But now the war has lasted for nearly four years. Despite the best that has been done by everyone – the gallant fighting of the military and naval forces, the diligence and assiduity of our servants of the state, and the devoted service of our one hundred million people – the war situation has developed not necessarily to Japan's advantage while the general trends of the world have all turned against her interest.

No mention that a Soviet invasion of Manchuria and other Japanese-held territories had also begun a few days before. That in itself would have been cause for alarm, but had clearly become a side-sow to the main event.

The enemy has begun to employ a new and most cruel bomb, the power of which to do damage is, indeed, incalculable, taking the toll of many innocent lives. Should we continue to fight, not only would it result in an ultimate collapse and obliteration of the Japanese nation, but also it would lead to the total extinction of human civilization.

Prompt and utter destruction. Now I am become death.

How are we to save the millions of our subjects, or to atone ourselves before the hallowed spirits of our imperial ancestors? This is the reason why we have ordered the acceptance of the provisions of the joint declaration of the powers.

Surrender as atonement, then, the honourable thing to do. Acceptance of the inevitable.

The hardships and sufferings to which our nation is to be subjected hereafter will be certainly great. However, it is according to the dictates of time and fate that we have resolved to pave the way for a grand peace for all the generations to come by enduring the unendurable and suffering what is unsufferable.

We cannot go on. We must go on.

Unite your total strength. Cultivate the ways of rectitude, foster nobility of spirit, and work with resolution, so that you may enhance the innate glory of the imperial state and keep pace with the progress of the world.

The poor quality of the recording and the arcane language of the speech had made the broadcast hard to understand. There was sure to be much confusion. To allay this, and to appeal to the general public to remain calm, there was an announcement by a well known radio presenter Tadaichi Hirakawa, stating in simple direct terms that Japan had indeed surrendered.

There had been no call for The Honourable Death, the ultimate sacrifice. I reassured Tomiko but she was still shaken, still fearful. She laughed again, cried again. For my part I was genuinely afraid that there might still be widespread despair, mass suicides. After we had listened I was unable to sleep, I got up in the middle of the night, sat in zazen, tried to focus my attention on the great chaotic koan all around. One hand clapping? The soundless sound? Death the destroyer of worlds.

At first light I stepped out into the street, left Tomiko asleep with Harumi held in her arms.

Even this early it was still hot and humid, the air clammy. There were no gatherings, no assemblies, no mobs. The few people I passed looked stunned, every face a bland mask of incomprehension. Some of them stared at me, at my pale skin, my round eyes, my shock of thick lightbrown hair. Was I some kind of advance guard, the *gaijin* walking among them already? I nodded to each of them, greeted them in Japanese, formally, with respect. But that only seemed to deepen their confusion and they walked on, eyes glazed. I found myself walking towards the centre of town, buildings on every side flattened by the bombing, the acrid smell of burning in the air, catching the throat.

For no reason I headed towards Mark's House where I had first been imprisoned. No reason at all, except to orientate myself, take my bearings from somewhere I knew. I thought I must have lost my way, taken a wrong turning, as I couldn't see the house. Then I recognised the garden wall where the neighbour's children used to climb and pass us food. Their house, next door, had been damaged and looked empty. Mark's House itself, our temporary prison, was gone, reduced to rubble and ash, nothing left standing but that wall and a fireplace chimney, the ruin still smouldering.

The building must have taken a direct hit.

If we had not been evacuated, not moved out to Futatabi.

If....

All forms are burning.

8

GAKUSHUIN

If this were a film the screen would fade to black. Then there would be a long shot of downtown Tokyo, razed after the bombing, Ueno and Asakusa blitzed, almost obliterated.

A cloud of cherry blossoms.
  The temple bell –
    Is it Ueno? Asakusa?

What would Basho have made of this? Ueno and Asakusa unrecognisable, a scene of utter devastation, hardly a landmark left standing save a solitary tall building, the Asakusa Tower, precarious above the burned-out plain. The Kannon temple (where Basho's bell perhaps sounded) was gone and with it the jumble of wood-and-paper buildings, the shops and tea-houses, markets and noodle bars, the thousands of flimsy homes huddled in the warren of streets, just kindling and tinder, flared up and gone.

Is it Ueno? Asakusa?

Ashes and dust.

If this were a film…

Fade.

Things had moved quickly. Tomiko and I, with little Harumi, had moved to Tokyo, encouraged by Yamanashi and Suzuki who had resolved to find me employment as soon as possible after my sojourn in Kobe. They sensed, rightly, that the teaching of English would be of crucial importance after the war. And who better to teach it than this cultured Englishman already living among them? And where better to teach it than at Gakushuin, the Peers School where sons of the aristocracy had studied – the rich and powerful, even the Imperial family – where Yamanashi had recently been Chancellor. Suzuki had also studied and taught at the school, and was held in the highest regard. With recommendations from both men – the Doctor and the Admiral – I was what the Americans would call a sure thing.

I was summoned to a meeting at Gakushuin. Yamanashi had been Head of the School since resigning as Deputy Minister for the Navy. Ironically that resignation had been forced on him because of his pro-Western sympathies, his opposition to the war. Now he was effectively to be purged from his position at the School by an edict from the occupation forces, removing anyone who had ever been tainted by association with militarism. Even his designation, his rank of Admiral, was enough to condemn him.

Damned if he did, damned if he didn't.

I expressed my sympathy and he thanked me but said he was having none of it. He accepted the situation as he had no doubt accepted every setback in his life, with a true Samurai spirit, a stoicism and fortitude.

He said, *Shikata ga nai* – It can't be helped.

It was an expression I heard everywhere, repeated like a mantra. Poverty, hunger, the sheer devastation after the bombings. None of it could be helped. But uttered by Yamanashi it did not sound trite or banal. Instead it resonated with his own inner strength, with all the quiet power of Hakuin's *Is that so?*

Besides, he said, I am seventy years old. I look forward very much to having time to tend my garden.

His eyes, those *ancient glittering eyes*, crinkled.

But first, he said, I have a proposition for you…

Yamanashi met me at the main gate, close to Mejiro station. On the way through the grounds, he stopped and pointed out four inscriptions on the walls. He explained they were maxims by the Emperor Ninko, and he translated them for me.

Walk in the paths trodden by the feet of the great sages.

Revere the righteous canons of the empire.

He that has not learned the sacred doctrines, how can he govern himself?

He that is ignorant of the classics, how can he regulate his own conduct?

So, he said. Those are the ideals, the spirit of this place. Unfortunately, like most of Tokyo the school has taken a pounding.

He indicated where an entire teaching block had taken a direct hit, been completely destroyed. The playing fields were overgrown, nets sagging, fences torn down. A large central building which he said had beed a handsome centrepiece, had been commandeered for the billeting of troops and was in a state of disrepair, windows broken, doors hanging from their hinges, plaster walls once white, now grey and scarred.

But it will be rebuilt, he said. It *must* be rebuilt. And this is where you come in...

His *proposition* was something of a ploy, albeit with serious intent. He had called me to meet him here at the school, partly to confirm the offer of a teaching post, subject to a few formalities. But there was more to his plan, as I was about to find out.

He led me into one of the older buildings, all old pine and sliding doors, which had clearly, and mercifully, not suffered damage. At one of the inner rooms he took off his shoes. I did the same and he opened the door, called out a formal greeting and indicated I should follow him.

Two distinguished-looking Japanese gentlemen in well-cut suits stood to greet us. They were of Yamanashi's generation and he introduced them as Professor Abe and Professor Koizumi. It took me a moment to realise that I had met Professor Abe before. Some years had passed but I recognised him as the Abe who had been Head of the Law Department at Keijo, the very same man who had negotiated my salary there and told me I was doing a good job.

Mister Blyth, he said. I don't know if you remember me.

Abe-Sensei, I said. I owe you a debt of gratitude.

I am happy to meet you again.

Likewise.

Yamanashi had spoken to me very highly of both men. Abe had succeeded him as Chancellor, Koizumi was, I knew, involved in the education of the young Crown Prince, Akihito. They bowed to me, the bows respectful but not too deep, then they both stepped forward and shook me by the hand. Koizumi said he was delighted to make my acquaintance. I noticed he had some scarring to his face, as if from burns, and he leaned on a cane as he stood. But his handshake, like Abe's, was firm. Both men had a kind of dignity about them, a quiet strength. They shared with Yamanashi that quality of the samurai, poised and self-contained.

In the centre of the room was an old but elegant hardwood table round which four chairs had been arranged, western-style.

Please, said Koizumi, indicating that I should sit, and they did the same.

As if summoned, a young Japanese woman slid open a side door and brought in a tray bearing teapot and cups. Again the style was not Japanese but European, the delicate china cups resting in saucers, each with a silver teaspoon. The woman, however, was entirely Japanese in her manner, her movements, picking up the pot and swirling it round, pouring tea into each cup, making the event a little tea ceremony before bowing and leaving as quietly and gracefully as she had come.

Cha-no-yu, I said.

Afternoon tea! said Koizumi.

They had clearly gone to some trouble in deference to my Englishness. In a little bowl was a quantity of granulated white sugar, and in another was a similar amount of pale powder I took to be dried milk. Please, said Koizumi again, indicating that I should help myself. Both items must have been in short supply, and I was happy to spoon two heaps of the sugar into my cup. The milk was another matter – I had encountered something like it before and not been impressed. But it would have been churlish to refuse so I sprinkled on some of

the powder, watched it clot and coagulate then spread out when I
stirred it, a spiral nebula.

I raised the cup to my lips, sipped, grateful for the sweetness but
tasting the powder on my teeth.

Good, I said. Thank you!

My hosts had taken neither milk nor sugar, preferring their tea un-
adulterated, the thing itself.

Professor Abe handed me a plate on which four little hard sweet
biscuits were laid out, one for each of us.

You can dunk, he said. That is the word? Dunk?

It is indeed, I said. And a fine word it is too.

Dunk.

For some reason I was back in Wormwood Scrubs, dunking stale
bread in a tin mug of stewed tea, three decades ago, in another world.
Dunk.

So, said Koizumi, spreading his hands. Welcome to Gakushuin.

I recalled what Yamanashi had told me about the two men. Like
him, they were cultured and cosmopolitan. Like him they had
spoken out against militarism and criticised the rush to war. For
this they had been treated with hostility and investigated by the
Kempeitai, the none-too-secret police. Now, Yamanashi had said,
in this time of rebuilding, perhaps they would come into their own.
Abe had travelled in Europe, studied Kant at Heidelberg Univer-
sity. He had visited China and spent that time in Korea, in my
old stamping ground of Seoul. Since the war he had served as the
Government's Minister for Education, and now he was taking over
as Principal at Gakushuin.

Koizumi had also spent time in Europe, studying economics in
London and Berlin, returning to Japan via New York. He was a
respected scholar and had been persuaded to take on his new role
as Counsellor to the Crown Prince.

Gentlemen, I said, I am honoured.

Strangely, looking back, I find it hard to recall the detail of our
conversation. I simply remember the range of it, and the depth. We
talked about Kantian ethics and Mahayana Buddhism, the Dhamma-

pada and the New Testament, Bach and Spinoza, Shakespeare and
Dickens and Noh. We had much to share, and I found it stimulating
and invigorating. At some point I referred to those maxims by Em-
peror Ninko which Yamanashi had shown me, inscribed on the walls,
said how much they had impressed me as a declaration of intent.

There was a natural lull, a comfortable hiatus, a drawing breath.

So, said Koizumi, setting down his teacup.

There was another little pause, then he continued.

There is something we would like to discuss with you.

Yamanashi's proposition perhaps.

There has been much…deliberation… about the teaching of the
Crown Prince in these changed times.

Changed utterly, I said.

Ah, he said. Your Mister Yeats.

Yes.

Things fall apart.

The centre cannot hold, said Abe.

So, said Koizumi. We who have survived have a great responsibility
to ensure mere anarchy is *not* loosed upon the world.

We have to rebuild, said Abe, echoing what Yamanashi had said to
me. A mantra.

We have to rebuild.

It begins here where we are, said Yamanashi, Here at Gakushuin.

The next generation, said Abe.

The future Emperor is in our care, said Koizumi. It is essential that
his education should be broad. He should learn about the wider
world, beyond these shores.

Its history, its philosophy, its literature – in general, its culture.

Its poetry, I said. Most important of all.

Yamanashi nodded, twinkled at me.

By the end of the meeting it had been agreed. I would be employed
as a teacher at Gakushuin, working to a curriculum of my own
devising but based on English language and literature. The salary
would be very reasonable given the times and circumstances, and I
would be provided with accommodation on campus. In addition to
my regular teaching duties, I would tutor the Crown Prince privately

for one hour every week.

Not for the first time in my life, I felt I was a beneficiary of some di- ⟩
vine providence. Karma? The roll of the dice? Whatever the truth of ⟩
it, benign force or random unfoldment, I was unutterably grateful.

Well, as Alice might have said, that was the strangest tea-party I
was ever at in all my life.

The house was in a little row, set aside for teaching staff, near the
stables. It had lain empty for a while, felt cold and smelled musty,
but Tomiko was happy we had a place of our own where we might
be settled at last, and Harumi was delighted, ran from room to
room, laughing.

There were a few old bookcases, left by the previous resident (now
retired). I set about building more – a whole wall of shelves in what
would be my study. I unpacked my books – those that had survived
the bombings – transported from Kobe via Kanazawa along with
boxes of other belongings, old clothes that were still serviceable,
bedding and blankets, a padded quilt.

With my first wage I made what I thought would be a necessary
investment – I bought a bicycle. Markets had already sprung up
everywhere, folk showing a remarkable if desperate resilience,
picking themselves up, providing necessities, eking out a living. One
of the biggest markets was not far away in burned-out Ikebukuro,
close to the station. I made my way there on foot from Mejiro,
followed the line of the railway track. I returned home on my new
bike, a sturdy old bone-shaker, complete with shopping basket on
the front. I would use that to carry my books, wrapped in a trusty
furoshiki cloth.

The old fellow who sold me the bike was was like a caricature from
one of Hokusai's sketchbooks. He wore a headband, a padded
kimono jacket tied at the waist, wooden geta on his feet. When he
grinned he showed a single tooth, his gaunt, lined face lighting up.
He was next to a stall piled high with sweat-stained army surplus
tunics, khaki leggings, forage caps and steel helmets, a stack of
mis-matched boots. He said he could get me cigarettes – Imperial

Chrysanthemum and American Lucky Strike, and bottles of pre-war Kirin Beer. When I said No he mimed disappointment, the corners of his mouth turned down. But he was astonished and amused to be selling his bike to this crazy tweed-suited gaijin. He pointed out that it came with a pump in working order, and for good measure he threw in a little tin box, an image of Fuji on the lid, containing a basic puncture repair kit. I thanked him enormously and we laughed, exchanging deep bows (each trying to outdo the other). He was still laughing, waving in benediction as I cycled off down the road. He shouted, *Gambatte!* Go to it. And I would. I had a job, and a place to stay, and now my own transport. I was ready.

If I hadn't bought a bike, the only way to get around would have been on foot. The trains and streetcars were overcrowded to the point where boarding meant risking serious injury. All the windows had been smashed, no glass left, and passengers would climb in or out through the gaps where the panes had been. The insides had been stripped of any padding or upholstery, ripped out and carried away to patch torn clothes or blankets. I heard stories of ribs broken in the crush, a pencil snapped in an inside pocket.

One of my students told me about his journey. My foot are stood on. My hands are caught. I feel like sardine in can.

So yes, I cycled everywhere, whatever the weather. As I did, I realised once more how fortunate I was, how blessed.

I saw whole families living on waste land, each hunkered down in a hole dug in the ground, covered over with tarpaulins. They cooked on a smoky open fire by the roadside, women fetching cold water from a communal tap. I knew the market at Ikebukuro was thriving but here on this bomb site, this scorched earth, it was sheer desolation, the poorest of the poor trying desperately to sell anything. I dismounted and pushed my bike, took a closer look at their pathetic wares, scraps and detritus laid out on frayed straw mats – a hank of wool, a shoelace, a ball of string, a toothbrush, a comb, a tin of boot polish, a half-used tube of toothpaste, old chopsticks, a baby's rattle, an inkstone, a single wooden geta, a cracked teabowl, a chipped cup, a moth-eaten sweater, a tea-strainer, battered pots and pans, bamboo utensils – a rice paddle, a whisk, a pair of wire-framed glasses with no lenses, a fountain pen with no cap and a broken nib...

My neighbour, how does he live?

I noticed rows of little orange discs laid out on stone steps. I asked Tomiko later and she told me they were slices of sweet potato spread out to dry. She said sometimes it was all poor families had to eat, that and cornmeal distributed by the Red Cross. She mimed moulding the meal into little patties, dumplings. *Gyoza*, she said but wrinkled her face in distaste at the thought of how unpalatable they would be.

At Ikebukuro Tomiko was able to buy the essentials, rice and flour, vegetables, tea (for herself), sometimes fish (for herself), as well as garlic and ginger, sesame oil, soy sauce, tofu, buckwheat, all at a price, at a price.

Yami ichi, she said. Black market.

Then she gave a little sideways tilt of the head I had come to recognise as a kind of resignation.

Shikata ga nai, she said. It can't be helped.

That mantra again. At one level it was an admirable stoicism, an acceptance. But I was wary of a kind of fatalism, and found myself wanting to add something more, especially with Tomiko. I gave her my own mantra, a pronouncement by Ikkyu, the wild old Zen reprobate. It was said he'd left his followers a message locked in a box, only to be opened in case of emergency. It read, *Nantoka naru.* Somehow things will work out.

I repeated it to Tomiko. *Nantoka naru.*

Hai! she said. Yes.

In the matter of the black market, even Yamanashi said they were a necessary evil, a way to get trade and commerce up and running again. I realised he knew infinitely more about the subject than I did, so I did not presume to argue with him. Rather, I remained silent, kept my own counsel.

The Admiral was instrumental in commissioning a memorial stone to the young boys of Gakushuin killed in the war. They had marched off in their uniforms, marched off to die. The class of '44,

graduating before their term was ended, so they could go to the war.
Yamamashi said he had wept as they went, and he wept again as he
unveiled the little stone monument in the campus grounds.
The boys had each composed a waka poem ending with the same
lines.

To bloom
With the cherry blossoms
Of Mejirogaoka.

The words were carved on the stone, in the admiral's calligraphy.
The waste of it, a generation lost. The cherry blossoms of Meji-
rogaoka.
I bowed my head every day when I passed the stone, on my way
to work.
At home I have another beautiful piece of Yamanashi's calligra-
phy, trailing elegantly down the page. It is written on a scroll of
handmade paper and it hangs on the wall in my study. A rough
translation would be: *Changes arise one after another. Even the gods do*
not know how things will turn out.
That the words are inscribed by the admirable Admiral makes them
all the more profound. profound.

My heart went out to the boys I was teaching. Their world had been
turned on its head, their city blitzed and fire-bombed, their nation de-
feated. Now here they were, back at school, getting on with their lives.
As we moved into winter, the rooms were freezing, unheated, and
the boys wore only their thin school tunics with at best a wool
jumper underneath. Their uniforms were for the most part ill-fitting,
outgrown, sleeves and trouser-legs too short, leaving wrists and
ankles exposed. Often their hands were red-raw with cold and they
rubbed them together for warmth, their breath clouding in the chill
air. I saw some of them had chilblains, knuckles itching and sore.
Nothing daunted, I continued with my lessons, teaching the ne-
cessity of poetry and of zen, insisting they were one and the same.
From the outset I tried to convey more than mere sentence patterns

and rules of grammar. I taught through question and answer, where the question itself teaches some useful fact or raises an interesting problem. Or, I would give an answer and ask them to make up a question.

It's usually made of wood.
It's made of feathers.
Because a razor is very sharp.
We call it a spade.

They were rather like reverse koans, beginning with the answer and working back.

Another technique I used was the correction of sentences. Like the strange contrivances of the White Knight, they are my own invention.

He saw her earnestly.
He always insists his opinion.
War began to break out.
I feel regrettable about it.

My approach was, one might say, unorthodox. But then I never did believe in orthodoxies of any sort. (No -isms or -ologies please).

Away from the rather cloistered atmosphere of the school, the world continued on its own chaotic way, at its not-so-sweet will. My apprehension about the black market proved prescient. Tomiko came home one day from Ikebukuro, shaken and upset. She said there had been violence – a gang of thugs had smashed up some of the smaller stalls and beaten up the stallholders, getting away before the police arrived.
A week later there was a major incident near Shibuya Station. The papers described it as a confrontation between Taiwanese gangs and Japanese *Yakuza* over control of the markets. Hundreds of gang members were involved, fighting with clubs, metal pipes and

even firearms. Policemen trying to contain the violence were among
those injured and killed.

A necessary evil?

Yamanashi said time would tell.

Tomiko shopped where she could, paid a little more. We managed.

The very heart of my work, it might be said, was the teaching of
the Crown Prince, Akihito. I had actually seen him before we were
formally introduced. Close to my accommodation at the school,
next to the stables, was a small open field, and one day as I was
passing, I looked up and saw a young boy riding a white horse round
the perimeter. Two attendants who looked like military men were
stationed by the gate, and I realised the boy on the horse was the
Crown Prince himself. I stopped for a moment to watch, surprised
and intrigued. The scene was utterly matter-of-fact – nothing special
– a young boy on horseback, trotting round a field – and yet at the
same time it was quite extraordinary. This was the future Emperor
of Japan, riding a white horse. The moment was timeless, the im-
age heraldic. One of the guards looked across and caught my eye.
I bowed and walked on.

My first formal meeting with Akihito was in a little ante-room at the
Palace. I was accompanied by Yamanashi, and two or three officials
were also present, among them the Chamberlain Mr Sumikura..
The boy stood to greet me, gave a little bow and held out his hand
to shake mine. I was touched by the gesture, and by just how young
he actually was. The effect was heightened by the fact that his hair
was cropped short, close to the skull, a cut that might be military or
monastic, but only seemed to emphasise his youth, the fine shape of
his head. He wore the regulation school uniform, navy blue, with the
tunic buttoned up to the neck. His, however was embellished with
a little crest at the collar in the form of a silver chrysanthemum, the
symbol both of his Imperial family and of Gakushuin.

He said, as he had no doubt been instructed, I am very happy to
meet you, Mr Buraisu Sensei. Thank you for coming from England

to teach me.

I did not think it would be polite (or politic) to explain that I had not crossed oceans and continents for the express purpose of being his tutor, but had lived in Japan for some time, notably as a guest of the Japanese government in Kobe. No. Instead I bowed and thanked him and said it was a great honour and privilege for me to be here.

My sessions with the Crown Prince were every Thursday at the same time – two o'clock in the afternoon at the Imperial Palace. So I came to think, Thursday is the Crown Prince's day, and I sometimes wondered if perhaps the Crown Prince thought, Thursday is Blyth Sensei's day. Who knows? (I never asked him!)

In the end (if it be the end) I taught the Crown Prince for some eighteen years, until my recent demise – no, not demise, not yet! The word I am looking for is decline.

In those early days there was a certain awkwardness. The Prince was young, with a natural, innate deference towards his elders (and in my case, a respect towards one designated as his teacher). He had also been born to privilege in the highest degree – the boy would be the 125th Emperor of Japan. Our circumstances, our everyday lives, could not have been more different.

All of this, combined with the fact that his English was as yet limited, made for a kind of restraint between us.

I noticed it was worse when, as was usually the case, there were other adults in the room – one of the Chancellors or a teacher from the school. The boy would invariably defer to them, glancing in their direction before speaking. I would also sometimes wonder how much he was following what I said. I found myself recalling my own earliest schooldays, in Leytonstone, my young self gazing intently at the teacher in the hope that my wide-eyed earnestness would deflect him from seeing I was taking in not a single word. When the teacher eventually realised this, he became very angry at me. Looking back I realised the teacher must have felt insulted by my behaviour (and understandably so). I was regularly bottom of the class because of

a congenital inability to master anything arithmetical. (Even today
I am unable to add up a column of figures, or do simple multipli-
cation or division). I can only assume that part of my brain never
quite engaged. The only things that interested me were insects and
religion – subjects more connected than many might suppose.

At secondary school, the only aspects of mathematics that held any
interest were a few elements in geometry, an explanation or a proof
that worked visually, with an inherent elegance, a clarity that gave
a sense of structure, an underlying pattern. This gave an occasional
frisson of excitement, but it was as nothing compared to the awak-
ening I felt when I first read poetry.

At secondary school I had a teacher called Mr Goodspeed who for
some unknown reason was known to his pupils as Mr Bloodknot.
He taught us English and music, and in retrospect I must owe him a
great deal. But my abiding memory of him is his animosity towards
anything that smacked of religion, he himself being a self-declared
atheist (and humanist, and socialist). His naturally red face would
get redder still as he argued some moot point of religious teaching
(which he dismissed as dogma) with any of us who dared to men-
tion God or quote scripture.

The only thing that incensed him even more was when he found
a boy eating sweets in class. I was guilty of it myself, breaking off
a square of chocolate from a bar in my pocket and surreptitiously
munching it. (My love of chocolate has become a recurring theme in
these pages). If Bloodknot did catch a boy out he would confiscate
the sweets and make a great show of eating them himself while he
carried on teaching.

This, not surprisingly, annoyed the boys, and some of them decided
to take revenge. They bought a small box of chocolates, scooped
out the insides and filled them with pepper. One boy by the name
of Evans volunteered – he hid the box under the lid of his desk and
pretended to eat. The teacher pounced and snatched the box, select-
ed one of the sweets and popped it in his mouth. His discomfort was
clear, he sweated as his face grew redder still. He glared at Evans
and around the room at the rest of us. But he kept chewing the sweet
and swallowed it down, all the while looking fierce but continuing

with his lesson, closing the chocolate box and throwing it in the bin. Strangely, the effect on the boys was to engender admiration for the teacher, for the sheer stoicism of his response, and thereafter we simply stopped eating sweets in class.

Mr Goodspeed, I remember, was killed at the Somme, as was the boy Evans.

War and the pity. A foreign field.

At some stage I found myself telling the Crown Prince about Mr Bloodknot-Goodspeed.

The Crown Prince was mainly interested in science, which I have always believed to be the enemy of mankind. I made no secret of this, or of my love for poetry and religion. The Crown Prince had grave doubts about both, thinking that they could easily be used to hoodwink mankind.

He enjoyed the school story immensely, awed by the audacity of the boys, laughing at the thought of the red-faced teacher and full of admiration for his strength and restraint.

So we persevered, His Royal Highness and I. We stuck to our task, and gradually a mutual respect began to grow, which flowered into fondness and a kind of friendship. From the beginning I enjoyed bringing him books to read. (Some of them I asked Ma to send from home). I gave him books on nature study, field guides to British wildlife, and he liked them very much. It was not far from there to how the poets saw nature, to the world of haiku, seeing-into-the-life-of-things, to animism and zen. Little by little, we found common ground and learned from each other.

I first met Emperor Hirohito in person at a reception in the Imperial Palace, a low-key affair I was told, connected with the re-opening of Gakushuin. I had no idea what to expect. I had seen photographs of the Emperor, this controversial figure, in uniform, in traditional robes, in formal western dress, a dinner suit and white tie. The English and American press had published brutal caricatures of him, dressed as a military leader, or in an ill-fitting business suit, affably doffing his hat while standing on a mountain of skulls.

On this occasion he wore a morning coat and striped trousers. I stood in a line of guests, waiting to be presented to him. He stopped briefly in front of each one, gave a slight nod of the head and spoke a few words of acknowledgement, recognition, benediction. I noticed that everyone without exception seemed to take a little half-step back away from him, as if fearful of encroaching on the divine presence. Any courtiers or attendants taking their leave of him did so with a curious crab-like movement, stepping backwards, bent double.

As he and his entourage moved along the line towards me, I was overwhelmed, not for the first time, by an air of utter unreality. This small, slightly-built man pausing before me was Hirohito, Emperor of Japan, still seen by many of his subjects as an incarnation, a direct descendant of Amaterasu the Sun-Goddess.

From every kind of man / Obedience I expect / I'm the Emperor of Japan...

So sang the Mikado. I silenced that particular voice and bowed from the waist. The Emperor gave a barely perceptible nod of the head, caught my eye briefly, registered a momentary curiosity and said he had once visited England. He had been very well received there, and King George V had made him very welcome. In England, he said, there was much to admire.

Then he moved on, along the line.

Later I was introduced to the Empress Kojun who said she had heard about me from the Crown Prince. Once again I gave my deepest bow and said how honoured I was to be teaching her son.

That was when she surprised me, saying something in Japanese which her attendant translated after a moment's hesitation as, You are solid built.

I must have registered confusion. Her Majesty said, in English (with a most definite twinkle in her eye), Mister Buraisu, you are very fat. I have told this story often, and it always makes me smile. I gathered myself, said it was probably on account of my vegetarian diet. (Elephants are large, I said, and they eat nothing but leaves...) I patted my stomach.

She laughed and repeated what I had said.

An elephant!

There was one more member of the Royal family I had yet to meet, and that was the Dowager Empress Sadako, mother of the Emperor, grandmother of the Crown Prince. The opportunity arose when I was invited to a kind of *soiree* at her official residence. (Part of the building had been destroyed in an air raid but it had been rebuilt, restored. Her philosophy, often stated, was that life-must-go-on, and with as little fuss as possible). When she entered the room, she impressed with her sheer presence. Small, though no smaller than most Japanese women, she was also sturdy, had an air of strength and poise. She wore a black ankle-length high-collared dress, offset by a long necklace of pearls. She looked about her with a brightness in the eyes, a keenness, a genuine engagement.

She approached me, gave a smile, said she was very happy to meet me and had heard about my interest in Buddhism. She asked if I was familiar with the Lotus Sutra. and the Nichiren faith.

I bowed, recited, *Namu Myoho Renge Kyo*. I bow to Kannon Bodhisattva.

She looked delighted.

A most powerful mantra, she said, nodding.

I said I very much liked the story of Nisshin Shonin, the founder of the Nichiren sect. He had fallen foul of the Shogun Yoshinori, been tortured to make him give up his faith. As a red-hot cauldron was placed on his head he chanted the mantra and was unharmed. Yes! she said. The fire did not burn him!

I thought at the time (and I think it still) that my old Ma would have been quite taken with her and the liking would have been reciprocated. (The Dowager Empress taking tea and scones in Ma's front room. Ma sipping green tea and eating mochi in the Imperial Palace. Both of them setting the world to rights).

The more I read about the Dowager Empress, the more impressed I was. She had been unashamedly outspoken in her opposition to the war. (Perhaps for that reason she had spent the better part of the war years out of the public eye, at the Imperial residence in Numazu). She had long been a patron of the International Red Cross – there

were newspaper photographs of her visiting victims of the great
Kanto earthquake, speaking with what looked like real concern to
a group of awe-struck children.

This, perhaps, was a way forward for the royal family, a way the
Dowager Empress had been showing them all along.

I had liked the Americans I met in Kobe, Bob Aitken chief among
them, and *pace* Mr Olsen from Pittsburgh. But I had no idea what
to expect from the occupying forces. I was afraid they might behave
with the brutishness of the conqueror, trampling roughshod over
their defeated enemy. And no doubt there were many who did be-
have like that. I heard harrowing stories. But the men with whom I
had direct dealings were intelligent, urbane and remarkably cultured.
Faubion Bowers was as exotic and aristocratic as his name. He had
actually travelled to Japan as a student before the war. He had devel-
oped a love for Japanese culture, particularly *Kabuki*. Then he had
served as a translator and had risen through the ranks to be General
MacArthur's aide-de-camp, and found himself part of the advance
party, sent ahead to prepare for the General's arrival. So he was the
first enemy soldier to be received on Japanese soil after the war.

The delegation of Japanese officials sent to greet the Americans
at Atsugi Air Base waited with understandable trepidation. How
would these rough barbarians treat them? What demands would
they make? I could imagine their astonishment when this tall, eager
young man strode towards them, hand outstretched in greeting,
and the first thing he wanted to know was whether Kabuki Master
Uzaemon was still alive.

Another member of MacArthur's delegation was Lieutenant-Col-
onel Harold Henderson. On first meeting he impressed me as a
quiet scholarly man. It was only when he started discussing haiku
and saying how much he admired my book, that I realised he was
the Harold G Henderson who had published a book of his own
translations – *The Bamboo Broom* – which I had read and appreci-
ated. I said in its way it was a little masterpiece. (His versions of

the poems were rhymed, which to my ear was jarring, but this was nitpicking pedantry on my part). I was overjoyed that men of this calibre, showing this degree of empathy with Japan and its culture, had been given a role to play.

As had I.

Part of Henderson's remit was to look at the future of Gakushuin which was under threat of having its funding withdrawn. The school was effectively owned by the Imperial Household. Its very name, The Peers School, was a reminder of its elite, elevated status. There were strong voices from the Occupation forces calling for the abolition of the peerage altogether, the transfer of all the Emperor's assets to the nation. This would inevitably lead to the school itself being abolished. Understandably, Yamanashi was not in favour of this and appointed me to liaise with Henderson and work towards a solution. Once a week I was picked up in an official car and driven to the headquarters of SCAP – the Supreme Command, Allied Powers. This was in the imposing Daiichi Seimei building, a huge block owned by an insurance company but commandeered by the occupation forces. Armed guards manned the front entrance, and inside I had to show my accreditation before being led to Henderson's office on the third floor where he would welcome me with great warmth and eagerness. On the wall behind his desk was a scroll down which trailed a beautiful piece of calligraphy I recognised as the famous epigram from the Heart Sutra.

Form is Emptiness.

Indeed it is, I said, the first time I saw it.

I looked out of the window across the bomb-damaged city.

Indeed it is.

Part of our task involved discussing the minutiae of the Emperor Meiji's Rescript on Education. This was important work, but it was slow and painstaking and grindingly dull. Mercifully we had haiku to talk about in our tea breaks. We shared favourite poems, sometimes comparing our own translations of the same verse.

He offered this, his rendition of a poem by Basho (in fact the poet's death-verse).

> *On a journey, ill*
> *and over fields all withered, dreams*
> *go wandering still.*

I noted the rhyme, countered with my own version.

> *Sick on a journey —*
> *My dreams wander over*
> *A withered moor.*

We nodded in approval at each other's efforts, each preferring our own.

Henderson and I could be formal and long-winded when the occasion demanded. Together we drafted a document for the school authorities.

It is our intention not to continue the Gakushuin in its present form, by merely changing its legal status, but rather to embark, unhampered by past traditions, on building a truly democratic institution which will focus on creating courses of thoroughly cultural education, and give unprecedented attention to the art and science of government, the study of every aspect of social and political life.

You could have been a politician, said Henderson, or a diplomat.

A smiling public man, I said. God forbid!

The aim of the school, we agreed, would be *to train students to develop individuality within a democratic framework.*

Both men and women equally, said Henderson.

Of course

To combine the duties of citizenship with a deep appreciation of internationalism.

Yes.

To give a practical understanding of general political life in a rejuvenated Japan as a preparation for active participation in that life nationally and internationally.

You've nailed it, said Henderson.

And I shall help bring this about, I said, by talking to them about poetry.
No better way, he said.

The poetry lesson is the most important part of schooling. If it is neglected, if it is a failure, all is lost and God created the world in vain.

We are poets in so far as we live at all.

Poetry is not emotion, not philosophy, not religion, not morality, not beauty, not comedy or tragedy, not love or hate, not God, not truth. It is none of these, though any or all of them may be subsumed into poetry.

What are the enemies of poetry? Shallowness, sentimentality, vulgarity, hypocrisy, bad taste, snobbery.

Poetry is recollection of identity. Poetry is forgetting the differences. (Take care of the differences and the identities will take care of themselves).

The leaves fall by gravitation. This is one hundred percent true. But equally the leaves fall because they *want* to fall. This is poetry.

9

DECLARATION OF
HUMANITY

The way things unfold.

Ma had replied to my anxious letters, assured me all was well with everyone I knew and loved. Now she sent me a picture book on the activities of the British Royal Family during the War. There were many photographs of the royals visiting communities that had been blitzed and bombed, and bringing, as Ma put it, a kind of comfort by their very presence.

On a whim, or sudden inspiration, I had Tomiko wrap the book and I gave it to Yamanashi to pass on, if he thought it appropriate, as a gift to the Emperor. He thanked me and said he thought it *most* appropriate and was sure the Emperor would be delighted.

There was another book I owned, a history of Russia which contained a photograph of the Romanov family – the Czar, his wife and their five children, posed, stiff and formal for the camera, looking out uncaring, unknowing, at a world moving beyond them.

Official reports indicated only that the Czar had been executed, by firing squad, on the orders of the revolutionary government, for crimes against the state. But stories had circulated that the whole family had been brutally murdered in the basement of a remote country house, their bodies butchered and buried in bleak woodland in unmarked graves.

Dictatorship of the proletariat. The killings were justified as necessary, to put an end to dynastic succession.

Dynastic succession. By official reckoning Hirohito was the one hundred and twenty-fourth Emperor of Japan. There were pho-

tographs like those of the Romanovs, showing the Emperor and
Empress, the Crown Prince and his younger brother, their four
sisters – this family I knew, the child I taught.

The rational part of me did not believe the same fate could befall
them. But the rational part of me would not have believed the atom-
ic bomb would be dropped.

The Americans might still decide that *long term historical purpose*
required an end to dynastic succession. They might still decide to
put the Emperor on trial and force him to abdicate. He might face
imprisonment, or worse.

It was unthinkable, but not unimaginable.

During that time I had a recurring dream in which the whole family
were put on trial in a scene that borrowed equally from *Alice and
Wonderland* and *A Tale of Two Cities*. A judge shouted *Off with their
heads!* as they were bundled into a tumbril, struggling to maintain
their dignity. The Crown Prince looked to me for help but I was
frozen, unable to move, unable to speak. The way it is in dreams.
That awful paralysis.

In the *Mumonkan* it says grappling with a koan is like swallowing a
red-hot iron ball, which you cannot spit out even if you try. When
you try to communicate you are a dumb man in a dream.

I have often been questioned, occasionally interrogated, about my
own part in it all, the way events played out. Chance or grace or the
randomness of fate – call it what you will – conspired to place me
in an interesting situation, between the Americans and the Japanese,
MacArthur and the Emperor. A rock and a hard place, some might
say. For good or ill I was in a position to influence the course of
great historical events.

Not that I laboured under any illusion of my own importance.

Nimitta matram bhava savyasachin, Krishna told Arjuna in the *Bhaga-
vad Gita*, on the battlefield of Kurukshetra, before he went into
battle against his own family, his own kin. *Be thou a mere instrument.*
My aim was always to keep myself, my self, out of the way. At the
same time I did my utmost to effect a result while striving to stay
detached from any hope or expectation. Act, said Krishna, but

surrender the fruits of your actions.

A mere instrument.

It helped, perhaps, that each side thought I was acting on behalf of the other, but with the aim of bringing them together, finding common ground. And in effect that was not far from the truth of it. At the palace I was received as an honoured guest, but one who, they understood, was trusted by the occupying forces. They also knew I would negotiate with those forces on behalf of the Japanese and for the wellbeing of my adopted homeland.

On one occasion I was received by the Emperor himself, with only two or three of his courtiers in attendance. The room was immaculate, dark polished hardwood, high-backed upright chairs. On the walls, in addition to brush drawings, hanging scrolls, were framed images, I assumed, from his textbooks on marine biology. On a sideboard, surprisingly but perhaps tellingly, was a bronze bust of Napoleon. Tea was served, with the usual formality and restraint. On the low table between us, carefully placed, sat the book I had given him on the British royal family. He gestured towards the book and gave me the slightest nod of the head, said simply, and quietly, Thank you.

The contrast with General MacArthur could not have been greater. The general's office, like Henderson's, was in the Daiichi Seimei building, close to the Imperial Palace but worlds away. The General welcomed me to his sanctum with a vigorous handshake and told one of his aides to bring a pot of coffee, strong and black, which he poured himself into two sturdy china mugs. He was a tall man, powerful for his age and square-jawed, and he carried himself like one of the cowboy characters in a Wild West film. He declared how happy he was to meet me, then proceeded to deliver a rumbling (and rambling) monologue, speaking *at* me rather than to me, pausing only to refill our coffee cups. He himself drank three cups, each one rapidly. I did not finish the second, fearing its effect, the sudden rush of wellbeing followed by intense agitation.

You can't beat a good cup of java, he said, then continued to harangue me, *filling me in*, as he put it, on his thoughts and impressions, his plans for the transformation of Japan.

Effectively he saw himself as a proconsul, maintaining order in this far-flung outpost of empire, a country of close on a hundred million people who differ from their conquerors in language, customs, attitude.

We have to clean up and use the existing government machinery as a tool, he said. That way we save time, manpower and resources. We require the Japanese to do their own house-cleaning, but we provide the specifications.

Eminently sensible, I said.

They have to make the transition from a centuries-old feudal system to full-blown democracy.

Perhaps emboldened by the coffee, I managed, briefly, to interrupt his flow and point out that such a transition would be difficult, might not be entirely welcome, and would certainly not happen overnight.

Exactly! he said, jabbing the air. And that is where people like you come into the picture. (People like me!)

Now, he said. Tell me about their religion.

A long thing is the long body of the Buddha. A short thing is the short body of the Buddha.

Walking is Zen, sitting is Zen – talking or silent, moving / unmoving.

When you are hungry, eat. When you are tired, sleep. When walking, walk. When sitting, sit.

Your everyday mind is the way.

Tell me about their religion.

Have you read the works of your countryman Thoreau? I asked. Or Emerson?

I may have done, in my West Point days, he said. But now I don't have much time for philosophy, or poetry.

I recalled the puffed-up rhetoric of his famous declaration on leaving the Philippines. *I shall return.*

What about Whitman? I ventured, thinking he might appreciate the swagger, the bravado. *Do I contradict myself? Very well, then I contradict myself. I am large, I contain multitudes...*

The General narrowed his eyes, fixed them on me. Flint.

I understand the man indulged in certain...*questionable*...practices, he said.

I sing the body electric...

Nevertheless, I said.

Tell me about their religion.

Consider the lives of birds and fishes. Fish never weary of the water. But you do not know the true mind of a fish, for you are not a fish. Birds never tire of the woods. But you do not know the true spirit of a bird, for you are not a bird. It is the same with the religious, the poetical life. If you do not live it, you know nothing about it.

That was from my *Zen in English Literature*. I could quote the passage by heart, and still can. But I decided against reciting it to the General. He would not have understood. I imagined he might have had me forcibly removed from his office as a kind of madman who had gone native.

In the world in which he lived and moved and had his being, the General was a good man, an honourable man. (Are they not all honourable men?) But he was first and foremost a soldier, a warrior, and that was both his strength and his limitation.

Tell me about their religion.

The General had done some cursory reading into Shinto and Zen. But his interest was pragmatic, political, rather than spiritual.

You know it has been suggested at the highest levels in Washington, he said, that the Emperor should abandon his Shinto faith.

At the same highest levels, I said, where it was proposed the Emperor be tried as a war criminal and publicly hanged.

I was determined, he said, it would never come to that.

I had read reports of the General accepting the Emperor's surrender
on board the USS Missouri, and by all accounts he had conducted
the ceremony with dignity, choosing his words with care and tact.

It is my earnest hope, he had said, and indeed the hope of all man-
kind, that from this solemn occasion a better world shall emerge out
of the blood and carnage of the past, a world founded upon faith
and understanding.

Again it was rhetoric, pure and simple, but entirely appropriate for
the occasion. Sufficient unto the day.

I commended him on the tone of the speech.

I was adamant, he said, there should be no sense of gloating, or
baiting a beaten enemy.

Indeed, I said.

And yet I knew he had insisted on a particular photograph being
issued to the press and printed on the front page of every newspaper.
It showed the Emperor, who was not much above five feet tall, and
next to him the General, towering, drawing himself up to his full
six feet four.

No gloating. No baiting.

When I mentioned the photograph, the General allowed himself
a wry smile.

Hell, yeah, he said. Sometimes you have to make a point. And
you know what they say, a picture's worth a thousand words. Was
the same when the Imperial delegation came here. I made sure
the guard of honour was made up of soldiers who were six-five
and over.

This time he chuckled.

Hell, yeah.

The invasion of Japan had been codenamed *Operation Downfall*.

You know, he said, I intervened forcefully to head off those elements
in Washington who still felt the Emperor should be indicted for war
crimes.

I had gathered as much, I said. And I am grateful.

It would have caused a tremendous convulsion among the Japanese
people, he said. The repercussions would be unthinkable. Destroy
the Emperor and the nation would disintegrate. To contain the

situation we would need a million troops deployed here for God knows how many years.

Might I suggest, respectfully, I said, that allowing the Emperor to retain his Shinto faith would also ease the situation.

Agreed, said the General.

However, said the General, I understand the Emperor is still a living god to his people. And let's face it, ruling through a living god is going to make my job a hell of a lot easier.

Indeed.

The line taken by MacArthur was that Tojo and his generals were militarist extremists who had hijacked Japan from 1931 on. The Emperor was a pro-Western moderate, a reformer who had been powerless to stop the military juggernaut.

I said I was sure that version of events would be effective and well received.

A long thing is the long body of the Buddha. A short thing is the short body of the Buddha.

Over the next few days, when I thought over my meeting with the general, there was one thing that troubled me, a little piece of grit in the memory, an irritant. As I was making to leave, he mentioned again the usefulness of the Emperor being perceived by his subjects as a living god. Then he paused as if pondering, looked at me hard, said, However......

His fear, I understood, was that those same factions in the US that had called for the Emperor's removal and even for his execution might need to be further placated by some diplomatic gesture on the Emperor's part, a declaration perhaps, a written statement.

Disavowing his own divinity? I asked.

Something like that.

To which he never laid claim in the first place?

I guess we want it both ways! he said, and laughed.

The idea took hold of me, and with it came a certainty that this course of action was the right one. I raised the matter next time I spoke to Yamanashi and he took it very seriously indeed. In fact he said he would bring it up that very week at a meeting with Ishiwata-san, Minister for the Imperial Household.

A few days later I attended the Palace for my weekly session with the Crown Prince, and as I was leaving I was surprised to see Yamanashi waiting for me in the entrance hall.

Please, he said, guiding me into a little anteroom where I was even more surprised to find Ishiwata seated. His face was a mask, like something from Noh drama, blank and impassive.

There were the usual deferential politenesses, but more quickly than usual they got down to business.

As it happened, they too had been discussing just such an initiative on the part of the Emperor, and my suggestion chimed perfectly with their own thinking. It had been put to the Emperor – subtly and deferentially – that a formal statement would be well received in the wider world beyond Japanese shores.

I suggested that like the Jewel Box speech, ending the war, this message too should be transmitted as a radio broadcast.

That too has been discussed, said Yamanashi. It will be called *Ningen Sengen*. The Imperial Declaration of Humanity.

I nodded. That seems well chosen. It has a ring to it.

Yamanashi continued. You are good friends with Mr Henderson at SCAP?

We share a love of haiku, I said.

And I have been telling Minister Ishiwata of the good work you have been doing together on behalf of the School.

The Minister gave a slight nod.

It has been suggested, continued Yamanashi, that you and Mr Henderson also work on a draft of the declaration, in English.

It would be an honour, I said, with a little sideways nod to Ishiwata. I understood the delicacy of the situation. It was important that the initiative for the declaration should be seen as coming from the Emperor, but also that it met with the full approval of the Americans.

This is where you come in, said Yamanashi. Hakuin says the sound of one hand is difficult to hear.

He held up his right hand.

In this case we need both hands.

He held up his left hand, brought his palms together in a loud clap.

Which hand made the sound?

He laughed. You are man-in-the-middle, can bring both sides to-gether.

He clapped again.

Ha!

Mindful of the Japanese love of formality and their rambling circu-itousness of discourse, I was reluctant initially to be too bold in my suggestions. But it was clear we were in agreement – we had to come up with a form of words that could be open to interpretation, that would keep both sides happy, as it were. In relation to the Emperor's supposed divinity (which of course he had never claimed in the first place), this should be seen as fulfilling a symbolic, a ceremonial function. Might it be viewed as a kind of metaphor, a myth in the broadest sense of the term?

Of course the Minister flinched at the word *myth*, and I had to side-step, ramble about mythos and logos, the very structures by which we understand our humanity, our place in the universe, our sense of hierarchy. I spoke of *Nama Rupa* – name and form. (I actually heard myself saying this!)

He began to glaze over.

Yamanashi intervened, said it was a matter of framing the Emper-or's declaration in a way that allowed him to retain his dignity in the eyes of his own people, but which would also placate the Americans and reassure them that his position was not a threat to them.

Ishiwata made one of those little sideways movements of the head with which I had become so familiar. noncommittal, prevarication in the smallest gesture.

Anno...

He sat in silence for a few moments as if in deep contemplation, fin-gertips pressed together in front of him. Then he gave a low guttural grunt that came from deep in his gut, and he stood up.

So...

He bowed, a stiff nod of the head, thanked me most courteously and said the Admiral would be in touch with me soon about how to proceed.

Later Yamanashi took me aside and explained that the Minister was absolutely ferocious about the need for tact and secrecy. I had heard of the bloody events surrounding the Emperor's Jewel Box broadcast, the rebel army officers who had tried to prevent it going ahead. What I hadn't realised was Ishiwata had been caught up in the chaos and had only narrowly escaped with his life.

The uprising had become known as the Kyujo Incident and had been nothing less than an attempted coup, a refusal to surrender. If it came to it, the rebels would prefer the honourable death of the hundred million.

Led by two disaffected officers, Hatanaka and Shiizaki, they had invaded the Imperial palace trying to find the recording of the Emperor's speech. Ishiwata had concealed it and had it smuggled out (as myth had it, in that laundry basket full of underwear). He himself had hidden in a dank cellar, a vault beneath the palace while the rebels searched for him, intending to disembowel him. All the telephone lines were cut and the whole place was in darkness due to a black-out in anticipation of an air raid. The rebel leaders, realising the tape had gone, hurried to the broadcasting studios of NHK, hoping to stop the transmission. When that failed, the two ringleaders left and headed across town, Hatanaka on a motorcycle, Shiizaki on horseback, throwing off leaflets as they went.

As the Emperor's speech was broadcast, both men shot themselves, each with a bullet to the head.

Good God, I said to Yamanashi. A real blood-and-thunder story.

I think they saw themselves like the Forty-Seven Ronin.

I'm sure.

And at least you can understand why Minister Ishiwata takes this whole matter so seriously.

I can only imagine, I said.

I pictured him, cut off in the cellar, a dungeon, in complete darkness – a descent into the abyss – not knowing when it was safe to move, or what carnage to expect when he finally did emerge.

And at least I understood the Minister's intensity, his inwardness, that Noh-mask of a face.
So.

Word came through very quickly, just a few days after our meeting at the school. The intention was that the Emperor's declaration be broadcast on New Year's Day. It was already the first week of December so the whole thing was a matter of some urgency.
I was picked up as usual in the official staff car and taken to SCAP headquarters where I went directly to Henderson's office.
Henderson was surprised at my announcing we had important work to do, and as he said later, slightly alarmed at my 'state of high excitement.' I told him our work on Gakushuin would have to wait. We had been asked to prepare – *immediately* – a draft of the Emperor's forthcoming Declaration, for transmission on January 1st. Henderson's reaction was akin to panic, and he retreated behind protocol, saying he could do nothing in the meantime as his immediate superior, General Dyke, was away for a few days. The matter would have to wait.
As patiently as I could, I explained that we didn't *have* a few days, and that the very future of Japan might depend on our getting it just right. My rhetoric had an affect, and he started jotting down notes as I outlined what was required.
I thought there should be a preamble to the message, making a virtue of the fact that it was being broadcast at New Year.
Happy Holidays! said Henderson.
A resolution on behalf of the nation.
Should we introduce a *kigo*, a season-word?
We settled to it, got to work.

The ties between us a matter of trust and affection... not dependent upon myths and legends...not based on the idea of the Emperor's divinity or of the superiority of the Japanese people...

Henderson said the crux of it was right there in that one word, *divinity.*

For the Westerners, I said, that's certainly the case. But for the Japanese not at all. It comes down to a misunderstanding, perhaps a misinterpretation of the word *kami*. Yes it means god, but not with a capital G. It carries the sense of someone or something superior, worthy of respect and even worship. But Shinto is inherently animistic. It might worship a stone or a tree.

Or any one of eight million gods.

Indeed.

And yet as I understand it, said Henderson, Japanese are essentially agnostic. They worship their ancestors, they marry in Shinto ceremonies and take part in Buddhist rites.

And to my mind they're none the worse for it!

So where does that leave us? asked Henderson, looking perplexed.

With a job to do, I said. A koan to be solved.

After two hours we had a draft of the speech written out on his yellow notepaper. I copied it out, word for word, in a notepad of my own and returned his draft to him, telling him to destroy it.

He looked confused, as if he thought I might be joking, or I had become unhinged. But I assured him I was being perfectly serious and that secrecy was essential.

Real cloak and dagger stuff, he said, and in truth there was something faintly ridiculous about it all. But these were the roles we had been assigned, and we had to play them well or not at all.

I sat up all night working and reworking the short statement, wrote several drafts on the same kind of yellow paper that Henderson had used – he had given me sheets of it from his own supply.

Ningen Sengen.

Getting it just right. The best words in the best order.

We met again in the morning, went through it sentence by sentence:

The ties between Us...capitalised, as the royal We... *and Our people*

*have always stood upon mutual trust and affection. They do not depend
upon legends and myths....*

This was a decent beginning. But for the Japanese consciousness,
the Japanese sensibility, there had to be a slight change in emphasis.
I made a suggestion:

*The Ties between Us and Our people do not only depend upon legends and
myths, but also upon mutual trust and affection...*

Henderson liked that. He said it left a door open, gave room for
manoeuvre. I told him the Japanese version would depend on that
slight ambiguity. In a sense we were trying to make one statement
to the Japanese and another to the Americans.

When I use a word, Humpty Dumpty said in rather a scornful tone,
it means just what I choose it to mean, neither more nor less...
The question is, said Alice, whether you can make words mean so
many different things...

Nama Rupa.

Again I had a sleepless night as I stayed awake, fine-tuning my
version of the speech. I presented it to Henderson early the next
morning, after he had solemnly assured me he had burned his own
draft in a metal bin in his office, then poured water over the ashes
and emptied it down a drain.
To make assurance doubly sure, I said.
Indeed.
Henderson was impressed. He said I had come up with a sophisti-
cated way of making a very fine distinction.
Damn it, he said. You're good!

The message was transmitted on Japanese radio. The English ver-
sion was aired on the American Forces Network and the BBC World
Service. Tomiko and I listened, in our new home in Mejiro, on the

Gakushuin campus. New Year's Day 1946. Showa 21.

Even now, almost twenty years later, I can recall the statement, word for word.

It began with what I had suggested, the (very Japanese) reference to the season, the auspicious date, a time of new beginnings.

This is a new year, a new year for Japan, a new world with new ideals, with Humanity above nationality, and the Great Goal, Brotherhood, based upon natural affection, that of the family, that of the nation and that of mankind. In our country, love of the family and love of the nation have always been specially strong. Now let us work towards love of mankind.

There were a few other formalities, then the passage which Henderson and I had delivered.

The ties between us and our people have always stood upon mutual trust and affection. They do not only depend upon mere legends and myths. They are not predicated upon the false conception that the Emperor is divine and that the Japanese people are superior to other races and fated to rule the world.

Translations were broadcast in Russian and French.

Henderson and I had contributed our tuppenceworth, our ten cents worth, our little footnote to the history of the time. We celebrated, moderately, with a drink in a little bar in Shinjuku, in a street that had survived the firebombing.

It takes a kind of resilience, I said, and courage, to reopen for business like this, to carry on.

Like London in the blitz, said Henderson.

Exactly so.

London. Another life. My mother had survived and was well, as was Dora, and after VJ Day, Ma had received a note from Annie, saying she and Lee had made it through, unharmed

I closed my eyes a moment, consciously sent them all goodwill.

Henderson raised his little glass of *sake* – it was all that was on offer in the meantime.

To the Declaration of Humanity, he said.

Humanity, I said, raising my own glass of soda water.

On the wall behind the bar was a framed portrait of the Emperor and a Rising Sun flag. On the counter was a little Daruma doll, like the one that had sustained me during my detention in Kobe.

The barman was looking across at us, face blank. I raised my glass to him.

Nana korobi ya oki... I said.

Seven times down, eight times up.

His look was still uncomprehending, but he gave the slightest nod of the head.

Hai.

Yamanashi and Ishiwata thanked me for my work on the Declaration, and passed on the thanks of the Emperor himself.

I have another of my sheets of lined yellow paper from this time on which I had written – quickly, to judge by the headlong forward slant of the script – notes for Yamanashi, outlining my further thoughts (for what they were worth) on the Emperor's role.

The Emperors of Japan have always been the supporters and the symbol of Japanese culture. But no culture is possible without a world view, a religion. In Japan this has largely been that of Mahayana Buddhism, and the unique contribution of Japan to world culture is the putting into practice, especially in daily life, of the principles of Kegon Philosophy. This is the power of Japan, the origin of its self-respect, and the only foundation for its future influence.

The model of Kegon philosophy was one that I thought would have great appeal, at least in its structure. The Kegon school taught that the Buddha himself was the centre and ground of the universe, and all phenomena emanated from his own being. In ancient times the imperial court had appreciated the imagery of a central power to which all subsidiary things owed their being.

Yamanashi agreed it was a powerful image.

The Emperor, I argued, should be the *spiritual* leader of his people. Without this, his cultural leadership would become mere dilettantism, and have no moral or spiritual power. He should be himself religious and show great interest in all practical religion as socially effective. He should be principally Buddhist in vocabulary and flavour but should welcome all Christian religious experience and thought.

(I said modern Buddhism should assimilate all the good of Christianity without the shortcomings).

No easy task, said Yamanashi.

Take the King of England, I said. (Please!) He is head of the Church, but influences culture very little. The Emperor should be head of the spiritual church of Japan. He should be an international leader in the fields of universal brotherhood, freedom of religion and belief. He should propose a poetical world view, putting beauty before comfort, significance before beauty. He should be leader in the country of Shakespeare, Hakurakuten, Basho, Plotinus, Spinoza, Eckhart, Gandhi, Christ, Buddha...

Yamanashi applauded.

And would the bible of this country, he asked, be *Zen in English Literature and Oriental Classics*?

I laughed.

I shall insist on it being used as a textbook in every school!

At a practical level, I suggested to Yamanashi that the Emperor alone could provide the emotional motive power for the proper distribution of food, to put an end to the black market. He should make a trip round Japan, visit the coal mines and farming districts. He should listen to the people, talk to them, ask them questions. On his return he should make a statement about the hoarding of food. He should stress the importance of making sacrifices now, just as in war time. He should uncork some feeling, pull out the stop marked *vox humana*, and appeal to Japanese to share their supplies for the greater good.

Once again Yamanashi thanked me and he said my suggestion was timely. Plans were already in place for just such an initiative.

It was not long before the Emperor was visiting the devastated areas, making speeches, redefining his public role.

If I am honest – and I hope I always am – I watched with a curious detachment (or detached curiosity) as things took their course. I had played my own small part but found it unsettling, almost surreal, to see the grainy newspaper photographs of the Emperor, uncertain, endeavouring to embrace his newly-declared Humanity, walking with his entourage through blitzed and burned-out cities – Yokohama, Kagoshima. It was particularly poignant to see this small figure in his overcoat and homburg hat, standing on an open-air platform in Hiroshima, addressing a crowd of thousands, all standing to attention, bare heads bowed in reverence.

It all had an air of unreality, or perhaps heightened reality. It was like a scene from a film, as if it had been stage-managed, which of course it had. Reality framed to make it more real, and paradoxically, rendered more true for being filmed in black-and-white. An artifice then, but as I looked on I felt a certainty that this process was essential. In the interest of the greater good, the good of the nation, this was how it had to be.

The Buddha spoke of *expedient means*.

Whatever it took.

I was sitting one evening at the US staff club with Henderson. I was giving him a report on Gakushuin and how it was faring in its move towards democratisation, egalitarianism. We were both eager to move on to discussing haiku, and in particular our differences of approach to these little jewels of verse. (For what it's worth, I see haiku as direct experience, a way of living – not a substitute for Christianity or Buddhism, but their fulfilment. Henderson's approach, I suppose, has always been more literary, less existential, and he stresses the importance of imagination in composing the verse).

I shall return to this later, leaving it for the moment as Henderson and I were forced to do when we were joined by a journalist by the name of Roberts, recently arrived from the US. He was an acquaintance of Henderson's and said he had heard my name and was happy to meet me. However he then proceeded to tell us about his own experience of observing the Emperor at first hand on one of his majesty's walkabout tours, meeting-the-people, the very process of 'humanisation.'

He said he and his companions referred to the Emperor as Charlie (after Chaplin) and it seemed they were determined to see him as a figure of fun. He mentioned the Emperor's ill-fitting Western-style suit, the awkward way he walked.

And you wouldn't believe how uncomfortable the guy is, said Roberts. He doesn't know what to do with his hands. And he doesn't know how to talk to people. It was like he asked everybody the same question – Where are you from? And whatever the answer, he would say, *Ah so*. As if it was truly amazing that somebody came from Gifu, or Kanagawa, or wherever. And that was it. That was all he had to say. *Ah so*. Getting more and more high-pitched. It got so our guys were waiting for it, and when they heard it they nudged each other and copied the sound and tried not to crack up!

I was finding this Roberts irritating in the extreme. His manner was straining my patience to the limit. When he started mimicking the Emperor again I could take no more and I interrupted him.

Mr Roberts, I said. Where are you from?

He looked confused. Pittsburgh, he said.

Ah, so, I said, then I stood up and bowed, nodded to Henderson and took my leave.

Later I apologised to Henderson for my rudeness, but I said I couldn't help myself.

On the basis of being in Japan for all of five minutes, I said, this fellow shows nothing but scorn for all the efforts being made here.

I know, said Henderson. The man's a boor. But for what it's worth, I don't think he took offence. In fact he was quite amused and rather admired your gumption. He thought your exit was 'very Zen.'

Again, I said, based on his vast knowledge of the subject. But in spite of myself I laughed. Buraisu-san the Zen Master!

Ah so, said Henderson.

Henderson and I did eventually get back to our discussion of haiku. The here and now is all, I said (rather pretentiously). The poem has to catch that *lived* moment of insight, that seeing-into-the-life-of-things.

Henderson argued that imagination was all important. Surely, he said, the poet is primarily a maker of imagined scenes.

The danger there, I said, is that it leads the poet further into a world of illusion and make-believe instead of rooting him...

Or her!

Or her, I continued ...in the real world, this world, the here-and-now.

So, he said, narrowing his eyes. Are you saying subjectivity has no place in writing haiku?

Consider Basho, I said. Surely he is at his greatest when his subject matter seems most insignificant – the neck of a firefly, the sound of hailstones, the chirping of a cricket, a dead leaf.

Not to mention a frog jumping into an old pond.

Indeed, I said. So I won't mention it. Except to say it has absolutely nothing to do with symbolism or metaphor or embodying-the-infinite. The meaning is the thing itself, clear, direct, unmistakable. It's like plunging the hand suddenly into boiling water, or for that matter freezing water. It's the shock of what's real.

I rather liked that. The shock of what's real.

I enjoyed these exchanges with Henderson, which is why they are vivid in the memory and I can recreate them at will. On occasion we were joined by the flamboyant Faubion Bowers, still assigned to MacArthur's office, still in love with Kabuki and Noh. He had tried his own hand at translating haiku and spoke of compiling an anthology, but he deferred to both Henderson and me, bowing (with a theatrical flourish) to our wisdom and experience. He did, however, enjoy setting us against each other as we agreed to differ.

Issa or Buson? he asked.

Gritty existentialism or artistic refinement.

Neither, I said. Both. Neither *and* both. Neither one is better. Both are absolutely the best.

But Buson wrote poems that were purely imaginary, said Bowers. The one about stepping on his dead wife's comb.
I knew the poem he meant. I had made my own translation of it.

In the bedroom, I trod
On my dead wife's comb:
The cold penetrated my heart.

The very one, said Bowers. And I understand he wrote it many years before his wife actually died.
Exactly, I said. It's like something by Poe. And I mean that disparagingly. It seems to me everything a haiku should *not* be. Haiku has nothing to do with bedrooms or dead wives or treading on this or that imaginary object conjured up for its emotional associations. This particular poem is artificial and sentimental and manipulative.
And other than that, said Bowers, I guess it's not too bad.
Why did you translate it? asked Henderson.
Sheer contrariness, I said, and they both laughed.

Once, when on my couch I lay, in vacant and didactic mood, I drew up a list of what I considered the characteristics of Zen in relation to the writing of haiku.
Selflessness. Loneliness. Grateful acceptance. Wordlessness. Non-intellectuality. Contradictoriness. Humour. Freedom. Non-morality. Simplicity. Materiality. Love. Courage.
It's a mighty impressive set of attributes, and if I felt I had achieved any of them (in the sense of *realising* them, integrating them into my very being) I might feel entitled to be rather pleased with myself. But that's the difficult part, that integration. It's what Hakuin grappled with for the greater part of his life.

I can truly say I love haiku. Haiku show us what we knew all the time but did not know we knew. So much in so little. *Multum in parvo*. Infinite riches in a little room. A good haiku catches an inherent humour, a sudden realization that life is fundamentally contradictory. This is not the too-obvious humour, the punning and witticism from which haiku grew. Instead it is a momentary leap out of the relative into the absolute and back again, an intense perception of the true nature of things.

The first haiku I wrote (God help me!) was in Japanese.
Hagakure ni aoi yume miru katatsumuri.

I made my own translation.

> *Behind a leaf,*
> *Dreaming its blue dream —*
> *The snail*

A small thing, but mine own.

The thing about haiku, the thing about Zen, is an essential simplicity. The sun shines, snow falls, mountains rise and valleys sink, night deepens and pales into day, but it is only very seldom we attend to such things:

This is by Kito.

In the shop,
The paper-weights on the picture books;
The spring wind!

Yes.

Just so.

10

THE MUSIC OF WHAT HAPPENS

I had often thought of my old friend and colleague Dr. Shinki. I had not heard from him since our parting outside Keijo station when the boys sang *Hotaru no Hikari*. Light of the Fireflies.

I had kept Shinki's painting of Autumn on the Han River – it had survived the bombing of Kobe and hung on the wall in our living room, a reminder. On one particular day I found myself thinking of him most powerfully, remembering his face, seeing it, vivid and clear. As if I had invoked him, I received that very day a letter from my publishers, Hokuseido. I tore open the envelope, and inside was another with a Fukuoka postmark, Shinki's name and home address in the top corner in his characteristic neat, spare calligraphy.

The letter explained that he had only recently returned from Korea to Fukuoka, his home town. He had come across a copy of my *Zen in English Literature* and written to me care of the publishers who had passed it on.

With some measure of excitement, I wrote back to him immediately, gave him my own address and said if he could manage a visit to Tokyo he must come and see us. In fact, I added, the sooner the better.

Four days later, in the early evening, I was sitting at home reading when there was a quiet knock at the door. Tomiko was busy in the kitchen, little Harumi in her own world, playing, so I opened the door myself, saw a middle-aged Japanese man standing there in an old brown suit, a small knapsack at his feet, a soft fedora hat in his hands.

I did not at first recognise him, was about to say, Yes, can I help you? Then he smiled and spoke.

Blyth-san.

The unmistakeable articulation, almost pronouncing it just-right.

His face came into focus. I recognised the younger man he had been.

Shinki-san! I said. My friend!

Neither of us was inclined to give the other a hug – we settled for a firm handshake, a manly pat on the shoulder. But our joy at seeing each other was profound.

Wordsworth and Coleridge, he said, and I laughed, picked up his knapsack and brought him inside.

Shinki stayed with us for a week – I insisted upon it and Tomiko made him welcome, set another place at mealtimes. He slept on a spare futon we laid out in the living room, rolled up and put away every morning. He kept saying it was too much, he did not want to impose, but we were having none of it.

At first Harumi was a little shy of him, hid behind her mother, peeking out. Then he saw one of her drawings – a bear or a cat – pinned to the wall, and he told her how good it was. He asked if he could have a piece of paper and borrow a pencil, and in no time at all, with just a few strokes, he made a sketch of her, handed it to her with a show of formality, saw her eyes grow wide with delight.

It had not been easy for Shinki to come home after the war. But he had felt less and less comfortable in Korea, where anti-Japanese feeling was strong. Eventually he had packed up and made his way on a cargo ship to Fukuoka where he was trying to find work. He told me a sad story – in those days they were many – about the fate of Hanayama Roshi, the Abbot at Myoshin-ji in Seoul. After the war he was to be appointed to the prestigious Nanzen-Ji temple in Kyoto. He had been travelling to Japan when his ship hit a mine and sank. Everyone on board, including the Roshi, had been drowned. We sat in silence, offering a prayer.

I took Shinki to meet Admiral Yamanashi who was in his shirt-sleeves, tending a vegetable patch in the little garden behind his house. I introduced Shinki and the Admiral greeted him with great warmth and kindness, said it must have been a real upheaval to repatriate. I said Shinki-san was looking for work and Yamanashi said he hoped he would be successful.

I also took Shinki to Kamakura to visit Suzuki. We sat on cushions on the verandah looking out over Engaku-ji, Suzuki chatting, sharing his wisdom in that relaxed way of his, Shinki in awe at being in the presence of the great man. He told me afterwards that being with Suzuki was like sitting in front of a vast serene ocean.

Within a week or two, after he had returned to Fukuoka, Shinki received the offer of a job at the Fourth Kanazawa High School. He had been hoping for something closer to Tokyo, and miraculously, another post became available at Seijo High School, not so far away in Kanagawa Prefecture. When he had been teaching there for a few months, Yamanashi told me they thought it might be a good idea to appoint a Japanese teacher of English Literature to work alongside me at Gakushuin. I told Shinki who applied and got the job. Once again we were colleagues.

By way of thanks, Shinki gave me another of his paintings, *Snowy Mountains,* which I hung beside his *Autumn on the Han River.* I further returned good for good by gifting him a bag of rice from a supply I had received from Henderson courtesy of the GHQ canteen. Such commodities were scarce and would cost a great deal on the black market.

Worth its weight in gold, I said.

Words cannot express, he said, and he bowed, quite overcome with gratitude.

It was Henderson who alerted me. There had been a suggestion that the Crown Prince might benefit from the appointment of an American tutor.

Of course, he said, that would be *in addition* to your good self, not *instead.*

Of course, I said.

Enrich his experience even more.

Yes, I said.

Widen his understanding of democracy.

The American Way of Life.

Not to put too fine a point on it.

We wouldn't want to do that now, would we?

We were in Henderson's office at SCAP headquarters.

It's another...*delicate*...business, he said. It seems the Emperor is quite keen and has in fact given his approval.

I see.

But it's rather like the situation with the Declaration of Humanity. We wouldn't want anyone to think SCAP was interfering or applying undue pressure.

Exactly.

I said I was surprised I had heard nothing about this from Admiral Yamanashi.

Henderson said it was all still *hush hush*, on a *need-to-know* basis.

Still, I said. I'd have thought...

Quite.

We both fell silent, then he continued.

There have been some proposed guidelines. The candidate should not be an old Japan hand but someone fresh to the country and with no knowledge of the language or culture.

No preconceptions.

Precisely. Middle-aged. Christian but not fanatically so.

No indoctrination.

Right.

Might I make one suggestion?

Please do.

Perhaps this new American tutor should be a woman.

It seemed this *need-to-know* restriction had even excluded Yamanashi. He was taken aback, resolved to find out what he could. Yes, he said, getting back to me after a week. It is so. Plans are being made. And your idea to appoint a woman has been welcomed.

Good, I said. Then might I make another recommendation?

Please.

If this tutor is to be Christian, that may cause difficulty. Catholic and Protestant can be equally evengelical, hell-bent, as it were, on saving mankind. The urge to convert may be strong.

Heaven forbid!

Indeed, I said. So it may be advisable to seek someone from, say, a Quaker background.

The appropriate wheels were set in motion, advice was sought, a shortlist drawn up. At my behest (and on the basis of my immense wisdom) a choice was made. The lady in question was invited and she accepted, crossed the ocean on a former troopship, the *Marine Falcon*.

Mrs Vining.

Mrs Elizabeth Gray Vining.

Mrs Vining was a very impressive young woman, tall and imposing, dignified in her bearing but with a lightness about her, an easy grace. More than that, I sensed in her a true inwardness, a stillness and strength. As a Quaker she would not be unaccustomed to silence. But there was nothing severe or rigid about her. On the contrary, her eyes sparkled with what I recognised as that rarest of qualities, a sense of humour.

The day before she was due to meet the Imperial family for the first time, I prepared her for her introductory exchange with the young Crown Prince.

I explained that the Prince would say to her, Thank you for coming so far to teach me.

She looked slightly quizzical.

And how do you know he will say this? she asked.

I replied, It is what I have instructed him to say. And you should respond, Thank *you* for welcoming me so kindly.

I see, she said, and there was that twinkle in the eye. It is more artificial and formal than I had intended. But I promise I shall try to remember my line in this little dialogue.

By chance, if there be such a thing, I bumped into her a few hours after her formal introduction to the Royal household, and I asked her how she had fared.

Very well, she said, although I had to abandon the prepared script.

Indeed?

I'd had the foresight, or presumption, to send in advance a small gift for the Crown Prince – a few chocolate bars I had brought with me from Philadelphia.

He has a sweet tooth, I said.

Like most twelve-year olds! And before I could say one word, he beamed at me and said, Thank you for the candy!

I laughed. A good beginning then!

Yamanashi – now very much in the know – told me that Mrs Vining was a widow and that her husband had been killed in an automobile accident.

Very strong character, said the Admiral. Strong faith. And I sensed that some of his initial misgivings had been laid to rest.

I also discovered that Mrs Vining had written a number of books, including novels for children, and she was kind enough to give me a copy of her most recent volume, *Adam of the Road*, a historical yarn about a young minstrel boy.

In return I gave her my *Zen in English Literature* and told her she was under no obligation to read it. But she persisted, persevered, said it was wonderful that I had written on English literature for the Japanese and Japanese poetry for the Westerner.

In a nutshell, I said, thanking her.

Since the day of her arrival, Mrs Vining had been besieged by the press. An American, and a woman at that, being appointed to teach the Crown Prince, was deemed newsworthy in the extreme. To her surprise she found many of the American journalists intrusive in their questioning to the point of rudeness.

She asked if I, in my time, had endured similar treatment.

I said this boring old Englishman was not of much interest to them and they left me alone.

Yamanashi, ever the gentleman, ever the diplomat, said, Mister Blyth has been among us so long he is more Japanese than English!

I took that then, as I take it still, as a great compliment.

It had been agreed that Mrs Vining would observe one of my private sessions with the Crown Prince, and she accompanied me to the little classroom. We were led into the room by the Chancellor, Mrs Matsudaira. The Prince stood and bowed to her, then he stepped forward and shook hands, first with me, then with Mrs Vining. I noticed he gave the American woman his most charming smile, perhaps in anticipation of more chocolate. If he was disappointed that none was forthcoming, he did not let it show. On the contrary, he sat up straight in his hard-backed chair and was the very model of attentiveness.

His answers to questions were as clear and precise as always. But as the lesson progressed, I noticed him glance across at Mrs Vining, as if expecting her to speak. She responded by smiling encouragement at him.

Eventually he began to manifest the faint signs of boredom I had come to recognise, a slight restlessness, a quick look down at his watch while pretending to straighten his cuff.

It did occur to me that if I were a 12-year-old boy being drilled by a middle-aged *gaijin* in a language not his own, I might well be aching to run from the room and out to the playing fields.

I am walking to the door, he repeated after me, dutifully. *I am opening the door. I am closing the door. Now I am sitting down....*

Perhaps I should vary it. *I am opening the door again. I am making a break for it. I am running as fast as my legs will carry me, out into the wide world...*

That might well make him laugh, as he did now and then if I said something that amused him. That mask of politeness and reserve would drop and his face light up with a momentary delight, a puckishness as brief as it was unexpected.

Poor little fellow, said Mrs Vining. Such a weight of expectation on his young shoulders.

Indeed, I said. It is unimaginable.

His little hand was cold, she said. I felt it when he shook mine.

I found myself strangely moved by her observation, and in that moment I knew it had been the right choice to appoint a woman, this woman, as the Prince's tutor.

His little hand.

Che gelida manina.

Mrs Vining made me laugh out loud when she told me of a ploy she had used in teaching the Crown Prince with his classmates at Gakushuin. She learned all the boys' names (not an easy task for someone to whom the Japanese names were unfamiliar and perhaps repetitive). Then one day she announced that she was giving them new names – English names – which they would use within the confines of the classroom. Here we speak English, she said, so you should have English names. She told the first boy his name was Adam. He repeated it, tentative, uncertain. The next boy's name would be Bill. On she continued, the boys increasingly amused, trying out their new names for size. Finally she came to the Crown Prince.

So, she said. You are Jimmy.

She said the other boys held their breath, not sure what would come next.

No, he said. I am Prince.

She wasn't sure if he was refusing to join in the game, or didn't quite understand, thinking perhaps she didn't recognise him amongst his classmates. (Did she even think all-Japanese-boys-looked-the-same?)

She explained again (acknowledging she most certainly knew who he was). She made it clearer, the names were only for here in the room, to help them feel English (or American), to help them learn. He looked very serious, taking it in. He said, Jimmy.

Yes, she said.

He nodded. Jimmy!

He laughed, and so did the rest of the boys.

After that, she said, it was the best lesson she had taught. The game seemed to allow them to relax, feel more at ease.

Democratisation at a stroke, I said. Supreme Command Allied Powers should put you in charge of their operations!

Was it my imagination, or did she tense a little at that, and was there the slightest flush to her cheek?

Certainly here were those who thought while she might not actually be in the pay of SCAP, she was at least working in their best interests, not so much toward democratisation as Americanisation. My own sense of it was that she herself was true and worked in good faith, and she certainly had no idea of my own involvement in her appointment.

Over time, the Crown Prince's English improved dramatically (as much through Mrs Vining's input as my own). I saw in the boy a genuine warmth and humanity struggling to come to the fore, and he saw that I was not, perhaps, as stern and patriarchal as he might first have feared.

It took us by surprise, though I'm not sure why. It was five years since Harumi had been born and I suppose I had thought that was that. But we had not, as they say, been taking precautions. Tomiko, of course, recognised the signs. She was once more with child. There had been talk worldwide of what they called a baby boom after the war, a reaction, a surge of new life. Now we had our own boom-baby, a little sister for Harumi, born in Seibo Byoin in Shinjuku. This was an international Catholic hospital – a fact that seemed as appropriate as it was unlikely. I recall sitting, standing, pacing the hospital corridor, yet again conscious of my uselessness in the face of events. But at least I had managed to leave Harumi with our next door neighbour, Mrs Nabeshima, and cycle to the hospital where I sat, stood, paced, sat, stood, paced. I had not slept well the night before and once or twice when I closed my eyes I drifted off to sleep, woke startled to see a nun glide past, surreal in black and white. Or I found myself staring without comprehension at a framed Sacred Heart, the image lurid and sentimental yet somehow reassuring. It offered solace, compassion. *Come unto me...*
Mr Blyth.
The voice that woke me was soft, Irish. A young Sister, her eyes kind.
Would you like to come and see your wee girl?
So I did, I went and saw her, my wee girl, red-faced, eyes shut tight against the brightness, little being wrapped around herself. My sec-

ond daughter, new arrival in this harsh world.

What was her original face, before she was born? A sleep and a forgetting?

Tomiko was exhausted but deeply at peace. She said we should call her Nana. It meant seven. She was born on the seventh of July, 7/7. So.

I laughed, loving it, the repetition, the music.

Nana.

Nanako, said Tomiko.

Little Nana. Our wee girl.

Was it Nana's birth that spurred me on to even greater effort in my writing?

My *Zen in English Literature* had been well received.

Mister Aldous Huxley, no less, had given it a favourable review in The Times.

The book deals with the relation between moment-by-moment experience of things-as-they-are and poetry. It is a bit perverse sometimes, but very illuminating at others.

I would settle for that as an acknowledgement and a fair description (perhaps even an epitaph?) A bit perverse sometimes, very illuminating at others.

We does our best.

The first of my four volumes of Haiku translations was ready for publication, and the other three were in preparation. Volume One was subtitled Eastern Culture. (I decided to let that pass – my publishers, Hokuseido had been extremely kind and generous in their dealings with me). The other volumes would be titled, more simply, according to the seasons: *Spring, Summer-Autumn* and *Autumn-Winter*. (I found that altogether more pleasing).

I asked my friend Shinki to do the calligraphy for the covers and he did excellent work. (His non-ego would not quite allow him to bask in satisfaction, but I could see he was pleased with it, a job well done).

As for the content, it was the mixture as before, my translations interspersed with notes, comments, asides, exegeses, non-sequiturs.

There are those who say my explanations are better than the original poems. Others say they add nothing and should be omitted. I myself agree one hundred percent with both views.

Once again, in moments of stillness, I realised how lucky I was, how grateful for the life I had been given. If I had stayed at home in little England with its rigid hierarchies, its class divisions, its snobbery, where would I be? My books unpublished, unread (perhaps unwritten). I might be an assistant professor at some provincial university, supervising graduation theses on, say, the colours of the beards of Shakespeare's clowns.

No, I chose the right path (or it chose me).

Through those immediate post-war years I made regular visits – I would still call them pilgrimages – to Suzuki's home in Kamakura. I always went with a head full of endless questions, on some obscure aspect of Zen doctrine, on the exact translation of some Japanese word I found confusing or ambiguous. He was never less than gracious, answering me at length and with infinite patience. One particular week, however, he sent a message to apologise for cancelling our appointment. He said he hoped I might come the following week as usual. I assumed, therefore, that there was not a problem with his health, but rather that his self-imposed workload, his intensely busy schedule, had simply not left time for our meeting. When I turned up the next week, he welcomed me as he always did with great warmth and we sat drinking tea, looking out over his garden, watching the spring rain fall. We sat in comfortable silence, then he told me why he had, regretfully, had to cancel our session the week before.

He had indeed been busy, but in a rather unusual capacity. He had received a visitor who had interviewed him at length about Japanese philosophy, and in particular its effect on what he called the nation's ethical code. But the visitor, Suzuki explained, was not some academic, studying these things in the abstract. He was in fact a Dutch judge by the name of Roling, currently presiding in the on-going war crimes tribunal taking place in Tokyo.

It was quite extraordinary, said Suzuki. The man wanted to speak to me because he was trying to understand what he called the Japanese mind.

No easy task! I said.

Quite.

I said I had actually heard of the man. To my surprise, Mrs Vining had taken a great interest in the trial, to the extent of attending one of the sessions – whether simply to keep herself informed, or observe history-in-the-making, or as a semi-official observer, I couldn't quite ascertain. But she had certainly mentioned Judge Roling, and the Indian Radha Binod Pal, both of whom had impressed her. (She had, I recalled, been particularly taken with Mr Pal, describing him as tall, fine-looking and dark-skinned).

She said there had been much discussion over the fact that no Japanese voices were being heard. It was very much a case of the victors trying the vanquished.

It was ever thus, I said. History is always the story told by the conquerors.

Suzuki said Judge Roling was very aware of this potential iniquity, and Mr Pal, perhaps because he was the only Asian taking part, was an even stronger dissenting voice.

I understand Judge Pal is a pacifist, I said, anti-war and anti-colonialist. Asia for the Asians.

I believe so, said Suzuki. But can a pacifist defend the war as a just one?

And can he be anti-colonial *and* anti-war, if the war itself is seen as anti-colonial?

I think for him this must be a kind of koan.

And for Judge Roling?

He seems to feel great respect for some of the defendants, especially Shimada Shigetaro.

Shimada, I knew, had been an Admiral in the Imperial Navy. Unlike our friend Yamanashi, he had not voiced opposition to the war, taking instead the anti-colonial line, the avowed aim being to put an end to American domination. Japan's own colonial ambitions, on the other hand, he thought entirely justified.

Nevertheless, Shimada's bearing and dignified presence had made an impression on Judge Roling who described him to Suzuki as a good man, fired by patriotism and working in the service of a higher cause.

This is the paradox the judge is trying to resolve, said Suzuki. He was even more impressed when I told him Shimada-san writes poetry.

Perhaps if he had written better poetry....

I am not sure if Mr Roling will ever quite understand, said Suzuki. But he has come to like the Japanese and to see that our philosophy might have much to teach the West.

And yet...

And yet.

There is a rumour that the Russians want everyone punished, as an example.

Pour decourager les autres.

Exactly. They want a purge, and I fear if they had their way, they would try the Emperor himself.

I recalled those photographs I had seen of the Romanov family, the dreams that had so disturbed me.

But that will not happen, said Suzuki, his voice firm, certain.

No, I said.

Outside, the spring rain continued to fall. We sat in silence, then Suzuki poured me more tea.

So, he said.

So.

It was around this time I finally met Mr Christmas Humphreys, to whom I owed an inordinate debt of gratitude for making Suzuki's writings available in English. Bizarrely, Mr Humphreys was a High Court judge and was in Tokyo to participate in the same war crimes tribunal which so interested Mrs Vining.

I found it extraordinary (or shall we say paradoxical?) that a practising Buddhist, committed to respecting all sentient beings, could be in a position where he might have to sentence a man to death.

We actually met – stranger and stranger still – at a display of excessive pomp to mark British Empire Day. Mr Humphreys and I were seated together at a parade ground opposite the Imperial Palace. A Message-From-The-King was read out then a military band swung into view followed by a detachment of the Navy, marching with colours flying and swords drawn.

Personally I was rather uncomfortable with the whole spectacle, but Humphreys was quite taken with it all. In fact he seemed deeply moved and looked almost tearful.

Damn fine, he said. Brings a lump to the throat, eh? Makes one come over all gulpy.

He also insisted on referring to the young Englishwoman accompanying him as his fanny, by which (as I later discovered) he meant FANY, a member of the First Aid Nursing Yeomanry.

Yet this was the same man who sat with me a few days later at Dr Suzuki's home, discussing the finer points of Mahayana Buddhism and the distinctions between Zen and Pure Land. Suzuki told him of my *Zen in English Literature*, which he promised to read, and about my planned four volumes of haiku translations.

A Herculean task, he said. I wish you well, but I fear it can't be done. The little blighters just defy translation.

He said he had tried his hand at it himself, not from the Japanese, but from rough versions in English which he'd tried to render into verse.

Entirely without success, he said. Couldn't make head nor tail.

It's a challenge, I said. But I shall do my best.

Bon Voyage, he said, saluting, and he laughed.

I couldn't help myself. I asked how he would face the dilemma I had imagined, how to reconcile Respect for All Beings with donning the black cap and passing the death sentence on a convicted murderer. *You shall be taken from here to a place of execution...*

His eyes were clear, his gaze piercing. I could imagine that gaze withering some poor shrivelled defendant in court. But for a moment those eyes clouded. He steepled his long thin aristocratic fingers in front of his long thin aristocratic face. Then he focussed again, and when he spoke his words were measured, considered.

The rule of law must be upheld, he said. Karma is a complicated business. It is karma that has made me a judge. It is karma that makes criminals commit their crimes. It is karma that punishment be meted out. I like to think that when the time comes I shall be able to temper justice with compassion.

A Herculean task, I said. *Bon Voyage!*

I saluted, and he threw back his head and laughed again.

I found myself wondering if the act of passing the death sentence would bring a lump to the throat, make him come over all gulpy.

It must have been a few years later I read an article about Humphreys in the Manchester Guardian, saying how much he had courted controversy in two high-profile murder trials. He had handed out the death penalty in both, the first to a young man named Timothy Evans, described as illiterate and possibly mentally retarded, the second to an attractive young woman, Ruth Ellis, who had killed her abusive lover. In both cases there was an outcry at the sentencing, fuelling calls for the abolition of capital punishment.

Suzuki also told me Humphreys had again been heavily criticised, but for exactly the opposite reason insofar as he had given lenient sentences for violent crimes, in particular for rape and serious assault. Was he trying to restore some kind of balance? Did he go from one extreme to the other in search of a Middle Way? Tempering justice with compassion?

The next time I had the opportunity, I asked Mrs Vining if she would tell me a little more about her experience of the trial. I understood from reading about it in the press that Judge Pal had become quite outspoken in his criticism of the whole procedure.

We were in the grounds of Gakushuin, at the end of a working day, the air pleasantly warm. I was pushing my bicycle, she walking alongside.

He is certainly a firebrand, she said.

A pacifist firebrand?

Yes!

I understand he has put the case that the Americans also should be charged with war crimes, because of the atomic bombings.

Exactly so, she said. He argued that the tribunal had the opportunity to judge both Japan and the Allies, to put war itself on trial.

The words struck me with great power. To put war itself on trial.

If only, I said.

It happened that we had stopped by Yamanashi's memorial to the Class of '42, the Cherry Blossoms of Mejirogaoka, fallen.

We read the inscription, stood a moment in silence, bowed our heads.

I remember the time of year, the month, though not the precise date. November in Japan was still autumn, the maple leaves a glorious overblown riot of colour, all reds and golds and every shade in between, all of it blazing, bright in the sunlight, and yet, with that first hint of chill, there was the sense that it was soon to fade.

That day the young Crown Prince was taking part with his classmates in a boisterous round of games, a tournament known as *kibasen* – a cavalry charge. The teams formed into groups of four, three of them linking arms and forming a horse, two to the front, one to the rear. The fourth member climbed up and sat astride as if on horseback. On a chant of *ichi-ni-san* they let out a yell and charged towards their opponents, jostling and grappling at close quarters. The aim was to barge or drag the opponent to the ground, or steal the coloured bandana from the rider's head. The last team standing were the victors.

I stood on the sidelines with Mrs Vining, looking on and cheering. I wondered aloud if this little game would be banned under the new regime as overly militaristic.

I sincerely hope not, she said.

We watched these young men, in their uniforms, their high-necked tunics, running and playing in the autumn sun, celebrating their little victories, stoical in their little defeats, and neither of us acknowledged our trepidation over an announcement to be made later that day.

The long drawn-out trial of Tojo and his generals had finally reached its conclusion, delayed even further by an adjournment until after the US general election. No doubt this was to ensure the political will to enforce the decision of the court.

The verdicts had been announced. The Japanese Nation was declared guilty of an 'aggressive war.' (Was there such a thing as a passive war?) Tojo and his fellow defendants had likewise been found guilty of war crimes and atrocities. All that remained was for the sentences to be imposed, on this bright, clear autumn day.

Mrs Vining and I tried not to appear too sombre as we took leave of each other, she to accompany the Crown Prince back to the Palace, I to return to my lodgings. But as we parted, we saw it in each other's eyes, and we nodded in silent acknowledgement.

The Crown Prince's team had won. He came over and bowed to us, saluted, then ran off laughing.

The evening had grown cool and I was glad to close the shoji screens and keep warm with my legs tucked under the little *kotatsu* heated table. Tomiko poured me some miso soup and I switched on the radio, waited while it whined and droned into life. I turned the dial, tuning through static and interference and eventually, crackling over the airwaves, came the voice of Sir William Webb, chairman of the tribunal. In a thin tinny monotone he read out the judgements. Sixteen of the accused, including Shimada, were given life imprisonment. Togo and six of the other military leaders were sentenced to death. They would hang by the neck till they were dead, at a date yet to be announced.

After all that had gone before, it was strangely perfunctory, and rather shabby, and very sad.

I said as much to Tomiko, and once again we exchanged mantras.

Shikata ga nai, It can't be helped.

Nantoka Naru. Somehow or other, things will work out.

Then, in English, she managed, Maybe now Japan no more war.

We can hope, I said. We can hope.

I had seen photographs of the defendants during the trial and they had looked beaten and dispirited, weary of it all and longing for an end to it. The day after the sentencing, the Nippon Times carried a front-page picture of the same men standing to attention, dignified as they faced their fate.

The accompanying article called for calm. It urged the Japanese people to hold emotion in check and view the verdict calmly and objectively. What it represented was a return to the rule of law, the only hope of the world. The execution of a few misguided and exhausted individuals, it argued, was a relatively minor episode and must not obscure the greater significance of the verdict in the light of its long term historical purpose.

God save us all from long term historical purpose.

The sentences were carried out on a cold drab December morning, unannounced, with no newspaper coverage, no final photographs of the accused. (There would be a small formal notice the following day). They went to their deaths unheralded, and largely unmourned. But Mrs Vining told me the mood at the Palace was sombre, and the Crown Prince was unable to celebrate his fifteenth birthday, as to do so on such a day would have been deemed inappropriate and inauspicious.

The Emperor's Poetry Party, *Utakai Hajime,* was formal in the extreme. It followed a thousand-year-old ritual, precise in every detail and strictly hierarchical.

The ceremony was to welcome in the New Year and let the court poets recite their verses and also to appreciate the poems written by the royal family for the occasion. In modern times there were submissions from poets outwith this gilded inner circle, and the best poems, as chosen by a panel of judges, were also read out at the ceremony. These commoners – the word was used without irony – were granted the privilege of being allowed to attend and hear their poems chanted aloud in a ceremony that was part performance, part ritual. It was worlds away from Basho on his narrow road to the deep north, or Issa in his flea-ridden hut.

And yet....

That year there were three Westerners in attendance, Mrs Vining, Mr Edmund Blunden and myself. Mr Blunden, as English as his name, was the poet-as-official-observer to the Japanese Nation. I had thought him a cold fish, like many from his country and class, aloof and withdrawn. But on reading his poetry I realised his demeanour was due, at least in part, to what he had endured in the First World War. He had enlisted as a boy, straight from school, and served for two years on the front line. It was clear from his work that the experience had brutalised and traumatised him, and it tortured him still.

It was yet another irony that we sat here, exchanging literary pleasantries across a polished table. Neither of us could have imagined such a thing when we were young men, when he had fought for his beliefs and I had gone to prison for mine. Yet here we were, here we were, in a room redolent with thick musky incense, in the Imperial Palace, in presence of our (former) foes.

Blunden and I had not submitted poems. As *gaijin* we thought that would have been stretching protocol to breaking point. But Mrs Vining, entering into the spirit of things, had written a poem in English and sent it to one of the judges. She had given a copy to me, written out in her elegant script. The theme for the year was *Asano yuki*: Morning Snow.

The morning snow
  Lies deep and white
And gleaming in
  The early light.
I wonder what
  Footsteps will mark
Its innocence
  Before the dark.

To her surprise it was translated into Japanese and distributed around the palace, and it was even published in a newspaper. Part of her was pleased, but overriding that was a kind of embarrassment. It was only meant as token, she said. I'm not a proper poet at all, just an amateur. I mean *everyone* in Japan writes poetry. And *almost* everyone writes better poetry than this!

Nevertheless…. I said.

Come on Mister Blyth, she said.

I'm mindful of something I read by Rilke in one of his letters to a young poet. He said nothing touches a work of art so little as words of criticism.

Nevertheless…. She said, and laughed.

I told her one of my own early poems had been called *Snow in Moonlight*. it was one of the pair that had been published in the London Mercury.

I copied it out from memory and handed it to her.

Returning good for evil, she said.

Hardly, I said.

On one dark trunk he laid
His brow of thought.
On all around, the snow
A hush had wrought.
There birth and life and death were stayed,
A silent pause, a quiet made
In nature's ceaseless flow.
All things were one,
Changeless eternity
At last begun.
Upon the pine tree crest
Of that bright hill,
All thought dissolved in peace,
In calm and still.
His was enough of joy and rest,
Only to be, made quiet his breast,
Only to stand where trees

Laid, far below,
Moon-shadows, soft and grey,
Upon white snow.

It's beautiful, she said, when she'd read it through.
Thank you, I said. It was written by a very young man.
All thought dissolved in peace, she said. That's very fine.
I believe it's my own favourite line, I said. And we sat for a while in a comfortable, companionable silence.

That had been some weeks before. Now I caught her eye as she came into the grand room where the Poetry Party was to take place, and she gave me a little half-smile I could only describe as complicit. By now she would know, to her great relief, that her poem had not been chosen as one of the winners.

The room had been decorated for the occasion with exquisite good taste. There were gold screens painted with scenes from *The Tale of Genji*, and above them hung an embroidery depicting a magnificent peacock with tail-feathers outspread. In front of this display, facing the rest of us, sat the Emperor, the Empress and the Dowager Empress on lacquer chairs decorated with gold. My gaze was drawn to the young Princess Kazuko, attending her first public engagement. She sat poised and still in a kimono of a deep wine colour embroidered with snow-covered plum branches, and little birds flying from branch to branch, the whole thing so delicate and subtle it took the breath away.

How to reconcile this utter refinement, the sheer love of beauty, with the brutality of the warmongers who had so recently driven this nation towards annihilation? How had the rigour and discipline, the code of *bushido,* been so wilfully misunderstood or misused? How could this *civilisation* have allowed itself to be so degraded?

The seven men who were to chant the poems came forward and took their places at a special table draped with purple brocade on which the poems had been laid. The men were all middle-aged and came from ancient noble families. As always it struck me as incongruous to see Japanese men dressed on an occasion like this in formal Western suits, like the Emperor himself, with high wing collars. But then the men began to chant and the mode was entirely other, entirely Japanese.

I followed the words, made sense of the meaning, as they chanted poem after poem.

The scent of early plum blossoms – my garden covered with morning snow. I translated as I listened, made my own versions in English. *In the morning sun, snow glistening on the pine trees.* The chanting swelled, each line repeated, overlapping, like a round or a canon, but with subtle variations in volume and pitch. It was atonal but not discordant, and as it washed over me in waves, it went beyond language and became pure sound, abstract. The sound filled the room, resonant, and I felt I was moving out beyond myself, yet observing it happen with a kind of strange detachment, a clarity I had known from time to time seated in zazen or listening to the sutras.

The chanting subsided and I was back here, in the moment, in the room. All attention was now focussed on the Emperor and I realised his poem was about to be recited. He sat straight-backed, attentive, as everyone else in the room stood, as if to receive a blessing or a prayer.

The main cantor sang the first line, his voice high but powerful, as if delivering a line from a Noh drama. *Snow deep in my garden this morning...* Three of the others joined in, *My thoughts go out...* All seven voices sang the last line, *... to the people shivering in the cold.* It wasn't quite Lear's *Poor naked wretches, wheresoe'er ye be...* But it was something, an attempt.

I looked at this small dignified man seated before me and I felt some sense of what he had been through. There had been calls for him to abdicate, to give up his religion, to go into exile. He could have been tried as a war criminal with Tojo and the generals. He could have been hanged with them. It was only two years since all of that had happened, the trial, the executions.

There was a story in circulation that when Tojo and his Supreme

Council had made their irrevocable decision to declare war, they came to the Emperor not for his advice but for his approval. Those present reported that the Emperor sat in silence for what seemed a very long time. Then he recited a poem by his ancestor Meiji.

In this world we are all one family.
Why then on every sea
Do wind and wave storm and rage?

After another silence he had stood and recited the verse again, then left the room without saying another word. Maddeningly oblique, it was as far as he could go, finally powerless in the face of the military. The horror and carnage that had followed. War and the pity of war. Defeat and surrender.

And here he sat, quiet, scholarly, utterly human, listening to his poem.

Snow deep in my garden...

The verse was chanted five times, again with that overlay of voices, chiming against one another, expanding, filling the space.

My thoughts go out...

The last note died away, left a hush, a wash of no-sound.

Mr Blunden, beside me, cleared his throat, as much, perhaps, to break the silence as out of any necessity. I looked again at Mrs Vining and thought she was fighting back tears.

The royal party rose to go, and we all stood and bowed. Still a little dazed, I raised my head and found myself looking straight at the Dowager Empress as she passed. She smiled as she acknowledged my gaze, gave a nod of the head, glanced back at me as she left the room.

Namu Myoho Renge Kyo

Mrs Vining had decided to go back to the United States and return to her previous incarnation as a novelist. I wanted to pay my respects, wish her well, and after her last lesson I made my way to the little classroom where she had been teaching. I found her there, as I had expected. She sat quite still behind her desk, looking straight ahead into the middle distance, her eyes fixed on nothing, in what might be a moment of meditation. On the blackboard behind her were chalked the words *Hope, Despair, Knowledge.*

I considered leaving her to her reverie, but then she turned and saw me, brought me into focus.

Mr Blyth, she said, composing herself, smiling. How delightful to see you.

Likewise, I said. I had hoped I might see you before you left.

That's kind, she said.

It must have been an interesting lesson, I said, indicating the words on the board.

I hope so, she said, then fell silent, and we sat and let the silence deepen, something shared, unspoken, a kind of prayer.

As it happened, Mr Blunden also left Japan around this time, heading home to London. Before he did, we had occasion to meet a few more times at this or that reception, and I found myself appreciating the man's fine qualities, his intelligence, his reticence, his love of Japan. What I had taken for an aloofness was instead a kind of innate shyness and reserve, a genuine humility.

A mutual acquaintance told me he thought Mr. Blunden was modest to the point of extinction.

I replied, He is modest to the point of genius.

Not long after Blunden's departure, Harold Henderson also returned home, to take up a teaching post at Columbia University. We had shared much and I would miss our disagreements on haiku.

One by one my peers were leaving Japan. I could not imagine myself doing so. For better or worse, for better *and* worse, this was my home.

A few months after the Poetry Party the Dowager Empress died, quite suddenly, of a heart attack. Hers had been a warm, benign, humorous presence in the Imperial palace, looking on with what had always seemed to me a kind of amused detachment, watching events unfold as they must.

I tried to say as much to the Crown Prince, her grandson, not quite sure if I was communicating what I felt. But he nodded, lips tight as if controlling his own emotion.

Yes, he said. We shall miss her.

I remembered Yamanashi describing her as a wise and thoughtful woman, adding that she was a wonderful judge of men.

Perhaps, I'd said, if the Japanese constitution had allowed for female succession, and she had become Empress in her own right, then the course of history might have been changed, and the carnage we had lived through might not have come about.

Perhaps, he'd said. But that was all impossible. It could not be.

Three weeks after her death there was a ceremony at the Palace, assigning a posthumous name to the Empress. Yamanashi described the purpose of the ceremony, which he said was called, as I understood it, the Rite of Informing her Spirit of the Posthumous Title. This was to acknowledge and honour her contribution and declare the name by which she would be remembered, which was Teimei, *Tei* meaning righteousness and constancy, *Mei* meaning light, enlightenment. He said the Emperor himself had chosen the name, and had read out at the ceremony a passage from Confucius.

Nichigetsu no michi wa Teimei nari. The path of the sun and moon is that of righteousness and light.

I folded my hands, bowed to her memory.

Teimei.

Namu Myoho Renge Kyo.

Namu Myoho Renge Kyo.

When I taught I was committed (and there were certainly those who thought I should be).

I wanted to give – and receive – something more than mere sentence patterns, more than grammar or structure. I believe I once wrote that in teaching I wanted to achieve the object of life, the communication of souls. And if that sounds high-flown and overblown, well then, so be it, let it stand.

My method, or non-method, was to extemporize, quoting passages from books and poems from memory, seemingly unprepared, seemingly at random, and leaving room for the unexpected. It was not teaching in the traditional sense, but a way of opening doors, creating opportunities for the students, letting them gradually get the feel of things for themselves.

That was the idea.

One day I was talking to a class about the Seven Wonders of the Ancient World – The Pyramids, The Colossus at Rhodes, The Hanging Gardens of Babylon, and the rest. The students were moderately interested and one or two could even name a few of the so-called Wonders.

I heard myself ask, Don't you think there is something vulgar about Wonders, especially these huge man-made monstrosities?

For a few moments they were silent, as they often were when I challenged them. Then one or two tentatively agreed, others looked unsure, as if I had asked a trick question.

All right, I said, What in *your* opinion is the most wonderful thing in the world?

Now their discomfort was palpable. They sat rigid, stared straight ahead, or they gave a strained apologetic smile, with that slight inclination of the head I had come to recognise.

Well? I asked.

Silence, awkwardness.

Nobody?

One of the bolder students asked, Please, Buraisu-sensei, what is *your* answer?

I thought for a moment, then said, Haiku.

Now they were really flummoxed.

The music of Bach, I said.

They looked miserable.

Wait! I said, and I laughed. I have my answer. The most wonderful thing in the world is Zen.

As I spoke the word, I felt the absolute truth of it.

Zen is not only the greatest thing in the world, I said, it is the *only* great thing. It is what makes things great. It is greatness itself.

Now they knew, beyond any doubt – they were being taught by a madman.

My exchange with the students put me in mind of an old Celtic story about the legendary hero Fionn Maccuill. One day Fionn was walking in the forest with a few of his followers, and he asked them the question, What is the finest music in the world?

They thought it over (as my students had done) and one by one gave answers.

The song of a skylark.

The sound of the wind in the pines.

The happy babble of a child.

A young girl's laughter.

The rush of summer rain.

Fionn said these were all good answers, but there was something more.

And they asked him, How do *you* answer, great Fionn? What is the finest music in the world?

And he answered, The music of what happens.

This story too I told to the students. One of them asked, What is Celtic?

It's an ancient culture, I said. Scottish, Irish, Welsh. The opposite in many ways of Teutonic, Germanic.

How opposite?

I took a piece of chalk, wrote two headings on the blackboard, *Celts* on the left, *Teutons* on the right, and underneath each I wrote a list of qualities.

I wrote *Vivacious* opposite *Stolid*, *Reckless* opposite *Fatalistic*. I wrote *Music & Beauty* opposite *Science and Logic*, *Dramatic* opposite *Epic*.

The same student who had spoken out said, These are difficult words.

Very well, I said, and I scrawled up *Fun* opposite *Dull & Humourless*, and I underlined them with a flourish.

So Celtic is better? said the student.

They were all painstakingly copying the lists of words into their notebooks.

It's different, I said. But then, a long thing is the long body of the Buddha, a short thing is the short body of the Buddha.

Both good? He was genuinely trying to understand.

Both equally not-good, not-bad. But maybe Celtic is more not-bad. So, he said.

Ha! I said, and I picked up a duster, wiped the board clear with great sweeping strokes, and I stood a moment looking into the abstract patterns I had made, losing myself in them.

The boys found my methods (and madnesses) challenging, but that was, after all, the intention. Among these boys were the future rulers of the country, the businessmen and captains of industry, the elite. Theirs would be the responsibility for building a new nation on the foundations of the old. They *had* to be challenged, cajoled into open-mindedness. They didn't always take it well. The more ambitious among them, the academically gifted, those eager to *get on*, were often the most puzzled, the most resistant.

During one session I asked them (not unkindly, I thought, and with a measure of good humour) what they understood to be their purpose in life.

Their discomfort took me back to that earliest class in Korea, the student rebellion. I am Spartacus.

I let the silence sit for a few moments, then said it was an important question to ask, if not to answer. I was, after all, asking myself the selfsame question.

I am asking it still.

11

THIS VERY PLACE

Another New Year, another poetry party. But this was not like the Emperor's formal *Utakai Hajime* which I had attended the year before. (Was it really only a year?) This gathering was entirely different – it was hosted by the Crown Prince, and it really was, first and foremost, a party. It centred round a popular collection of verse, *Hyakunin Isshu,* One Hundred Poems by One Hundred Poets, and it took the form of a game. The poems formed an anthology spanning the period from the seventh to the thirteenth century, and had been gathered together by a nobleman named Fujiwara No Teika.

Some of the verses were slight and (I would have thought) forgettable. But some were from the Manyoshu and were very fine indeed. The poems were printed on cards – about the same size as our playing cards and beautifully illustrated. One set of a hundred cards featured the opening lines of the poems, another set the closing lines. Someone appointed as Reader would take charge of the set of opening lines. The other set, the closing lines, would be scattered on the floor. The Reader would shuffle his cards and read out the lines from each card he turned over. There would then be a scrabbling to find the matching card which completed the poem. Whoever found it first scored a point, for himself, or herself, or for their team.

To my great delight, on this occasion the Crown Prince had asked me to accept the role of Reader, and I said I would be honoured. He said I would be a good intoner. He very much liked the sound of my voice and the way I recited poems, saying I did it with a kind of dignity. Gravitas, I suggested.

But also with humour.

Equally important, I said.

I was quite touched that he had asked me. It was very much a gathering of young people, The Crown Prince's schoolfriends, his younger brother and sister, Prince Masahito and Princess Kazuko, all elegantly dressed in honour of the season. They gathered in a circle round the cards on the floor, eager and intent, ready. I sat at the centre of the circle, the Reader, the Dealer. I did my best Mississippi card-sharp routine, shuffling the deck. Then with a theatrical flourish, a flick of the wrist, I turned over the first card and read out – *intoned* – the lines written there.

> *Nagaraeba*
> *Mata konogoro ya*
> *Shinobaren*

In my head I translated as a I went.

> *If I should live long,*
> *Perhaps these present days*
> *Will be dear to me,*

But before I had even finished, there was a cry of delight and a scrambling on the floor. To my amazement – though I should not really have been surprised – the Crown Prince had beaten everyone to it, found the right card and held it up in triumph. He read out the lines.

> *Ushi to mishi yo zo*
> *Ima wa koishiki*

Again, for my own sake, I translated.

> *Just as sad times past*
> *Come back in quiet thought.*

The Prince bowed to the round of applause and placed the card on an exquisite little side-table, set there for just that purpose, then he turned back to the game, braced and alert.

I turned over the second card.

In all my years in Japan I had never seen such unrestrained merriment, joy unconfined. These bright young things, sophisticated and privileged, in public all restraint and composure, were suddenly children again, shouting and laughing, losing themselves completely in the game.

By mere playing we go to Heaven.

It filled me again with that unreasoning sense that, in spite of the carnage mankind had wrought on the world, all might still be well, and all might be well, and all manner of things might be well.

I was told once that in appearance I looked like a cross between Laurence Olivier and Charlie Chaplin. I would take either as a compliment, but it might be difficult to combine the two, would risk confusing one with the other. I am not sure that Olivier could play the tramp, and his Great Dictator would probably owe more to Mussolini than Hitler. But Chaplin as Hamlet would be something to behold. Enter the Prince of Denmark, shuffling, twirling a cane. The film is black-and-white, silent, with captions. *Outrageous fortune!* it reads, as he dons his bowler hat against a hail of slingshot and arrows flying over his head.

Take arms! His cane becomes an umbrella which he opens and holds up as a defence, only to find it is full of holes.

In one of my boxes of documents is a set of tape-recordings to which I was a contributor. I may have resembled Olivier and Chaplin, but my acting career began and ended with these recordings, *Obunsha's Educational Record-Books*.

The one I recall was called *Home Life*, and my episode was entitled *A Friend Pays a Visit*.

The *dramatis personae* featured an American couple, Henry and Mary Jones. Mr Jones was described by the narrator, Mr Sasaki, as a very kind gentleman who looked remarkably young even though his hair was greying. Mrs Jones, according to the eager Sasaki-san, was a wonderful and charming lady of striking personality. Henry and Mary's children, the *gay and loveable* Emily and *extremely active and handsome* Dick, completed the family.

I (Ahem!) was the eponymous Friend-who-paid-a-visit, an Englishman by the name of George Smith.

The action began with a knock at the door (rendered in the studio by a technician rapping on the table).

The dialogue is seared into my brain.

Why, hello, George.

Hello Mary, I haven't seen you in ages.

This is a pleasant surprise.

How's Henry?

Oh, he's fine. I bet he'll be surprised to see you.

Well, hello George.

Hello Henry. How've you been?

Just fine, thanks. And you?

I've never felt better.

Sit down and take the lead out of your feet.

Thank you.

What men will do for money!

It's all there in the memory, on tape as it were, reel-to-reel. (Real to real?) George Smith explains why he is in Tokyo, (*Sudden business made it necessary for me to come*). He comments on the Jones home. (*By the way, this is a very comfortable home, a bright home with a pleasing Oriental atmosphere*). There is then some prattle about using chopsticks and wearing kimono and geta, before George gives some advice on their teenage son who is reaching *that difficult age*, telling them Dick's a good boy and they have nothing to worry about. George then refuses tea, saying he would love to stay, but he has *a thousand things to do yet today*, before riding off into the sunset.

Hi Ho Silver, away!

The Joneses were played by two charming American academics, Bill Moore and Jay Callender. Between scenes, Bill had us laughing with his coarse take on the storyline, providing his own sub-text.

Oh yeah? he'd say, his voice gravelly from the cigarettes he smoked. *Old George just happened to be in the neighbourhood, eh? Sudden business made it necessary? Damned disappointed if you ask me, finding Henry at home. Henry will be surprised to see you? I'll bet he will!*

The recording is accompanied by a book containing the script, preserved for posterity. There are photographs of the cast, posing in a mocked-up living room. In one shot, Bill, Jay and I are laughing, probably at Bill's risqué commentary.

Oh yeah?

The studio. The recording. A time, a moment, caught.

I am aware that in these pages there is little of what might be called the domestic. I have not written a great deal about my home life, time spent with my family, with Tomiko and above all my two daughters. I make no apology for this reticence. It is quite beyond my capacity to put into words what these girls have meant to me. Nana and Harumi. Harumi and Nana. It would be the worst kind of sentimentality. (Is there a best kind?) So I shall not make the attempt. *Wovon man nicht sprechen kann, darueber muss man schweigen.* Whereof one cannot speak, thereof must one remain silent. But I acknowledge it. They are dear to me. I hold that truth in the deepest part of my being. There. Sentimentality avoided (though only just).

In his *Narrow Road to the Deep North*, Basho wrote that days and months are travellers in eternity, and travellers too are the passing years. This is profound and true, but most often we perceive time passing, not as a flow but in fits and starts. So I watched the girls grow up, become who they were. The time passed, but not in any measured, linear way. Rather it resembled a home movie with its jumps and cuts, now slowing, now speeding forward, moments flickering, glimpsed then gone. Nor can I choose the moments I remember. The images arise unbidden then fade.

I gave the girls the gift of music, as it had been given to me. I taught them with my accustomed rigour, had them practise scales and arpeggios, scales and arpeggios, Harumi on viola, Nana on a little violin. Tomiko, like Annie before her, suffered, and not always in silence. Why not a tune? When they were ready the girls played simple melodies, *Tannenbaum, Twinkle Twinkle Little Star* (telling them it was by Mozart, aged five), *Au Claire de la Lune, Row, Row, Row Your Boat....*

I imagined us playing Bach together, but Harumi rebelled, said she would rather play on the ukulele. She insisted on it, learning to strum *O Susanna,* and making me laugh. Sometimes too she would sing along and I thrilled at the quality of her voice. She was pitch perfect, sang with a warmth and sweetness, a slight huskiness in the tone.

In time, and with patience, I taught her Bach's *Jesu, Praise to Thee be Given.* I accompanied her on cello, quietly awed, filled to the brim with gratitude.

What else?

I bought the girls bikes (again, a smaller one for Nana), taught them on the pathways round campus at Gakushuin. I showed off (I admit it), pedalling hands-free, or just on the back wheel, the front wheel in the air. *Ladeez an genulmen, I give you the amazing trick cyclist, Mister B....* I succeeded in making it look like fun, and the girls, after their initial wobbling uncertainty, grew quickly confident, were soon cycling round with assurance, ringing their little bells so students would get out of the way. One trick I refrained from showing them was something I had done since my own childhood. Cycling behind a truck or a lorry, I would catch hold of it at the back, the tailgate. I could then stop pedalling and be carried along, freewheeling. My mother had scolded me, told me it was dangerous. Now the thought of my own daughters doing such a thing filled me with dread, made me feel sick to my stomach. So quietly, if reluctantly, I gave it up, rode more sedately like the middle-aged English gentleman I was.

On Sundays, unless it was raining, the three of us would cycle on quieter roads to a cafe and cake shop I had learned to love. (Memories of my time in Korea with Akio's little daughter Katsura). We ate cake, drank lemonade. I carried something home in a little box for Tomiko (who could not cycle and had no inclination to learn). I would also stock up on my own supply of chocolate, buy two or three bars to see me through the week.

I have spoken before of my love of chocolate. Let me take it further and state it is my considered opinion that chocolate constitutes a teleological argument for the existence of God.

I made the same point to the girls, albeit in simplified form. I bit into a thick chunky square, rolled my eyes, said, Ah!

Yes. There must be a God.

In my jacket pockets there was often a residue, crumbs or flakes of it, perhaps a little piece that had melted then hardened again, that and chalkdust from teaching. Tomiko would grimace, turning the pockets inside out to shake them clean.

Chalk and chocolate. A poet would make something onomatopoeic of that.

How did Mr Eliot put it? I have measured out my life?

My life.

Chalk and chocolate. Chalkolate?

Enough.

That gift of music I gave the girls was also one I gave the Crown Prince. I recommended (as strongly as I dared) that he should learn a musical instrument, and I was gratified when he told me he had obtained a cello and would begin taking lessons. I like to think my own enthusiasm for the instrument influenced his choice. (I am sure the royal household would not have thanked me if I had pressed him to take up the tuba, or the trombone!)

My years of teaching Akihito also come back to me as moments, little vignettes from those weekly meetings at the palace. They have the quality of parable – Tales of the Young Crown Prince.

The time I asked him which he thought was better, to be born as he was, into the Imperial family as Crown Prince, into a life of duty and responsibility, or to be born into an ordinary family and have an ordinary life. He gave it serious thought and replied, I don't know, because I was born to this life and never knew any other.

What did I teach him?

The time I had dropped a pen on the floor (intentionally or otherwise, who knows?) The Prince was seated, as usual, not far from my desk. The pen rolled to a point in between us, and I asked, Well? Which of us is going to pick it up?

He caught my tone, challenging, teasing.

Perhaps it is a little closer to you, he said.

Perhaps, I said. Shall I get a ruler and measure the distance?

He thought for a moment.

Perhaps, he said, with a smile. But then again, I am the Crown Prince. Perhaps it is not my place to pick it up.

You are most definitely the superior, I said. No doubt about it. But, on the other hand, perhaps the superior man reveals his superiority by bending and showing humility.

Perhaps! he said, and after another moment of thought, he bent and picked up the pen, held it in both hands and returned it to me with a little bow.

I laughed and bowed deeper.

For some years our household had another member.

Tomiko had a cousin, who had a good friend, who had a daughter...
(Japanese bonds of family and friendship are strong!)

The daughter, Chieko, was in her late teens. She was a quiet, intelligent girl who had studied at a Christian school where she had learned English. Now she was enrolled at Gakushuin women's college and Tomiko suggested that she move in with us.

Home-stay, said Harumi, giving the idea credibility by putting it in English.

Tomiko said it would help the girl and her family, who were not wealthy (and an education was not cheap). She would be another pair of hands about the house, a companion for Harumi and Nana. She could type and would be a kind of secretary for me, improving her English and helping me with translations.

What could I say against such a barrage of good reasons? Surely only an unfeeling brute would have any objections. And when I met Chieko I saw why she had touched Tomiko's heart. She seemed much younger than her years, perhaps because of her sheltered upbringing, her Christian faith. She gave the impression of being serious, studious, a little shy. The girls had already taken to her, saw her as an older sister.

As with most domestic issues, the women were complicit, the matter had already been decided, and I was the last one to find out. It was decreed. The eternal feminine was to surround me even more. Now, like Lear, I would have three daughters.

Very well, I said. Home-stay for Chieko it is.

Chieko's mother wanted to repay us in some small way for looking after her daughter. It happened that the family had a small house on the Izu peninsula. The accommodation was simple, she explained, and quite basic, but it was in a beautiful spot and not too far from the town of Numazu. She would be honoured, she said, if we would be her guests there in the summer. We agreed.

The girls were particularly excited. It would be the first real holiday we had taken as a family. Tokyo was hot and humid in summer, sometimes unbearably so, and the prospect of time away from all that, somewhere remote, refreshed by sea air, was exhilarating in itself.

There were other reasons I was eager to go. The Crown Prince would be spending the summer at the Imperial villa in Numazu, and when I mentioned our family holiday to him he was delighted that I would be close by.

The Izu peninsula was also associated in my mind with Zen Master Hakuin. I had read a story by him – a parable? a tract? – called *The Precious Mirror Cave*, in which Hakuin described a kind of vision experienced by a local fisherman who chanced on a sea cave where figures of the Buddha and his two closest disciples miraculously appeared, granting illumination to all who made the difficult pilgrimage to see them.

As a teacher, Hakuin was ferocious, a hard old taskmaster who battered his students with unsolvable koans till they broke (but only after he had travelled the same gruelling road, driving himself beyond, always beyond).

> *This very place is the Pure Land.*
> *This very body is the Buddha-body.*

Everything he said and did was teaching, for the sake of his students, for the sake of humanity. Expedient means. Whatever it took. He was a Bodhisattva, committed to saving all sentient beings.

In the story of the Mirror Cave he depicted himself visiting the sacred shrine in person, ferried there by a boatman and at first not seeing the figures which were hazy, indistinct. (A hallucination? A trick of the light?) Undaunted, he returned a second time, humble, surrendered, chanting the *Nembutsu* with simple devotion, and this time he saw clearly, he was granted a vision, the three figures radiating light.

I tried asking around, in Numazu when we passed through, and more locally when we arrived in Izu, but nobody had any idea where the cave might be. I was disappointed, but resigned. In any case, what would I have seen? The effects of phosphorescence? A trick of the light? The chance weathering of old rocks into something resembling three holy figures?

Hakuin made it clear that what the seeker saw in the cave was a reflection of his own consciousness, and that was what he had to face.

In another story, *Idle Talk on the Night Boat*, Hakuin spun a yarn about how he went off into the mountains above Kyoto to sit at the feet of an ancient sage – reputed to be 300 years old! – and learned from him how to cure what he called his Zen sickness, a complete and utter exhaustion of mind, body and spirit, engendered by years of austere discipline.

In re-reading these tales, I was reminded of Bob Aitken's description of koans as folk-tales, passing on the deepest wisdom, down through generations.

> *This very body is the Buddha-body.*

What was most engaging about Hakuin was his sense of humour.
I saw it first in his drawings, vigorous, briskly executed, displaying
warmth and humanity in every line, and wickedly, surreally, funny.

Two mice, sumo-wrestling.
Two bumpkins, beneath a sign reading *No Graffiti*. One has climbed
on the other's shoulders to write, *Sorry For Defacing This Sign!*
Hotei, the pot-bellied god of good fortune, adrift in a small boat,
lolling back at ease, hands behind his head. The poem underneath
reads:

> *Steering his boat*
> *Where it wants to go –*
> *Hotei all at sea.*

There are photographs, black-and-white, in an album, taken during
that visit to Izu. That time and that place, those people we were.
The three girls, Harumi, Nana and Chieko, on the beach, smiling,
smiling.
Tomiko, outside the little house, shielding her eyes from the sun.
Yours truly, His Nibs, Mr RH Blyth, not in a suit and tie, but wearing
khaki shorts and an open-necked shirt, the sleeves rolled up. And
again, shirtless, bare-chested, posing, giving my best impression of
Johnny Weissmuller in the Tarzan films (though with, admittedly,
a rather less impressive physique).
All five of us, one behind the other, straddling the long low branch
of a tree.
(Who took that particular photo? A neighbour? Chieko's mother?
I have quite forgotten).
I look and look, and each picture becomes a frame, a little window
through to where we were, a reality that still exists, outside time.

> *This very place is the Pure Land.*

The days were warm and sunny, the balmy sea air a welcome respite
from the heat and fug of the city. One day a visitor appeared at the

door, a young man bearing gifts. He was like many of the students I taught, formal and polite, his high-necked tunic buttoned up in spite of the warmth of the day. He had been sent by the Crown Prince with a box of fresh fruit – *momo* and *kaki* – exquisite pink peaches and what must have been the first persimmon of the season.

After handing them over, the boy took a letter from his satchel and held it out to me, bowing. The envelope bore the Imperial chrysanthemum crest, and the boy was respectful to the point of reverence, mindful of his sacred role as messenger. We invited him to stay and eat with us, but he said he did not have much time and had to return to the palace. I thought I sensed his resolve weaken when he saw the girls and their obvious delight at the gift. But then he steeled himself, and after accepting a glass of water, he stood to attention, clicked his heels, bowed again deeply and was gone.

I opened the envelope and read a brief note from the Crown Prince, in his own handwriting, saying he hoped our time at Izu had been pleasant and that we would enjoy the simple offering of seasonal fruit. He said he very much looked forward to renewing our conversations on our return to Tokyo.

Chieko's mother was looking across at me, concerned, perhaps, that the letter might contain bad news. (How often is that our reaction – to fear the worst?) I laughed and showed her the envelope with its crest, told her what the Crown Prince had said, and she was overwhelmed, happy and flustered, not quite able to believe a personal letter from the Prince had been delivered to her door.

Her door!

Chieko had taken the fruit to the kitchen, washed and peeled and sliced it, divided it into equal portions in little bamboo bowls, and we sat outside and ate.

I think I can truthfully say there is no fruit I love more than persimmon. Even peeled and sliced, they have to be eaten with the fingers, which have to get good and sticky in the process. (I swear the fingers can *taste* the fruit). That golden-yellow flesh, the texture almost slippery, the taste both astringent and sweet, lingering at the back of the palate.

Ah!

I could completely identify with Shiki who wrote a late haiku which might well have served as his death-verse and epitaph.

Think of me
As one who loved poetry
And persimmons.

If I could pass it off as my own, I might well use it as my own *jisei*, my death verse, instead of that anonymous piece about leaving my heart to the sasanqua blossom.

As Tomiko had hoped, Chieko effectively became part of our family, like an older sister to the girls. Her English was good, which was immensely helpful to me as she could help when I was translating poems from the Japanese.
She was also musical, could sight-read and had taken violin lessons as a child. So with Harumi on viola (though she still said she preferred the ukulele), Nana as second violin and my esteemed self on cello, we had a string quartet. We worked on a repertoire, practised of an evening if my school work allowed, and performed little recitals on a Sunday afternoon to an audience of Tomiko and the dog.
We always had dogs, this particular fellow being a doughty character of doubtful lineage. I named him Joshu.
Did *this* dog have the Buddha nature?
Hear him bark!
Occasionally Joshu would join in, add an unscripted counterpoint to what we were playing, an improvised solo for howling dog

Let dogs delight to bark and bite
For God hath made them so.

There is a Sufi poem which begins, The dog barks, the caravan passes.
Chieko married, moved away.
The dog barked.
Our lives flowed on.

The Crown Prince was eager to tell me his news. It had been agreed he would travel to London for the coronation of Queen Elizabeth. I knew from conversations with Yamanashi that this had been proposed, and that in some quarters there had been considerable resistance to the idea. The Crown Prince was too young. He was inexperienced. So soon after the war, he might encounter anti-Japanese sentiment, perhaps even outright hostility.

Yamanashi had said the diplomatic trick was to turn these arguments into something positive. Yes, Akihito was young, but so was the new Queen – they were of the same generation. He was inexperienced, but that meant he was not jaded. He had the freshness of youth, and as a mere boy throughout the war years, he was free of any taint or blame for those years.

As Yamanashi put it, he carried no baggage! He was the New Japan. Now, clearly, the moderate and progressive elements had prevailed. Akihito would indeed go to London and, for the first time, represent his country at a great state occasion.

What do you think? he asked, eager but perhaps just a little apprehensive.

I think it's wonderful, I said. *Subarashi.*

Yes, he said, grinning. Wonderful!

He had come directly from playing tennis, in his white shirt and v-neck sweater, his wide flannel trousers – his *sport-wearing* – and he was indeed the embodiment of youthful well-being, a natural poise born of wealth and privilege, not hidebound by the past but truly international, open to it all.

I told him the lines from Shakespeare I had framed on my wall, written out like a poem in Suzuki's own hand.

> *O wonderful.*
> *wonderful,*
> *and most wonderful wonderful!*
> *and yet again wonderful…*

And yet again. Wonderful.

My acting career may have been short-lived – in fact it ended after my brief supporting role as Mr George Smith. But I did make a radio broadcast, a spoken commentary describing – in Japanese! – the coronation of the young Queen Elizabeth. I watched a screening of the event, the first television broadcast I had ever seen, in a studio in Tokyo, and I spoke into a microphone, giving my own measured account of the proceedings.

Ma had told me a neighbour had bought a television set and invited her round with a few other folk to watch the whole thing, live, as it were, on a nine-inch screen, the images black-and-white, a flickering *kamishibai*, a little moving picture show. All the grandeur and spectacle were reduced and framed, the pageantry diminished. And yet I could imagine how it would be viewed back home. Ma would be seated in the neighbour's front room, just a few miles from where this Great Ceremony was being staged. She and her friends would be gathered round the screen, history being played out right there in front of them as they ate cheese and ham sandwiches, and no doubt scones and cakes, and drank strong sweet tea, hearts swelling with patriotic pride. It would be a national holiday, the schools and factories closed. Outside there would be street parties, gardens decked with bunting and Union Jacks. They would quaff warm beer and sing *God Save the Queen* and *Roll Out the Barrel* and *Knees Up Mother Brown,* in Leytonstone, E11.

Home.

And I watched it on my own little screen, headphones over my ears, microphone picking up my every word, every plosive and sibilant, in a dimly lit studio in downtown Tokyo, half a world away.

I thought of my charge the Crown Prince, my responsibility towards him, the great weight of expectation on his shoulders, and I felt a kind of empathy towards this slight figure, this young Queen, robed and sceptred, the great heavy crown on her head.

> *'To the looking-glass world,' it was Alice that said,*
> *'I've a sceptre in hand, I've a crown on my head.*
> *Let the Looking-Glass creatures whatever they be,*
> *Come and dine with the Red Queen, the White Queen and me.'*

And however ridiculous it all was, however outmoded and anachronistic and downright surreal, it might somehow be necessary, or at least useful, as a symbol, of order and unity, life restored after the dark years of destruction.

On the wall of the little studio where I sat was a framed photograph of Emperor Hirohito. It would have been from this very building that his speech had been broadcast at the end of the war, the recording smuggled from the Palace under attack from armed extremists. *Gyokuon-hōsō.* Jewel Voice Broadcast. Imperial Rescript on the Termination of the Greater East Asia War. Tomiko and I had listened in our little rented apartment, straining to hear the message, eerily unreal, as if transmitted from a distant universe.

Then later we had tuned in to hear *Ningen Sengen,* the Imperial Declaration of Humanity, which I – incredibly – had helped to compose. That too would have been broadcast from this building, perhaps even from this very studio.

From his frame on the wall, the Emperor looked down at me, dressed in full military uniform, his expression composed, giving nothing away. My connection to this great Imperial household has been, and remains, a mystery to me, some unfolding of karma.

Swami Vivekananda, the Hindu monk, once wrote that a memory of the spiritual life often haunts the throne, that some souls were actually born to this kind of role because of past merit, that they might be in a position to do good in the world.

Was it actually conceivable that the world might yet move into an era of peace and co-operation? In my own time on earth – a mere half-century – I had already lived through two World Wars, and as an atheist / agnostic, lapsed Christian / faithless Buddhist, crypto-anarchist / sometime nihilist, I prayed with all my being to Christ, Buddha, Siva, Allah, Yahweh, the Cosmic Joker, the Great Self beyond the beyond, that I would not see a third, and, more important, that Nana and Harumi might live in a world at peace with itself.

But I had my doubts.

And yet…

The choir sang, settings of Vaughan Williams. *All people that on earth*

do dwell... The voices rose and swelled. *O taste and see...* The young
Queen stepped out, into her fairytale coach. The crowds cheered.
The broadcast ended.

I removed my headphones, switched off the microphone. I bowed
to the producer, and the sound engineer, and they bowed more
deeply to me, in deference to my status as resident *gaijin*, expert on
all things royal. *Buraisu-sensei.*

They accompanied me to the main entrance. They were amused,
and perhaps impressed, that I had arrived on my bicycle. They
dispatched a young man from the front desk to fetch the bike from
the car park, and all three stood in a row, bowing in unison as I
pedalled off.

It was a pleasant evening, and the studio was in Uchisaiwaichō,
not too far from the Imperial Palace, so I cycled past the old walls,
so familiar to me, and out into the traffic, through the city streets,
home to Mejiro.

Apart from horse riding, tennis was the Crown Prince's favourite
sport, and I grew used to him turning up to see me in those immac-
ulate whites, his *sport-wearing*, either before or after a game.

Someone in the staff room asked me one day if the Crown Prince
was playing a lot of tennis these days, and whether he was enjoying
it more than usual.

I said he had always enjoyed the game and as far as I knew he played
it very well.

I didn't quite understand the import of the question, then I saw
an American magazine with an article about the Crown Prince,
featuring a photograph of him with his tennis partner, a beautiful
young woman by the name of Michiko Shoda. The article dropped
none-too-subtle hints that this was the future Princess. The headline
was *Love Match.*

It was typical that I should be oblivious. The Prince had said noth-
ing. The main Japanese newspapers, no doubt by agreement, had
not run the story.

Tomiko, of course, knew all about it, as did Harumi and Nana.

Some small magazine had published the photograph, fuelling speculation, and then it had appeared in the American press.

Don't you know anything? asked Tomiko.

Apparently not.

Harumi said since the Prince's coming of age, they had been searching for his Princess. They had considered hundreds of candidates.

Hundreds?

At least!

Candidates?

Of course.

That makes it sound like they were running for public office.

They said the marriage had to be arranged. It could not be left to chance. The Chosen One had to be someone appropriate, from the right background.

Naturally.

Also it could not be someone taller than the Prince.

Or older than him.

Unthinkable!

But surely the Prince would have some say in the matter.

Nana said he had declared, I will have this girl and no other. (She pointed dramatically). No other!

When I next spoke to Yamanashi, he explained further. Traditionally the future Empress would be chosen from Imperial relatives or a very small group of aristocratic families.

But, he said. Much has changed since the war. These are modern times. The Crown Prince, as you well know, is a young man with his own ideas and a strong will.

But the marriage must still be arranged?

Think of your King George and Queen Mary, he said. Their marriage was arranged, but it was a long and happy one. On the other hand, when things are left to fortune, it may be a situation like the Duke of Windsor, marrying someone inappropriate, with resulting chaos.

But by all accounts, I said, a decision has been made.

I think everyone will be happy, he said. Then he laughed. Well, almost everyone! There has once again been...*resistance*...in some quarters.

I understand the young lady is not of royal birth.

Not even aristocratic, he said. But she is from very good family. Her father is a wealthy industrialist. Of course, and again *as you well know*, the Imperial Rescript, which you helped to translate, has gone at least some way to reducing the gulf between the Emperor and his people.

Still...

Yes, he said. Still!

I imagine it will be difficult for the young woman herself.

Indeed, he said. She has been, shall we say apprehensive. But the Crown Prince is determined. He is very keen on this *Love Match*. Perhaps you should ask him about it next time you meet.

The next time Prince Akihito came to me for his lesson, straight from the tennis court, I asked if he had, as usual, enjoyed the game, and this time I also asked if it had been a love match.

For a moment he looked surprised, wrong-footed. He actually blushed a little, then catching my eye he laughed and said, So, the cat is out of the bag!

I'm afraid so.

He asked if I had married for love and I said Yes, neglecting to add, Both times...

He said he hoped it would not be too long before I could meet the future Princess Michiko in person. I said I was greatly looking forward to it. He was a young man of rare good taste and discrimination. How could the young lady be other than enchanting?

Yes, he said. Enchanting.

There were dissenting voices. These were troubled times – the threat of a general strike, fear of full-blown revolution. There were those who denounced the royal betrothal as a distraction, a side-show to deflect attention from harsh political realities. (It certainly served that function). The novelist Shichiro Fukazawa wrote a vitriolic diatribe expressing the hope that the Imperial family should die out completely.

Just a few years ago this same Fukazawa published a short story called *Fūryū Mutan* – An Elegant Dream. It imagined the Emperor and Empress beheaded by a revolutionary guard, while the Crown Prince and Princess lay on the ground, awaiting the same fate. The story provoked outrage, and Fukuzawa was forced to apologise and go into a kind of exile, shunned and unable to publish his work. For me the story brought back an uncomfortable memory of my own dream, prior to meeting MacArthur, in which the royal family, like the Romanovs, were taken away and executed.

It is curious what details stay in the memory. In Fukuzawa's story, for some reason the Emperor wore an expensive overcoat labelled *Made in England.*

The mind is its own place.

Tomiko and the girls wanted to see the first interview with the Princess to be broadcast on television. I had no intention of buying a set, so we went to the home of a neighbour, Mrs Tomira, to watch the programme. (It brought back that image of my mother and half of Leytonstone crowding round a small set to watch the coronation)

It could not have been easy for the Princess facing the cameras, the questions posed by eager journalists. But she stayed poised, and dignified, and also displayed that quality I had seen in her, a lightness touched with humour, that *chame.*

What country impressed you most on your recent trip abroad?

That is difficult to answer because my visit was so short.

Very diplomatic, I said

The girls shooshed me.

Is it true that the Crown Prince told you on your trip to be sure to visit Scotland?

He did not say, Be sure!

Good! I said. Set them straight!

Sssshhh!

Who is the better tennis player, you or the Crown Prince?

The Crown Prince, without doubt.

At this the girls laughed. I had told them the Crown Prince had confessed that she had beaten him more than once when they played doubles.

She beat him! said Nana. She is better!

They were in total agreement that the Princess was wonderful. Harumi was much taken with her dress – she explained it was ivory brocade – and the little white hat she wore. Tomiko said the Crown Prince was very lucky. Nana was the most enthusiastic of all, said the story was like a fairytale. They all called the Princess Michiko Sama, claiming her as their own.

Yamanashi was delighted with the broadcast.

You see? he said. Surrounded by wary, scrutinising reporters, she dispersed all anxieties completely.

I couldn't have put it better, I said.

She was not a bit swayed or tottered in that occasion.

Not in the least.

I am sure she charmed all observers and showed she will bring peace and happiness to the Crown Prince.

Peace and Happiness, I said, as if proposing a toast.

Peace and Happiness.

Eventually I met the Crown Prince's betrothed, his beloved, Michiko Sama, and found her every bit as charming as we had been led to believe.

I understood I was to turn up at the Palace as usual for my weekly session with the Prince, as usual park my bicycle by the palace gate, as usual remove my trouser-clips, dust myself down and straighten my tie, run a hand through my hair. But on this occasion the Princess-to-be was to grace us with her presence. And that was the truth of it. She had all the qualities we had seen in the TV interview – the lightness, the poise – but heightened and enhanced on meeting her in person.

She spoke English with fluency and ease, albeit with the trace of an American accent. She told me she loved the language and had done her student dissertation on Galsworthy.

Conflict and Reconciliation in The Forsyte Saga, she said, smiling.

Most useful, I said.

Yes!

I told her she spoke beautifully, and she did. She thanked me and said she very much looked forward to our conversations.

As did I, I told her, bowing deep. As did I.

At my next meeting with the Crown Princess-to-be, I was delighted when she spoke to me about poetry. She said certain poems had helped her and sustained her through difficult times, especially during the dark days of the war. She said there was one particular poem by Robert Frost...

An exceptional poet, I said.

Yes, she said. I think so too. I first read this one in translation by Tomoji Abe.

A firebrand, I said. Quite radical in his views.

A pacifist, she said, when it was not acceptable to be so.

Something I understand only too well!

Blessed are the peacemakers... she said.

Indeed.

Abe-san's translation was quite charming and childlike, she said. It moved me deeply.

I don't suppose, I said, the poem was *The Pasture*?

Yes! she said, clapping her hands.

I recited the first verse.

> *I'm going out to clean the pasture spring;*
> *I'll only stop to rake the leaves away*
> *(And wait to watch the water clear, I may):*
> *I shan't be gone long.—You come too.*

She continued, spoke the second verse, her voice confident and with an innate musicality.

> *I'm going out to fetch the little calf*
> *That's standing by the mother. It's so young,*
> *It totters when she licks it with her tongue.*
> *I shan't be gone long.—You come too.*

It's quite remarkable, I said. In one volume of my haiku translations I quoted that very poem in its entirety. I believe I said the poem expresses almost the whole meaning of human life, and with it the nature of haiku.

That is very beautiful.

We see these things, the pasture spring and the water clearing, the cow and her calf, and we feel fulfilled.

It's so vivid.

But that's not the whole story. The poem reaches out to humanity, to you, to the reader, to everyone. You come too.

Yes, she said. You come too!

She turned and smiled at the Crown Prince who smiled back at her, clearly captivated.

Whatever forces of reaction and conservatism might be arrayed agains this young woman, whatever she might have to endure, I felt in that moment she would prevail.

I recall a little interlude from this time – a music recital at the palace. I took some pride (another besetting sin, I know) in the knowledge that the Crown Prince had followed my advice and learned a musical instrument. Quietly and without fuss he had been taking lessons on the cello. I had never heard him play but was sure he must have acquired a level of competency at least. When he set his mind on something, his concentration was one-pointed.

I understood his Michiko-san was an accomplished pianist and I imagined he had arranged the evening for her sake. I had no expectation, felt rather like a parent attending a school concert.

A little printed invitation card explained they would perform a short composition by Faure, *Sicilenne*. I was not familiar with it but assumed it would be a kind of dance, light and melodic, sweet to the point of sentimentality. I resolved to be uncritical, to listen, as it were, with an open heart and not a closed mind. I sat upright, ready. But I was completely unprepared for how the music affected me. Nor was it just the music, it was the very fact of these two young people playing it. The whole feeling of the piece was autumnal, bittersweet, imbued with a sense of what they called *mono na aware*, the pathos, the *touchingness* of things. And that was rendered all the more poignant by its contrast to the very youthfulness of the performers, the immense weight of expectation on them, the role they were to assume, their place in history. And yet, and yet, they were still just this young couple, vulnerable in their humanity, trying their best to express something timeless and beautiful and true. It affected me deeply and I was grateful to have a large handkerchief with which to blow my nose and, discreetly, dab away my tears.

After the royal wedding there were grand celebrations and receptions, great state occasions in their own right, attended by visiting royalty and heads of state, grandees and dignitaries of every hue. Then there was a smaller gathering, described as *intimate* and attended by a mere two hundred guests of the Crown Prince and Princess Michiko – former tutors, chamberlains, family friends and business associates.

The Crown Prince had told me I was one of only three foreigners invited to the reception, and I was happy to hear that one of the others was to be Elizabeth, Mrs Vining. She had sent me a note the year before, saying she was back in Japan, briefly, for a literary conference organised by PEN International, where she had been thrilled to meet some of the delegates, particularly Steven Spender, John Steinbeck and Yasunari Kawabata, declaring Kawabata to be, in her words, easily the most colourful and appealing of all those in attendance. Kawabata was close to sixty, and she described him as a wisp of a man with huge eyes and a shock of thick grey hair. She said he seemed like a deer, tentatively emerging from the forest. Reading Mrs Vining's letter, I was happy to be reminded of her unabashed enthusiasms, her largeness of heart and sheer goodness. I was very much looking forward to meeting her again.

We found ourselves standing together at the reception, waiting in line to be presented to our royal Host and Hostess, and she greeted me with great warmth, said I hadn't changed a bit in the seven years since we'd met.

I said she was too kind, and that there was definitely rather more of me these days.

For my part, I added, I was happy to find her much as I remembered her, but even more so.

She seemed to have grown into herself, become who she was – charming, gracious, composed, and still with that twinkle of humour in the eye.

When the royal couple entered the great hall they made their way along the line of guests waiting to be presented, pausing briefly with each one, exchanging a greeting, a word of thanks, and moving on. Elizabeth said to me, *sotto voce*, that the poor dears must be exhausted from all that deep bowing.

Indeed, I said, it must be quite strenuous. I also knew that earlier in the day they had attended an outdoor rally in the drizzling rain, listened to interminable speeches and responded to the thousand-strong crowd shouting *Banzai!* at them.

When they reached us, the Prince and Princess stepped forward and shook hands with us, nodding and smiling. They said they were delighted we could be there.

I said we knew the day must have been a tiring one. One thousand *Banzais* and two hundred deep bows were no joke.

The Princess smiled and the Crown Prince laughed, was immediately the young boy I had taught all these years.

It is good to see you both! he said, and they continued along the line.

Elizabeth nudged me.

I see you have not lost your sense of humour, she said.

I can think of nothing worse, I said. That would indeed be hell. *Lasciate ogni speranza...*

Dear Mrs Vining, dear Elizabeth. She had prayed for the young Crown Prince, prayed that she herself be a worthy teacher. She had prayed that he might be a latter-day Prince Shotoku, a bringer of unity and peace, prayed that he would lead his country in its hour of need. *Bless this child to whom one day will come great responsibility. Endow his teachers with wisdom and courage and grant that we may serve his best development...*

Amen.

12

BARBARIC YAWP

There is a verse by Whitman I have on my office wall, beside a sharp, jagged drawing of a crane by Mu Ch'i.

I too am not a bit tamed, I too am untranslatable.
I sound my barbaric yawp over the roofs of the world..

If I were ever to gather these scribbled pages together and publish them as a volume, I might consider that as a title.
My Barbaric Yawp, by the untranslatable RH Blyth.

The best things are inexpressible.
The untranslatable words are good.

I shall continue writing these pages as long as I keep my faculties intact.
Who wrote that? JD Salinger, I think. Yes, in his short story. *For Esme with Love and Squalor.*
Keep my f-a-c-u-l-t-i-e-s intact.
Mr Salinger, who told his readers about me.
There was the young American woman who tracked me down at Gakushuin, asked if she could interview me. She was writing a paper, or a dissertation, or a thesis, on Vedanta and Zen in the work of JD Salinger. She happened to be in Tokyo and asked if we might meet.
Why not?
She quoted to me a passage from Salinger's novel *Frannie and Zooey*

– a passage I noticed she had underlined.

'Bore that I am, I mentioned R. H. Blyth's definition of sentimentality: that we are being sentimental when we give to a thing more tenderness than God gives to it.'

She looked at me eagerly, as if expecting me to comment. I breathed deep. She turned the dog-eared page, found another underlined passage.

'Regarding R. H. Blyth: Blyth is sometimes perilous, naturally, since he's a high-handed old poem himself, but he's also sublime – and who goes to poetry for safety anyway?'

Did you know about these passages? she asked.

They have been drawn to my attention, I said.

A high-handed old poem!

She had clearly familiarised herself with my own work, and at one point she ventured to take me to task, albeit gently and with a smile, for what she called a discriminatory attitude towards women.

I said perhaps she had read too much into one or two throwaway remarks about women haiku poets.

What then is your position? she asked.

Let me put it this way, I said. Zen distinguishes between what it calls *dai-ich-gi* and *dai-ni-gi*, the absolute and the relative.

Are you going to bamboozle me with philosophy? she asked.

Not at all, I said.

The absolute and the relative?

And we may speak from either. For example, absolutely speaking, men and women are the same and their enlightenment is the same. But relatively speaking they are different and their enlightenment is different.

And what does Zen say?

Zen means speaking from both at the same time. And we must speak from both at the same time. All the time.

Bamboozling! she said, showing an admirable grasp of Zen.

I might have said to her that the object of life is to understand one another, in particular, for men to understand women (which some think should be easy but is not) and for women to understand men (who seem mysterious but are not).

The process is as difficult as it is for one nation – if such an illusion has any real existence – to understand another.

A very old friend of mine, Cycill Tomrley, had recently written to me from home, not quite taking me to task, but challenging me, teasing me about the selfsame matter, and I managed to find the letter, show it to the young American.

(I have the letter here as I write this. It is written on the same kind of blue airmail paper my dear mother always used).

No one ever writes about Zen for women, she wrote, *except you, and that with a tinge of dubiety. A western woman like myself, doing for many hours each week the sort of work men do, feels neither fish, flesh nor fowl. I am not one who believes men and women are built to the same plan. But if psychologists such as Jungians take especial pains over women, why not the Zen teachers? Could you write a book for British women? Obviously you could, but you can't. (Answering my own questions is still a speciality!)*

Occasionally women, usually old hags, appear in Zen anecdotes, but the enlightenment of women is conspicuous by its absence (and sex problems are conveniently ignored).

Buddha accepted women into his order with the utmost reluctance and prophesied they would be the ruin of it. A reaction to this has been to say he should not be judged by the standards of the 20th Century. I agree, but say he should be judged by the standards of the 30th Century. If a man's view of half the world is wrong, then so must his view of the other half be wrong.

Woman is man's joy and all his bliss. That was Chaucer.

But then Byron wrote, *There is a tide in the affairs of woman / Which, taken at the flood, leads God knows where.*

I would add that God does indeed know where, and that *where* includes randomness, spontaneity, unpredictability, all absolutely essential to our very existence.

Woman represents nature, and in criticising women, men criticise the universe itself.

> *'All women...'*
> *He declares, looking*
> *Over his shoulder.*

I myself like women. If I were the only man in the world, as the sentimental song does *not* say, then I would be perfectly happy!
Do I contradict myself? Very well, then I contradict myself.
I've quoted that before, often. Many a time and oft.
Do I repeat myself? Very well, then I repeat myself.
(Very well, then I repeat myself!)

Dickens called critics and reviewers the lice of literature, rotten creatures with men's forms and devils' hearts. But even Dickens was stung by them, by their pigmy arrows, and had to steel himself against them, overcome his rage and gain victory over them by being indifferent and bidding them whistle on.
There was one critic, however, who got to me and shattered my hard-won equanimity. My volumes of haiku translations and commentaries, published by Hokuseido, had gained me some small reputation, and for the most part they had been well received. But one day I received in the post a long angry letter from some old man who clearly regarded himself as (God help us!) an authority. He took me to task, mercilessly and at great length, saying that I did not understand haiku at all, neither in the particular nor in general, neither the individual poem nor the underlying spirit of the form.
I read the letter a second time to make sure I had not misunderstood. I folded it up again and put it back in its envelope, and I realised my hands were actually shaking I was so angry. I continued to be angry for three days, making life miserable for poor Tomiko and the children. Eventually Tomiko suggested, tentatively, that I go to Kamakura to visit Dr Suzuki at Engakuji. I thanked her and set out forthwith.

As usual the good Doctor and I sat with the tea-bowls, the little rice-cakes, on a low table between us. His secretary had brought in the tray, set it down and left us to it.

The pent-up rage came out of me all-in-a-rush. I ranted about the unfairness of the criticism, the unthinking dismissiveness of it.

Whatever I know or don't know of haiku, I said, at least I can say I know nothing of Zen!

Nothing, he said, and nodded.

I waited for him to say more, to remonstrate with me. I braced myself for a reproof, hoped for teaching, advice.

Tea, he said, indicating the bowl in front of me.

I raised the bowl to my lips, sipped, breathed in the fragrance, the *greenness*. Vegetation after spring rain.

We sat in silence. The creak creak of cicadas came through the open shoji screen. I took in the deeper background smells, redolence of old timber, pine incense.

Finally he spoke.

People with poetic mind, he said, are more sensitive to things than others, and sometimes they take longer to forget.

To praise instead of blaming.

I was overwhelmed and burst into tears.

I look back at my younger self (and even my older self). Why that anger? Why the stupid tears? What was wrong with me? Who did I think I was? Puffed up and foolish, full of myself. And still Suzuki treated me with kindness.

O wad some power the giftie gie us, tae see oursels as ithers see us.

To see ourselves. That would be blessing and curse, in equal measure.

Critics aside, it seems my reputation has grown and I have been credited with the creation of an entirely new form of poetry, English language haiku. Existentialists, imagists, zennists, japanologists, all-sorts-of-other-ists have sung my praises and found in my little translations (or reworkings) something fresh and liberating. Apart from Mr Salinger, and that passage where he called me a high-handed old poem, I have been acknowledged by Alan Watts, himself a successful populariser of Zen. I am grateful to him, though his *Beat Zen, Square Zen and Zen* left me cold. And as for that Beat Zen (or beat zen) a whole host of those younger poets have quoted me and thanked me – Messrs Ginsberg and Kerouac and Snyder (who is by far the most interesting of them all). Beat, they say, is drumbeat or heartbeat, it is beaten, it is upbeat or beat up, it is blessed as in beatitude. (Beatitudinous?) I cannot say I particularly enjoy their excesses, but I admire their chutzpah. At their best they echo Whitman and Blake.

I sing the body electric.

Energy is eternal delight.

I am amazed that they have read my work and responded to it so positively and wholeheartedly.

At the other extreme, one outraged critic wrote, *Blyth talks too much. He should have been strangled at birth.* There's just no pleasing some folks.

I have a cutting from The Times in which Aldous Huxley reviewed Zen in English Literature.

The book deals with the relation between moment-by-moment experience of things-as-they-are and poetry. It is a bit perverse sometimes, but very illuminating at others.

I would settle for that as an acknowledgement and a fair description (perhaps even an epitaph?) A bit perverse sometimes, very illuminating at others.

We does our best.

As for those self-styled Beat Poets, Mr Ginsberg's *angel-headed hipsters*, Suzuki has his own view. The subject came up recently and he delivered his opinion in a controlled monotone, his words measured, his gaze steely. More than ever these days, with his eyebrows and nose-hairs overgrown and uncut, he resembles some ancient fierce-eyed sage, a Zen patriarch in a painting by Hakuin.

The aim of Zen, he said, is to open the eye of vision and knowledge, the *aryajnana*. It is to see directly into the true reality, to confront a world which is entirely new, and yet at the same time not new at all. This is where there is gross misunderstanding, he said, a complete misinterpretation by those who have never actually had the Zen experience.

Those who know do not speak, I said, mindful of the fact that I myself was prone to speaking at great length on the matter in hand, and in fact on anything under the sun.

I refer, he said, to the modern-day addicts of the so-called psychedelic drugs.

Mr Huxley, I said, is a great advocate of mescalin as an aid to opening the doors of perception.

Indeed, said Suzuki. And I believe there are other drugs in use – psilocybin and LSD. It seems they conjure up 'mystic' visions which the users claim have some connection with Zen.

Instant samadhi, I said. Satori in a pill.

It is preposterous, said Suzuki. They will do anything for realisation except work for it. And these visions have nothing whatever to do with Zen, either psychologically or spiritually. The Mumonkan makes it perfectly clear. Zen is not concerned with visions but with the person. The drug-users can never have the true inner experience of identity. They stay forever on the surface of reality and never look into the secrets of the here-and-now which transcends the relative.

When he'd finished his rant, his little discourse for this audience of one, I bowed and smiled, like Maha Kashapa after the Flower Sermon.

Suzuki sensei, I said, you are the only man who can speak about Zen, or write about it, without making me loathe it.

Good, he said, laughing. Good!

Later I wrote down what he had said while it was still fresh. Lest I forget.

Among the unlikeliest of my admirers is Henry Miller who wrote to me to say how much he appreciated my work. I tracked down his *Tropic of Cancer* after he had contacted me and I could see why there has been such an outcry about his novels. He has stirred things up as much as Lawrence ever did, and for the same reasons.

I replied to his gracious letter, thanking him and saying in spite of all the outrage he has provoked, I had the impression he was a man of great modesty (and obvious frankness).

I said that perhaps my years of living in the East had inculcated the idea that what is hidden is best, a philosophy seemingly at odds with his own approach.

He said he hoped to come to Japan some day, and I said if he did it would be a shocking pleasure to meet him. (And I chose that adjective carefully, another example of the hidden!)

I might have told him that any criticism of the universe, its wasteful cruelty, its perverse purposelessness, its glaring inconsistencies, is improper.

Sadly I never experienced that shocking pleasure – we never met and now we never will. We exchanged a few more letters and I sent him in return for his novel, two of my small pamphlets on Zen. It would be hard to imagine work more different from his own, but they delighted him and he thanked me with great effusiveness.

I seem to recall him expressing a fondness for Japanese women, for their charm and reserve. I mentioned this to my American colleague Bill Moore who said Mr Miller probably wanted to marry one to add to his collection. His attitude to Japanese men was rather different. With a nod to Hobbes he dismissed the ones he had met as nasty, brutish and short. While disagreeing with the generalisation (as with all generalisations) I found that made me laugh out loud. I think Mr Miller would appreciate senryu.

Politically, nationally and cosmically we have to cheer on both sides, all sides, rejoicing with the brutes and weeping with the brutalised. This is no easy matter. For my part I find it difficult to share in superficiality, to wade in sentimentality and to wallow in vulgarity. But on all these fronts perhaps I have made some little progress.

(Do I contradict myself? Not only that, I have full-blown arguments with myself, both of me equally vehement).

There was another contemporary writer who acknowledged a debt to me, the black American novelist Richard Wright. I received a handwritten letter from him, addressed to me at Gakushuin, in an envelope with a Paris postmark. I hadn't read his work, but I knew he had made an impact with his novel *Native Son*, and a memoir, *Black Boy,* drawing on his experience of growing up in the Southern States.

His letter moved me deeply. His suffering as a child had been unimaginable, and one lasting effect, he admitted, was that the countryside, and by extension the natural world, only reminded him of the misery and poverty, the sheer unremitting bleakness of his early years.

But then latterly, as if by some kind of miracle (his word!) he discovered my four-volume *Haiku* and (again, his words) the veil was lifted and he saw things clear. The brevity of the form was a revelation, as was the simple mathematics of it, the elegant 5-7-5 structure. (I write them all the time, he wrote. I'm always counting syllables on my fingers!)

He had been in poor health, and work on a full length book, *Island of Hallucinations*, was exhausting. Discovering haiku, he said, had been a liberation, and he just wanted to thank me, from the bottom of his heart, for opening up new worlds, or rather for showing him *this* world with new eyes.

He said he had written hundreds of poems. But don't worry, he added, I don't intend to bombard you! Instead he enclosed with his letter a sheet of thin paper with a single poem typed out. (Not strict form, he said, unusually for me. But I think it works!)

The poem described a light fall of rain, raising a smell of silk from umbrellas.

There was a return address, and I wrote back telling him how touched I was that he had taken the trouble to write to me, and that, like me, he had found the way of haiku a solace, a consolation and a joy. I told him the silk umbrella poem was very fine, made real by that sensory detail, the faint smell of silk, linking it to the thinness of the rain, the suggestion perhaps that the season might be spring. I also said I was glad to see he was not straitjacketed by the strict

5-7-5 form. Catching the moment, in just the right words was more important than the arithmetic of the thing.

Finally I said if he wanted to send me a few more of his poems I would be delighted to read them.

I fully expected a response but nothing came. I was hard at work with the teaching, and the work on my own books, so I thought no more about it. Then a month or two later I was in the library at Gakushuin, reading a week-old copy of the London *Times*, and I read a notice that he had died in Paris, 'after a long illness.'

I sat for a time then folded up the newspaper. Yamanashi happened to pass by and he bowed, asked if something was troubling me. I told him about Mr Wright and his passing, said I was unexpectedly affected by it, considering I had never met the man.

Yamanashi was silent, then said simply, Life is tears.

I said I only wished I had written more in my letter to Mr Wright. Things are as they are, said Yamanashi. I am sure what you wrote was perfect.

The writing of haiku worldwide, in other languages, was something I did not foresee. (Though I myself have been told I must accept some of the blame!)

It would be a good thing the Japanese to see that writers in America and elsewhere might equal or even surpass them in their own field, beat them at their own game.

I looked forward to reading haiku from Russia – all the vast energy, the intense bleakness of the Russian soul, contained, or constrained, in a three-line poem. War and Peace reduced! I cannot, however, imagine (nor could I countenance) a communistic haiku, any more than a capitalistic haiku, or a nationalistic haiku. Such things are a glorious impossibility. Haiku are universal, international. What an Earthly Paradise it will be when the Eskimo blow on their fingers as they write haiku about the sun that never rises, the sun that never sets. Or when African tribesmen compose jungle haiku about the gorilla or the python. Or nomads of the Gobi or the Sahara pause, wipe the grit from their eyes to see a world in a grain of sand.

I have always been rather resistant to most contemporary haiku about the realities of modern life. I stubbornly held to my view – of course I did! – even though a poet as great as Shiki had written passable verses on baseball. But poems on the mechanised city life of commerce and work held little appeal. *However* (a most useful word) I recently came across this in a newspaper:

> *The pattering of the hail,*
> *The sound of the telegraph machine,*
> *The night-scene outside the window.*

This is good in that it finds meaningless meaning in the present day world, the urbanised industrialised world with its noise and harshness and clatter.

There is an American poet, Charles Reznikoff, who does this kind of thing very well. He has a poem exhorting the reader not to despise a shining green jewel simply because it happens to be a traffic light.
This is very good indeed.
Do not despise…
That could be a credo.
Yes.

At different times in my life I have returned to Basho's frog haiku, *Furuike ya….* I have written about it excessively. But then even the inestimable Dr Suzuki has been driven to excess in discussing it. He told me once that he thought the little leap of the frog was just as weighty as Adam's Fall from the Garden of Eden, for here too was a truth revealing the secrets of creation.
I nodded, sagely, then I laughed, and he asked why.
I said there had been some execrable translations, especially of that untranslatable last line.
The best, I said (and worst), going for full onomatopoeic effect, was *Waterish splish-splosh.* It makes it sound as if Basho has fallen in.
Suzuki gave a low chuckle, did his best to pronounce the line.

Waterish splish-splosh.

There goes Adam, I said.

Nevertheless...

The power of the poem persists. Like a koan it opens out, expands beyond itself.

Furuike ya kawazu tobikomu mizu no oto

The old pond:
A frog jumps in –
The sound of water

The pond is old, in an old garden. The surrounding trees are ancient, the trunks green with moss. The silence is timeless, it reaches far back beyond man and all his noise.

A frog jumps in.

The silence is broken. The whole garden, the whole universe is contained in one single plop! It is the soundless sound, a sound that is beyond sound, and silence, and yet, *and yet*, it is the sound of the water of the old pond.

In my *Zen in English Literature* I gave a laboured explanation of the poem, covering eight pages. I have changed my mind.

My translation obscures something fundamental in the original, something that belongs to the Japanese mind and language.

The empty spaces in pictures.

The absence of things in rooms.

The silences in conversation.

This *something* is a lack of division and separation, a sense of the whole when dealing with the parts.

What was it Basho omitted to say?

When he heard 'the sound of water,' the sound of *this* water, he heard the sound of all nature.

This might be better, more true.

The old pond:
  The sound
    Of a frog jumping into the water.

But Basho's real and imagined experience might be rendered:

The old pond:
The-sound-of-a-frog-jumping-into-the water.

Or perhaps the best rendition after all would be simply:

The old pond:
  A frog jumps in –
    Plop!

There. Let that be an end of it.
Plop!

I have written much (some would say *too* much) on my love of hai-ku. They have been a consolation and a joy. But in my later years I have to say I have loved senryu even more, in their ability to thumb the nose at humanity, to cock a snook at authority, to laugh in the face of adversity (and of prosperity).
And after all, solemnity and sanctimoniousness are not, let us hope, inevitable to religion.
Thank God.
(And I do actually believe God laughed the Universe into being).
In the beginning was the joke.

> *A blockhead bit by fleas put out the light,*
> *And chuckling, cried, 'Now you can't see to bite!'*

Zen is the religion of disrespectful respect and respectful disrespect. It has something of Sam Weller in it, and nowhere more so than in *senryu*.

A good senryu is no respecter of persons, or rather it respects all persons utterly and not at all. It is most definitely no respecter of rank and position and privilege.

The T'ang Emperor Genso was the most powerful man of his age, and his concubine the Princess Yokihi was regarded as the most beautiful woman in China (and therefore in the world).

Here they are, pinned to the page.

The Emperor Genso
  Sobs and sobs,
    Picking his ears.

Princess Yokihi,
  Her beautiful face,
    Eating pork chops.

And a wry look at their relationship, rendering them as everyman and everywoman:

Making him grateful to her
  That she loves him
    More than her own life.

Of course no poet of the time could have written these lines and kept his head, unless, perhaps the Emperor Genso and the Princess Yokihi were blessed with a sense of humour. And it seems to me humour is a kind of practical transcendence. It raises us above the mundane while keeping us grounded in it.

And yet I doubt if senryu will ever be as popular as haiku. After all, who can object to haiku? They are small and inoffensive, are generally about nature. (And who does not profess a love of nature?) So haiku are allowed, even admired, by people whose lives are diametrically opposed to the haiku way of living (as long as they can keep their television set, their luxury home, their fast car...)

Senryu are something else again – scathing, satirical, often downright vicious. They do not make comfortable reading.

The husband –
  When his wife dies,
He sends a letter to the other.

The other here is, the other woman.
It was ever thus.

Of course there is a danger inherent in senryu, that they may descend into vulgarity, as waka can descend into sentimentality and haiku into insipidity and inanity.
Them's the risks.

I find myself once again thinking of Thoreau..

  How hard it is to remember
  What is most memorable.
  We remember how we itched,
  Not how our hearts beat.

But then again, perhaps in itching we are most fully alive.

  There was a young lady from Natchez,
  Whose clothes were in tatters and patches.
  When asked to digress
  On the state of her dress,
  She replied, 'When I itches, I scratches.'

Did I write that? What it lacks in profundity it gains in vigour.

Let me turn once more to senryu.

The weaknesses of men –
  They escape from them
    To the graveyard.

I can no longer remember who wrote that, but the translation is my own. As is this:

The way back from the cemetery.
  How far away...
    How long ago...

And this:

Watching the stream
  Watching
    My life.

Have I become jaded and cynical in my old age? Or have I always been so?
Whatever the truth of it, I have to say my favourite senryu is this:

  Someone trying his sword
  On a chance wayfarer –
  Jizo looks on, calmly

An arrogant disaffected samurai has purchased a new sword. To test the quality of the blade, he tries it out randomly on some hapless innocent who just happens to be passing by, cutting him down and killing him without a qualm. A statue of Jizo looks on, impassive. Jizo, the god of mercy, patron saint of travellers and children.

I suppose what I like in the poem its serene detachment and, simultaneously, its savage irony. (Or its serene irony, its savage detachment).

Master Ummon said this: When you meet a swordsman, meet him with a sword. Don't offer a poem to anyone but a poet.

The sword, sadly, is mightier than the pen.

It is written that those who live by the sword shall perish by the sword. But there are times when the opposite holds good, and those who draw not the sword shall also perish by the sword, dragging down the innocent and the guilty alike to share their doom.

I have watched Kurosawa's *Seven Samurai* thee or four times and even though I am a lifelong pacifist I find it thrilling. When I think of the film there is one particular scene that comes to mind. It features the character Kyuzo, the stern-faced Zen warrior, a master swordsman, played by Seiji Miyaguchi. In the scene in question, Kyuzo is on guard at the edge of the village he is trying to protect against marauding bandits. From the quality of the light it is late afternoon, moving towards evening. He is seated beneath a tree, still and unmoving as if in zazen. He is surrounded by small white flowers. He lets his gaze rest on them. He reaches out and touches one, acknowledging its presence, its being. Two bandits, perhaps thinking he is asleep or daydreaming, have been creeping up behind him, ever closer. Alerted by the slightest sound he responds. All-in-one-movement he is on his feet, sword drawn, all-in-one-movement he cuts his enemies down. His concentration is total, his focus one-pointed. Flashing blade. This is the Sword of Manjushri, the sword of discrimination, cleaving ignorance.

I asked Suzuki about this symbolic nature of the sword, and he said it was twofold. One function is to destroy anything that opposes the will of the sword's owner. The other is to sacrifice the instinct of self-preservation. The first relates to the spirit of patriotism or militarism, while the second has a deeper, religious connotation of loyalty and self-sacrifice. In the first, the sword may mean destruction pure and simple, the symbol of force, sometimes devilish. It must therefore be controlled and consecrated by the second function. Then destruction is turned against the evil spirit. The sword comes to be identified with the annihilation of things which lie in the way of peace, justice, progress, and humanity. It stands for all that is desirable for the spiritual welfare of the world at large.

I wrote all of this down in a little notebook, intent on recording what Suzuki actually said on the matter. The danger, of course, is of glamourising or fetishising the actual swordblade, glorifying the actual hacking to death of actual human beings.

Suzuki has been accused of this kind of mythologising, condoning violence. And yes, in these times he too has his critics, many of them hostile in the extreme. They point to his writings on *Bushidō*, the way of the warrior. He has praised the samurai spirit, the virtue of *Hagakure*, translated as *Hidden under the Leaves*, the ideal of working selflessly for the good of mankind. But he is accused of conflating this with ideas of military conquest, pan-Asian expansion, colonisation. He is even accused of sympathising with the Nazis, identifying with their reliance on the Will.

Yet when the Pacific War came to an end, he spoke of the conflict as useless and meaningless, caused by the ambitions of ignorant and power-thirsty militarists.

At the outset of that war, he wrote – memorably, I think – that all things move along a line of the inevitable, and mere human powers are altogether helpless to shape their own course.

For my part I have already put it on record that Suzuki is the sanest and wisest man I have ever known.

He operates from a level of understanding rarely encountered, where the immanent and the transcendent are one. He knows that everything is relative, and that at the same time everything is absolute. He understands the void in the full and the full in the void. Does he contradict himself?

(He is small, he contains multitudes).

I must take time in these pages to attempt the almost impossible and pay tribute to what Suzuki-sensei has meant to me. He has been an unfailing guide, mentor, friend, and I have always found it difficult to disagree with anything he wrote – well, *almost* anything, and if I have ever ventured to criticise him, it has simply been biting the hand that fed me. (No more could I disagree with anything Mozart composed, or Paul Klee painted, or DH Lawrence wrote). A great writer is great in every sentence. A great man is great in every action, as the sea is salt in every drop. Dr Suzuki is a great man, in every cell, in every atom.

There are some Zen practitioners I have met who seem – how can I put it? – not sufficiently human. They are lacking in human warmth. Oh, they are transcendental all right, but there never seem to have any emotion to transcend. Dr Suzuki is a notable exception.

He has been criticised (of course he has) for not engaging in political discourse. But I believe his wisdom transcends all opposites, including political differences.

I once asked him if the human race is more taken up with war than peace? And has there always been more war than peace in our world? And if that is the case, what is the zen man to do?

His eyed narrowed under those bushy brows and he replied, Zen does not bring about peace or war. How could it do that? Instead it shows us how to live properly in either.

Sadly the universe was not made for happiness. Our lives may have peace, but they must also have sorrow.

> *Man was made for joy and woe*
> *And when this we rightly know*
> *Through the world we safely go.*

To *rightly* know is the whole story.

Bob Aitken wrote to me, years ago, about hearing Suzuki speak during a lecture tour of the US.

He said the Master would begin, in a quiet voice, and with a raising

of those ferocious eyebrows, *Lately I have been thinking...*
And the audience would immediately be attentive, alert, leaning
forward in their chairs.
What? What is it he's lately been thinking?
I knew exactly what Bob meant. I experienced it every time I heard
Suzuki talk. His every utterance felt like the beginning of an ad-
venture. There was a narrative that led the listener on, ever deeper.
Come along with me and let's see where this leads, through twists
and turns and chance encounters, challenges and reversals, puzzles
and insights and moments of dazzling illumination. And where
does it end? With luck, back where we started, in the here and now,
ready to begin again.
Begin again.

Suzuki is the hub of a great wheel of interconnectedness. He is a
one-man Indra's Net, extending beyond time and space, linked to
everything everywhere, and, or so it seems, to everyone.
I recall him speaking of his former pupil at Gakushuin, Yanagi
Soetsu, who had founded the Folk Art Museum in Seoul (the very
one I had visited with Akio and Shinki so long ago). Yanagi had
opened a similar museum in Tokyo, the Mingeikan in Komaba.
At one stage, not long after the war, there had been a move by the
occupying forces to requisition the building (and indeed Yanagi's
house next door) as a residence for the Dutch military attache. This
would have been an act of cultural barbarism and I added my voice
to the widespread protests which in the end were successful.
On one occasion Suzuki himself took me to the Mingeikan. He told
me he thought Yanagi and I had much in common, in our eclecti-
cism, in our borrowing from East and West, our efforts to bridge
the gulf between the two.
For example, he said, he is inspired as much by Blake as by Dogen.
This was intriguing, but what really caught me was the actual qual-
ity of the work. I picked up a little tea-bowl (and that in itself was
telling, the fact that I *could* pick it up – it was not in a glass case as
some of the rarer items were). It had a simple rightness about it, the
roughness and texture of the glaze, the weight, the perfection of the

not-quite-perfect shape, comfortable (and comforting) in the hand.
I told Suzuki it reminded me of the cheap, everyday bowls I had
bought in the markets in Seoul. This had the same feeling of being
made for use – form following function – but shaped by something
more, the artist's hand and eye, his consciousness.

Suzuki nodded and said he was sure Yanagi-san would agree. Then
he led me through to a back room and introduced me to the man
himself who was bright-eyed and intense, stocky-built with a wide
clear forehead, a swept-back mane of thick iron-grey hair. He bowed
then shook my hand vigorously, said he was very happy to meet me.
He laughed when Suzuki told him what I had just said about the
pottery. Yanagi was particularly delighted by the Seoul connection.
For too long, he said, the heavy hand of Japanese militarism had
lain on the Land of Morning Calm.

I thought of Akio Fujii, refined and cultured, secure in his certainties.
Yanagi had countered what he called this cultural imperialism by
opening that small museum in the old palace building.

I was there! I said. I went with a colleague.

Yanagi smiled. It was a place where politics could be left at the door
and people could meet together to discuss the things that really
matter.

Art, love, truth and beauty, I said.

Exactly so!

Over tea – which I had to drink – a smoky, fragrant bancha he said
was from the 200-year-old Ippodo teahouse in Kyoto, served, of
course, in exquisite bowls – he spoke with great enthusiasm about
his aesthetics, his philosophy. (They were one and the same thing).
Beginning with the tea – he took a sip, savoured it – he said *Cha-no-
yu*, the *art* of tea was the *way* of tea. They could not be separated
from each other, or from the craftsmanship involved.

True craftsmen, he said, work without ego to create a kind of natural
beauty. They make things that are plain and simple but marvellous.

And yet this, I said, holding up the bowl from which I had been
drinking, is particularly fine.

Yes, he said, and I am glad it pleases you. It is by Shōji Hamada.
But he works in a tradition. He owes great debt to those who have

gone before, to generations of artisans.

Anonymous, said Suzuki. Unsung.

Yes, said Yanagi.

But this, I said, again indicating the bowl, this is special.

It manifests *mekiki*, said Suzuki. You might call it the seeing eye.

Mekiki, I said, savouring the word, saving it for future use.

Yanagi said he was not denying the existence of individual talent, even genius. But real greatness, he said, lay in humility. This was not negating individuality but transcending it.

I nodded, laughing at the clarity of his insight.

Yes!

Suzuki said, It is letting the Buddha-nature shine through.

Now it was Yanagi who nodded and laughed. He clapped his hands.

Hai!

Suzuki continued. The best quality of Yanagi-san's work is *shibui*.

This time Yanagi simply bowed.

How to translate *shibui*? Austere? Subdued? But more complex than these (and at the same time simpler!) the word held a suggestion of quietness, purity, depth, all born of an inwardness, something innately spiritual.

Like this, I said, holding up the bowl from which I had been drinking.

Yanagi bowed again, leaned across and re-filled the bowl with tea.

We talked the afternoon away, moving easily from Zen and the Pure Land to Blake and Ruskin, Basho to the French Impressionists, the Bible to the Dhammapada.

When it was time to leave he handed me a little package, a gift. I opened it back in Mejiro, found it contained the tea bowl I had used and admired. He had obviously asked one of his assistants to wash it and wipe it dry, wrap it for me in beautiful rough-textured handmade paper.

A few weeks later I returned to the museum at Yanagi's invitation to meet his old friend, the potter Bernard Leach who was visiting from England. I knew Leach by reputation, and he was also an admirer, almost an acolyte, of Suzuki (who had sent his apologies and could not attend on this occasion). Grateful for Yanagi's generous gift of the tea bowl, I brought, by way of thanks, a signed copy of my *Zen in English Literature* and another copy for Mr Leach.

Yanagi thanked me with much enthusiasm, grinning and touching the book to his forehead. He pointed to the inscription, delighted, thanked me again. Leach was much more restrained, in a way I remembered as peculiarly English. It was there too in his appearance, tall and thin in a well cut suit, a collar and tie, white hair neatly combed, moustache trimmed. His manner was rather scholarly – a visiting professor – as he scanned the contents of the book.

Interesting, he said. Thank you. Then offhandedly, almost diffidently, he gave me a copy of his own volume, modestly titled *A Potter's Book*, which I took gratefully and touched to my own forehead.

Arigato.

Thank you.

Leach's voice was pleasant enough, urbane, not too Home Counties, with a slight lilt to it, perhaps from spending time in St Ives.

He asked where I was from, how I had come to be in Japan.

Like Yanagi he was intrigued that I had spent time in Korea, and he asked about my Zen practice there. Was there a touch of amusement in the eyes when I told him how many years I had done *zazen*?

Excellent, he said. Dr Suzuki speaks very highly of you.

And of you. I said.

He told me he had first been drawn to Japan by the magic of Lafcadio Hearne's prose. I resolved to put that aside and not hold it against him. He then spoke at length of his connection with Suzuki, linking through Gakushuin to the group of writers and artists known (rather too poetically for my taste) as *Shirakaba*, or Silver Birch.

As on my previous visit, we sat together drinking tea (I had one cup then switched to warm water) and setting the world to rights. Leach had a tendency to hold forth, a self-styled expert. But he was a clear thinker and it was no great hardship to listen to him expound, especially with Yanagi contributing a counterpoint, making his own enthusiastic interruptions. My own role, I felt, was to add the occasional grace note.

We spoke of beauty and pattern, vitality and stillness, the joy of imperfection. We returned again to Blake, the holy madman.

Yanagi spoke about Blake with something approaching reverence. Blake loved nature, he said, but he knew we could not copy nature. Yanagi denounced those who dismissed Blake's visions as pathological. No! he said, his own eyes shining. Blake saw beyond the senses. He saw the infinite in all things. He saw God.

In this world, I said. Here and now..

This. A rainy day in Tokyo.

Amen! said Leach, and he laughed.

Most of all, said Yanagi, Blake hated the kind of mechanistic rationalism we see everywhere.

I told him I was given to ranting about exactly that, whenever the opportunity arose.

Once again we talked the afternoon away.

When it was time for me to go, both men shook my hand. Leach asked if I ever visited Cornwall.

I've never been, I said.

You would love it, he said. The quality of the light…

He left the sentence unfinished, the words trailing, his eyes bright with remembrance, and in the moment I saw the life of him, his inwardness, the quality I had seen in his vases and pots, a kind of delicacy combined with robustness.

You must visit, he said, next time you are in England.

I will indeed, I said. But even as I spoke the words, I sensed that I never would. I would not return home. Not never no more.

13

SACRED TREASURE

One day at the school, after a lesson, Yamanashi took me aside.
He looked thoughtful, serious, enough to cause me a little flurry of
concern. I waited for him to speak.

There was a faction, he said at last, certain *friends* of the school, who
would be happy to see me removed.

I know I can be difficult, I said, perhaps even anarchic. But I'm
damned if I'm going to show up at those endless faculty meetings
that start in the early morning and go on till late at night and end
up resolving absolutely nothing. They are my idea of hell.

He nodded, smiled.

I understand, he said. And yes, your non-attendance must annoy
some of your colleagues. But the problem is deeper than that.

He had my full attention.

What have I done?

These people have short memories, he said. They forget that Ga-
kushuin owes its continued existence to your efforts. They want
things to be as they were, without foreign interference. And when
they see a *gaijin* teaching their sons, teaching the Crown Prince, the
kind of people we are talking about can be very disapproving.

The kind of people who had disapproved of the Emperor's Declara-
tion of Humanity, and the very act of surrender. The kind of people
who had approved of the war in the first place.

I understood what the Admiral was telling me. I had to be circum-
spect.

Around this time I was cycling home one day from the Palace and heard a blast of martial music, tinny and loud, blaring from a loud-speaker van up ahead. I felt a sickening emptiness in my gut as I recognised the melody, remembered it from Kobe, crackling on the the camp commander's old gramophone, *Roei no Uta*, the Bivouac Song. The van pulled over and three men got out, all in dark suits and wearing armbands. They began handing leaflets to passers by as the music carried on the air, above the traffic noise, ridiculous and chilling, for all the world like the out-of-tune soundtrack to some old flickering newsreel film in a pre-war cinema, an anachronism, a time gone.

Yamanashi's none-too-veiled warnings about those hostile *factions* proved prescient. A few weeks after I had spoken to him, I came out of the classroom after a day's teaching to find that the tyres on my bicycle had been slashed. A close examination showed it could be no accident – the rubber had been cut through. I had to push the bike and walk home where I found Tomiko distraught and the girls close to tears. While we had been out in the afternoon and the house had been empty, someone had broken in and slashed the tatami mats in the downstairs room.

The authorities were apologetic, the damage was repaired immediately and there were no further attacks, but the whole business left us uneasy. I thanked God that Tomiko and the girls had not been at home. But the threat was clear. I had been warned.

Message received and understood.

Even now after living here for almost half my life, and immersing myself in the culture, and being, as Yamanashi-san would have it, an honorary Japanese, or in Dr Suzuki's eyes, an old Japanese soul, I am still regarded as *gaijin*, outsider, alien. (And, looking as I do, how could I ever be anything else?) Even the very word, gaijin, holds within it the idea of the other, and beyond that a sense of taint, impurity, uncleanliness – the foreigner as the great unwashed, the dirty barbarian. (And who can blame the Japanese for that? Do we not wallow in our own filthy bathwater, rather than washing first? Do we not wear our outdoor shoes inside, bringing all manner of muck from the street into our homes?)

I have long had a fondness for the films of Ozu, which I have been watching avidly since just after the War. They catch unerringly the texture and timbre of everyday life, portraying the nothing-special of it with profound insight and humanity. They are zen-without-Zen (and perhaps that is the best kind!) – understated, casting a clear eye on the everyday, the tangle and complexity of family life. They are suffused with utter melancholy but succeed in being affirmative. They always move me to my core, make me weep. And yet I have a Japanese colleague who prides himself on his knowledge of Ozu, and who insists that as I am not Japanese, I cannot possibly understand the films or appreciate them fully.

And why might that be? I ask him.

Simply *because* you are not Japanese, he answers.

I neglect to tell him that I once watched *Tokyo Story* with Tomiko and realised she found it slow and dull, the lives portrayed just too familiar.

Instead I tell the colleague that there may be subtleties and nuances I have missed, but I understand the spirit of the films, their intrinsic meaning (or non-meaning). And after all, I have lived in Japan for a very long time and immersed myself in the culture here far more than most.

It's true, he says. You are almost Japanese, so perhaps you can *almost* understand Ozu. But not completely.

We agreed to disagree.

I think when we westerners, we *gaijin* – especially men – first come to Japan, we see it through enchanted eyes. Then after some time that changes and we see through a glass darkly, we see the flaws and the shortcomings, the complexity and the sheer incomprehensibility of the place. Finally, perhaps, we see it as it really is, good and bad and neither, simply and utterly itself.

It is like the old Zen saying. Before studying Zen, the men are men and the mountains are mountains. While studying Zen, everything gets mixed up and it's hard to distinguish one thing from another. After studying Zen, once again the men are men and the mountains are mountains.

I once asked Suzuki, So what then is the difference between the before and the after? He answered, Afterwards you are maybe six inches off the ground!

So.

During a period of my own disenchantment with the place (the *during,* as it were, rather than the *before* or *after*) I found myself exasperated by the constraints and limitations I encountered. For a time I had been consumed by the notion that I should make a visit to London to see my mother. It was long overdue – I had not been home in almost twenty years – and I began, with some eagerness, to plan my trip. Then I came up against the brick wall of bureaucracy. Currency regulations forbade the taking of Japanese Yen out of the country. I would have to pay for my whole trip in Pounds Sterling. I thought, foolishly, that this would not be a problem. I was still earning a decent salary. I had sufficient funds. It should simply be a matter, surely, of making the exchange, buying what I needed.

Not so.

The office, in Shinjuku, was a characterless concrete monolith, one of the new monstrosities that had been thrown up – I use the term in both senses – immediately after the war.

The room was a clutter of wall-to-wall filing cabinets (in gunmetal grey) on top of which were cardboard boxes on top of which were stacks of dusty papers, the whole edifice looking as if it might topple at any moment. The scene was Dickensian – Jarndyce v Jarndyce. Or then again I might have wandered into a novel by Mr Kafka, or a play by Mr Beckett. And yet there was something about it all that was peculiarly and particularly Japanese, a resolute holding fast to some sense of order amid the chaos.

The young man dealing with me epitomised this. He explained to me, politely, the limit on the amount of Yen I would be able to buy. I did a quick calculation, told him, politely, that this would not be enough. It would barely cover my travel costs, allow for nothing extra, not even the basics. He said this was unfortunate but there was nothing he could do. I countered by telling him of my exalted status as a respected academic with money-in-the-bank. I even, to my shame, mentioned my role as tutor to the Crown Prince. Friends in High Places. He looked momentarily flustered then expressed his regret, came out with that old familiar mantra, *Shikata ga nai* – It can't be helped.

When I asked what on earth I was supposed to do, he said it was not for him to say....

There is another Japanese expression I had picked up. It refers to the habit of prevaricating, of talking round a subject, holding something back. I have to say it is something to which the Japanese are particularly prone. (That inclination of the head. *Anno...*) The way they put it is this: *Okuba ni mono ga hasamatta youna iikata o suru.* It literally means to speak as if there is something stuck between your back teeth. That was exactly what this young man did. He said perhaps I might make other arrangements.

I was blunt, asked him, What other arrangements?

I was being disingenuous. I knew what he meant but wanted him to come right out and say it. He meant I could buy US dollars on the black market and exchange them for pounds in the UK. Tomiko had mentioned this as a possibility, and even Yamanashi had reluctantly alluded to it, though he stopped short of recommending it as a course of action.

I asked the young man if he was indeed suggesting I buy black market dollars, no doubt at a greatly inflated rate. That figurative something, a prawn, an un-chewed piece of chicken, stayed lodged between his molars.

Anno...

I stood up and bowed, thanked him with exaggerated civility and made my way, raging, out of the building.

An earthquake, a toothache, a mad dog, a telephone message, and our house of peace, so painstakingly built, tumbles like a pack of cards.

I thought of the monk who asked his master how to conquer his overwhelming anger.

Can you show me this anger? said the master. Where is it to be found?

Back home I told Tomiko what had happened. I said I had made up my mind and I would not bend. She said something that might be translated as, Now *there's* a surprise! That made me smile, but I meant what I said. I would not do business with the black marketeers. And if that meant I could not yet return home, then so be it.

So be it.

I never made that trip home, never saw my mother. Now I fear I never will.

Swings and roundabouts. Yamanashi told me I had been nominated for an award from the Japanese Government, in the name of the Emperor. The particular honour was the the *Zuihosho*, the Order of the Sacred Treasure, (Fourth Grade!) and it was rare for such a thing to be awarded to a foreigner.

I was honoured, I said. Or rather, I would be once it was bestowed. I assumed it was the equivalent of an OBE back home, or an MBE. I really had no idea.

In general I had no truck with honours of any kind, found the whole idea repellent. But I was rather tickled at the thought of this prophet-without-honour being recognised in his adopted home. There was also a certain bittersweet irony in the thought that my old mother would have taken great pride in the award. It might be some small recompense for my having been denied the opportunity to return to England to see her. For that reason alone (I told myself) I would be happy to receive the Order. Sacred Treasure. Fourth Grade.

There was one sticking point. For some reason the presentation of the award to a British national had to be sanctioned by Her Britannic Majesty. And with my history of pacifism and conscientious objection, my lifetime of living in exile, in might be that Her Majesty would dismiss me as a knave, consign me to the outer darkness. *Off with his head!*

Yamanashi said he would keep me informed, and in due course he told me permission had been granted and I was invited to receive the award from the Emperor himself in a special ceremony at the palace. On the appointed day I travelled to the palace by taxi rather than on my bicycle, and instead of my chalky tweeds I wore a formal black three-piece suit, hired for the occasion, with a stiff-collared shirt and black bow tie. I might almost have passed for a gentleman of some standing.

The Emperor seemed genuinely happy to be presenting me with the award – an exquisitely crafted gilt medal, shaped like a Maltese cross, its ribbon pale blue trimmed with gold. He smiled as he pinned the medal to my lapel and I bowed with a truly heartfelt respect. He said he was grateful to be able to recognise my years of service to Japan, to his family and to Gakushuin. He also handed me a commemorative scroll bearing the Imperial chrysanthemum crest and his signature, with a reproduction of the medal, and my name spelled out in *katakana* lettering. RH Bu-Rai-Su. Mister Timeless. Reggie Blyth from Leytonstone. My old Ma would indeed have been proud, and the thought moved me greatly.

I always meant to frame the scroll, hang it above my desk, but that was one of a great many things I never quite got round to. So it stayed rolled up in its cardboard tube, and the medal in its elegant black-lacquered case sat on a shelf beside a little bronze figure of Amida Buddha and the wooden Daruma doll I had kept since Kobe. Reminders all. Sacred treasures.

I knew it would come to this. I had reached retirement-age – ripe and old – and bureaucracy being what it was, my contract came to an end. I would be pensioned off, put out to pasture, my golden coach turned into a pumpkin.

I could still teach classes, at the Girls' School and at a number of other locations, But I no longer had tenure at Gakushuin itself. Worst of all, we had to vacate our accommodation on campus, our home these fifteen years. In all that time we had been sheltered, protected. In Tokyo even small apartments were expensive and ideally we wanted a traditional Japanese house. But then I needed somewhere with substantial walls to take my 6,000 books. Tomiko said moving would give us a chance to have a clear-out, sell the books or give them away to a library. More than once she said we should

lug them to the nearest waste-ground, pile them up, make a pyre
and set them alight. All forms are burning. A bonfire of my vanities.
I had further requirements (demands?): a little breathing space, per-
haps a small garden, a decent distance from aeroplane flight paths
in and out of Haneda. Not too much to ask, I would have thought.
Not too much at all, said Yamanashi. As long as you don't mind
moving out of Tokyo.
Strangely, the thought had not occurred to me, but when he said it
I experienced a moment of illumination. Yes. As long as it was not
too far, that might be the answer.
Yamanashi said he would make enquiries, see what he could do.
Given the circles he moved in, I should not have been surprised
when he got back to me. He had an old friend who was the daugh-
ter of Viscount Eiichi Shibusawa the well-known industrialist. The
daughter had a house in Oiso which was lying empty and in need
of some repair. Yamanashi said he could negotiate a good price.
Yamanashi accompanied us on the train-ride to Oiso, a little over
thirty miles along the Tokaido line. The very name Tokaido still
thrilled me – the ancient trade route from Tokyo to Kyoto. Both
Hokusai and Hiroshige had made woodblock prints of views from
the road. Hakuin had been born at a way station in Hara and set
up his temple Shoin-ji close by. I was intoxicated at the thought of
it all, the connections.
Tomiko was disgruntled at the thought of moving from Tokyo, the
friends she had made there, the comfortable life we had led. She had
said as much, but she bore it well, tense but smiling and nodding,
smiling and nodding, saying it couldn't be helped.
I had read that Oiso had a population of just 20,000. After Tokyo
it felt like a village, a backwater. We stepped off the train and could
smell the sea. I could see Tomiko relax, perhaps reminded of her
home in Hagi. The girls breathed it all in, laughed, exhilarated. We
looked out across the town and there, emerging from mist, sat great
Fuji, timeless and familiar, a reassurance.
The house was on a low wooded hill at the edge of town, quiet and
sheltered, a little run down but somehow full of character. Inside
it smelled musty, but fresh air would clear that. We slid open the

shoji screens, let the outside in. Tomiko looked around, smiled approval at the kitchen, the size of the rooms. The girls ran outside, all excitement, to the back garden where a single pine tree grew tall. They ran back in, laughing the way they had when they were small, ran upstairs and called to us to come up and see, come up and see, there, through the window, in the distance the glint of sun on the water, a glimpse of the Shonan Sea.

Well? said Yamanashi, eyes twinkling.

Yes, I said. Yes.

This would be our home, perhaps my last.

I adjusted quickly to the new routine, the extended commute to work. I invested in a Green Car train ticket, giving more comfort, greater leg room. I used the journey time to read and even to write, scribbling in a notepad on my lap. If anything, my output increased. Did I know my time was short, even then? Time's winged chariot shunting me back and forth along the Tokaido?

Certainly my schedule was quite ridiculous. I taught at the Gaimusho for three hours in the morning, then at the Girls department of Gakushuin from 1-2:30 in the afternoon, at Waseda 2-4 at the Jiyu Gakuen 3.30-4.30; and at Kyoiku Dai 4.30-5.30. These times overlapped in the most interesting way, leaving me a minus quantity in which to pass from one place to another.

Someone commented on how much I managed to accomplish. How do you find the time? he asked.

I make the time, I replied, with a rhetorical flourish.

So there it is. I find time. I make time.

I continued work on my *Zen and Zen Classics*, on a two-volume *History of Haiku* and on *Japanese Life and Character in Senryu*.

In addition, and perhaps as a necessary counterpoint, I threw myself into the physical work of repairing and restoring the house. I built those bookshelves for the 6,000 books, I patched and replaced torn shoji screens and laid new tatami. I fitted new tiles on the roof where the old tiles had slipped or broken. I built in a *kotatsu* heated table for the winter, over a pit sunk into the floor, a brazier to take the coal briquettes, old blankets tacked in place to keep in the heat. When I was too exhausted even to lift the lightest hammer, I busied myself with translating the Mumonkan, struggling with the koans. Does a a dog have the Buddha nature? Why did Bodhidharma come to the West?

Pass me the hammer!

I stood one day looking at the lone pine tree in the garden behind the house, and I had a moment of revelation, inspiration. I would build a little outhouse *around* the tree, the trunk running up through the middle, living, growing. A tree-house! The spirit of Crusoe was strong in me.

I worked hard at the building all through autumn and there it stood, ramshackle but sturdy, my retreat.

There was someone else Suzuki wanted to introduce to me. (I should simply have handed over my entire social calendar to him). I was aware that the novelist Yasunari Kawabata lived in Zushi, near Kamakura, so he and Suzuki were almost neighbours. I recalled Mrs Vining speaking of him with great respect and admiration after meeting him at the PEN Conference in Tokyo.

I had not read his novels, but Suzuki said they were very fine. *Yuki-guni* Suzuki translated as Snow Country. Then came *Meijin* The Master of Go, *Senbazuru,* The Thousand Cranes, and most recently *Yama no Oto.*

The Sound of the Mountain, I ventured.

Yes, he said, nodding approval.

They are good titles, I said. Resonant without being overly poetic.

Sadly, said Suzuki, they have not yet been translated into English. But I think you would appreciate them. They are filled with love, melancholy and loss.

Perfect themes for the novelist!

Suzuki had arranged for us to meet, perhaps surprisingly, at a fashionable coffee shop close to Kamakura station. It was in Koma-chi-dori, a little street I had always loved, lined with craft shops and tea houses, shops selling nothing but incense, or kimono, or hanging scrolls. The cafe was called Iwata and had opened after the war, the decor stylishly western, menus in English and Japanese, plastic-topped tables, upright chairs covered in some kind of faux-leather.

From where to where, I said to Suzuki, looking around. To have come to this in a few short years.

Indeed, he said.

Kawabata, when he arrived, was unmistakeable. He wore a warm kimono jacket and a fedora hat. He doffed the hat and bowed to us, swept a hand through his thick white hair.

Mrs Vining's description of him as *deer-like* was a good one. He was thin and almost delicate, but wide-eyed and alert, and I had the impression he was a man of sharp intelligence and insight.

He sat down at our table, looked around with a kind of amused wonderment. We ordered coffee (water for me) and Suzuki suggested we try the special pancakes, saying they were famous.

Kawabata nodded, perhaps a little bemused that pancakes could be famous. When they arrived, stacked, inch-thick and drenched in jam and cream, he set to, laughing and declaring them delicious. He had a lightness about him that I had not expected. Suzuki had told me his novels were elegaic and that quality had only deepened since the war. He was unlikely, said Suzuki, to write anything frivolous.

Over more coffee he lit a cigarette (after ascertaining we didn't smoke, and asking our permission). Somehow the cigarette looked large between his thin fingers. He inhaled, held, breathed out, relaxed.

Suzuki took the opportunity to ask him how his work was progressing. He said he was very lazy so perhaps he had less time to work than other writers. But then, he continued, by the time he thought about putting in effort, the work was already done.

Suzuki laughed, said to me, He knows where to put his strength so he doesn't waste it. It's like the strongest position in kendo, using power without exerting it.

Mugamae no kamae, said Kawabata. Nothing position.

Busy doing nothing, I said.

Buraisu-san is a great student of Zen, said Suzuki. He knows all about *Mu*, all about nothing.

Or I know about nothing at all!

I think there is a great deal of Zen in Kawabata-san's novels, said Suzuki. They flow, like a composition that does not know where it will begin or end.

Kawabata said he was tired of novels that depended on a twist.

The story ends when it blossoms, said Suzuki.

Kawabata smiled.

So.

They drank more coffee. Kawabata lit another cigarette, spoke about European culture, his love of Debussy and Turner, Flaubert and Mann.

Where is east? he said. Where is west?

When we emerged from the coffee shop, afternoon was darkening into evening. We walked together to the railway station, waited on the platform for Kawabata's train to Zushi, just one stop along the line. Suzuki would go a single stop in the opposite direction, to Kita Kamakura and I would continue, back to Oiso.

I noticed Kawabata staring across the tracks towards the neighbouring hotel, the name spelled out in English, in wrought iron lettering, *Hotel New KAMAKURA*.

He explained it used to be called Hotel Yamagata and the novelist Akutagawa Ryunosuke had spent time there, writing.

A troubled soul, said Suzuki. A terrifying talent.

Akutagawa had killed himself, aged only 35.

So, said Kawabata, a look of great sadness in his eyes. Then his train arrived and he composed himself, smiled and bowed and thanked us, said goodbye and climbed aboard, bowed to us again through the window as the train moved off.

We crossed the platform to wait for our own train, almost due.

A remarkable man, I said.

He works in solitude and pain, said Suzuki. But the result is a kind of flowering.

He burns very bright, I said.

Yes, said Suzuki. But I fear he may be consuming himself.

This meeting with Kawabata came back to me yesterday. As I walked along the hospital corridor, I saw a visitor to the ward, a young woman waiting till it was time to go in. She sat on a bench, poised, completely absorbed in reading a paperback book. I couldn't help but notice it was Kawabata's latest novel, just published, *Utsukushisa to Kanashimi to*, which I believe translates as Beauty and Sadness.

I resisted the temptation to engage the young woman in conversation, tell her I had met Kawabata in person. She might have thought I was a sad old lunatic, an aged man, a paltry thing, a tattered coat upon a stick. (Unless soul clap its hands and sing, and louder sing). So I showed restraint, said nothing.

Beauty and sadness.

Love, melancholy and loss.

I had been told it would be difficult, but still I found myself completely unprepared.

Harumi had been courted (I still liked that word) by an entirely acceptable young man, a Mister Kikkawa. (If he had a first name it was not proffered and he remained resolutely Kikkawa-san).

My first reaction had been the rather incredulous protest that Harumi was just a child, to which Tomiko pointed out she was almost 20 and as such was not younger than Tomiko herself had been when we first met.

I spluttered, Be that as it may…. then found I could not finish the sentence. I began to feel like the pompous father in some comedy of manners, or one of the farces I'd read about that were gracing the West End stage.

My own fears (and sense of disappointment) deepened when I found out Mr Kikkawa was effectively a mathematician and a scientist. He was considering a number of job opportunities including, to my trepidation and alarm, a position at the University of Utah where he would be working on some gigantic computing machine taking up its own enormous room.

I was further appalled to hear the work would be directed towards the continuation of what was known as the Space Race, which I suspected was more about weapon systems and military advantage than communication for its own sake.

We had read the newspaper reports of the Russian sputniks launched into orbit, first unmanned, then carrying the little dog Laika (Nana had wept for him) and finally with the intrepid Yuri Gagarin, glorying in the designation *cosmonaut*, a latter-day Jason sailing among the stars. The whole continuing story was thrilling but nevertheless created an undercurrent of unease.

I think in my attempt to carry the discussion onto higher ground, I terrified the young man. I heard myself quoting Spengler, saying so-called practical requirements are simply the mask of a profound inward compulsion.

New York has a great many skyscrapers, I said. Why is this? (I might have added, as now does Tokyo. But that would have muddied my argument).

Kikkawa-san looked bemused to the point of panic, smiled and nodded his head.

The standard answer, I said, is because land is scarce, so it is more convenient and cheaper to build upwards than to build outwards.

He glanced across at Harumi, that rictus smile still on his face. She stared straight ahead.

Spengler's answer, I continued, would be that this is an excuse hiding the real reason, which is a desire for infinity, for the vast and limitless. Beyond and beyond!

(I gestured, spread my arms wide).

Another sideways glance.

In this case, I said, it expresses the American desire for the biggest, the highest, the mightiest. It is what Stevenson called the divine unrest of humanity. Perhaps it is this urge, in its purest form, we see in the space race. This is the poetry of it, the thing that inspires us. Nevertheless...

I recognised the look in the young man's eyes, a look I often saw in my students, a complete bafflement.

Nevertheless.

I thought (perhaps unconsciously I even hoped) Kikkawa-san might be frightened off, fearful lest this madness run in the family.

Nevertheless, a few short months later (no time at all), I found my-
self, tearful, waving goodbye to Harumi at Hanada Airport as she
headed through the check-in desk for her transpacific flight. She
was to join her husband-to-be. Mr Kikkawa had gone on ahead to
take up his post. They would settle in Utah among Mormons and
computing machines, make a new life there.
Harumi turned, ticket and passport in hand. She wore a pale blue
coat, a little pillbox hat. She waved one last time and was gone.

I am thinking of that Ozu film, *Banshun*. Late Spring. Technically it
is a masterpiece. For the interiors, the camera almost never moves,
holds its point of view, the eye-level of someone seated on a tatami
mat. Ozu said the lens he used was the closest to the human eye.
The final scene is almost unbearably melancholy. The old widowed
professor returns alone to his home, sits at the kitchen table and
begins to peel an apple. His concentration is total as he removes the
peel in one continuous spiral. The peel grows longer and longer until
his hand finally stops and the peel falls to the floor. His shoulders
slump and he bows his head.
Cut to the last image, the ocean in the half-dark.wave after wave
washing onto the shore.
I watched the film for the first time in the early 1950s. The girls
would still have been very young, and perhaps Tomiko was at home
looking after them. In any case, I remember going on my own to
the little cinema in Shinjuku. I sat there in the darkness, alone, and
I watched that last scene and I wept. I had to compose myself be-
fore emerging into the daylight and the busy city street. The sight
of a corpulent tweed-suited *gaijin* coming out of the cinema would
have been unsettling enough in those days, but for said *gaijin* to be
blubbering like a child would have caused consternation.
When I saw the film again just recently, an old man myself, it moved
me even more. I was startled to notice something I had forgotten, or
hadn't registered at the time. The opening frame shows the railway
station at Kita Kamakura, just yards from my own grave at Tokeiji.

From time to time when I was in Kamakura, I visited the Daibut-su, the Great Buddha at Kotuku-in temple. It was a different place entirely from Engaku-ji. The main temple grounds, the monks' quarters, were hidden away from public gaze. But for a few yen visitors could gain entrance to the gardens and the open courtyard where the colossal Buddha sat.

I liked the fact that he had sat there for centuries, windblown and weather-beaten, his original bronze worn to a dull patinated green. I liked the fact too that he had originally been housed indoors in a spe-cially-constructed temple building. But the building was destroyed in an earthquake, leaving the Buddha unharmed but exposed to the elements. The temple authorities decided, wisely in my view, that his will was clear – he actually preferred to sit outside in the open air instead of being constrained and boxed in.

I think he had the right idea.

On the whole I am not greatly taken with monumentality and gran-diosity. Those Wonders of the World I decried to my students leave me cold – examples of man's overweening pride and inflated sense of himself. But this is different.

The statue has an unmistakable spiritual presence, a remarkable combination of power and gentleness, strength and compassion. Like Fuji it sits unmoved and unmoving – it looks on tempests (and earthquakes) and is never shaken.

I like to walk round it, clockwise, chanting the *Nembutsu* as I go. *Namu Amida Butsu*. I bow to the Buddha of the Pure Land.

What is your religion Mr Blyth?

I would have to declare myself an atheist.

But are you a Christian atheist or a Buddhist atheist?

Thy will be done.

Namu Amida Butsu

There is a little door at the side of the Buddha, towards the rear, down a few steps and right inside the statue, which is, of course, hollow. I like it in there, especially when it is quiet and I can have it to myself. It is a cool and quiet space, the light dim. A rickety flight of wooden steps leads up to a little platform which is actually inside the Buddha's head. I can climb up there and look out through his eyes at the temple grounds, the green surrounding hills, the world beyond.

I am in the Buddha's head.
I look out through his eyes.
Namu Amida Butsu.

These days, especially in the summer season, it is much visited by tourists and pilgrims. (Tourist-pilgrims? Pilgrim-tourists?) They are invariably respectful, genuinely awed by the statue, immense and benign, looming over them. They light incense, waft the smoke over themselves, clap their hands and bow. More and more often a camera is produced and snapshots are taken, individuals and family groups posing, the moment recorded. They were here.
I imagine one of those film sequences in time-lapse, hundreds and thousands of little figures, there a moment and gone, the Buddha behind them, continuing.
I once went with Suzuki into the temple itself where he had been invited by the abbot as a special guest. A few of us sat round a low table, eating a simple meal, making spiritual smalltalk, a sharing that was civilised and timeless.
As a result of the conversation, I found myself being asked to translate a tanka poem by the redoubtable female poet Akiko Yasano. In her lifetime she scandalised the establishment, speaking out for women's rights, condemning, at least for a time, the traditional values of bushido and the cult of war-mongering, and, most heinous of all, writing poems that were unashamedly erotic in content.
The verse I translated was less contentious, a simple homage to the Daibutsu.

> *Here in Kamakura*
> *Sits Sakyamuni*
> *The Holy Buddha*
> *A handsome figure*
> *Among the Summer Trees*

Although the poem is serious, you can sense the poet's personality, her playfulness, in that one unexpected word, *binan*, beautiful man, which I translated as handsome figure.

Aesthetically the statue is perfect in its scale, its proportions. From whatever angle you choose to look up, it is pleasing to the eye, harmonious, and that harmony communicates a sense of wholeness, completeness.

On one particular day I stood in front of the statue and looked up at that great head, the face in turn looking down at me, calm and serene, all-knowing but non-judgemental, the full lips curved in a faint but unmistakable half smile. And for a moment I felt the selfsame expression on my own face, my eyes half closed, my own smile coming from within. Everything else faded away and I was looking at the reflection of my own inner being, which was looking back at me with infinite kindness and love.

The moment passed and I bowed once more.

Namu Amida Butsu.

The poet's name was Akiko, a name that would come to mean a great deal to me.

Akiko.

As I read this I realise I am writing it in the past tense. A time gone. A life ending.

So.

That tiny little word, so expressive, so ubiquitous, in English as in Japanese.

So.

Suzuki once said to me, If he believed in reincarnation, he would say I was an old Japanese soul who had lived here for many lifetimes.

If he believed in reincarnation.

It would make sense of a great deal, more so than the idea that life is once-round-the-block then over.

I suppose I had always thought of reincarnation as a useful metaphor, explaining some aspect of the way the universe works, as the theory of evolution is another metaphor, or the law of karma, or original sin, the structure and function of DNA. These all offer a glimpse, tell a part of the story, but not the truth the whole truth and nothing but. Expedient means.

There are times when I have been overwhelmed by a feeling of recognition, a sense of knowing a place, a person – *deja vu*, easily dismissed as some random chemical reaction in the brain.

But.

Those few days in India. Not this, not this....

The fact that when I first heard Spanish, and German, I felt I understood both languages at some deep intuitive level, and in fact I learned both without difficulty.

The years I have lived here in Japan, utterly alien but utterly at home.

An old Japanese soul.

If I believed in reincarnation.

There is an anonymous tanka poem I translated, touching on an aspect of it.

> *To have lived*
> *so many lives –*
> *how many loves*
> *I know but*
> *do not know.*

Then there is a Tagore poem I can almost remember.

In the dusky path of a dream I went to seek the love who was mine in a former life...
She raised her large eyes to my face and silently asked, Are you well, my friend?
I tried to answer, but our language had been lost and forgotten....
I thought and thought; our names would not come to my mind.

If I believed.

It would explain (if not justify) the reality of my own current situa-

tion. Perhaps for that very reason I should reject it.
Let me leave it there.

Over the years I had maintained intermittent contact with Bob Ait-
ken (and he with me). It was with the usual anticipation that I saw
among my letters an airmail communication from him, postmarked
Honolulu, Hawaii. I tore it open (carefully) and saw it was the latest
issue of his *Diamond Sangha*, a single page broadsheet, typewritten
and mimeographed. Across the top Bob had written, *I am sure you
have been amused at the earlier reviews, all of them either scornful or
strident in their condemnation!*
Underneath was a review, anonymous though clearly by Bob, of my
Zen and Zen Classics, Volume 7.
I settled at my desk, read with mounting gratitude.

*Mr Blyth writes with authority of something he has understood for twen-
ty-five years. It is the very liveliness of his mind that seems to create so
much resentment; the Buddhists are upset to find an artist in their midst.*
I remembered Bob as I had first seen him at the camp in Kobe, thin
and gaunt, an eager acolyte.
*When Blyth rushes pell-mell at Sacred Institutions, slaughtering and
ravishing, he is like the storms mentioned in the sutras – the trees with
shallow roots are blown over.*
Yes.
*It is a healthy thing to understand that a large measure of Zen, as it
appears in organisations, books and individuals in both East and West,
is downright fake.*
Beautifully put.
*It is a healthy thing to understand that men and women are different, and
if Blyth's protests against the curse of chivalry becomes too shrill, we need
only to look about to sympathise.*
Ha!
*The point is, that after the beneficent nuclear explosion of Blyth's writings
has cleared away, we are left with poetry and the attitude of poetry, which,
as he has been telling us since Zen in English Literature, is Zen itself.*
I felt exhilaration rising, a great bubble expanding in my chest.

Mr Blyth is an extraordinarily interesting human being. We need him at
every step of our training to puncture our self-importance and to teach us
really to laugh.
I banged the desk and threw back my head and laughed myself, a
great all-consuming roar that brought tears to my eyes.

I never tired of browsing in book shops, and finding books for the
young Crown Prince was an added stimulus. Books Kinokuniya
in Shinjuku – a dealer dating back to Hakuin's time – had a decent
stock of books in English and I was always happy to check their new
titles, losing myself there of an afternoon. The Crown Prince was
fascinated by the natural world and I had bought him field guides to
British wildlife. So for his birthday one year I bought him a copy of
Born Free, the story of Elsa the Lioness, and he was quite delighted
to receive it, reading it eagerly through and through again.
More recently I picked up a copy of *Lady Chatterley's Lover*. I had
followed the sensational stories in the press, the public outrage, the
publisher tried for obscenity, and inevitably the massive increase in
sales of the book. My beloved Lawrence was once more causing
a stir!
I picked up a copy in Kinokuniya, refused the offer of a paper bag
and carried it instead, unashamedly, under my arm, made a point
of reading it on the train.
What did I teach the Crown Prince? Life.

Among my papers is a letter from Harumi, sent last year from her
home in Utah. She had enclosed a photograph, clipped from a mag-
azine, of President Kennedy with his elegantly beautiful wife Jackie
and their two small children. What comes from the picture is a sense
of relaxed ease. There is none of the stiffness and over-formality of
our own politicians (or for that matter, of any world leaders whose
images I have seen in the press). Harumi said looking at the picture
filled her with hope. I wrote back to her, saying simply, Brave new
world that has such people in it.
A few months later, on a bright November day, Gakushuin still rich
with those autumn colours, always the same always new, the red and

gold of maple and ginko, I heard the announcement on radio that President Kennedy had been shot dead.

I am not given to rhetoric, but when I stood in front of my class the next day, I felt moved to give a short speech, urging the students to take care in their own lives lest they murder not men, but principles. In the staffroom I sat down and wrote a short note to Harumi, enclosing two haiku by Issa, in the original Japanese and with my own translations.

We walk
  On the roof of hell,
    Looking at the flowers.

This world of dew
  Is a world of dew,
    And yet…

I walked across the campus grounds to post the letter, pushing my bicycle through the fallen leaves, hearing the shouts of young boys playing baseball.

The roof of hell.

And yet…

Another letter from Harumi sent the good news that she was with child. A few months later came a telegram announcing the birth of her son, Taro. Mother and Son Both Well. Later still came a photograph, a colour snapshot. Taro, the grandson I have never met.

One of the last lectures I gave before taking my leave was on a Saturday afternoon at Gakushuin. The lecture was not part of any course, and attendance was not compulsory, but there were perhaps eighty students packed into the classroom. It seems they were still eager to hear this old gaijin speak.

I was aware I would be causing a stir as I wrote the title, in white chalk, on the blackboard.

WHY I HATE BUDDHISM.

There was indeed a little ripple round the room, an apprehensive intake of breath, some nervous uncertain laughter.

So.... I began.

Of course I was not criticising the Buddha, or his teachings. (Not today, at any rate...) What I hated was that it had become an -ism, a system, a philosophy. In fact I hated all -isms without exception – communism, capitalism, colonialism, imperialism... A pox on all their houses. God save us from religion.

Worst of all was when the great spiritual truths became ossified and codified into dogma and ritual, in other words when they degenerated into a religion – Hinduism, Judaism, and yes, Buddhism (which was why I could truly, if paradoxically, say I hated it).

Did they know the story about tying the cat to the bed?

No? Then I would tell it to them.

There was once a spiritual master who lived in a small community with just a few close followers. Once a week they visited him in his hermitage and sat with him in meditation.

Now it happened that this master had a cat. He was very fond of the cat, but sometimes it would cause problems during the master's meetings with his disciples. The cat would run around the room, or come to the master purring and seeking affection. This was very distracting, so the master came up with a solution. When the disciples arrived, he would tie the cat to the bed in his room. The cat learned to accept this, and the routine was established. They met once a week, the master tied the cat to the bed, he meditated with his disciples and afterwards they all went home and the master untied the cat.

This went on for a number of years. Then the master passed away, and the disciples continued meeting in his room once a week. As before, they tied the cat to the bed, meditated, then released the cat and went away.

In the fullness of time, however, without the master's presence, they lost intensity and in the end they simply met once a week to tie-the-cat-to-the-bed and then go home.

And that, says the punch-line, is religion.

Another story.

Always a story.

Of course, I said, I could just as easily have called my talk this...

I rubbed out BUDDHISM from the blackboard, replaced it with CHRISTIANITY.

And yes, I said, I hate Christianity just as much. An -anity is every bit as bad as an -ism.

Think of the rhymes, I said. Inanity. Insanity. Profanity. (I said I could have added Humanity, but that would have spoiled my argument!)

I may have no truck with Christianity, I told them. But Christ is a different matter entirely. He was, without doubt, one of the greatest poets the world has ever known, and it is the poetry in his life and words that is eternally true.

Consider the lilies of the field how they grow. They toil not neither do they spin. Yet I say unto you that even Solomon in all his glory was not arrayed like one of these.

I read these words as a boy, as a young man. They moved me to tears in a way I could not understand (as I could not understand the words themselves). But then the point was not to understand the lily, but to consider how it grows.

Perhaps I could edit Christ's words into more of a haiku.

Consider
 The lilies of the field
How they grow.

So, yes, I said, Christ, like Buddha, was a very great poet, and that is why both still speak to us today, because poetry is the most important thing in life.

I paused.

And what is life? I heard myself say. Life gives us the the opportunity to be in Heaven here and now. Until our being dissolves in death we have a chance to live an eternal life as often and as long as we have the will and the power.

Finally I looked round the room, said, What are you all doing?

Why are you sitting here listening to me on a beautiful day like this? You should be out on the playing fields. Or walking with your sweethearts!

Motes of chalk-dust hung in the air, caught in the shafts of sunlight filtering through the windows.

Go! I said, sending them off with my benediction, a last wave of the hand.

My goodbye.

Chalk-dust in the air.

My head ached.

I still have at home an old bible that belonged to Ma and Pa, leather-covered, the pages of thin onionskin paper, edged in gold. It has survived two world wars and sits on my desk beside my collected Shakespeare, the Mumonkan, the Gita. I dip into it from time to time, and always read from it on Christmas Day when I get up early and light the big pot-bellied stove, filling the place with smoke.

I begin the day by playing a record on the gramophone, Handel's *Judas Maccabaeus*, its ending loud and triumphant. I know I have said before that Handel has no Zen and his music is mere shouting. Very well. But sometimes Zen is not what is required, and a great swell of emotion fits the bill very nicely. (And if not on Christmas morning, then when?)

    Sing unto God…

Harumi said Handel and woodsmoke were the sound and smell of Christmas.

My old friend Shinki often visits us on the day. One year when the girls were young, he pinned a blank sheet of paper to the wall and, to their utter delight, did a watercolour painting of the Three Wise Men.

I had tuned up the piano, the old joanna, and banged out *We three kings of orient are…* followed by a few other carols, and ending with a rousing hymn from those far-off days in Leytonstone.

    Give me oil in my lamp, keep me burning.
    Give me oil in my lamp, I pray. (Halleluja!)

Give me oil in my lamp, keep me burning.
Keep me burning till the break of day.

Keep me burning.

Looking back, looking back. What of all the poetry and music I loved? What of art, truth and beauty? Was it merely ornamental, like flowers on the coffin of this life? What did it have to do with eating or breathing, being generous or lustful, angry or weary?

Of all the stories of Buddha, the tales and parables, the story of his flower-sermon is one of my favourites.. It tells of how the Buddha came to give a lecture, a dharma discourse, in a particular town. Word had spread and a large crowd gathered to hear him speak. The Buddha appeared and everyone sat, attentive and expectant, eager to receive his wisdom. But instead of speaking, the Buddha simply sat, in silence. Time passed and still he did not speak. Then he picked up a single flower and held it up in front of him. Most of the crowd were confused, but one of the Buddha's followers, Maha Kashapa, understood what the Buddha was saying-by-not-saying. It was not to be communicated in words but in profound silence. Maha Kashapa showed his understanding by smiling, and in that smile the Buddha said his disciple had received everything he had to offer, his entire teaching. It was all there, nothing held back, nothing up his sleeve.

Always a story.

I have recently read the flower-sermon as a love story, and in love, anything will do – raising a flower or not raising it, words or silence. The beloved understands, and the understanding is beyond words. The wordless is expressed when it is not asked for.

Ah sweet mystery of life at last I've found you. (No you haven't!)

The mystery of life is grasped when we misplace something, or lose some money, or when it starts to rain unexpectedly and we are caught out, drenched.

Then we catch the winged joy as it flies, and live in eternity's sunrise.

14

THE SPACES BETWEEN

There's a poem by Ikkyu which I translated.

Why do I write?
To leave something behind?
That's just another dream.
I know when I awake
There will be nobody
to read my words.

So what have I been writing? A tale told by an idiot? A tale told by *this* idiot? Full of sound and fury?

And yet...

I have been working on these pages – while I still can – busying myself with organising them into something more coherent (or sometimes, for the fun of it, into something *less* coherent). I have been shaping the material as the fancy takes me, sometimes interspersing passages already written with what I'm writing now.
This and that and the next thing.
Each day the effort is more exhausting, my energies are waning. The headaches are becoming more severe.
Perhaps someone else, someone I shall never know, will find the pages decades hence, gathering dust in an old cardboard box, and edit them, embellish them, pull them into shape.
Perhaps.

I suppose what I have been writing is what Shiki would have called *watakushi shosetsu* – an autobiographical novel. This shilling life (or ten yen life!) has certainly found its own formless form. I have come to realise in filling reams of paper with my scribblings, in looking back and trying to make sense (as if such a thing were possible), that the truth of the story is in the gaps, the silences, the things left unsaid, the spaces between.

I recently read some translations of Spanish poems into English, and the translator described them as *versions* of the originals. I rather liked that in relation to my own efforts. I have made versions of haiku, rendered them new. Similarly this has been a version of my life, unashamedly partial. I have been what novelists call an unreliable narrator. But who, after all, could be more unreliable that a man telling his own tale? (Or blowing his own trombone!)
So yes, look to the gaps, the silences, each one a pause, a caesura, a rest.
Something understood.
I've said it before and I'll (un)say it again. Zen is what we don't talk about when we're not asked about it.
The silence is the thing. Everything and nothing. The void in the full and the full in the void. The nothing at the heart of it all.
Form is emptiness.
Mu.

I find this difficult to write about, more difficult than anything else I have set down in these pages.

Akiko.

I would not have believed it possible, thought myself long past any of this, thought it could not happen. Not this. I was a middle-aged man, settled into family life (or perhaps it would be more accurate to say I had settled *for* it).
Akiko had been my student, years ago, and she had made an im-

pression.

Kobayashi Akiko, she had said, introducing herself. Kobayashi like haiku poet Issa.

Akiko meant bright, and yes, she was in every sense. Her English was good, her intellect clear and sharp. But there was a brightness too in her demeanour, her being. She shone and I was dazzled.

But then I was often (and easily) charmed by young Japanese women, and it was no more than that, at most an innocent flirtation that could never be anything else.

She graduated, moved on, and that was that. Until she came back. It was a bright spring afternoon, warmth in the air, a sense of promise. I felt it, even at the end of a long day's teaching. I breathed deep, taking it all in, ready to get on my bike to cycle home. I loosened my tie, took off my tweed jacket, shook off chalk-dust as I folded it and stuffed it in my saddlebag. I was about to start off down the path towards the main gate when she spoke.

Buraisu-sensei.

I looked, shielding my eyes, at first not recognising her.

Kobayashi-san, she said. Akiko.

In the few years between she had grown even more beautiful, a young woman. She still had that brightness but with it a new-found poise, a kind of ease.

Yes, I said. Akiko!

We bowed to each other, slightly awkward, then she bowed again, more deeply, and we laughed. That was it, we laughed.

Kobayashi like Issa, I said.

Yes.

Akiko like Yasano Akiko who wrote of the handsome Buddha at Kamakura.

Yes.

How had it happened that Tomiko and I had grown apart? Had we simply tired of each other, sharing less and less?

Was it simply what happened to men at a certain time in their lives, a kind of biological imperative, a desperate need for change? I have spoken of disappointment in love, but is the very nature of human love to be disappointing?

Not this. Not this...

Certainly the man I saw in the mirror – to my occasional shock when the mist cleared and I saw him clearly – was noticeably ageing, the jowls heavier, the once thick dark hair now thinning and grey. There was a tiredness too in the eyes, a world-weariness. The face I deserved? Was this all Tomiko saw when she looked at me? She certainly took pains over her own appearance, wore fashionable western clothes and make-up, her hair cut and styled, given a 'permanent wave.' None of this particularly delighted me.

Akiko dressed stylishly but subtly, wore little or no make-up. Her hair hung long and straight to the shoulders, glossy and lacquer-black, her look altogether more natural and unaffected. But there was more to it than mere appearance.

Not only had Akiko returned to Gakushuin to do research, she had been assigned to work as my secretary for two or three days a week. The fates had conspired. She was to help with my backlog of paperwork, and, more important, finding haiku and senryu to translate. Her own knowledge of the forms was broad and deep and her suggestions were invaluable. Not since Motoko back in Korea had I worked with someone who had such a profound and intuitive understanding of the poems, an awareness of their power. Like Motoko she opened my eyes.

We make a good team, I said, and she nodded, blushing in a way I found utterly disarming.

On another occasion we were discussing the intricacies of *kigo*, the season-words so essential to haiku. They were like a code – an image or a single word indicating the time of year being described. *Ume no hana*, plum blossom, was spring. *Suzukaze*, cool breeze, was summer. *Yosamu*, cold night, was autumn. And you could feel winter in *hatsuyuki*, first snow.

The way she spoke each word, the shapes her mouth made, filled me with a longing, a kind of sweetness tinged with melancholy.

She stopped and smiled. I am spring, she said. You are autumn.

A good combination? A counterpoint?

Could I not have seen it coming? Could I have prevented it?
In one way it was a cliché, a matter of time and chance, propinquity.
It was ever thus. But it felt much deeper than that, a kind of recognition, something shared.

Akiko was helping me translate a series of *renga*, linked haiku,
by Basho and a few of his disciples. She was explaining that the
link from one verse to the next should be subtle, not overstated or
obvious.
It's like this, she said. You sit close to someone, but not so close you
are touching.
She put her hand on my arm, let it rest there lightly, the briefest of
moments, took it away again, moved her chair a little away from me.
But close enough you smell the other person's perfume. So.
Another moment. I breathed in her fragrance, light and delicate.
So. That's how the link should be.
I moved my chair closer to hers again, reached over and put my
own hand on her arm.
Not like this? I said.
No, she said, her eyes bright.
Not subtle enough?
Not subtle, she said, putting her other hand on mine. Not subtle.
But is OK.

Tomiko and I had less and less to talk about, less and less in common. We were jaded, often irritable with each other for no real
reason – my getting back from work later than usual, spent and
exhausted, she feeling numbed by the sheer dull monotony of domesticity. When we did try to converse, to find common ground,
we found language a problem in a way it had never been when we
were younger. Her English had never been strong, but we managed.
Now when exhaustion took hold I could lose the ability to think
in Japanese or express myself clearly, and the effort of it made my
head ache.
I might also, as it were, be banging my head against some intractable

koan from the Mumonkan (*It is like trying to swallow a red-hot iron ball...*) while she would be trying to decide which plastic kitchen containers to buy from a range known as Tupperware. One of her friends had visited the house, bringing samples and inviting her to a kind of party where they would be on sale. With the same friends Tomiko would sometimes go to a coffee shop while the girls were out at school, or she would watch a performance of some popular Kabuki show. I had no objection to any of this, but neither was it of any great interest, just as the Mumonkan was of little interest to Tomiko.

Sometimes too – even after all these years – she would balk at having to cook me separate vegetarian food. (A fishbone of contention, as it were!) Again this was worse if I came home late. She and the girls would have long since eaten. (Often the smell of fish would linger, clinging, in the hallway). I grew used to tasting *bonito,* fish-flakes, in the noodle broth! I accepted this with what I am sure was a sullen lack of grace.

These were small matters in themselves, but cumulative.

Looking back I think the worst of it was that we simply lost the ability to laugh together, and love without laughter, without humour, is an abomination.

At the end of last term – was it really so recent? – I had a session with one of my students, a very earnest intelligent young man named Munakata who had come to me for a seminar on Shakespeare, in particular on the theme of Love in Shakespeare. (No small subject matter!) He began by reading aloud the passages from Julius Caesar relating to Brutus and Portia. I listened, attentive, as he read, his voice at first shaky then gaining in confidence. When he had finished he fell silent and I waited for him to say something more, perhaps venture an opinion.

I allowed the silence to continue until finally, hesitantly, he broke it. I have no words, he said.

Ah, I said.

I could see he was struggling but I felt very kindly towards him.

Their love is so beautiful, I said, that you cannot find words to say what you feel.

Yes, he said, grateful. Yes, that is it exactly!

I understand, I said, and their love is indeed beautiful, and true. But somehow it is not complete. It is lacking in humour.

> *Is it excepted I should know no secrets*
> *That appertain to you? Am I yourself*
> *But, as it were, in sort or limitation,*
> *To keep with you at meals, comfort your bed,*
> *And talk to you sometimes? Dwell I but in the suburbs*
> *Of your good pleasure?*

Tomiko, Tomiko. How did it come to this? The suburbs of each other's good pleasure.

Things came to a head. There had been niggling quarrels over nothing, a constant annoyance at each other, a prickliness, a readiness to take offence. Eventually it erupted in a full-blown argument, a shouting match, each in our own language only half understanding the other. But things were said, on both sides, that could not be unsaid.

It ended with Tomiko, in frustration and rage, by accident or design, with a sweep of her arm knocking something from the top of my desk. I heard it smash on the floor, saw it was the little tea bowl Yanagi had given me, the one made by Shōji Hamada. I looked down at it, shattered to shards and fragments. I felt nothing, a kind of emptiness, as I knelt to gather the pieces, pick them up. I watched myself doing it, found myself taking refuge in a story.

When master Ikkyu was a boy he once knocked over and broke his teacher's favourite tea-bowl which was very old, a priceless antique. He hid the pieces then asked the teacher why everyone had to die. It is the nature of things, said the teacher. Everything has to die when the time comes. Very well, said Ikkyu. It was the bowl's time to die. Always a story. Even at a time like this.

Tomiko left the room, in tears. The door was a sliding shoji screen but she still managed to slam it shut, shaking the partition.

Always a story. There was another. The Shogun Yoshimasa also had a favourite bowl which was accidentally smashed. Instead of throwing it away, he had a craftsman repair it, painstakingly piecing it together. But instead of trying to disguise the cracks, the craftsman accentuated them by using a mix of lacquer and powdered gold. The random patterning of gold lines was appreciated and greatly valued. *Kintsugi.* Repairing with gold.

But this, this was beyond repair. Sweeping up the bits of broken bowl I cut my fingertips, felt the sting, saw tiny red jewels gather. Mind numb, I licked them, tasted my own blood, salt and warm.

I bade Mr Munakata farewell at the end of our session, fully expecting to see him again in a few short months, after the summer break, but it was not to be.

A few short months?

Time is behaving strangely, as it always does.

If you talk to a beautiful girl for an hour, says Mr Einstein, it seems like a minute. If you sit on a hot stove for a minute it feels like an hour. That is relativity. (And in matters of relativity, Mr Einstein is absolutely correct).

It would also explain why these few months have felt so long, often unendurably so.

And yet in general, the time has gone faster, year by year.

Explain me that if you will.

You're dancing round a maypole, holding the streamer attached to the top. Every round the cord gets shorter, the distance less, the steps fewer, till there's nothing left and you stop.

Or is it that say, when you're five or six years old, a year is a very long time indeed, a huge percentage of the time you've known on earth. Then by the time you're, say, sixty-five, a year is nothing, a blink, a tiny fraction of your allotted span.

Time and change. Time and change and death.

Some interviewer once asked me what had sparked my interest in Zen. Without hesitation I said, Disappointment in love.

I laughed as I said it, so perhaps my reply seemed flippant or throwaway, even cavalier. But at the time I meant it.

And what, pray, did I mean by it?

There was Dora, the one-that-got-away. A walk by the Serpentine. Many a time in the Rialto.

I shall not circumscribe our love.

Then Annie who gave up on me. Annie in the lecture room, bringing in the cold. The warmth of her in heavy coat and thick scarf. Always a story.

Then Tomiko, soft hand cupping mine as she placed my change, a few coins, in the palm of my hand. A palm-of-the-hand story.

Love is not love.

Tomiko.

Who was it who said to lose a wife is tragic, to lose two is downright careless?

I thank yew!

Every one a gem.

But was it really love that disappointed me? Or was I the one who was the disappointment? Or is it simply that love can never really be anything other than disappointing?

Now at the very last there is this late love, true love, but at what cost? Akiko, teaching me about renga – not so close you are touching, but close enough to smell the other's fragrance.

At what cost?

A colleague once told me that his marriage of twenty years had come to an end. I asked if things had been going wrong for some time. He looked thoughtful for a moment, then said, Oh, about nineteen years.

Tomiko moved out, went back to live with her parents. Nana was torn but decided to stay with me. After some time, Akiko moved in.

When did the headaches begin?

I recently read again a few letters from my mother, written on thin airmail paper, pale, sky-blue. Each sheet when folded, stuck down, made an envelope containing itself. Hold the page to the light you can see right through, see the writing on the other side.

The words are faded here and there but still clear, the handwriting firm.

Each one began differently: *Dear Boy, Dear Reg, Reg Boy, Dear Son,* and signed off *Mother, Ma, Loving Ma,* and once, near the end, *Ma Ma Monkey.*

I look through them, my eyes blurring.

Did I tell you I've worn a thick coat and snow boots all winter long? All winter long by the fire with a blanket over my knees. The snow boots are to keep chilblains off my toes.

Just that one word *chilblains*, resolutely Anglo-Saxon, brings her fully to life. I remember the misery of chilblains from my childhood, on knuckles and toes, red and swollen, itching and painful at the same time. My mother's remedy was to rub it with half a raw onion. It would hurt at first, nip and sting, then the pain would subside miraculously, bring analgesic ease.

In another letter, from a few months later, she wrote, *We have had a very mild March and there has been no need for fires.*

Cold and warmth, perennially. Then further down the page is a clear-eyed observation, haiku-like in its sharpness. *I saw a rook, sitting on eggs, at the top of a bare tree.*

With a little surge of recognition, I see the poet in her.

> *A rook,*
> *Sitting on eggs,*
> *At the top of a bare tree.*

Later on again she's writing pure senryu, full of punning delight in language and social manners as she tells of being at a tea party. *An Indian boy said, 'If you have no mind, I should like a second cup.'*

Her mind always active, well into old age.

I had several people to see me yesterday. They all say I look well just because I'm cheerful. But sitting all day by the fire is not stimulating to the brain-box.

I can hear her voice, see her tapping her forefinger to the side of her head.

The brain-box.

Now my own brain-box is malfunctioning, packing it in, giving up the ghost.

Behind our accommodation at Gakushuin there was a low enclosing wall with a little gateway, a back way out. It was the way I usually came and went, sometimes just walking, sometimes pushing my bike. But the lintel, a solid beam of hardwood, was low, and I was often distracted, lost in thought. It was a regular occurrence that I banged my head on the beam, sometimes quite painfully. I consoled myself with the thought that perhaps the universe was trying to knock some sense into me.

I recalled the story of Hakuin taking blows to the head in his quest for enlightenment, first from his teacher, Shoju Rojin, then from an old woman wielding a broom when he was begging for alms.

Breaking through.

Katsu!

But these encounters I had coming through the gate had no discernible effect on my own awakening. All I experienced was shock and pain and dumb rage. (Dumb Reg!)

The first few times it happened, Tomiko and the girls were all sympathy, anxious that I might have injured myself. But it became commonplace, my thick British skull was obviously resilient, and the sympathy faded.

Tomiko said more than once that I was a typical gaijin who never learned to bow his head.

(And perhaps that was the lesson I was meant to learn and never did).

But just now, as I thought of this and wrote it down, I realised the memory might have been stirred by the present pain in my head that builds and builds till it stops all thought.

This. This. This.

And I wonder if there might be a connection, if the battering caused lasting damage.

This.

I resisted seeking medical advice. It was nothing serious, simply a bad headache, perhaps a migraine. Grit my teeth. Carry on. But the pain became more and more persistent, less easy to ignore. I made an appointment with the local doctor at his surgery near our home. He made a few tests, took my temperature and blood pressure. He shone a light into my eyes, which was most uncomfortable. (It dazzled and hurt). He scribbled notes, said something I couldn't quite understand (but which I took to mean he couldn't quite understand). He sent me, direct, to the nearest hospital, Kyoundo in Hiratsuka. There they ran more tests, gave me painkillers, said they would keep me in for observation. It seemed they too couldn't-quite-understand. I was an anomaly, a mystery, a conundrum. They gave me more painkillers and a course of antibiotics, sent me home still shaky but able to function, just about. I had to work on the final volume of my *Zen and Zen Classics*, trawl through my dusty boxes of papers, write more of these pages in my yellow notepads, make sense (or nonsense) of it all. Look back. Retrospect.

Akiko and Nana were anxious, wanted to pamper me, but I was having none of it. All would be well and all would be well and all manner of things would be well. And indeed for some months there did seem to be an improvement in my condition, a reprieve (an interesting choice of word). I experienced what I felt was a remission (another interesting choice – remission of my sentence, time off for good behaviour). Then it began again, the decline.

I was on my way, late one afternoon to see Suzuki-sensei at his home. On the train I felt wretched, unable to focus, unable to read. When I got off at Kita Kamakura I was overcome with nausea and I vomited right there on the station platform. The others on the platform, arriving or waiting, probably thought I was drunk, confirming their worst fears about gaijin. They looked away, disengaged. The arrivals kept walking towards the exit. But the stationmaster recognised me from my visits to Engaku-ji. He ushered me to a seat, brought me a glass of water. I managed to thank him, apologise for the mess. Ridiculously, I tried to say I would clean it up, but he said it was nothing, mimed filling a bucket, sluicing.
I was inordinately grateful. I told him he was a Zen man, a Bodhisattva. I had no idea if he understood, but he clearly took what I

was saying as a garbled compliment.

I was shaky as I walked along the road, slow, and up the steep steps to Suzuki's residence. The autumn colours were vibrant, intense, red of the maple, gold of gingko. A bird sang, piercing, clear. I climbed past the dead of Tokei-ji, the dead I will soon be joining.

Suzuki-sensei took one look at me and insisted I be taken to hospital forthwith. I should go to St Luke's in Tokyo, where his wife Beatrice had been treated. When his mind was fixed on something there was no gainsaying him. He had decided and that was an end of it. He instructed his secretary Okamura-san to make the necessary phone calls. He told her to use his name and explain the situation was serious, his good friend was in need of emergency treatment. I listened as at a great distance, tried to stay calm and centred as the pain pulsed and thudded in my head and the room was a vortex spinning round me. Suzuki said we shouldn't wait for an ambulance, then I was in the back of Okamura-san's car and she was driving me through Yokohama and Shinagawa, the landscape slipping past as I drifted in and out of wakefulness. At one point Fuji was there, itself, that unmistakable shape, great sacred presence, silhouetted stark against the evening sky, just a glimpse then gone as we drove on through miles of urban sprawl, on into the metropolis, the city flashing and flickering around us. I was exhausted, drained, washed up on some far shore. Then I was in a ward, in a bed, dressed in some coarse hospital-issue smock, and a young doctor was giving me something-for-the-pain, and I slept.

I was walking in the rubble and ruins of burned-out Tokyo. I was looking for my mother and trying to make sense. I knew she shouldn't be there, dear Ma, in her overcoat to keep warm. Suzuki was speaking, trying to guide me. All forms are burning. The individual fire returns to the All-Fire. In the dream there was something I had to solve but the answer was just out of reach. I came in at the back door of our house in Mejiro, through the gateway. I remembered to duck but banged my head anyway. I heard Tomiko's voice, You still haven't learned to bow your head, and she laughed. Inside, it was the house I remembered, but at the same time it was the home in Oiso with the tree growing up through it, and yet it was also my childhood home in Leytonstone and I was walking up the stairs thinking my mother would be there. I heard her call out to me. Dear Reg, she said. Your poor head. You've damaged the old brain-box. It's nothing, I said, though my head really did hurt, even in the dream. It's nothing. And the word resonated as if with some huge significance that made me want to laugh and cry at the same time. Nothing.

I returned to consciousness, to this time and this place, here in the hospital ward. I was pressing my head with my hands and my cheeks were wet with tears.

I can smell burning, an acrid charcoal smell like burnt toast or rubber. It comes and goes, but when it comes it is unmistakable.
The first time I smelled it, I mentioned it to the nurse, who looked puzzled.
Was it coming from the kitchen? Had something been charred on the stove? Was it somebody smoking in the corridor? Had some papers caught fire in a bin?
Her confusion increased. She repeated what I had said, to make sure she understood what I was saying in Japanese. She clearly didn't want to offend me or upset me. She nodded her head rapidly, wrinkled her nose as if sniffing the air. But no, she was sorry, there was nothing burning. She couldn't smell a thing.
She had obviously mentioned it to the consultant who came to see me later. He too was sorry, but for a different reason. The smell of burning, when there was none, was a symptom, a side-effect of brain tumour.
The medical term for it is *phantosmia*. He pointed to the word in an English language medical dictionary. Imaginary odours. Olfactory hallucination.

All is burning.
And what is the all that is burning?
All forms are burning.

There is another radio station – the reception always loud and clear – which plays only Japanese music. Today I heard on shakuhachi and koto – flute and harp – that exquisite piece by Michio Miyagi – *Haru No Umi*. Spring Sea.
Harumi, so far away.

Have I already become, as it were, institutionalised, used to being here?
There has been great excitement in the ward over the Olympic Games being in Tokyo. Apparently it's the first time the Games have been televised live, all over the world, through the miracle of some new technology involving satellites. They say it is even being shown in colour in America, but the set we have here is small and ancient, and the flickering images are in black-and-white. I think I prefer it that way. Somehow it reduces the whole thing, undercuts the bombast and pageantry that remind me too much of the militarism I abhor.
Much has been made of the fact that a huge typhoon has just swept the country, over the last few days. It kept me awake at night, the gale force, the rain hammering the windows. The nursing staff arrived quite bedraggled – battered and drenched – and had to towel dry and change their uniforms. But the storm has already been mythologised. Now that it has passed it is being seen as a cleansing wind, clearing the dust and filth from the city in readiness for the great occasion. One commentator said it was the Shinto gods showering their blessings, sweeping away the past, ushering in the future. Perhaps.
Those of us who were still mobile were ushered by the nurses and orderlies, with characteristic politeness, to the patients' lounge where the television had been set up at the far end of the room, in an alcove that could easily have held a shrine. A televison *tokonoma*. As the set warmed up the images on the screen came into focus and the sound crackled then became clear. There was a long shot of the stadium, raising a little cheer round the room. Then the patients and staff were up on their feet, standing to attention as the camera closed in on the Emperor, himself standing, a small figure in the vast

crowd. He wore a simple black, three-piece suit, and with an ordinariness that was as touching as it was unsettling, he took a piece of paper from his inside jacket pocket. peered through his wire-framed reading glasses and read out his short speech, welcoming everyone and declaring the Games open.

On one of the last occasions when I spoke to the Emperor, he surprised me by telling me of a trip he made to Europe in 1921. He surprised me even more by telling me his memories of that trip were among the happiest of his life. From a little wallet made of silk he took out a ticket and handed it to me. It was from the Paris Metro and he had kept it all these years, a memento. It occurred to me it might have been the first and last ticket he bought for himself. I bowed and handed it back to him, carefully, proferring it with both hands as if it were a holy relic.

He smiled, gave a brief nod of the head.

He said when that European trip was first proposed, the traditionalists in the government had opposed it vehemently. They said he would be exposed to corrupting Western influence. Happily, he said, the more progressive element prevailed.

He said he had not forgotten that in the dark days after Japan's defeat I had given him a gift, that book about the British Royal family. It had served as a reminder of his own meeting, on that trip in 1921, with King George V, and the kindness he had been shown.

Decades later, was that a factor when the war cabinet had to decide whether or not to surrender? The Emperor had, it was said, the deciding vote, and his decision, it was said, saved the nation, and the world, from further catastrophe.

He smiled again, put the Metro ticket back in its silk wallet, then tucked it away in his waistcoat pocket.

In the stadium there were shots of the Japanese flag fluttering alongside the Olympic banner. A brass band struck up the national anthem and everyone in the ward started singing along, if possible standing up even straighter. I found myself joining in, hand on heart.

Kimigayo wa
Chiyo ni yachiyo ni...

I knew the translation.

May your reign continue
for a thousand, for eight thousand generations,
Until the pebbles grow
into boulders lush with moss.

We sang, the halt and the lame, as we watched these flickering images on this latter-day *kamishibai* screen. There was an utter unreality about it all, the passing show. But as the ceremony progressed I found myself unexpectedly moved. The one chosen to light the Olympic flame from the torch he carried into the stadium, was Yoshinori Sakai, a young man born in Hiroshima on August 6th 1945, the day the atomic bomb was dropped.

For the nation to have come so far, from Hiroshima to this, in less than twenty years, was nothing short of miraculous.

The young man ran briskly up the long steep flight of steps, light on his feet. He stood for a moment, at attention, then raised the torch to the great cauldron and lit the flame. Again the camera closed in as the fire caught and blazed.

All forms are burning.

By an almost unbearable irony, the coverage of the Games was interrupted by reports of China testing its first atomic bomb, in the Gobi Desert, close to the ancient Silk Road. The strength of the bomb was estimated at 22 kilotons, more powerful than the *Little Boy* dropped on Hiroshima. The race is on, it seems, to develop ever bigger, faster, more powerful weapons. And to what end?

Now I am become death, the destroyer of worlds.

I have heard it argued that the correct translation is not death, but

time. Now I am become time, the destroyer of worlds. But for Mr Op-
penheimer's purpose, for his grim rhetoric, death was the right word.

The best words in the best order.

Sometimes I think the Way of Haiku, the Way of Basho, can hardly
be said to exist any more, and that is a testament to the stupidity,
vulgarity, sentimentality and unpoeticality of human beings. At
such moments I view the possibility of their total self-destruction
with equanimity

They speak of the Four-Minute Warning, saying with bland fatalism
and numb resignation, that this is all the time we would have from
the launching of a nuclear attack to our total annihilation.
Some years ago there was an old nun, visiting Tokei-ji, who was
introduced to me by Suzuki. I was quite taken with her – wrinkled
face, gap-toothed smile, eyes sparkling with clear-eyed inquisitive-
ness – and she seemed equally taken with me. We were comfortable
with each other, at ease, with a shared sense that the universe might
in the end be some huge joke.
I asked her what she would do in the event of such a warning. How
would she spend her last few minutes on earth?
Without a moment's hesitation she said she would sit in zazen,
enter into emptiness.
Nothing returning to nothing.
Mu.
She patted my hand and smiled, her eyes, her old eyes, bright with
compassion and acceptance, true and hard-earned.
So, I asked her, where do we go when we die?
I have no idea, she said.
Neither do I, I said. But let's go there together!
She laughed and bowed, laughed and bowed.

Don't mourn for me now, don't mourn for me never.
I'm going to do nothing for ever and ever.

Have I been following what my karma demands, or simply being a foolish old man? Or does my karma demand that I be a foolish old man?

Long ago I came to the realisation that karma was not moral, but causal. It is not a case of punishment and reward, but the simple (or complex) unfoldment of cause and effect. Follow *this* course of action, and *that* will be the result. It follows, as the night the day.

To thine own self be true.

Where, then, is free will?

Suzuki once said, when we follow our desires we are bound. When we follow the dharma we are free.

Thine own self.

According to Ramakrishna, everything is maya, illusion, even the name of God. But some maya leads us deeper into illusion, while some can lead beyond itself, to liberation.

I like the sound of that, beyond its inherent paradox (in fact, because of its inherent paradox).

I have also realised that men are good at inventing intellectual excuses for what they have done. We wish to be loved without incurring any duties or responsibilities or reciprocity.

This is how men behave. Blyth is a man. Therefore…

Expense of spirit in a waste of shame.

I have taken to scribbling little hospital haiku in the margins of these pages, after the manner of those anonymous Celtic scribes in the Middle Ages who wrote out laboriously the great manuscripts, like the Book of Kells, with their elaborately embellished lettering. From time to time they would take respite from their labours and jot down a little observation.

How pleasant to me is the sunlight on these pages as it flickers so.

That is pure haiku.

My own marginalia owe much to Shiki, and his poems of sickness, of convalescence

The light through the window
  tells me it's evening,
    tells me it's autumn

The small hours, the dog watch –
  the young nurse, wakeful
    in the light of her lamp.

Beside the sickbed
  the persimmon
    uneaten

15

BLYTH'S SHADOW

Among my papers I just found a list of words copied out by Nana when she was small, the words written out in crayon with such concentrated care.

A fox. An ant. A cat. A camel. A doll. A dog. An egg. A box. A man. A lamp. A plum. A zebra. A violin.

Nana.

The simple power of lists, like those of Sei-Shonagon in her Pillow Book – *Things that quicken the heart*. Or my favourite, *Disagreeable things*.

A long-winded visitor when you're in a hurry.
A man, when he's with you, praising a woman he previously knew.
Nasty little fleas that get under your clothes.
A dog that barks when it sees your lover coming to visit you secretly. (Such a dog, she says, should be killed).

That long-winded visitor brings to mind an old blowhard I know – an Englishman – who once came seeking me at home in Mejiro. I saw him from the upstairs window and knew he was coming with the full intention of boring me entirely to death with relentless small talk about the Japanese and their inscrutability, their exotic and mysterious ways. Nana was the only other one at home, and I called down to her to send him away, tell him I had gone out and she had no idea when, if ever, I would return.

I listened from above as the poor child, with infinite politeness, explained that the man would not be able to see me on this occasion. Undaunted, he kept talking, asked if I had gone far, and when I might be back, and whether he might come in and wait.

In the end I could take no more and I shouted to Nana that she should tell the gentleman I was most definitely not at home and that was an end of it.

I heard the door close and his footsteps down the path, and I threw back my head and laughed, and Nana, released, laughed too, the pair of us wonderfully complicit.

I heard later he had taken to blackening my name, calling me a cantankerous old misanthrope. I have been called worse.

There's a drawing by Sengai which shows him sticking his head out through the open window of his dwelling. The caption says he was in the habit of calling out to visitors, announcing his own absence. I'm not home!

My favourite calligraphy by Sengai shows a briskly executed zen circle, incomplete, drawn with a single stroke of the brush. The injunction underneath reads *Eat this and have a cup of tea!*

Eat the void.

Nobody home.

I used to have another list on the wall above my desk. I had written out by hand a series of exhortations to myself.

Not to be sentimental.
Not to be cruel.
Not to be selfish.
Not to be snobbish.

One of my students – nothing if not direct – asked me if those were faults to which I was particularly prone. I laughed and told him he had hit the nail on the head, and that I hoped in time to get round to addressing other failings I was yet to recognise or unwilling to acknowledge.

Nana came to visit this afternoon, as she does most days. I had teased her that as my old brain grew more and more tired I was finding it more difficult to think and converse in Japanese. This was actually the truth of the matter but I tried to make light of it, telling her she would have to improve her English. So today she brought the little book I had edited for use in schools, Easy Poems. These were simple, but to my mind profound verses that could be committed to memory. I had taught them to Harumi and Nana when they were younger. (Tomiko had stubbornly resisted, thinking the poems were childish).

Tell me one to read, said Nana, handing me the book.

Rain, I said, knowing the little verse by Stevenson was one of her favourites. In fact she knew it so well she did not have to read it, but recited it from memory. By heart.

The rain is raining all around,
It falls on field and tree,
It rains on the umbrellas here,
And on the ships at sea

Perhaps, I said, my living has not been in vain.

Too difficult, she said.

Everything's good, I said.

A rough translation.

I could draw up yet another list, of things I might have learned from the Crown Prince. Not to overstate or exaggerate things. Not to go to excess. To consider all questions from both sides. Not to condemn others. To give careful consideration before making a decision. Not to tell lies.

People ask what I taught the Crown Prince. The better question might be, What did he teach me?

I received a most unexpected gift from him yesterday. He sent a note, handwritten on his own notepaper embossed with the Imperial chrysanthemum crest, expressing his sincere hope that I make a speedy recovery. It accompanied a little package, exquisitely wrapped, in a special container to keep it cold – a carton of ice cream from Princess Michiko who had added a message of her own, saying the ice cream was home-made by the palace chef, and she hoped it would cheer me up.

As has happened so often recently, I found myself tearful at the sheer kindness of it all. I have been eating less and less and my once portly figure is much diminished. But I sat up in bed and set to with a spoon. The ice cream was indeed delicious but to finish it was beyond me. I asked the duty nurse, who was most impressed at the source of the gift, if what was left could be kept for me in the refrigerator, and she bowed and carried it off like an acolyte bearing a holy relic.

It occurred to me after she had gone that I might never finish it. If that is the case, I hope the nurse or someone else will polish it off. Do this in remembrance of me.

How it will be. I will eat even less, continue to diminish physically, fade away to skin and bone. This too, too solid flesh (or sullied flesh) will melt. The care will become palliative as they concentrate on easing my pain.

Existence is suffering, its cause is desire. Suffering can be conquered, there is a way.

The four noble truths. The noblest of them all. Its cause is desire. Ay there's the rub. If I were tickled by the rub of love. It can be conquered, if only.

I heard more Bach today on the hospital radio, the aria from his St Matthew Passion. *Mache dich mein Herze rein.* Make my heart pure. What would Bach have said if he had been told on his death-bed that he was not going to Heaven, that God was not going to wipe all tears from all eyes, that his sleep was to have no awakening?

Would he have answered that this too was God?

And would he change the music by a single note?

Would he still speak of God's *loving* hands? Or would he remove that one word?

I think he would not change the word. In fact I believe its meaning
would be more deeply painful for him, as it is for me.
Loving.
I think Bach believed in God as absolutely and without doubt as I
believe in Bach.
He is beyond compare. He breathes an altogether more rarefied air
than, say, Handel. Handel has no Zen. His music is mere shouting.
Music is not emotion. Music is Zen. And the Art of Fugue is pure
Zen, from beginning to end.
There. I have had my say. Contradict me who dare!
Shoot me down in flames.

The fallen.
Those young boys from Gakushuin, marching off to die.
Akiko came to visit one afternoon (not so long ago it seems, but
who can say?) She was taking away a stack of these pages I've been
writing, with the intention of typing them up, keeping them in order.
I told her it would be easier to burn them but she insisted. She sat
for a while beside my bed, saying nothing but saying it loudly.

If dirt is matter in the wrong place, sin – or evil – is energy in the
wrong place.

But the whole question of sin is a vexed one anyway. I like the
mediaeval idea that without Adam's sin there would be no need of
salvation, and Christ would still be loitering in Heaven, waiting for
someone to die for.

Knock, knock.
Who's there?
Answer came there none.

So, what is Zen? (Yes, I'm still asking this at the last).
Zen is what we don't say when we're not asked about it.
(The wordless is expressed when it is not asked for).
To write about Zen (or poetry, or beauty, or love) has something

disgusting about it.

The question is, how much love has the writer in his heart, in his pen?

There is no truth in the world unless we are true. There is no beauty unless we are beautiful, no love unless we are loving.

So what is the realised man to do?

He could play the violin – very badly – in front of 2000 people at Carnegie Hall.

Or...

He could tiptoe through the tulips, dwell in marble halls, work endlessly on building a perpetual motion machine.

He could go to sea in a sieve, or eat with a runcible spoon. Hear the soundless sound of one hand. Believe six impossible things before breakfast.

He could just walk. He could just sit. He could just have a cup of tea. See a grain of sand in a grain of sand.

Come on, Blyth. What *is* the realised man to do?

The answer, I suppose, is whatever he chooses, and with all his heart.

And how are we to understand Nirvana?

The annihilation, the transcendence, of the self?

A state of bliss?

The individual fire returning to the All-Fire?

Questions, questions.

Why did Daruma have a beard?

Why did he have no beard?

Why did he have five-and-a-half beards?

How do we even begin to answer?

I hear Harumi is flying from America to see me and bringing her baby boy Taro, my grandson. I hope for her sake she is not too late. I shall do my best to hold on. *Deo volente. Inshallah.*

It is with increasing surprise and sense of shock these days that I confront my reflection in the mirror. I have lost a great deal of

weight and the face that looks back at me is gaunt. The fancied re-
semblance to Olivier (or even Chaplin) is long gone. My white hair
has grown wispy and if I do not allow myself to be shaved for a day
or two, I resemble no one more than Abraham Lincoln.

I once dismissed Lincoln's entire speech on the Declaration of In-
dependence as humbug, empty rhetoric.

And yet.

Life, liberty and the pursuit of happiness...

If only.

Often in these last days my thoughts have turned unbidden to young
Lee and what befell him.

I heard about it much later, in a rare letter from Annie. It pained
her, she wrote, to tell me what had happened.

Lee had gone back to Korea, intending to teach English. But when
war broke out there, his very fluency in the language meant he was
under suspicion, and the North Koreans placed him under arrest.
They then forced him, on pain of execution, to broadcast propagan-
da aimed at US troops. After the war he returned to the South and
was arrested by the authorities there as a traitor. A Quisling. A Lord
Haw Haw. There was no proper trial. He was denounced, charged,
sentenced, taken from the court and executed by a firing squad.

Did heaven look on, and would not take his part?

The question of questions. Answer Yes or No.

If there is an answer it is not Yes and it is not No.

It is in asking the question, as Shakespeare does.

It is there in Hamlet, in Lear, in Othello, in Macbeth. If we read
them or see them performed, it is there, perhaps only for a short
time before the glow dies away. We know the answer. Not Yes and
not No.

Not-Yes, and Not-No.

Not Not-Yes, and not Not-No.

What, then? Joshu's *Mu*?

Nothing.

Nothing is but thinking makes it so.

Nothing is but putting it into words makes it so.

But now, sometimes, language is slipping. Slipping away. Slipsliding. Slippage.

I cannot remember things I once read...

I was asking for a pen the other day, and the word for it escaped me. I knew what it was, the object, but it had slipped free of its name. I knew it was the thing-you-write-with, but what it was called I had no idea.

I got to it through the Japanese loan-word. *Borupen*. Ballpen.

Yes.

A pen.

This pen I'm holding now, as I write.

Nama rupa. Name and form.

I have another pen, one I've had for years, a gift from dear Dora on my departure from England. So long ago. It is a fountain pen with a gold nib, a blue marbled pattern on the barrel. Everything about it was pleasing – the feel of it in my hand, the flow of the ink, the sound of the nib scratching on the page. Scribble, scribble.

There were times when I thought the squeak of the nib on the paper held more meaning and less error than anything I was trying to express. I loved that pen, loved its suchness, its fitness for purpose. I loved the *pen-ness* of it.

But refilling it with ink has become too finicky. I had to put it aside and use this *borupen*.

I'm forgetting the names of places and people.

The Scotsman who was in the cell next to mine in Wormwood Scrubs.

Did ye hear about the lonely prisoner?

He was in his sel.

His self.

His cell.
Robertson. That was his name. Davie Robertson.
There was a young fellow named Reg...
And Bishop the butcher who wouldn't kill men.
And the other one, younger than me. Dickson, Paul. Poor, poor Paul.

The other night I heard my mother's voice, her voice when she was young, so long unremembered, but speaking to me now down fifty or sixty years. When I was very, very small, a little nipper, a tiny wee lad, she would tell me stories, or sing to me, or recite scraps of poetry – nursery rhymes, nonsense verse.
And this was the one that came back to me:

Yesterday, upon the stair,
I met a man who wasn't there.
He wasn't there again today,
I wish, I wish he'd go away...

I would shriek and laugh at the sheer ridiculous mystery of it, the hilarious impossibility
Again! I would shout, and she'd repeat it, and I'd laugh even more as if being tickled.
Again!
And she came and told me it again, a few nights ago, her remembered voice so clear and close.
I wish, I wish.
I could even smell the house, dark redolence of furniture polish, tang of camphor, reek of my father's pipe smoke, all comforting beyond measure. I was back there, five or six years old, in Leytonstone, E11. 93 Trumpington Road. Then waking to this.
This.
Those unmistakable hospital smells, cloying and metallic, chemical. And the burning.
Women's voices, quiet and singsong.

This morning I woke from a vivid dream of Korea, the Sushi Hisa restaurant and its mad zen chef Momota-san with his samurai blades.

Oi!

Hai!

That was almost thirty years ago and I found myself salivating at the memory. Perhaps that persistent odour of burning was transformed in my dream into the smell of the food. I could almost taste it. Sadly, the hospital food is dull fare, unimaginative and bland. Once again the vegetarian's lot is not a happy one. It is back once more to rice and vegetables, vegetables and rice.

Nana saves my life by bringing me a bento box, lovingly prepared, beautifully packed, wrapped in a *furoshiki* cloth for ease of carrying. What have I done to deserve this? I ask, and we laugh. But I mean it. I mean it.

She fills the box with my favourite items, like the *inari* tofu pockets I love. They are also said to be the favourite of the fox-gods (and why should I doubt it?) and are placed as an offering at Shinto shrines. There are *tamagoyaki* rolled omelettes, folded into layers and sliced. Nana has even included two *temaki* sushi, the nori folded round the rice, and through the middle a dash of *umeboshi* salt-pickled plum, sharp and tart but fragrant, an explosion of taste.

I am becoming the poet of the bento box!

The consultant tried to say it in English, but the word was beyond him. *Inoperable.*

That's easy-for-you-to-say!

So he said it in Japanese. *Shujutsu fukano.*

But the English word drums in my brain. Inoperable. Inoperable. Inoperable. And some inconsistency in the word itself keeps niggling. A system is inoperable – it cannot be operated, it does not work.

But this, *this*, cannot be operated *upon*. And surely that is a different thing entirely, another matter, different ball game, kettle of fish. Name it – cancer, tumour, malignancy, growth. However you cut it (however you cut it!) it is inoperable.

Easy for you to say.

The condition is terminal, irreversible.
After me now, conjugate the verb.
I die, you die,
He, she or it dies,
We die, you die, they die.

Do not go gentle. But at this stage going gentle has great appeal. I do not want to go screaming and kicking, or for that matter mewling and puking, into that good night.

Earlier this year I picked up a copy of the *Maniichi Daily News* which had been left in the library at Gakushuin. I flicked through the pages, glancing at the headlines, and saw a photograph from Seoul. It showed two South Korean soldiers standing guard at a memorial to General Douglas MacArthur, who had died on April 5th in Washington. The service had been attended by the South Korean President and the commander of UN forces in the peninsula. The article mentioned the general's heroic peace-keeping achievements and said it was believed he had died of cirrhosis of the liver. He was 84 years old.
I shall return.
Not this time he won't.
I recalled my first meeting with him, the jolt from the coffee he poured me. *A good cup of java.* He had spoken of the new Japan, told me how people like me would be crucial in effecting the transition. People like me.
His Pacific campaign was called *Operation Downfall.*
A war hero, laid to rest. An honourable man.
Look on my works, ye mighty…
Cirrhosis of the liver.
And here I am with my in-operable tumour, counting the days, counting down.
The thousand natural shocks that flesh is heir to.
Perhaps I will know the exact time of my departure, like the monk Hoshin. He announced it to his disciples who thought he was joking. He had a grave dug and an open coffin placed beside it. He climbed in. Still the disciples thought he was teaching them some

lesson about accepting mortality. One of them, entering into the spirit of the thing, suggested the master write a death verse. Hoshin thought for a moment, then shouted out.

From brilliancy I came
To brilliancy I return.
What is this?

Then he let out a roar, lay down in the coffin and died.

That I should have such certainty, such courage.

The fear comes sometimes, inevitably, in the wee small hours, the middle of the night when life is at its ebb. *Brahma Muhurta*, the hour of the gods. The thin time between worlds. I surface from uneasy sleep, dragged up by the scruff, gasping, panicky. There's the thud of pain in the head, deep in the core of the brain, and the clench of sick agitation in the gut, in the chest.
There are presences here in the ward, death-forces all around.

Thou hast made me, and shall thy work decay?
Repair me now, for now mine end doth haste,
I run to death, and death meets me as fast,
And all my pleasures are like yesterday...

Donne.

Done.

I try to fight the fear, face it down, and a memory comes to me of Tomiko and a story she told.
When she was young, in her teens, she and her sister Kazuko often had to walk home along a lonely road, by a forest, near a graveyard. Tomiko was always terrified – even when her sister was with her she was fearful of demons and ghosts. And one day Kazuko said to her, I will come here alone, at midnight. I will wear a white kimono

and whiten my face. I will stand under the pine tree and wait. I will embrace the fear. I will become a ghost myself.

I found that thrilling, as a statement, as an attitude – not just fac-ing-the-fear, but identifying with the ghost, becoming the other and realising her oneness with it. That seemed to me to be the embod-iment of Zen.

Hokusai drew ghouls and hungry ghosts, leering and grimacing in the night. Hakuin depicted fierce demons boiled down and sim-mered into soup, for the realised man to eat (and take into himself). He made one late painting of Jizo who was Yamaraj, the god of death, wrote in harsh black calligraphy, I BOW TO THE BODHI-SATTVA OF HELL.

An image I found genuinely chilling, from a Japanese horror film, the moment of terror when the ghost turns its face towards us, out of the screen. But there is no face, only a smooth featureless blankness. Nothing. No-self. Oblivion.

Kazuko with her white face, her white kimono, standing under the pines at midnight, waiting.

The hungry ghosts hovering around my bed.

I struggle to raise myself on one elbow. Draw breath in pain. The young nurse is at her station, in the glow of her light, an aura in the darkness. She is seated with her back to me, leaning on her desk and writing something. Her back to me. So I can't see her face. I will her to turn around but then am consumed with the fear that she will turn and have no face.

She turns, slowly. I want to cry out but cannot. It is unbearable. She turns, and she is herself, here, in the glow of her light. She turns and she smiles at me, concerned. She smiles and brings me back to this world, the only one.

My old friend Shinki has sent me a kind letter enquiring after my health (this in spite of his own wife being unwell). Knowing how much he thinks in visual terms, I have sent him a reply in the form of a graph, showing the change in my condition over these past months – my state of fitness on the vertical axis, the passage of time (inexorable as ever) on the horizontal. The graph shows a sharp decline, followed by a slight levelling out on my admission to hospital, then, sadly, a further, if wavering descent.

I hope it will make him smile, and also let him know that for the moment at least, I still have my wits about me. (God help me if I should lose those!)

Bob Aitken has also written to me. Perhaps the word has spread that I am not long for this world, and in his way he is thanking me and saying farewell. He graciously accepted my flaws, he said, as he accepted the flaws in his own father. His father brought him into being, he said, and shaped his character. I for my part put him in touch with himself (whatever that might mean) and with this great rich wonderful world. If we had not met, he said, he might well have spent his life mired in the mundane and the trivial. He said my words often come to him when he is teaching his own students, and my face sometimes appears to him in dreams. (God help him!) But I take all this in the spirit in which it is intended, and as a kind of absolution.

Aitken Roshi. Dairyu Chotan.
Great Dragon of the Clear Pool.
Bob.
Thank you.

There are letters too from Ma and from Dora, sending their prayers, wishing me well.
Dear Dora married some years ago, but still comparatively late in life, to a Mr Lord, a colleague at the bank where she worked. I wrote and congratulated her, said if her husband were ever knighted, she would be Lady Lord.
A fellow of infinite jest.
(Sand spilling from a skull).

Alas poor Blyth.

Padmasambhava instructed his followers to bury Buddhist scriptures for the enlightenment of future generations, a time capsule.

What would I bury of mine? What dross will I leave behind? An archive for some poor soul to catalogue and curate.

My old tweed jacket, lovat green, patched at the elbows. (Chalkdust and chocolate crumbs in the pockets).
My flute, my cello, my trombone...
The container for all of this will have to be on the large side. (I am large, I contain multitudes!) It will need to be expandable. (Expendable?)
Some well-thumbed sheet music. Bach, yes, but others also. Corelli, *Sonata for cello and piano*. Galliard, *Sonatas for trombone and piano*.
Perhaps as a farewell statement I could play a blast on the trombone, a final raspberry, a last rasping fart delivered *forte, con brio*. Perhaps *that* can be my death-verse. Paa-aa-arp!

I have always thought the desire to be nothing is particularly common among those who are practically nothing to begin with. And yet...

I am tired.

I have some old photographs that have somehow survived from a time long gone, another age, before two world wars – the War-to-end-all-wars and the one which followed with relentless inevitability less than twenty years later. The photos are sepia-tinted, faded and cracked. The oldest of them was taken in a studio and shows me as a very small boy, perhaps five or six years old. I am dressed in a kind of sailor suit with a loose striped blouse, a broad-brimmed straw hat pushed back on my thick dark hair. I am seated on what I assume was a papier-mâché rock on an ersatz beach in front of a painted backdrop depicting a wild dramatic sea, waves surging under a dark lowering sky. I lean jauntily on a long-handled spade, look straight at the camera, out into the world, into the future and all it holds. I look happy, ready to laugh, ready for play.

When I was down beside the sea
A wooden spade they gave to me
   To dig the sandy shore.

My holes were empty like a cup,
In every hole the sea came up,
   Till it could come no more.

I loved Stevenson even as a child (perhaps *especially* as a child).
I remember that little boy I was, travelling in the train with those free tickets my father had been given. It was always a thrill, and I would turn one of the knobs in the compartment, as if by that small act I was starting up the engine and setting it in motion. In my imagination I was driving the train. I caused the pistons to turn, the whistle to blow, the smoke to pour as we picked up speed and thundered through the countryside.

Faster than fairies, faster than witches,
Bridges and houses, hedges and ditches;
And charging along like troops in a battle,
All through the meadows the horses and cattle...

I eased back on the controls, brought the train to a stop at our destination, the seaside town at the end of the line.

Down Southend.

I would love (as my old dad would have loved) to travel on the *Shinkansen*, the high-speed bullet train. The service has just commenced – miraculously – in time for the Olympics. Every Japanese I know has been inordinately proud of the post-war rebuilding of the country's infrastructure, especially the railway system. It is fully integrated – everything seems to interconnect. And yes, the trains really do run on time! And the jewel in this particular crown is the Shinkansen. Sleek and futuristic, it travels at 125 miles per hour, can make the journey from Tokyo to Osaka in three hours. Faster than fairies. Faster than witches.

Here is a child who clambers and scrambles,
All by himself and gathering brambles....

It was one of the first poems I learned by heart, and the ending moved me in a way I didn't understand.

And here is a mill and there is a river:
Each a glimpse and gone for ever!

A glimpse and gone. Forever.

A Child's Garden was Stevenson's *Songs of Innocence*, offset by those dark little *Fables*, wry and sardonic, his *Songs of Experience*.
One of the fables is called "The Penitent" and has the quality of a ballad. I used to know it by heart.

A man meets a lad weeping and asks him, What do you weep for? I am weeping for my sins, says the lad. You must have little to do, says the man.
The next day they meet again and once more the lad is weeping. Why do you weep now? the man asks.
I am weeping because I have nothing to eat, says the lad.
I thought it would come to that, says the man.

Those beggars outside the temple in Seoul, freezing to death.

Does a dog have the Buddha nature?

Why should a dog a horse a rat have life?

That young boy, Paul Dickson, just the age I was then, not yet 20. He'd have effectively been pressganged, returned to 'his regiment' by force.

That heroic young conshie named Paul.

He finds himself on a transport ship, crossing the Channel. Cursed and beaten, spat upon, brutalised. On the battlefield he is ordered to fight. He continues to refuse but is willing to work as a stretcher bearer. Though he will not fight, he can still save lives, or at least ease suffering. He does his bit. He sees men die, blown to pieces all around him. He will not add to the carnage. He will not kill. He will not fight. They are losing the battle. The regiment is decimated. They order him to fight, they try to force a gun into his hands, but he throws it down onto the ground. He has never fired a gun, and he never will.

His voice from the next cell.

> *I didn't raise my boy to be a soldier,*
> *I brought him up to be my pride and joy.*
> *Who dares to place a musket on his shoulder,*
> *To shoot some other mother's darling boy?*

He is summarily court-martialled, summarily taken outside, summarily shot dead by a summarily-convened firing squad. He lies face-down in the mud. That wayward tuft of hair refuses to lie flat on his head. They drag his body away.

Lug the guts into the neighbour room.

Think only this. Some corner of a foreign field.

That Orwell story, set in Burma, about a prisoner being taken to the gallows to be hung, stepping round a puddle to avoid getting his feet wet.

I thought it would come to this.

This. Not this.

That other poor boy Lee. My son. Innocent and damned.
If we hadn't adopted him.
If I hadn't let him go back to London with Annie.
If he hadn't learned English.
If he hadn't returned to Korea.
If, if, if...
That way madness lies.

Above the gates of hell is written in letters of fire, IF ONLY...

Too little care.

Remorse. *Agenbite.*

Buraisu-san, the nurse says. Why are you crying?

Buraisu-san.

The boy I was. Reginald Horace. Young Reggie. Reg.

There was a young fellow named Reg. Who was frequently heard
to allege.

Blyth. Blithe spirit. Hail to thee. Bird thou never wert.
Never. Never. Never. Never. Never.

Who is it that can tell me who I am?
Blyth's shadow.

Not this. Not this. Not this. Not this.
Not peace, not joy, not love, not light. Not this.
Not prayer and meditation, satori or nirvana. Not this.
Not Brahma, Vishnu, Shiva. Not Father, Son and Holy Ghost.
Not Buddha, Krishna, Kali, not Christ. Not the Bible, the Gita, the
Dhammapadda.

Not Confucius. Not Lao-Tsu.

Not heaven and hell. Not sun, moon and stars.

Not earth, water, fire, air. Not this.

Not *Through the Looking Glass* or *Precious Mirror Cave.*

Not Shakespeare, Stevenson, Wordsworth, Eckhart, Blake.

Not Dante, Cervantes, Spinoza, Goethe.

Not Mozart not Beethoven. Not Bach, not even Bach.

Not Herbert, Donne, Traherne, Vaughan.

Not Lawrence, not Dickens, not Arnold, not Hardy.

Not Yamanashi, not Suzuki. Not Akio and Motoko.

Not Prince Akihito and Princess Michiko.

Not Hirohoto or Macarthur.

Not Henderson, not Bob Aitken, Great Dragon of the Clear Pool.

Not Basho, not Buson, Not Issa, not Shiki.

Not haiku not tanka, not senryu.

Not koans. Not *Mu.* Not the sound of one hand.

Not form, not emptiness.

Not Zen.

Not Hakuin or Dogen, Bodhidharma or Hui-Neng.

Not the rain on the window, the wind in the pines.

Not a song at twilight when the lights are low.

Not *wabi-sabi*, not *mono no aware.*

Not beauty or sadness, the transience of things.

Not a cup of tea. Not the bittersweet taste of persimmon.

Not Ma and Pa. Not Dora. Not Annie, not Lee.

Not Leytonstone, Not Soeul. Not Kobe, Kamakura, Tokyo.

Not Tomiko. Not Harumi and Nana. Not Akiko.

Not yesterday today tomorrow, not Time.

Not Death-the-destroyer-of-worlds.

Not anything, not anything at all. Not nothing.

Not this. Not this.

Tomiko is here. She has come to see me at the last. No. My eyes clear and it is Harumi. She has flown from America to be with me, and she has brought the boy, my grandson, the most beautiful little fellow I have ever seen. Taro.

Harumi props up the pillows behind me so I can sit up.

She takes my hand. My own grip is weak but I feel the strength and warmth in hers.

Nana korobi ya oki... she says. Seven times down, eight times up.

Not this time, I say.

Not this time.

Where am I?

St Luke's in Tokyo. Seiroka. No, they moved me here to Seiwa where no doubt I'll breathe my last.

My posthumous Buddhist name has already been chosen.

Buraisu Kodo Shoshin Koji.

The late not-come person. Shining mind. Zen spirit way.

Or some such.

He who followed, with illumined mind, the old path of Zen.

Better? Perhaps not.

I met a man who wasn't there.

My mother's voice.

Again! Again!

And what next? What else can it become?

Ashes. Darkness. Dust.

I also had my hour.

One far fierce hour and sweet.

Not leaving my heart to the *sasanqua* flower, the day of this journey.

Not-coming, not-going, not-born, not-dying.

A man who wasn't there.

Mister Timeless Blyth.

Thanks

The writing and publishing of this book would simply not have been possible without the help of a number of people, and I owe them all a huge debt of gratitude:

Ikuyo Yoshimura for her kindness and hospitality in welcoming me to Gifu and sharing her love of Blyth as well as the research material that had gone into her thesis, in Japanese, on Blyth's life and work, published as *The Life of R.H. Blyth* (Dohosha).

Norman Waddell in Kyoto for his encyclopaedic and personal knowledge of Blyth and for patiently answering my endless questions. His own lifelong involvement with Blyth has resulted in his recently-published *Poetry and Zen: Letters and Uncollected Writings of RH Blyth*. (Shambala).

Saeko Yazaki at Glasgow University for her enthusiastic response to early chapters of my book and for putting me in touch with the Blyth archive at Gakushuin University in Tokyo where Blyth himself taught for decades.

Motoko Ohkawa and Yuri Tomita, archivists at Gakushuin, for their extraordinary helpfulness and support in allowing me access to the Blyth papers and artifacts in their care. Their work is a labour of love.

Yuji Takeda for his encouragement and for kindly and courteously sharing family memories and his own unique insight into Blyth.

Chieko Iwamura for her priceless stories of the years spent in 'home study' in the Blyth household where she became part of the family.

Kuniyoshi Munakata, one of Blyth's last surviving former students, for his warmth and generosity, for introducing me to Nō theatre and for his memoir in Japanese, *Thank you, Professor Blyth* (Shohan).

Daisuke Matsunaga for tireless help with the research, translating material from Japanese, meticulously checking my work for linguistic and historical accuracy (keeping me straight!) and for his continuing friendship.

Alan Bett and Creative Scotland for financial support enabling me to make an invaluable research trip to Japan, thankfully completed just before pandemic restrictions would have rendered the visit impossible.

Elizabeth Sheinkman my indefatigable agent at PFD, first port of call for the completed manuscript, a positive voice, a reassurance in difficult times.

Eric Oey, owner of Tuttle Publishing, for committing to something new to their lists, a bio-fiction, the imagined autobiography of a real life character.

Terri Jadick at Tuttle, a sensitive and perceptive editor who really understood the book and its subject matter.

My wife Janani, as always, for spiritual and emotional support through the whole process of writing the book, for living through it with me, with love.

Also by Alan Spence

FICTION
Its Colours They Are Fine
The Magic Flute
Stone Garden
Wat to Go
The Pure Land
Night Boat

POETRY
Seasons of the Heart
Glasgow Zen
Still (with Alison Watt)
Clear Light
Morning Glory (with Elizabeth Blackadder)
zenscotlit
thirteen ways of looking at tulips (with Elizabeth Blackadder)
Edinburgh Come All Ye

PLAYS
Sailmaker
Space Invaders
Changed Days
On the Line
The 3 Estaites
No Nothing